The Viking's Shadow Lady

Vikings in the Bronze Age, Book 2

MAUREEN CASTELL

CHAMPAGNE BOOK GROUP

Published by Champagne Book Group
712 SE Winchell Street, Depoe Bay OR 97341 U.S.A.

~~~

First Edition 2023

pISBN: 978-1-959036-73-9

Cover Art by Sevannah Storm

www.champagnebooks.com

Version_1

To Alan, as always
for your love and support.

Praise for
The Viking Who Fell Through Time

"I love romance, science-fiction, time travel, paranormal, and prehistoric historical. I love stories told in all those genres about what happens when one culture meets another. Imagine finding a book that combines all of them in one absorbing tale! I was delighted to put Maureen Castell's *The Viking Who Fell Through Time* on my Kindle."
—ali macgee, author of *Sit, Stay, Love: A Romantic Comedy Where the Dogs Know Best*

"Without going into a lot of detail (i.e., no spoilers) I'll simply say that Ms. Castell has done her research, and crafted a believable and well-paced time-travel tale that manages to incorporate the sexy Vikings (as promised), alien technology, and a Bronze-Age warrior woman with all kinds of issues of her own. And it all turns out to be great fun...Top-notch enemies to lovers play here, and Ms. Castell makes the most of her characters and their wary dance. This is a very character-driven story (my favorite type) with believable stakes and motivations."
—Keith Willis, author of the *Knights of Kilbourne* series

"Although not the genre of book I usually read, I thoroughly enjoyed Maureen's book and am looking forward to the next book in the series."
—Happy Gardener, Amazon

"I was way out of my comfort zone reading this...[but] to my surprise, thoroughly enjoyed it. Maureen Castell is a skilled wordsmith but beyond putting pretty words on paper, she excels in her research. I look forward to more of Maureen's works."
—Bill Coe, Goodreads Reader

Dear Reader,

If you have read the first book in this series, *The Viking Who Fell Through Time*, welcome back to New Asgard and the Bronze Age. If you haven't, welcome to my world.

Sixteen years ago, a damaged spaceship dragged a trio of Norse ships into the ancient past before crashing into the side of a mountain. Since then, the Norse exiles have merged with a local village, built a thriving home, and harnessed the power of the spaceship's cargo to trade with other times for wonders that make their life easier.

This story is at the heart a romance between two people who are reluctant to admit they don't fit the expectations others have of them. I hope you enjoy watching both hero and heroine discover their true selves.

While I have attempted to stay true to historical detail, any errors are mine, either accidentally or intentionally. Specifically, I have taken some liberties with geography. As far as I am aware, there is no such place in England called Stag's Tor, and I have yet to find a coastline in Denmark that matches the Viking settlement.

For more information, including a complete pronunciation guide for the series, please visit my website at http://www.MaureenCastell.com.

Maureen

Pronunciation Guide

If you are like me, you prefer knowing how words sound when read, especially if you are reading them aloud to someone else, so I have included my best estimate of how some of the less obvious words are pronounced, based on several sources. For multi-syllable words, the emphasized syllable is in all caps. Any errors are, sadly, my own.

Names:

Arne (AR-neh)
Gudrin (GOOD-rin)
Kai (KYE)
Kaya (KYE-ah)
Kiana (kee-ANN-a)
Lida (LEE-dah)
Runa (ROO-na)
Sjørotte (Shure-OTT-ah)—Sea rat; derogatory name for raiders
Vider (VY-der)
Zabeth (ZAH-beth)

Words:

Anno Domini (anno do-mee-nee)—Latin for "year of our lord"

Bǫkk (thock—'th' as in 'breath')—Norse for "thanks"

Borð (thorth—first 'th' is as in 'breath', second 'th' is as in 'breathe')—Norse for "table"

Góðr (GOATH-rr)—Norse for "good" or "fine"

Ja (YAH)—Norse for "yes"

Keevah (KEE-va)—Warm milk, spiced, with a strengthening/healing potion in it, a combination of local herbs and medicine traded with a Shadow world; also used as birth control (invented word)

Klengodd, (KLEN-got)—Claw-shaped root from a Shadow world that, when treated with certain chemicals, has remarkable healing properties (invented word)

Knorr (NOOR)—Viking ship used primarily in trade (Norse)

Latine loqueris (la-TEEN-ay low-KWAIR-iss)—Latin for "do you speak Latin"

Lauga (LAU-gah, rhymes with HOWga)—Norse for "bathe"

Nei (NAY)—Norse for "no"

Parlez-vous Francais (par-lay voo fron-say)—French for "do you speak French"

Vel kominn (vel-COAM-en)—Norse for "welcome"

Chapter One

The Caribbean, 1764 AD

Lady Elizabeth Conroy smiled at her son while he suckled at her breast. She wouldn't be able to do this if her frugal husband hadn't insisted on leaving most of their servants behind on this move to the colonies.

"You can't go without a wet-nurse," her mother had protested in shock. "You'll have to feed the babe yourself!"

Women of Elizabeth's station were not supposed to perform such common tasks, but she'd never understood the restrictions. Aside from the messy chore of changing his clout, which she passed on to her maid, Maizy, Elizabeth enjoyed feeding and looking after her little boy. Edward David Conroy—Ned—was her world.

"Why does it have to take so long?" her mother continued. "It's not that far. Your Aunt Sophie's letters from Virginia only take a month."

The memory brought a grin to Elizabeth's lips. Lady Alice had no head for practicalities. How to explain sea currents and prevailing winds to a woman who couldn't even point you in the direction of London? She settled for a simpler, and in part fabricated, story. "We're joining a convoy of ships going to Jamaica in a few days. Once they get to their destination, we'll sail up the coast of the Americas to Connecticut. It takes longer but it's safer."

In truth there were no other ships, but David had assured her English warships often patrolled the same route, and the trip should be safe enough without the added protection. According to Geoffrey, the old seaman who now lived with his granddaughter on the estate, the southern route was the most practical way to get across the Atlantic. It avoided the strong west-east current that sped ships in the other direction farther north.

Lord David Conroy, third son of the Duke of Warwick, peered around the cabin door and drew Elizabeth back to the present. "Are you finished yet?"

She smiled at her husband and covered herself with her shawl. "Soon."

"Come on deck when you're done. There's a ship on the horizon. The captain thinks it's from the colonies, come to welcome us." David had always been fascinated with the Americas, and when he'd been offered the position of governor of one of the colonies, he'd jumped at the chance.

She grinned at his eagerness. "I'll join you after I put Ned down to sleep."

David blew her a kiss and shut the door behind him. Elizabeth removed her shawl and stared down at the baby again. He resembled David even at this tender age—wide mouth, a nose that showed hints of the distinctive Conroy hook. His eyes, though, green and inquisitive, he'd inherited from his mother, as well as the downy hair that already showed tints of red. Her beautiful boy. How lucky she was her first child survived his birth. Now almost four months old, he already had the hardened gums that hinted at his first teeth. She grimaced. Feeding him might not be so comfortable when they broke through. Gently she untangled his fingers from the cross around her neck and laid the baby in his cradle.

As she tucked the blanket around his small body, the door opened again and her maid slipped in. *Perfect timing. Maizy can look after Ned while I join David on deck.*

When the girl remained at the door, Elizabeth glanced up. Maizy clutched her apron and squeezed the cloth in her hands. Her breath came in rasping gasps, her eyes bulged as if she'd seen a horror too terrible to describe, and her lips trembled.

Alarmed, Elizabeth straightened. "What's wrong?"

"There's a s-ship, my lady." The maid whimpered and shook her head, as if in denial.

"What ship?" Elizabeth snapped. Something must be wrong for Maizy to stutter. "Pull yourself together. What ship?"

Maizy swallowed. "They j-just raised the b-black flag."

A chill swept up Elizabeth's spine. Before they left England, her mother had listed the risks of travel to the Americas in a vain attempt to persuade David to change his mind. The black flag played a prominent part in her pleas.

Pirates!

~ * ~

New Asgard

"Beren?" The shout reverberated through the huge chamber and fooled the listener into thinking the caller was in the next room instead of two hallways away.

Beren Torsson clutched the box to his chest and straightened. The flames from the torch wedged between two large chests danced in reflection across metal walls. In all the years he'd been coming here, the size and strangeness of the chamber still fascinated him. "Not so loud, Eskil," he called back. "You almost made me drop one. Come in and give me a hand."

Beren grasped the torch and pulled it from its niche. It lit Eskil's features when he strode into the chamber.

"How many more do you need?" Eskil gestured toward the boxes secured in individual nets to shelves that disappeared into the depths of the room. Each was the size of a man's head, the top covered in circles that turned at the touch of a finger and small metal sticks Beren's uncle Vider called *stangs*.

"The keepers asked for three." Beren indicated the crumpled cloth at his feet. "I brought a sack but it'll be safer if you carry two. I'll take the third and bring the torch." It was more common for the younger children to perform this task, but three boxes were too heavy for anyone but a strong warrior to handle. Besides, the *stangs* were flimsy enough to snap if the boxes were shoved haphazardly into a sack.

Eskil lifted two of the boxes and held them beside each other with the *stangs* on the upper edge. After placing them into the sack, he cradled it in his arms. Neither spoke while they made their way through the echoing hallway. Soon the ragged slash of the entrance came into view and sunlight slanted a welcome beam into the opening.

Beren doused the torch in the bucket of sand left for that purpose inside the opening, then helped Eskil maneuver through the narrow rift. Dirt and vines had softened the edges over the years, but the metal was still sharp enough to cut an unwary explorer.

"Now," Beren said once they stood on the shelf outside the entrance, "what was so important? Has the *Freki* returned?" Tor Olafsson led the trade mission to the Southlands. The *Freki* was a combination warship and trading vessel, which the keepers called a *hybrid*, a term they'd learned from the Shadow worlds. It was as capable of carrying a substantial cargo as it was of defending that cargo against enemy raiders. However, Beren wasn't in a hurry to see his heart-father. After all, a man of twenty-two summers should have accompanied Tor on several trading voyages by now. True, he wore the pelt of the bear he'd brought down in his thirteenth year, but he'd done little else, in his opinion, in the nine years since to make his parents proud. He preferred a scholar's life.

Eskil shifted the boxes for better balance. "Better. Keeper Magrim is going to open a full-size portal."

Beren tightened his grip on the box he carried. He was no stripling to exclaim in excitement, but he couldn't help a feeling of pride at the news. *I gave him the 'Link just yesterday. He must be confident in my work if he wants a demonstration so soon.* He hadn't told anyone else, even Eskil, about his success for fear of sounding boastful.

Magrim was by far the most dedicated of the five keepers, and the most studious. Ever since Beren's heart-parents, Tor and Kiana, discovered the cache of Shadow-Links sixteen years earlier, the keepers had sought for ways to make the artifacts more useful. The 'Links opened head-sized holes into other places, and allowed them to trade with the people on the other side of those holes. However, those exchanges were limited by the small portals. For years, the keepers had attempted to increase the size. They longed to trade for larger objects, perhaps even pass through the portals themselves to trade in person.

Beren had always been fascinated by the mysterious 'Links, and at times had borrowed a box to study and fiddle with. He hadn't told his heart-parents. Perhaps they suspected, but they'd never said anything, and he didn't want to disappoint them. They were both great warriors and he…was not. Oh, he'd gone through warrior training and was now a guard with fighting skills that couldn't be faulted, but his heart led elsewhere. He wanted to take things apart, learn how they worked, then put them together so they worked even better. If Beren hadn't known his own origins, he might have thought Vider was his true father.

Last month, Beren's tinkering had paid off. He'd succeeded where no other keeper had, and if this demonstration worked, it might give him the confidence to reveal his secret to his heart-parents.

"Because it's the first time," Eskil continued, "Magrim wants guards there in case something goes wrong."

Nothing would go wrong. Nothing *could* go wrong. "Makes sense. Let's get these back."

Eskil grinned. Without a word, he sat for the treacherous slide down the steep hill below the God-Hold entrance, followed by Beren. The longer path along the edge of the cliff was smoother, but neither wanted to take the extra time.

There had been talk of removing the gentle path by cutting away part of the flat area and creating a small landslide to cover the remaining trail. Many argued the 'Links were too valuable to allow such easy access to those who might want to steal them. The steeper trail might be tricky to maneuver, but easier to guard. More sensible heads had prevailed, though, pointing out the folly of leaving an unstable trail as the lone access. The alternate path was now hidden by trees and overgrown brush, and protected, of course, by the mysterious gray man who appeared as if by magic to warn intruders away.

When the two men reached the bottom of the slope, they set off at a run for the village two miles away. Beren never tired of hearing the tale of New Asgard's founding. He'd soaked up the stories of how Tor led his friends, family, and crew into exile in this new land, how he had met Kiana and the then-six-year-old Beren, and how he and Kiana had found the half-buried God-Hold in the fire ship that had brought his people here. Beren remembered when the fire ship had struck the mountain, a blazing ball of fire and metal larger than anything he'd ever seen. He and Eskil had been caught in the landslide of rocks. After the discovery of the God-Hold chamber, it had taken Tor's friend Vider less than two months to solve the mystery of the boxes and open the first link to the Shadow worlds. He it was who formed the company of Keepers of the Shadow-Links, though once he'd discovered the secret, he'd lost interest and abandoned the study. He married Tor's sister, Runa, and preferred to remain Tor's war-second.

Many had hoped to use the 'Links to make trade easier without the need for long sea voyages, but that hope proved futile. The keepers had come to realize the 'Links opened holes to different times as well as places. Instead of allowing trade with other lands in their own time, the boxes showed places stranger than any Beren's people had ever imagined. There were still plans to try to make a profit from them, though. The *Freki's* mission this summer was to discover whether the boxes, even with the small openings, were acceptable trade items. Kiana had accompanied the crew to act as interpreter in some of their destinations because Beren's heart-mother had a gift for understanding and speaking any language after hearing three or four words.

Beren's heart beat faster when they neared the village. He wanted to explore foreign lands, and what was more foreign than the Shadow worlds, lands even the gods didn't walk, reached without the need to sail on a ship? Even the horses Tor had traded for on one of his first land expeditions weren't acquired to carry riders. Their purpose was to plow and haul lumber. When anyone traveled overland, they did so on foot and used the sturdy horses as pack animals.

The beach was deserted when Beren and Eskil emerged from the trees, the fishing boats not expected back until sunset. The route to the Keeper Hall passed through the village square. Women washed clothes at the central trough, practiced with bows, or trained with the off-duty guards. A few of the women paused in their task when the two men appeared. Both ignored the giggling comments when they hurried past.

"Beren, looking strong today."

"What's the hurry, Eskil? Stay and share a kiss."

"When will you take me to the God-Hold, warrior?"

Beren scowled. He enjoyed the village women as much as the next man, but he'd never yet taken one up the hill, although many of the guards did. It didn't seem right to sport among the Shadow-Links. Perhaps he'd change his mind if he ever found his lifemate, but that was doubtful now. The village was small, and he knew all the women here. Although he had spent a night with a few over the years, none held enough special appeal for him to want to handfast.

With a sense of relief, he rounded the final corner and the Keeper Hall came into view ahead. Eskil looked flushed, but not with exertion. Beren suspected his friend yearned for one of the women they'd passed, but had yet to tell her. Even Beren didn't know who had caught Eskil's eye. Perhaps that was why, at twenty-one, his friend had never married.

When they arrived at the Keeper Hall, a large stone building surrounded and separated from the village by an open space fifty paces deep, the two men passed the precious 'Links to one of the acolytes, then proceeded to the trade chamber. Beren unstrapped his sword from his back where he'd fastened it out of the way. He slipped it into its proper loop at his belt and pushed open the heavy doors to the chamber.

Four guards waited, gathered in a rough half-circle behind Keeper Magrim. Beren and Eskil slipped into the two empty spaces in the line, stood at ease, and waited for instructions.

There shouldn't be any need for a guard. Beren had tested many of the Shadow-Links before settling on this one for his experiment. All the other 'Links opened into a room or a field. This one, though, opened to a seemingly empty sky, but if you stood close and peered down, twenty feet below the opening a vast ocean stretched to the horizon, as empty as the air above it. The only danger he'd ever faced with this particular 'Link had been the one time he'd opened it into a storm, and waves had washed through the opening to soak him and the floor around him. This time there should be nothing more dangerous than a stray bird to threaten the guards.

The keeper fiddled with the Shadow-Link, his actions blocked by his body. Beren shifted for a better view.

Magrim stepped back. "We'll open a portal the size of a man." The keeper fixed each of the six guards with a stern eye. The guards stood straighter, although some eyed the Shadow-Link with suspicion. "There should be no danger, but the chieftain insists you be present for this first trial." His gaze passed over Beren without a flicker of acknowledgement, then turned back to the pedestal that held the

Shadow-Link and ran crooked fingers through his thinning white hair. He gave a decisive nod, then used a single finger to rotate one of the circles in slow steps from one mark to the next.

Beren held his breath.

~ * ~

Elizabeth clutched her baby to her chest and shrank into the dubious safety of the cabin doorway. Behind her, flames already licked at Ned's tiny cot, while in front all was blood and death. Her husband had made her stay here while he searched for a boat, a way off this doomed ship for his family.

If he wasn't already dead.

The desperate fighting swept forward and she was forced to retreat into the smoky cabin. A whimper from Ned drew her attention away from the carnage. She soothed the child, then dared another peek through the crack between door and wall. Figures ran past her flimsy shelter, sailors in the red and gold uniform of the Dover Guild of Sea Merchants, wild-looking pirates in their wake. Maizy had already fled the cabin to seek the uncertain shelter of the hold. Elizabeth hoped the girl found a good place to hide. She didn't know what had happened to Toby, David's valet.

When the battle moved to another part of the ship, the deck in front of her cabin emptied of combatants. In the momentary lull, a figure darted from the shadows toward her cabin.

David.

Before Elizabeth had time to react, another body hurtled from the side. David crashed beneath the weight and lay motionless, eyes open in shock. A pirate disentangled himself from the fallen man. He rose to his feet and ran his sword through David's chest. Elizabeth stuffed a fist in her mouth to stifle her scream. The pirate didn't hear her, but dashed off to join his fellows in the slaughter.

Elizabeth jerked open the door, rushed forward, and fell to her knees beside her husband's body.

In the relative quiet of the isolated corner where he'd fallen, David lay on his back and gasped for breath. Elizabeth shifted Ned to one arm and lifted David's head into her lap. Blood seeped into her dress, but she ignored it. Although their marriage had been arranged, she'd grown fond of this impractical, impulsive man. The thought of him dying like this, so far from home, was more than she could bear.

"David, stay with me. Please don't die." A lump blocked her throat. She had to force the words out in a hoarse whisper.

He coughed, convulsed, and clutched at her arm to steady himself. He clasped her hand, pulled it down until the handle of his dagger pressed against her fingers. "Take it."

She stared in shock at the weapon, then raised her gaze to his.

He nodded. "No way off… You…know what…they will do…to you and…and…the child."

Yes. Her mother's warnings, of women raped and tortured, forced to watch their children disemboweled before their eyes, were nothing if not graphic. An unnatural calm drained away the panic. With trembling fingers, she drew the heavy knife from her husband's belt.

David smiled, but then his gaze shifted over her shoulder and widened in alarm. She twisted around. A pirate stood behind her, his sword already swinging downward, *toward David*. She flung up her arm. The sword hit the knife, slid down the blade, skidded off the hilt, and sliced through her shoulder.

She screamed. The knife dropped from nerveless fingers. With great effort, David lurched upward and flung himself on the pirate. The two men collapsed to the deck. Elizabeth rolled out of the way and scrambled to her feet. She chanced a glance back to her husband, but David lay unmoving atop the pirate, who cursed and shoved at the heavy body.

Clutching Ned to her breast, Elizabeth ran blindly into the thick smoke. The world had gone mad. The screams of dying men filled the air around her. She'd lost the knife. Only one place offered a clean death. The sea.

~ * ~

Keeper Magrim twisted the marked circles. A small hole appeared in the far wall. So far it looked no different from a normal trade-link, but now the keeper spun another circle, and the hole expanded to the size of a doorway.

Beren grinned. It worked! At first there was nothing but a blank darkness, then light beyond the portal flickered with a red glow through gray smoke.

Wait. Smoke? What's going on? Where's the water?

As if someone had indeed opened a door, sound and smell erupted into the room. Smoke. Fire. Screams. The clash of metal on metal.

There's a battle beyond the portal.

"This is not a good idea, Keeper," Dug, the oldest of the guards, remarked with a calm Beren found astonishing. Dug's knuckles were white where he gripped his sword. All the guards had drawn their swords.

The keeper fiddled with more circles, frowned. "Perhaps you're right." He reached for the cut-off *stang*.

And Beren saw the woman.

A bright light appeared before Elizabeth where the deck rail had been a moment ago. Unable to stop her forward rush, she stumbled from the smoke into a room full of bearded men.

She staggered into a gray-haired man who stood at the forefront of the group. The man held her in a firm but gentle grip, and his kind eyes expressed concern, not triumph. *Where did he come from?*

A roar behind her made her turn her head. The pirate had freed himself from beneath David's body and now dashed toward her through the smoke, teeth bared and sword raised.

Time slowed. The sword swung in an arc aimed at Elizabeth's head. With little time left to react, she thrust the baby at the astonished elder, then braced for the killing blow.

A bar of metal appeared in front of her. The sword, instead of cleaving her head, rang against the metal with a loud clang. The metal bar resolved itself into another sword, held by a dark-skinned bearded man. He flashed Elizabeth a reassuring smile and parried the pirate's attack.

The old man dragged Elizabeth out of range of the clashing swords. The other men crowded forward to form a wall between the pirate and the rest of the room. She lost sight of the warrior who'd saved her life, and when the old man pushed the baby back into her arms, Elizabeth stumbled into a corner and huddled against a stone wall.

The screams of battle still echoed through the room, counterpoint to the clang of sword against sword, the light of the flames, and the stench of blood. She didn't want to watch the fight but couldn't help herself. The pirate, faced with armed men instead of a terrified woman, leaped backward and retreated into the smoke. The old man did something to a metal box on the table beside him.

The smoke disappeared, the light winked out, and silence filled the room. No fire. No pirates. No ship.

Stone walls?

The old man turned his attention to Elizabeth. She shrank back. Reason returned. Had she traded one nightmare for another? Her impulse earlier to give Ned to the old man now seemed utter madness.

She huddled over the tiny form in her arms. "Leave him alone. I won't let you harm him."

The man crouched before her and spoke in a language she'd never heard before. She shook her head and tightened her grip until Ned squalled in protest. The man spoke again, his voice soothing. He glanced at the baby, smiled, then spoke over his shoulder. Two of the men left the room. Another stepped forward and crouched on his heels in front of

Elizabeth.

He, too, smiled, and she recognized him. The face of the man who'd saved her life was burned into her memory. He was younger than she expected. Although hard to tell through the shaggy black hair and beard, he looked about David's age, in his early twenties perhaps. Unlike the other men in the room, his skin was dark, not black but more swarthy, like the Arab prince who had befriended her father in Egypt and had come to their wedding last year. And his eyes... Dark as chocolate, their gaze made her feel warm and...safe.

Elizabeth's heart slammed in her chest.

He touched her cheek. Mesmerized by those eyes, Elizabeth couldn't move, and for a moment couldn't breathe. Instead she found herself returning his smile.

While your husband lies dead on a burning ship?

The treacherous thought snapped her back to reality. She stiffened, drew away. Guilt wiped the smile from her lips. The man's eyes softened in concern, but she forced herself to ignore the comfort they offered.

Three women entered the room, followed by the two men who'd left earlier. One woman nudged the black-haired man aside and plucked Ned from Elizabeth's arms.

Elizabeth cried out a protest, lurched to her feet, and reached for her baby, but she couldn't lift her left arm nor keep her balance. The other two women closed in from either side to support her. The woman who held Ned smiled at her, then walked backward toward the door.

Unwilling to leave her son in the hands of a stranger, Elizabeth followed, her steps uneven. Her limbs trembled and her head spun, but she was determined to get Ned back. She took another step. A dark cloud formed over her eyes and she swayed. The woman on her left tightened her grip. Pain lanced through Elizabeth's shoulder and she gasped. The dark cloud exploded into black fire, and she knew no more.

Chapter Two

Stunned by that smile, hesitant as it was, Beren found himself frozen in place even after the injured woman drew away. So when she was helped to her feet and began to shuffle toward the door, when she sagged and dragged her supporters to the floor, it was Dug who sprang forward and reached her first. He swept the unconscious woman into his arms, then stood with a bewildered expression on his face.

He turned to Beren's aunt, who cradled the squalling baby. "What shall I do with her, Runa?"

Runa shifted the baby into the crook of her arm, leaned over the woman, and felt her forehead. "Take her to the guest chamber in the west hall." She glanced at Beren and winked. "You'll have to be faster than that, nephew, to catch yourself a woman."

She didn't wait for an answer, but herded Dug and the women from the chamber. Bemused, Beren stared after them. Another time he'd have bristled at his aunt's teasing, but his vision tangled in hair the color of sunset and vivid sea-green eyes.

"Well," said Magrim after a moment. "That was interesting."

"Interesting?" Beren jerked his gaze away from the door. "That woman was almost killed, and so were you." Guilt made him snap at the older man. After all, Beren had been the one to discover the appropriate adjustments on the 'Link, even if no one but he and Magrim knew.

The keeper gave an indulgent smile. "She is safe now. Would you deny we saved her life?"

Beren was speechless. The keeper acted as if this whole disaster was the best thing to happen to that poor woman.

Eskil stepped forward and touched his arm. "He's right. Whatever happened in that Shadow world, she wouldn't have survived if we hadn't opened the door when we did."

Shadow world. All Beren's indignation seeped away, replaced by wonder. He'd met a real denizen of the Shadows.

A commotion drew his attention back to the door. Chieftain Garan limped into the chamber, his thick black brows drawn together in an intimidating scowl.

When the previous chieftain, Soren, died with his sons in battle twelve summers ago, his nephew was the obvious choice to take over leadership. That same battle had damaged Garan's leg beyond healing. Garan and his family took over Soren's quarters after Soren's wife moved to a nearby village to stay with her married daughter.

Now Garan fixed the keeper with a hard glare. "What's this I hear about an attack?"

Magrim didn't seem to notice the chieftain's mood. He stroked the Shadow-Link on the pedestal. The gray metal box still hummed with the power of its last use. "There was no danger, Garan. Your warriors were sufficient to avert any problem."

Garan's gray eyes narrowed and he tugged one of the braided points of his beard. "That's not the point. Is it true? You let a woman from the Shadow worlds through the portal?"

"She fled a battle. We could hardly send her back." Magrim offered a placating smile.

"I'm told she was chased by a berserker."

Magrim shrugged and covered the Shadow-Link with an embroidered black cloth. "Oh, I don't think he was a berserker. Merely a barbarian."

Garan scowled and clenched his fists. "A barbarian who almost killed you, who could even now be running loose in my village, terrorizing my people."

The keeper sighed. "You're overreacting, Garan."

"Overreacting?" The chieftain cursed, words Beren had never heard from this usually placid man.

Beren exchanged a worried look with Eskil. The other warriors shuffled their feet and avoided looking at each other. Garan the Relentless was known for an even temper. A good man, shrewd in judgments, it was rare for the chieftain to show anger, but when he did, wise men avoided him.

Garan paced around the chamber, the halting drag of his footsteps whispering on the rush-covered floor. He stopped in front of the pedestal and snatched the cloth from the 'Link. His jaw tightened and he fixed the keeper with a stern gaze. "There will be no more portals opened. We've survived well enough with the trade. I won't risk people coming through."

The smirk on the keeper's face slipped for the first time. "But we've spent years trying to widen the portals. How else can we learn if we don't visit—"

"No." The one word held all of Garan's authority and disapproval.

Magrim blinked. "But lord—"

"No." Garan took a deep breath. "No more portals. You will not continue with this madness. Do I make myself clear?"

The two men faced each other, one old and frail but with a will of steel, the other younger, half a head taller, his battle scars masked by the muscles on his arms and legs, his will just as strong, just as determined.

After a moment, Magrim bowed his head and gave a brief nod. Beren sighed out the breath he'd been holding.

Garan smiled and clapped a beefy hand on the keeper's shoulder. "Come, my friend. You have to admit it's safer this way." He paused, waited until Magrim looked at him before continuing in a more gentle tone. "You know it must be done."

"But the woman—we can return her when she heals. The battle will be over then. It should be safe."

Wait. If the 'Link opens to water, then she must have been on a ship, not dry land. The realization stunned Beren. *Even if the ship hasn't sunk, it won't be in the same place as the 'Link any more. She can't go back.*

"The woman stays. There is no other choice." The chieftain straightened his shoulders. "I will not risk my people again."

After a long moment, the keeper nodded.

Garan turned to Beren. "Your sword, warrior."

Startled at the sudden attention, Beren drew the heavy blade and held it out, but Garan shook his head. "No, don't give it to me. You're the strongest here." He gestured at the Shadow-Link. "Destroy it."

Destroy it? After all the trouble I went to getting it to work?

The meaning of the keeper's reluctance became clear. With the 'Link destroyed, there was no way the woman could return to her world, even if the ship was still there, and Beren's success was meaningless, the sole result a strange woman who didn't even understand their language.

He couldn't refuse the order. If he didn't do it, another would. At least he might be able to control the amount of damage.

He walked to the pedestal. Over the years, it had been discovered that, while the 'Links were impervious to fire and in general indestructible, they did have a weakness. If struck in the right spot, atop the colored circles, they shattered.

Beren raised his sword above his head, then paused. A pair of sea-green eyes, dark with pain and defiance, flashed into his mind. *No.*

He banished the vision, took a breath, and brought the sword down. Blade struck 'Link and produced a blinding flash of light.

Beren blinked away the after-image and stared. A pile of crushed metal remained on the pedestal, and at its foot, a pool of oily liquid seeped into cracks in the wooden floor.

Garan grunted. "It is done. Best clear up the mess before someone slips on it."

He limped away, leaving Beren to stare at the remains of the 'Link he'd worked so hard on.

~ * ~

Elizabeth opened her eyes. *Am I dead?* All around her was white—white walls that flowed like water, white ceiling that rippled and swayed in a hypnotic manner. She pushed herself up. Sharp pain lanced through her shoulder and she bit her lip to keep from crying out. For the first time she noticed her left arm was swathed in bloody cloths.

The dead don't feel pain, nor do they bleed.

A woman's face appeared above her, unwrinkled yet not young, reassurance in her smile. Her mother's age, or close to it perhaps. Elizabeth recognized the blue ribbons braided into her blonde hair. This was the woman who had taken Ned away.

The woman pressed a gentle hand against Elizabeth's good shoulder and forced her to lie down again. The surface beneath her felt as soft as any bed in her father's manor, softer, for the mattress, if she could call it thus, was covered in a wool that neither scratched nor made her sneeze with dust. She closed her eyes.

Someone pressed a cool cloth to her forehead. Words washed over her, their sound soft but unintelligible. Once more she opened her eyes. The room no longer spun around her. *Did I faint?*

"Ned," she whispered, unable to keep the fear from her voice. "My baby. Please?" She bent her good arm and rocked it, hoping the gesture, if not the words, conveyed her meaning.

The woolen blanket slid to her waist. Startled at the sudden rush of cold air, she dragged the covering back up to her neck. Her fingers brushed the chain holding her cross. She wore nothing else. *Where's my gown? My corset and chemise?*

The woman who tended her said something in that strange language, then moved from sight. She returned a moment later with a bundle of fur in her arms. She lowered it to the bed and pushed the fur aside.

Elizabeth's son lay cradled in the soft folds. His eyes drooped with sleep but he still gazed about him with curiosity. She let out her breath and raised her good arm to touch his cheek. He was alive, unharmed. He opened his mouth and turned his head toward her, pudgy fists pushing at the covers. Her breasts felt heavy and full, aching for release, but she couldn't risk feeding him. There might be poison in the wound, in the blood.

The woman touched her arm and indicated a cup she held in one hand. Elizabeth nodded. The woman slid her other hand beneath Elizabeth's shoulders and raised her head. She tilted the cup and Elizabeth took a sip. One swallow made her cough and sputter. She'd expected water, or perhaps wine, not warm milk.

"*Keevah*." The woman indicated the cup.

Elizabeth nodded, not sure whether the word meant 'good' or 'milk' or even 'medicine.' She took another reluctant sip, then pushed the cup away.

The woman laid the cup on a small wooden table and touched a hand to her chest. "Runa." She pointed a finger at Elizabeth and raised her eyebrows in an obvious question.

Elizabeth wet her lips. "Elizabeth."

Runa tilted her head. "Ee-liss-eth?"

"No. Za-beth. E-li-*za-beth*."

The woman laughed and shook her head. "Zabeth."

Elizabeth hadn't the strength to argue, but when Runa lifted Ned from her side, she clutched him tighter.

"*Nei*." Runa loosened Elizabeth's grip and held the baby out of reach.

Two other women stepped forward from the shadows. Like Runa, they wore ankle-length shifts covered in colorful tunics made of a heavy material that looked like sacking but felt, as Elizabeth learned when her hand brushed Runa's clothing, more like soft wool. Each woman wore a different colored tunic, one pale green, one yellow, and Runa's a bright poppy red.

Runa handed Ned to the woman in the green tunic, who sat at the foot of the bed and pulled her sleeve off her shoulder to reveal a plump breast. Ned lunged for the proffered meal.

"Little glutton," Elizabeth murmured with a fond smile.

The third woman leaned over Elizabeth and removed the bandages that bound her shoulder.

A doctor? In some distant lands women were allowed to do more than embroider pretty pictures and bear children. Elizabeth often wished she'd been born in such a place, where she was allowed to stretch her mind. Her brothers had scoffed at her when she'd hid in the schoolroom to eavesdrop on their lessons, although they'd soon learned the advantages of a sister who volunteered to do their schoolwork while they escaped to the stables or apple orchard. Even David teased her about her insatiable curiosity, her unfeminine love of books. He never understood her need to learn about other lands, her interest in other languages.

David. Tears filled her eyes, but she blinked them back. She couldn't allow herself the luxury of grief, not yet, not until she knew more about where she was and how she was going to get herself and her son home again.

Someone touched her good shoulder. "Zabeth?"

She looked up. Runa stood beside the healer and frowned. With trepidation, Elizabeth turned her attention to the wound. At her first sight of the cut, bile rose in her throat. The white of bone showed through. She'd be lucky not to lose her arm. She'd be lucky to live.

The healer pulled a claw-shaped root from a pouch that hung at her belt. "*Klengodd,*" she pronounced. The name of the plant? She crumbled the dried root into a pot she held on her lap, added water, mashed the concoction into a paste, then smeared it over the wound. Elizabeth flinched, but the pain wasn't as sharp as she expected.

When the healer was finished, she bound the wound again and pulled the blanket over Elizabeth. A pleasant numbness spread through Elizabeth's shoulder.

"Ned?" She yearned to hold her son again.

"*Nei.*" Runa shook her head, pointed at the bandaged shoulder, and waved her arms through the air.

Elizabeth understood. She already felt distant and feverish. She'd tended her brother, Jason, when a broken leg had resulted in fever. He'd thrashed about in delirium, and if she did the same she might hurt the child. She understood, but it took all her courage to nod her agreement.

Runa patted her on the shoulder and muttered something that might have meant *good*.

Ned had fallen asleep at his supper. Runa took him from the wet-nurse and laid him in a wooden cradle a few paces away. The healer and wet-nurse left. Runa settled on a bench near the cradle and removed a crude drop-spindle and wool from a bag at her feet. While she spun, Elizabeth stared at the rippling ceiling and waited for the fever to take her.

After a moment, she blinked. She was wrong. The ceiling wasn't moving. A canopy of white gauzy material was suspended over the bed. Hides of white fur covered the walls and floor. Where was she? On land, of that she was certain. She'd grown so used to the rocking of the waves over the last few weeks that their absence was noticeable.

How did she get there? How did she step from a ship in the

middle of the ocean into a stone room on dry land?

Or had she? Perhaps there was another ship, one sent to attack the pirates. In her flight she'd stumbled from one ship to another, and while she lay unconscious, the ship had sailed to land. She must have confused the stone walls of this building with what her panicked mind had seen on the ship.

So where was she? Was this one of the colonies they'd been sailing to, and these people…natives?

So many questions, and no chance of an answer as long as she couldn't speak their language. They'd saved her life, but why and how would have to wait.

A tremor passed through her. She huddled under the warm wool. Her head ached. Her cheeks felt as if they were on fire. The plant the healer had put on her wound must be drawing the poison. *I hope it doesn't kill me while it's doing its work.*

At least Ned was safe. She sensed these people were kind enough to care for him if anything happened to her, but she didn't know them, didn't even know if they believed in God. She preferred Ned be raised a good Christian and for that she'd have to survive.

The room spun and she squeezed her eyes shut. Her first duty was to get better, to help her son, help herself.

When the fever took hold, she dreamed of the early days when she and David had first wed. They were happy days, before David's obsession with the Americas uprooted the new family two months after the birth of their son. The first part of the voyage had been peaceful, and lulled her into believing David's promise of a fine new life.

Then came the attack.

Elizabeth whimpered, tossed her head. A rough hand brushed her hair away from her eyes. Gentle fingers smoothed the creases from her forehead.

As I used to do to David.

Tears spilled unheeded down her cheeks. Again, the healing touch of callused hands stroked her hair. She sighed, sniffed back another tear, and drifted deeper into sleep.

~ * ~

Beren resisted the urge to wipe the tears from the woman's face. She seemed calmer, her sleep peaceful now, and he didn't want to wake her. Leaving his hand in place, he shifted back on his stool and rolled his shoulders to ease the cramp in his neck.

"You shouldn't have come if you didn't expect to be put to work," Runa chided while she bustled around the room.

"I only came to tell you the 'Link's destroyed. You didn't have to drag me in here to play nursemaid." His protest was half-hearted. In truth he didn't mind sitting with the Shadow woman—Zabeth, Runa had called her. No, he didn't mind at all, especially if he was able to calm her delirium.

Runa smoothed a hand over the blanket that covered the child. "Now you've told me, and you've helped me calm her down without waking the baby. She'll be fine for a few hours. You don't have to stay if you don't want to."

Beren fisted his hand, pulled it back from Zabeth's hair—such soft hair, cool and silky, for all it looked like liquid fire. He waited for a moment but she didn't react to his withdrawal. He heaved a soft sigh of relief—or was it regret?—and pushed himself to his feet.

When he headed for the door, Runa called after him. "Any word from the boys?" The question was flung out as if in afterthought, but Beren heard the tension.

Guilt swamped him. He'd forgotten why Runa wasn't busy with her own household. Her husband was away on the *Freki* with the rest of the warriors, while her son faced his manhood trials in the woods with the other boys his age.

"Not yet." He turned to her. "They've only been gone a week." He'd passed his own manhood trial at thirteen, the same age as Runa's Mikkel. It had been exhilarating, exciting, and terrifying at the same time. At least the boys had adult hunters to back them up.

Runa sighed. "I know, but they say…" She paused. Fear flashed into her eyes but was gone so fast Beren wasn't sure he'd seen it. After a moment, she continued in a stronger voice. "They say the bears are bolder this year. The dry summer kept the berries from ripening in the foothills, and they're moving into the valleys in packs."

Garan hadn't wanted to worry anyone until the boys returned but word had obviously spread despite his efforts. Beren forced a reassuring smile. "You've been listening to the old gossips."

"Perhaps." Runa raised her chin and caught his gaze. "They also say the males are bigger, the biggest in memory."

He shook his head. "They're no bigger than when I took my first pelt." He stroked the fur of his cloak and hoped his aunt wouldn't remember how three of the boys in his year had been mauled before he'd managed to bring the beast down.

Runa nodded, gave a faint smile. It didn't fool Beren. "All right. I suppose Mikkel would die of embarrassment if he knew I worried about him."

Beren grinned. "Every thirteen-year-old wants to forget he has a mother during the manhood trials."

Runa remained silent, one of the few who knew better than to ask if he wanted to forget his own mother.

From the cradle by the window, an arm flailed in the air and a sound, half coo, half hiccup, issued from the tiny occupant. When Runa bent to soothe the child, Beren headed back to his room and the tasks that awaited him there.

Chapter Three

The next morning Beren rose just after sunup, hurried to the Keeper Hall, and made his way to the small storage room where he'd stowed the broken Shadow-Link. Despite Garan's order, he couldn't bring himself to throw it away. He pulled the bundled cloth from the back of the shelf, careful not to rattle the contents more than he had to. The hallway was deserted when he peered out the door. Good. No one to notice him sneak the bundle into his workroom.

When Beren had first given in to temptation to study the Shadow-Links, he had set up a small workspace in a far corner of the God-Hold. That had proved unworkable once winter came and the God-Hold was closed off until spring. He'd confided in Magrim, who offered a forgotten room behind the keepers' quarters. Relieved at the solution, Beren moved his tools to the Keeper Hall.

Now he made his way down the hallway, peering around corners and door frames before proceeding. Although the keepers knew about his interest, Beren didn't want anyone to see what he carried. He held his breath when he crossed the open space of the trade chamber, and didn't release it until he was past the sleeping quarters and shut in his workroom.

He spread the cloth on the wooden table he used as a workbench and peered at the tangled mess of broken wires and crushed metal.

Why did I think I could repair this? The damage is too great.

"It's not your fault."

Beren jumped at the voice and swallowed his surprised cry. Magrim stood in the doorway.

"Yes it is." Beren recovered quickly and waved at the table. "It's my fault Zabeth is here. If I hadn't fixed the 'Link—"

"If you hadn't fixed the 'Link, she'd be dead in that place." Magrim strolled around the table and poked a finger into various bits of metal. "What you did was a great achievement. How many years have we failed to solve this problem?" He didn't wait for Beren to answer. "You should consider formal training. You can't keep working in secret."

Beren shrugged. "I'm supposed to be a warrior."

"Bah. Any fool can be a warrior." Magrim stopped in front of him. "You've a sharp mind. We need you here."

"Tor and Kiana—"

"Tor and Kiana would approve."

Beren shook his head. "They expect more of me."

Magrim clucked his tongue. "You don't know that." He narrowed his eyes. "Beren, you once told me what your mother said before she sent you away. Do you remember?"

Be brave. Live a good life. Make me proud.

"I remember." She'd given her life to save his.

"Don't her wishes mean more than trying to do what you think your heart-parents want?" Magrim gentled his tone. "Tell them. They may surprise you." He straightened his shoulders, looked Beren in the eye. "And don't blame yourself for Zabeth. The gods sent her here for a reason. It's not your fault she came."

Again Beren shook his head. "Maybe so, but it's my fault she can't go back." He glared at the broken 'Link.

Magrim chuckled. "Blame that on Garan. You only acted as his hands."

"Still."

"Still, it is done and there's no changing that." He poked a finger at the metal again. "This can't be fixed. Throw it in the sea and be done with it." At Beren's instinctive protest Magrim rolled his eyes. "Or keep it here until a miracle puts it together."

Beren sighed. "It's just… It seems so final."

Magrim shrugged. "Do as you wish, but think about what I said. Talk to Tor and Kiana if you must, but don't let them make up your mind for you. You're a grown man. Time to follow your own dreams, not anyone else's."

With a final poke at the mess on the worktable, Magrim left the room. Beren picked up the sack he'd tossed on the floor, swept the pieces into it, and set it in a storage box in the corner of the workroom. A miracle might not be able to *put it together*, as Magrim suggested, but deep in his heart he was certain he had to keep the broken Shadow-Link. One day, perhaps, it might come in useful.

Even if only for parts.

~ * ~

Later, after the morning meal, Beren and Eskil sat on a tree stump on a hill east of the village. They often came here when they were bored, or needed a quiet place to think. Dominating the space below was the building that housed the kitchens, the Gather Hall, the quarters of the chieftain, and rooms for several families whose men folk had sailed on the *Freki*.

And Zabeth.

How did she feel this morning? The *klengodd* root would be well on its way to healing her injury. She might need to build the strength in her arm, but by tomorrow the cut should be almost closed. He narrowed his eyes and tried to match the location of her room with the windows he could see from this vantage point. Unfortunately, her window was on the other side of the building and overlooked the town that had grown over the years.

He remembered when the Gather Hall was built, a longhouse now enclosed by additional rooms on all sides, as well as a small courtyard in front of the main doors on the west side. A second level raised the roof of the Gather Hall so high the ceiling rafters sometimes disappeared in the smoke from winter braziers. Separate buildings now housed barracks for the warriors, both male and female, and stables for the livestock.

The forge, once located at the edge of the village, now stood near its center, engulfed by individual houses as the number of families grew and spread over the years until buildings sprawled from the forest to the beach and half the width of the cove from cliff to cliff. Like the Keeper Hall, the forge was surrounded by open space paved with stone to catch any stray sparks.

Attached to the back was the bath house, Beren's favorite building. Many of his ideas to improve the Shadow-Links came to him while he relaxed in the heated water.

"Stop moping, Beren." Eskil gave his friend a playful punch on the shoulder. "Anyone would think you'd never seen a woman before."

Beren scowled. "I'm not moping. And she's not just any woman. She's from the Shadow worlds."

Ever since Zabeth had stumbled through the Shadow-Link portal, Beren hadn't been able to get her out of his mind. It was puzzling. The fact she came from a world far from his shouldn't cause her face to appear in his dreams. Was she from the future or the past? Did his interest rest with her origins, or was there something else?

And therein lay the danger. Fascinated as he was with the Shadow worlds, with learning everything about them, still he didn't quite trust them. Who knew what lay on the other side of the 'Links? Treasures untold? Or savages and danger? At least with the smaller windows, the keepers had more control over what came through the 'Link. Garan was right to destroy the doorway.

Beren shifted on the stump and shied away from the memory of the broken 'Link.

"You won't learn much if you can't understand her," Eskil teased. "Why don't you ask the keepers to trade for a translating device?"

Beren shuddered at a memory. "You mean like the one they stuck in my ear last summer? I thought I'd go deaf when you all started babbling louder than a herd of dragons in rut."

Eskil grinned. "Magrim said it needed adjusting."

"Not much left to adjust." Not after he tore it from his ear and hurled it against the wall.

"A pity you can't just pick up her language like Kiana." Eskil chuckled, then went still. "I wonder if Gudrin…"

Beren rolled his eyes. "Gudrin's five." His heart-sister had inherited her mother's talent for understanding any language after hearing a few words, but the child was too young to form clear sentences in her own tongue, much less translate someone else's. "Anyway," he continued, "Zabeth's going to have to learn our language sooner or later. She'll be living here now."

Eskil picked up a stone and tossed it into the long grass, "Hopefully, Runa finds her some decent clothes. Did you see all that material she was wearing?"

"You should have seen what was under it," Beren retorted without thinking. Eskil gasped and Beren realized his mistake. "What I meant was…when I was there, Runa showed me…there was this…" How to describe the stiff vest Runa told him she'd found beneath Zabeth's clothes? She swore it had pulled the woman into such an unnatural shape it was a wonder she could breathe. Eskil grinned, and he had to grin back. "Never mind. I'm sure Runa will show you. Or the keepers. She said she might give it to them."

The keepers had traded for many items over the years. Most proved useful, but some even their best scholars were unable to understand. These ended up on display in one of the rooms set aside in the Keeper Hall for such things.

"She wore a cross, like the old seer," Beren continued, remembering the silver chain around the woman's neck. Jorvik, by his own admission raised in a monastery, had studied the old gods as well as the new one, and employed divination tools unknown to most priests of his order. The seer's death of a fever six years ago had left an unexpected hole in the community.

"So she follows the one god?" Eskil pursed his lips. "That means she's from the future, then."

Beren shrugged. Worship of the one god, he understood, was a fledgling religion in Tor's time. Here, of course, thousands of years before that time, a cross held no meaning. "When the *Freki* gets back, Kiana can talk to her."

Eskil nodded. "Do you think they'll make it back in time?"

Beren shrugged. "They're only two weeks late."

"But if they don't get back before the first snows, they'll have to dock in a southern port until spring."

"It won't be the first time."

"And then there's the raiders. What if they find out?" There was no fear in Eskil's voice. Mortal enemies didn't worry him.

Beren flexed his fingers on the hilt of his sword. "Let them come. We'll drive them off like we did the last time."

"Last time we had thirty warriors," Eskil reminded him. "Now there's less than half that."

"Plus the local farmers and hunters and those women with advanced skills Lida trained." But Beren grimaced. Most of the warriors had sailed with Tor. The *Freki*'s task this year had been exploration in addition to trade, and Tor wanted as many fighters with him as could be spared, even though it left the village, if not defenseless, at least short-handed. "We'll manage."

A shout drew his attention back to the village.

"What's going on?" Eskil squinted for a better look.

Dug appeared at the foot of the hill and waved urgently at them.

"What is it?" Beren shouted.

Dug pointed to the Gather Hall. "The boys are back. It's not good."

Chapter Four

Chaos reigned in the Gather Hall. The groans of injured boys mingled with the wails of their mothers and the imperious shouts of those few attempting to restore order. Beren glimpsed some of the returning hunters but before he could look for his cousin, Runa, distracted and frantic, rushed up to him.

"Beren, thank the gods. Mikkel's been injured! Can you watch over Zabeth?"

Alarm shot through him. "Mikkel? What happened?"

"I don't know yet. Please Beren. Zabeth's fever broke and she's sleeping but I don't want to leave her alone and I can't stay with her. I'll send one of the women to take over as soon as I can."

He'd never seen his aunt so upset. "Of course I'll watch her. Go." He gave her a gentle shove toward the pallets. He couldn't tell which of the several injured was Mikkel, and much as he wanted to stay, he'd been given a job to do. With one last glance at the chaos, he climbed the stairs to the second level.

Zabeth had been put into the room on the northwest corner of the sleeping quarters. He listened outside the door before he pushed it open. Because the room now held a healing patient, the walls had already been hung with winter furs and the shutters on the window were closed to keep the heat in. Even the lack of light, however, couldn't dim the bright red curls that peeked above a woolen blanket on the raised pallet.

Beren crept closer and gazed down at the woman.

The spark he'd felt when she'd first appeared in the portal, when he'd soothed her during her fever, was just as sharp now. With the blanket pulled up over her nose, all he could see were her closed eyes, but he knew the green of them. They reminded him of the magical hues of Bifrost on a cold autumn night, a green so bright a man could get lost in them. He'd never felt this way about any of the village women. Was this the lifemate he'd been waiting for?

A muffled scream of pain drew his attention to the door. Mikkel? No, the cry was too deep, a man's voice. On the way to the Hall, Dug had mentioned the bear had charged one of the hunters and broke his arm, exposing bone. Thank the gods it hadn't been one of the youths.

Worry had him moving back to the door. He'd stay there, where he could watch Zabeth and listen to what was happening below, at least until the woman Runa sent arrived. Then he'd see for himself how his cousin fared.

He glanced at the pallet, then leaned against the wall to wait.

~ * ~

Elizabeth woke from her fevered dreams and remembered where she was. She lay still, listening for Ned's snuffling breaths. He always snored a little when he slept. There, a snort. She smiled to herself, then froze. She wasn't alone. Someone else breathed nearby. *Not Runa*. A faint scent of cedar filled the room. Heart pounding, she turned her head.

A man leaned against the far wall, dark skin framed by dark hair and beard. Her breath caught in her throat. It was *him*. The man who'd saved her.

He still looked like a barbarian, but he'd tidied himself up. His black hair now hung in two long braids over his shoulders and half-way down a dark blue woolen tunic that stopped at his knees. A brown leather belt cinched the tunic at his waist. Below the tunic, brown breeches disappeared into high leather boots.

There was something familiar about his clothes, as if she'd seen someone dressed like him in a picture, but she couldn't place the memory. He'd braided the outer strands of his beard, but the rest flowed in a luxuriant mass that stopped below his collarbone. His beard hid the shape of his jaw, but he had high cheekbones, a straight nose, and eyes…eyes that held a gentle reassurance she found at odds with his uncivilized appearance.

At the moment, those eyes kept shifting their gaze from the far wall to the door beside him. She stirred beneath the woolen blanket. The material scratched her skin and reminded her of her nakedness. At her movement, the man transferred his attention to her.

She pulled the blanket down to her chin and held it with her good hand. Her injured shoulder protested the movement, but she ignored the pain.

"What are you doing here?" She was determined not to show any nervousness. "Where's Runa?"

A speculative look entered his eyes and he straightened away from the wall. Dear God, he was even taller than she remembered, and much more massive. He made her feel like a child by comparison. She swallowed hard, but held his gaze and raised her chin to show she wasn't intimidated by him. *After all, I'm the daughter of a viscount, born to nobility, while he's just...just a scruffy barbarian.*

As if understanding her bluff, the expression in his eyes softened. He touched his finger to his chest. "Beren." He pointed at the door and said something with the name *Runa* in the phrase.

Elizabeth shook her head, uncomprehending. She slid farther down in the bed and gripped the blanket so tight her knuckles ached. She shouldn't even be speaking to him. They hadn't been introduced.

Yes, it was irrational to think of proprieties under such circumstances, but she couldn't forget nineteen years of schooling in the proper way for a lady to act. Before her marriage to David, she'd never been alone in a room with a man, not even her father or brothers, and to be so now, naked as she was, made her shiver with...unease? Yes, definitely unease.

A cry drew her attention to the cradle a few feet away. *Ned.* Concern overrode modesty. She tucked the blanket beneath her chin, pulled her uninjured arm from beneath the cover, and gestured to Beren. "Can you bring him to me?"

Confusion filled his eyes. She gestured again, but instead of going to the cradle, he said something about Runa and hurried out the door.

"Wait." The door slammed behind him. "Men," she grumbled, but her anger was half-hearted. David, too, always found an excuse to avoid holding his son, as if his mere touch might shatter the child.

Memories of David as she'd last seen him flooded into her mind and threatened to swamp her with grief, but Ned continued to cry. Impatient sobs escalated to a demanding howl. Perhaps later, when she had a chance to think, to rest, she'd allow herself to grieve for her husband.

Right now, her duty was to her son. "All right, love. I'm coming." She pushed back the blanket.

She levered herself to a sitting position and swung her legs over the side of the bed. She couldn't' quite reach him. Chill air struck her body. She needed clothes or...something...before she dared go to Ned. Her gaze lit on another blanket at the foot of the bed. She grabbed it, wrapped it around herself, and tucked in the ends as best she could.

A wave of dizziness shook her. How many days had she been trapped in fever? She made it to her feet, but at once swayed and had to lean against the white furred hides on the wall. After a moment, the room stopped spinning. At least her shoulder didn't hurt as much as before.

"I can do this," she muttered. Although the floor still threatened to fall from beneath her, the surface beneath her fingers remained steady. A couple of steps, but it seemed like miles. Placing one foot in front of the other, Elizabeth slid along the wall, brushing her fingers against the silky fur until she stood beside the cradle.

"There now," she murmured, and stroked a finger down Ned's soft cheek.

Using her injured arm as little as possible, she managed to lift the baby and hold him against her shoulder. Someone had swaddled him in a soft blanket, but he'd managed to free one arm. He hiccupped, grabbed a fistful of her loose hair and stuck it in his mouth.

Elizabeth rocked back and forth, crooning at the impatient child. "Hush, there. I'll feed you soon, but I can't do it standing here. Hush."

Still chewing on her hair, Ned dropped his head on her shoulder and relaxed. Perhaps he wasn't hungry after all. He seemed warm enough in the blanket. Perhaps he wanted reassurance, as she did, that he wasn't alone.

She breathed in the clean baby scent of him, then sniffed again. Someone had washed him and, more recently, fed him. A stab of jealousy swept through her, then she gave a rueful chuckle. Ned may be her responsibility, but she'd not been able to do that job of late.

She looked back at the bed. Her body trembled from the little exertion she'd forced upon it. She tightened her grip on Ned, leaned against the wall, narrowed her eyes, and concentrated. At last, the trembling passed. *I can make it. I have to.*

A glint of light drew her attention farther along the wall—an opening, shuttered with wooden slats painted white to match the furs. Daylight filtered through the slats in narrow bars.

A window. A chance to see this new land she'd come to.

Curiosity banished the last traces of weakness. Perhaps curiosity wasn't a trait in which a lady should indulge, but she could no more change her nature than the color of her hair. She clutched Ned more securely and edged along the wall. Ten more steps to the window. Five. Two. One.

She eased open the edge of one shutter with her elbow and braced for her first view of the world outside.

One floor below lay a street. Cobbles lined the edges and packed earth sprinkled with small pebbles wound between houses unlike any she'd seen before. She wasn't sure what she expected. From her reading she knew places like Boston or Philadelphia had stone or wood buildings, but this place wasn't as big as those great cities and no such buildings graced its streets. Nor did the scene match the pictures of the native people's tents.No, she wasn't in a city or a native camp. None of these houses were more than one story tall, and all looked made from a kind of whitewashed plaster. Narrow windows were covered in shutters painted in bright colors. The scene reminded her of a painting she'd once seen of an Italian seaport.

A chill breeze nipped at her fingers. *Not Italy. Not any sun-drenched country.* Not even the nights in England ever got this cold, and with the sun overhead, it wasn't going to get much warmer as the day progressed. Where was this place? How far was she from the nearest English settlement? David had told her tales of the cities in the Americas, but nothing he'd described matched this place.

As if the plaster walls of the buildings weren't enough to confuse her, when she lifted her gaze higher, roofs came into view, not shingled or thatched. Flat as a meadow, each roof seemed made of living *grass*. More than half had goats grazing up there. Ramps covered in grass led from the ground to the top of each house, with a shed or small stable at the bottom of each ramp.

How curious.

To her left, the sea glistened vast and blue. A pebbled beach barred the street from the water, and, pulled up on the beach, tilted on its side like a wounded calf, lay a ship. About forty feet long, the vessel looked sleek and fast. A dark, barnacle-encrusted hull faced her, and rising high above the prow, jutting defiantly into the waters, was a figurehead she'd seen in paintings, the head of a fierce dragon.

A Viking ship!

"Oh dear God," she whispered.

She let the shutter swing shut, clutched at her cross, and stared at the covered window. That was where she'd seen the man's—Beren's—clothes before. She'd read all the tales, knew all the stories. Vikings were cruel, murderous heathens who destroyed good Christian churches and slaughtered innocent priests and nuns.

But Vikings hadn't been seen for over six hundred years. Those who hadn't converted to Christianity had killed each other in senseless battles. At least some, it seemed, had fled to the Americas and settled here.

Did her hosts plan to help her get back to her people or keep her as a slave? Had she escaped the pirates only to fall into the hands of more savage captors?

They saved Ned and me from the pirates.

The thought helped calm her panic. So far she'd seen nothing that made her believe she was a prisoner. They'd treated her wound, taken care of her son.

But…*Vikings.*

The tales she'd heard growing up were difficult to ignore, but Elizabeth also couldn't ignore the evidence of her own experience these last few days. Were these people potential friends...or duplicitous enemies?

Chapter Five

Beren stood on the wooden balcony that circled the open space and looked for his aunt's blonde hair among the throng. Hair color ranged from white-blonde through light brown, while his and Kiana's were true black. His sister's hair was dark brown and his brothers' lighter, but no one had the rich sunset color of Zabeth's.

The Shadow woman seemed healthier today, recovered from the fever. Her manner reminded him of one of the grand ladies he'd heard ran the households of the Gallic coast. She'd expected instant obedience when she'd gestured at him, although what she'd expected him to do was beyond him. Something about her injury, or the baby? Or maybe she needed to use the privy?

In the end he'd decided the easiest solution was to get Runa, or at least one of the women she'd promised to send to replace him. They'd be better able to care for the woman's needs.

Reminded of his task, he continued his scan. Ah, there.

Runa sat at the side of a figure so swaddled in furs Beren didn't recognize his cousin. The boy kept throwing off the furs, but Runa, with equal determination, forced them back on him. At least Mikkel and the rest of the boys were alive, if injured.

Beren descended one of the staircases and pushed through the women. "Runa."

She jumped and gave him an impatient look. "What are you doing here? I told you to watch Zabeth." She stopped, shook her head. "Oh, I was going to send someone, wasn't I?"

"You were busy." Beren placed a hand on her shoulder. "I'll find someone now I'm here."

"Why did you leave her?" Runa searched his face, "Has the fever returned?"

"No. She's asking for something but I don't know what."

Runa raised an eyebrow. "If she's awake, she probably wants

her baby. All you had to do was give him to her."

Beren refused to meet her gaze. Instead he bent over his cousin. "How bad?"

The boy pushed the fur away from his face. "I'm not hurt. A few scratches. Mother fusses too much."

Runa snorted. "A few scratches deep enough to scar and become infected. Really, Mikkel, what were you thinking?"

"There wasn't much choice." He turned to Beren, eager to share his adventure with someone who'd appreciate it. "There was a big bear, more than twice your size, Beren. We were passing the waterfall when it attacked us. It grabbed Bjorn, so I jumped on its back and kept stabbing it until it let him go."

"You jumped on its back?" The bears in this land were giants. Beren's heart stuttered in his chest but he forced himself to grin. "That was very brave of you."

The boy preened, but Runa snatched the fur from his fingers and forced it up to his chin again. "That was very foolish."

She glared at her son, but Beren heard the fear in her voice. He pulled her to her feet and hugged her. He'd long ago outstripped Kiana in height, but Runa was still taller than he by two finger-widths. She sighed and tilted her head to his shoulder.

"Runa." He rubbed her back to relieve the tension in her shoulders. There was one thing that might distract her. "About Zabeth…"

Runa pushed away from him. "Yes, Zabeth. If she wants the baby, why didn't you give him to her?"

He cringed at her tone. Why didn't anyone understand? He was a big man, and it would be so easy to crush or drop such a tiny creature. "The child is too small. It needs a woman's touch."

"*He* doesn't need anything you can't give him." Her expression softened. "He won't break. Just pick him up and give him to her."

Beren said nothing, and after a moment, Runa sighed. "Men. Why do you always panic at the thought of touching a baby? Vider was the same, and Tor." She smiled at a memory, then hurried on. "I can't leave here. You said you'd watch her and I thank you for taking time from your duties, but I can't come. You'll have to deal with this yourself."

She gave an encouraging smile, and Beren found himself returning a sheepish grin. "Look." She glanced once at her son then back to her nephew. "If you don't want to lift the child yourself, help Zabeth lift him. The root's been working for a good day. She should be strong enough by now."

Relieved at this solution, Beren flashed her a wide grin. "Yes. Thank you, Runa."

"Now go on." She gave him an impatient nudge toward the stairs. "I'll come as soon as I can."

Beren winked at Mikkel, then returned to the room where he'd left Zabeth. Not until he stood in the hallway did he remember he'd intended to ask one of the women to replace him.

He listened at the door. No crying. No sound at all. Concerned, he pushed the door open. Zabeth stood at the window, the child held in one arm, his head resting on her shoulder. Beren breathed a sigh of relief. She hadn't fainted or collapsed, and thank the gods, the babe slept.

Draped in the woolen blanket, Zabeth's head, bare feet, and one arm were visible. The heavy wool concealed her curves. Standing there in the semi-darkness, shrouded in the shapeless blanket, she looked like a goddess, not a Valkyrie but one of the gentler goddesses of Asgard, a shadowy figure like the Shadow world from which she came.

He took a step forward and a board creaked beneath his foot.

Zabeth spun around, gasped, and backed away. Her eyes went wide for a moment, then she raised her chin as if in challenge. Despite her determined stance, even in the dim light the pallor of her skin was plain to see.

Puzzled, Beren took another step, but again she retreated until her back pressed against the wall. She hunched over the baby, as if to protect it—him—from danger, and said something in a tone that left Beren confused. She wasn't terrified, but she didn't want him near her.

Beren stopped. He held up both hands in a placating gesture. "I won't hurt you." He kept his voice low and spoke in soothing tones, as if to a nervous horse, the way he'd spoken to her in the Keeper Hall. "What has frightened you?"

She said nothing. A tremor raced through her body. Her knees gave way and Beren sprang forward to catch her.

When he accidentally grabbed her injured arm, she cried out, and he released her at once. She sagged against the wall and braced her knees to keep from sliding down.

So much for not hurting her. "I'm sorry." He injected as much remorse as possible into his voice. "I want to help. Here, come to the bed. You need rest."

Slowly, so as not to alarm her, he held out his hand. She stared at it as if it were a snake poised to strike. He gave his best reassuring smile. After a moment of indecision, she raised her head. Anxiety still showed in her eyes, but her lips were pressed together in a determined line. She straightened and glared at him until he backed away, then she shifted the child to a firmer position on her shoulder and slid sideways along the wall. The winter furs both supported her and protected her back from the rough stone beneath.

Beren tensed. Every instinct screamed at him to help her, but he resisted. He knew stubbornness—he did, after all, have a sister and an aunt who embodied the word *stubborn*—and he knew courage. Zabeth might be afraid, but she refused to let her fear keep her from guarding her child. He respected that.

Runa had been the same with her children. He remembered six years ago when his aunt had stood with sword drawn at the door to her house, resisting all efforts by enemy berserkers to enter. He hated to think of the consequences if her husband hadn't seen them and run with Tor to help her.

But Zabeth didn't face raiders. For some reason she seemed to think of Beren and his people as her enemies. What had changed since he'd left her? How to convince her they wanted to help?

Once she was seated on the edge of the bed, Beren picked up the cradle and brought it closer. He gave her a questioning look. Gods, he wished she could understand him. She made no move to lay the baby in the cradle. Instead, she clutched him tighter to her.

Perhaps Beren's height made her nervous. He stepped back and crouched on his haunches. He held out his hands, palms up in a peaceful gesture, and waited. At last, some of the fear left her eyes.

Beren glanced around the room and spied a cup on the small table beside the bed. He lifted it and held it toward the Shadow woman.

"*Keevah?*" Her lip curled in a grimace, and Beren chuckled. "I know. It's not my favorite drink either, but it'll give you strength." He held the cup toward her. "Drink, yes?"

To his surprise, a tiny smile quirked the corners of her lips. She looked at the cup, then transferred her gaze to her arms, one holding the child, the other swathed in bandages. Finally she looked at him and raised an eyebrow.

Beren shook his head with a rueful grin. She'd not be able to take the cup with both arms occupied.

He tilted his chin toward the cradle, but she shook her head. Instead, she shifted, let the baby slide down her chest until he rested on her lap and freed her arm. She reached for the cup and her expression became serious again.

Beren laid his hand over hers to steady her. The touch sent a jolt of fire leaping to his loins. He released the cup faster than he intended, but she'd already gripped it and nothing spilled. He curled his fingers on his thigh as she took a few tentative sips. When she thrust the cup back at him, he was careful not to touch her.

She took a deep breath as if to say something, but at that moment the baby stirred on her lap and gave a pitiful sob. She glanced down. The child opened his eyes and made sucking noises.

Zabeth rubbed the baby's cheek, and when he turned his head toward her, she slipped a finger into his mouth. The child latched on, suckling with an eagerness that caused a sharp flare of desire to sweep through Beren at the sight. *If only her finger was in my mouth.*

He pushed the image away, backed up, and sat in the sole chair in the room. He had a good hour before he was due on patrol. Zabeth seemed more relaxed now. Once she'd finished feeding the child, he'd try to teach her some words. The sooner she learned, the sooner he could...could what? His mind went blank. Oh, he could ask her about her world. And about her...life.

To his surprise, Zabeth didn't lift the child to her breast. Instead, she stared pointedly at Beren and said something in her own language, then jerked her chin toward the door.

He raised an eyebrow in disbelief. "You don't want me watching you?" He shook his head at her shyness and grinned. "Gods, Zabeth, if every woman insisted on suckling in private, the children would all starve to death before they were weaned."

Her gaze never faltered. He sighed, rose to his feet, then crossed the room. At the door, he glanced over his shoulder at her. Her expression told him she'd accept no argument, though her hands trembled. Still grinning, he opened the door and left.

He leaned against the wall outside her room and considered the woman within. He had to admit he was attracted to her but it was clear she was married. Did her husband still live in that Shadow world she came from? Or had he died there? Was she a wife or a widow?

To some of the friends he'd grown up with it wouldn't make a difference. They'd think nothing of seducing such a woman, but not Beren. She deserved more. What was it about her that drew him? Her courage? Yes, she'd shown that in every gesture, every tone. Her beauty? That too, but there were more beautiful women in the village.

It was a puzzle, but now was not the time to ponder it. Runa had given him a task. He couldn't watch Zabeth if he couldn't see her, but if he kept his ear to the door, he was bound to hear her if she fell off the bed.

"What are you doing out here?" As if conjured by his reflections, Runa strode down the hallway toward him. "Did you find someone to watch Zabeth?"

Beren straightened. "Um..."

Runa clucked her tongue in annoyance. "You forgot, didn't you? And now I find you skulking in the hallway. Honestly, Beren, she won't bite."

He winced. He hadn't done anything wrong but Runa had a way of making a man feel like a wayward child when she was displeased. He needed a diversion. "How's Mikkel?"

Runa's expression softened. "Better. The healers said to let him sleep, so I came to relieve you of your charge."

Before Beren could prevent her, Runa pushed past him and opened the door. A startled shriek from inside informed him Zabeth didn't welcome the intrusion.

He grinned. He suspected Runa had met her match in stubbornness.

When the door closed behind her, he shrugged away from the wall. Almost time for his patrol. Bears didn't come this close to the village, but there were other dangers, and the guards took turns watching the forest around the village. He'd just have time to grab a quick meal before he headed out.

~ * ~

Two hours later, on his way to the Gather Hall after an uneventful patrol, Beren almost collided with Eskil.

"There you are." His friend grabbed his arm.

The urgency in the statement stilled Beren's words of greeting. "What's wrong?"

"I went back to check those traps we set last night north of the village, and…" He paused, his gaze troubled.

"And?" Beren prompted. "Don't tell me you found one of those bears in a rabbit trap."

Eskil didn't smile. "No. I found something else. I was going to tell Garan but didn't want to worry him if I'm wrong. Can you come see?"

A short time later, Beren knelt beside Eskil in the soft mud and studied the footprint. There'd been a frost the night before, and the melted ice defined the shape of a large boot in the pale afternoon light.

"Someone stood here for several hours." Beren rose and both men stared over the rocky outcropping to the village below. They had a clear view of the busy streets, the empty harbor.

"It could have been one of our men," Eskil argued, but his tone implied he didn't believe it any more than Beren did.

"There's no danger from the village so why face that way and for so long? And in darkness?" The footprint had to have been made overnight. It wasn't there yesterday when Beren patrolled this spot.

Eskil narrowed his eyes. "So I wasn't wrong. Who do you think it was?"

"I'm not sure." Beren searched the area and found another print, bigger than the first. "There were at least two of them. They came from this direction." He looked up the hill toward the crest a short distance away. "Come on." He set off at a run.

The track vanished on the rocky summit, but reappeared farther down the hollow, heading away from the village. The ground must have been frozen when the watchers first came this way.

The trail followed a serpentine route, parallel to the shore. The mysterious watchers chose a path far enough down the slope of the cliffs they were able to walk upright and remain hidden from anyone on the seaward side. Several minutes later, Beren and Eskil arrived at a small cove three miles north in a straight line from the village.

Eskil pointed to a groove in the sand. "A small boat beached here."

They searched all around the area, but found nothing more, no evidence to indicate who their overnight visitors had been.

"Whoever they are, they're up to no good," Beren decided.

He remembered the enemies who had spied on the village sixteen years earlier, but dismissed them. They hadn't survived to report their discovery, and no one had come looking for him or Kiana since. That part of his life was over. Besides, there were other, more obvious enemies, if his suspicions were correct.

Eskil nodded. "Otherwise why skulk around so far from the village? We'll have to warn the women not to pick berries alone. It's bad enough with the bears so far south. We should make sure no one goes out after dark, or travels by themselves."

On the way back to the village, Beren glanced at his friend. Eskil was always thinking of ways to protect the helpless, while Beren's reaction to any threat was to run after it and attack before it attacked him. "You'd make a good chieftain," he remarked.

"Right," Eskil scoffed. "And you'd make a good blacksmith. Leading's not in my nature."

"It wasn't in Garan's, either," Beren pointed out. "Or Vider's, and he's war second now."

Eskil shook his head and quickened his pace. A few minutes later, a slender body hurtled from the bushes and crashed into Eskil. They rolled into the dense scrub on the other side of the trail.

By the time Beren drew his sword and ran to the spot, the two figures had come to rest. The smaller sat on Eskil's chest and held a knife to his throat. Sunlight arrowed through the denuded treetops and glistened on the gold cord threaded through the blonde braids of the attacker.

"Astri." Eskil spat pine needles from his mouth.

Beren sheathed his sword. Eskil's father was a fisherman, but Eskil himself had longed to be a warrior like the Norse settlers who had joined them years ago. Vider and Runa, Astri's parents, fostered him for a few years to teach him the skills. The arrangement wasn't unusual in the Norse culture, so Eskil and Astri had grown up together. Astri, five years younger, took her role of foster sister seriously and teased him at every opportunity.

Grinning, Beren leaned against a nearby tree to enjoy the comedy taking place a few feet away.

"Some warrior you are," Astri purred. She pressed the point of her knife deeper into Eskil's throat and drew a pin-prick of blood. She wore the same tunic and trews as the male warriors and had trained with them and the other women who wanted more than defense training. "You were making more noise than a herd of dragons. Perhaps I should slit your throat and deprive the village of one of its least effective warriors."

Eskil narrowed his eyes. He heaved, twisted, and a moment later the two had reversed position. Eskil straddled Astri's hips, using his weight to hold her still and his hands to pin her wrists beside her head. The look of surprise on her face made Beren grin.

Most times Astri was the winner in their little skirmishes, but since Eskil had moved to the barracks with the other warriors, he'd learned a few tricks. As far as Beren knew, this was the first time Eskil had had a chance to use them.

With Eskil's face close to hers, his whispered response was too low for Beren to hear, but Astri didn't seem to like what she heard. She cursed and heaved, almost throwing Eskil off, but he shifted again and pressed a knee into her stomach. The air whooshed from her and she lay still, gasping. They glared at each other for several moments until Astri lifted her head and kissed Eskil hard on the mouth.

He was so startled she had no trouble tumbling him off her. She leapt to her feet and looked around for her knife.

Beren decided the time had come to interfere. "That's enough, children. Play time's over."

Astri spun around. Either she hadn't noticed him behind Eskil, or she'd forgotten he was there. She shrugged, grinned, and helped Eskil to his feet.

He stood. A frown of annoyance creased his forehead. "You shouldn't be wandering around here alone."

Astri flushed. "I wasn't wandering. I was looking for you—the two of you."

"Why?" Beren asked.

She raised her chin in challenge. "I found something in the cove back there."

"The boat mark?" Eskil snorted. "We saw it."

She huffed, deflated, but recovered with a smug grin. "Well, you didn't see *this* because I already picked it up."

She pulled a small object from behind her belt and handed it to Eskil. He studied it, and his gaze turned grim before he handed it to Beren.

It was a medallion from a war-dagger, a bronze oval with the familiar design of a sea-serpent engraved in the center and sharp holly leaves along the edge.

"Sjørotte," Beren declared, and closed his hand over the medallion. "I knew it."

"What do they want?" Eskil asked.

Beren bared his teeth in a grim smile. "What they always want, our land and slaves to work it."

Blood and riches, that's all the raiders loved. They weren't a new threat. Raiders had begun their attacks years ago, when Tor's people raised Beren's village from poor farmers and fishermen to prosperous traders of furs, woven cloth, mead, and metals forged into weapons and jewelry.

"We need to warn the village," Astri said.

Eskil brushed dirt off his backside and straightened his vest. "That's where we were going when you so foolishly interrupted us."

Astri raised an eyebrow in challenge and opened her mouth to speak. Eskil plucked a leaf from the top of her braid, turned, and pushed through the bushes back to the track. Astri closed her mouth with a snap and dashed after him. Beren shifted aside to avoid a collision.

The three of them proceeded in silence back to the village. From the angry looks Astri and Eskil exchanged, Beren doubted their thoughts were about raiders. A stray thought made him stumble. Was Astri the one Eskil pined for?

No, it couldn't be Astri. Eskil found her too annoying.

Back in the village, they made their way to Garan's quarters. As befitted the chieftain, Garan lived with his wife in several rooms off the Gather Hall. Garan's two sons were on the *Freki*, and when in the village they stayed in the barracks.

Garan sat before a roaring fire in his main room. Beren suspected the chieftain's leg injury made even the sunniest of fall days too cool. It was a tragedy he'd lain so long untended on the battlefield those many years ago. They hadn't known about *klengodd* root then, and when they did, it was too late to reverse the damage caused by the slash that almost severed his leg above the knee.

He didn't rise when the three entered, but waved to a bench on the other side of the fire. They sat, Beren between Astri and Eskil, and took turns explaining what they'd found, the conclusions they'd drawn, and the precautions they wanted to take. Garan didn't interrupt, and when they finished, he gave an approving smile.

"All good suggestions. Trouble is, most of the men here are fishers and farmers and cripples. If there came an attack now we'd need more than them and you six warriors. We'll need the women." He stared into the distance for a moment. "Tell Lida what's happening and have her step up the training, not just the young, strong ones like Astri here, but anyone who can hold a knife. Beren, you and Eskil can help when you're not on duty. Train in the horse barn so any watchers won't see our preparations."

The men nodded. Astri preened. Although few were a match for Kiana in swordplay, many of the women were expert archers and formidable foes. Lida, Kiana's first trainee, now trained all the women who wanted to fight, as well as every other female in the village to ensure they were capable of defending themselves. To Beren's surprise, although he had no liking for the skill, he found himself as adept at swordplay as his heart-mother. He couldn't refuse to help.

When they parted company, Beren and Eskil to pass the word to the other warriors and Astri to alert her fellow trainees, Beren saw Eskil glance after Astri, a thoughtful expression on his face.

Chapter Six

Her encounter with Beren had left Elizabeth shaken. It was more than his being a Viking. Despite the evidence of the ship, he hadn't acted like those fearsome ancient warriors. He hadn't assaulted her or attempted to harm her or Ned. She still had her cross. No one had taken it from her, even though the silver was a temptation to any thief.

In fact, everyone she'd encountered seemed friendly, helpful. At least Runa had managed to put her fears to rest when she returned to the room and used crude sign language to indicate Elizabeth was not a prisoner.

But there was that Viking ship. A puzzle, yes, but…not so much a puzzle as this strange warrior. Beren was gentle, calming, and she discovered she trusted him. There was something in his eyes that drew her, something she was afraid to acknowledge.

To distract herself from unwelcome emotions, she fussed over Ned. It had taken a while to communicate her wishes to Runa, but at last the Viking woman had nodded and opened the shutters. The light let Elizabeth see her son was safe and well.

"I need to learn the language," she decided, and smiled at Ned, fast asleep with one fist curled by his cheek. "If your father was here he'd insist *they* learn English." She paused, closed her eyes for a moment as the wave of grief swept over her, then took a deep breath and shook her head. "But there's only one of me and many of them. It's more polite for me to learn *their* language, don't you think?" Ned snuffled in his sleep and brought another smile to her lips. "Yes, that's what I thought. It'll be so much easier if we understood each other, if I can tell them what I need. Tomorrow, then. I'll ask Runa tomorrow."

The next morning Elizabeth broached the question as best she could. At first Runa didn't understand what she wanted. When Elizabeth pointed to her tongue, Runa picked up a plate of stew and handed it to her.

"No." Elizabeth shook her head and dropped her finger from her mouth. She looked around the room. How to get her meaning across? Inspiration struck.

She pointed at the mug of warm milk on the table. "*Keevah.* Milk."

Runa lifted the mug but Elizabeth stopped her hand. This time she pointed to the remains of the paste the healer had left in a little dish on the table. "*Klengodd.* Potion." She didn't know if that was the right translation, but at least it showed Runa she wasn't interested in something to drink. She tried other words she'd heard recently. "*Nei.* No. *Ja.* Yes."

The older woman tilted her head, narrowed her eyes, then pointed to the table. "*Bord.*"

"*Bord?*" Elizabeth repeated. "Table?"

With rising hope, she pointed to a few other items. When Runa supplied the words, Elizabeth repeated them, determined to get the accent right. Her tutors often told her she had a good ear for languages.

Once Runa understood what Elizabeth wanted to do, she said something and left the room. A few minutes later, she returned, followed by a little girl of about four or five, with skin darker than Runa's but a lighter gold than Beren's.

They stood in front of Elizabeth, and Runa put her hand on the child's shoulder. "Gudrin," she said in introduction.

The girl stuck a finger in the corner of her mouth and gave Elizabeth a polite smile, then switched her attention to the cradle beside the bed. She was a pretty child. Dark brown hair hung in two braids down her back. Not as pale-skinned as Runa nor as dark as Beren, she glowed with a healthy tan, which made her blue eyes more prominent.

Elizabeth smiled. "Is she your daughter?" She forgot for the moment that Runa couldn't understand her.

Gudrin looked up. "Auntie is Papa's sister."

Elizabeth gasped. The words were in perfect English.

Gudrin returned her attention to Ned in the cradle. Runa stroked her hair and spoke a few words. Gudrin muttered something, then turned to Elizabeth, a sullen look on her face. "Auntie says I have to tell you what she says and what you say to her."

For a moment, Elizabeth was stunned. "How old are you?" she asked.

Gudrin held up five fingers. "I have seen five summers, and my nameday is at midwinter."

Five years old, not quite six? "How do you know my language?" *And where were you when I needed you yesterday?*

Gudrin spoke to Runa, who paused a moment before answering. Gudrin nodded and switched her attention back to Elizabeth. "Mama taught me."

Satisfied she had answered the question, Gudrin bent over the cradle and stroked Ned's cheek. "What is his name?"

Elizabeth answered automatically. "Ned. His name is Edward, after his grandfather, but we call him Ned."

We. David and me. She swallowed back a sob and instead forced herself to ask the next question. "How does your mother know English? Could she come and teach me?"

At Gudrin's questioning look, Runa shook her head. Gudrin's translation dashed Elizabeth's hope. "Mama is away with Papa. She has traveled much and knows many lan...languages."

Runa spoke and waited for Gudrin to translate. "Auntie says she does not have time to teach you our words since Mikkel is injured, but she will send Beren. I can help a little but I don't know all the words yet."

"Beren?" Elizabeth ignored the sudden heat to her cheek, the stutter in her chest. "Why?"

As if guessing Elizabeth's question, Runa chattered to Gudrin, who translated. "My brother is pat...patient. He knows four, five languages but he cannot learn as fast as me." Her tone turned smug. Since Beren was so much older than Gudrin, Elizabeth suspected the child had reason to be proud.

Still... "Is there not a woman who can teach me?"

Gudrin shrugged. "Not until Mama comes back." Runa said something, perhaps asking what Elizabeth had asked. After a brief exchange, Gudrin sighed. "Beren will be a good teacher and I can come with him for the first few times. Why don't you want him?"

Because I do want him, and I mustn't. Elizabeth swallowed a gasp. Where had that thought come from? Instead, she offered a better—safer—explanation. "In my land we—women—are not supposed to be in a room alone with a man."

Gudrin tilted her head. "That's silly."

It was Elizabeth's turn to shrug. "That's my...do you know the word *culture*?" Gudrin nodded. "In my culture it is not...well, it's one of our rules."

"Ah." Gudrin rolled her eyes. "I still think it's silly." After exchanging more words with Runa, Gudrin smiled. "Auntie says she has heard of these rules. She says she has heard if the door stays open then the rules are satisfied."

If the door stays open... Elizabeth considered that and nodded.

"Yes, that will work." She remembered the rest of Gudrin's earlier statement. "Who is Mikkel?"

At the name, Runa's gaze sharpened, but Gudrin answered without hesitation. "Auntie's son."

"Oh." Concern filled Elizabeth. "You said he was injured. Will he be all right?"

"Oh yes." Gudrin gestured at Elizabeth's shoulder. "It's not too bad and we have lots of *klengodd* root." Again Gudrin bent over the cradle. "Can I come see Ned sometimes?" She seemed smitten by the baby.

Elizabeth smiled. "Any time you want."

Runa touched her niece's shoulder and pointed to the door. "Auntie says you need sleep so we will come back another time."

"Wait!" Elizabeth needed one more thing before the child left. "Can you ask your aunt to bring me some clothes?"

After Gudrin translated, Runa smiled and nodded.

Satisfied, Elizabeth lay back on the bed and watched Runa and her niece leave. How lucky to have someone who spoke English. That would make it easier for her to learn this other language. But Beren... To distract herself from the memory of that enigmatic man, she concentrated on the family relationships she'd learned. Beren and Gudrin were brother and sister. Runa was sister to their father, and Mikkel was Runa's son.

Somehow the idea of her hosts being a family eased the tension in Elizabeth's shoulders and neck, and with the beginnings of a headache averted, she drifted to sleep.

When she woke a few hours later, she found an ivory colored garment at the end of the bed. It wasn't a proper dress as she was used to, but at least it covered her. The sleeves were wide and the neckline had drawstrings that made it easy, even with her injured arm, to slip on.

Tightening the drawstrings made the neckline modest enough she wouldn't be embarrassed in front of visitors, although the garment itself was shapeless, falling straight from her shoulders to her feet. There weren't any shoes, but even this one piece of clothing made her feel more normal.

She suspected, however, that *feeing normal* was going to be difficult when Beren arrived tomorrow.

~ * ~

"You want me to what?" Beren stared at his aunt in disbelief.

"Teach Zabeth." Runa tucked a blanket around her sleeping son. "Keep your voice down. Mikkel needs his sleep." She straightened and fixed Beren with the gaze his heart-father called her secret weapon. No one could resist that commanding glare. "She wants to learn. She *needs* to learn."

"I thought you took Gudrin—"

Runa waved a dismissive hand. "The child knows the basic words, but Zabeth will want more and Gudrin doesn't have the vo...vo...what is that word Kiana learned last summer? The one about all the words in a language?"

"Vocabulary," Beren supplied.

"Yes. Vo-ca-bu-lary." Runa sounded the word. "Gudrin doesn't have that. You do, and you've learned other languages so you know how best to go about teaching someone else."

"But—"

"I can't do it," Runa continued as if he hadn't spoken. "I need to be here, and everyone else is busy."

"So am I." He was supposed to be guarding the village with the other warriors. He wanted to spend some time in the Keeper Hall learning from Magrim. He wanted...he wanted to see Zabeth again.

Runa gave him a satisfied smile, as if that final thought had appeared in his expression and gave him away. "You don't have to sit with her all day, just an hour or so before or after your guard duties." Her voice softened to a coaxing tone. "We'll take the baby to the nursery so Zabeth isn't distracted." She bent and brushed the hair from Mikkel's forehead. "And besides, it's not as if you'll be alone. Gudrin can be with you as long as she's able to help."

Beren sighed. Gudrin. A help, yes, with her talent, and the opportunity to sit with Zabeth for a whole hour...that was one argument he couldn't ignore.

So it was that after the midday meal the next afternoon, Beren found himself with Gudrin in the hall outside Zabeth's room. Remembering her distress when Runa had entered the other day, he called out and waited. A voice called back...bidding him enter?...and, heart pounding, he opened the door.

Zabeth sat in a chair by the window, dressed in a simple night-robe with a blanket across her knees and a green shawl around her shoulders. The color of the shawl contrasted with the flame-red hair she'd pushed behind her ears. A shaft of early afternoon sun lit her face and highlighted the scattering of freckles over her nose and cheeks. *Freckles*—a word he'd learned from one of the Shadow traders for the pale dots on many a fair-skinned man or woman. It sounded more exotic than *pale dots*, and the word fit Zabeth perfectly.

"Good day, Zabeth." He gave a polite bow, not taking his gaze from her.

"Good day, Beren, Gudrin," she repeated. She met his gaze for a long moment before red suffused her cheeks and she turned away.

He ignored the increased pulse in his chest and started to close the door.

"No!" At Zabeth's cry, he stopped.

Gudrin touched his arm. "Remember? We have to leave it open."

Oh yes. The culture rules of Zabeth's land. He shrugged and left the door. He didn't understand what difference it made but if the open door reduced her anxiety, he had no objections. Someone had brought in an extra chair so he crossed the room and shifted it to face her.

Gudrin skipped over to Zabeth and after a murmured conversation, turned to Beren. "Let me have one of your laces. That one in your beard should do."

Laces? Bemused, he untied the leather thong from the bottom of his beard, handed it to Gudrin, then speared his fingers through the woven hair to unbraid it. Meanwhile, Gudrin slipped behind Zabeth and used the thong to tie the woman's hair into a messy tail.

Beren raised an eyebrow and Gudrin grimaced. "Another culture rule. She doesn't like to have her hair loose in front of a man." From her expression, it was clear Gudrin thought this rule as silly as the open door one.

Finished with her task, Gudrin sat on the floor at Beren's feet. The moment she did, Zabeth spoke to her. Again they held a murmured conversation before Gudrin looked up at Beren. "In Zabeth's land, she learned some different languages. She wants to find out if you know any of them."

"All right." Beren leaned back in the chair.

Zabeth spoke something that sounded like *parlay voo fronsay*. At Beren's blank look, she tried a different phrase. He still didn't understand the words but recognized they were in a different language from the first. She tried twice more, and at the last phrase he sat up straight. *La-tee-nay low-kwair-iss. Latine loqueris.* He knew that one. *Do you speak Latin?*

Excited, he nodded and responded in the same language. "Yes, a little."

Elizabeth's eyes opened wide, and then she smiled.

The sight took Beren's breath away. For a moment he stared at her mouth, that upward bow at the corners, the lush lips—

"What is *Latin?*" Gudrin asked, and Beren could breathe again.

He smiled at his sister. "It's an old language Jorvik taught me. Remember when I wanted to learn the names of the star pictures and where they came from?" Gudrin shook her head. Oh yes, that was two years before Gudrin was born. Jorvik died before she had a chance to speak with him, so she'd never heard the language before today.

"Now we can speak…um…together?" Zabeth addressed the question to Beren in that other tongue. Her speech was slow, as if her knowledge of the language was as sparse as his own.

He returned her smile. "To begin, yes, to help learn the…the words of New Asgard."

"Yes, my words in Latin are few. It is many years I learn them." She still spoke them better than he.

Gudrin shifted her gaze from one to the other, then added her own opinion, in better Latin than either of them. "Now you don't need me so I'll go back to the Gather Hall."

Without waiting for consent, she jumped to her feet and dashed out the door. Beren stared after her for a moment, a whirlwind abandoning her post, then he offered Zabeth a sympathetic smile. "She is young and easily bored."

"Yes." Zabeth looked at the door, a puzzled expression on her face. "Did she learn Latin with you?"

"Not at the same time." Today was the first time Gudrin had heard it, but it would be too difficult to explain that until Zabeth had more words.

Zabeth took a deep breath that did wondrous things to the cloth under her shawl. "Then we begin."

Beren dragged his gaze away from her…shawl…and straightened in his chair. *Yes, time to begin teaching.* Pointing, he gave her the proper words for the objects in the room. Occasionally he'd switch to halting Latin when he needed extra explanation, like the difference between a chair and a stool.

The ringing of the supper bell a while later surprised him at how fast the time had passed. Zabeth pulled her shawl closer around her.

"Thank you for your time," she said in Latin, then repeated the words in his own language.

He grinned. "You learn fast."

"Tomorrow I learn faster."

Yes. I'll be back tomorrow. Beren smiled at the thought.

Chapter Seven

Well, that went well.

After the women who brought Ned and supper left, Elizabeth rose to make sure the door was latched. Although still weak, she was able to manage a few steps across the room if she took it slow.

Ned gurgled in his cradle and waved his arms about. She sat beside him. "Did you have fun in the nursery?" She played with Ned's fingers while she thought about the last hour.

She had a moment of panic when Beren began to shut the door on his arrival, but he'd respected her request to leave it open. She recognized the necessity of being alone in the room with him—Gudrin was too young to count as a chaperone—but she wouldn't abandon all propriety. A closed door invited so many speculations, but an open one proved nothing inappropriate was going on.

Thank goodness she'd planned what to say ahead of time. Her first sight of him after their scandalous meeting a few days ago had taken her breath away, and those practiced words had saved her from the embarrassment of stutters or awkward silence. She remembered Gudrin saying her brother spoke four or five languages and wondered if they might know the same ones. It had been a gamble, and after Beren's obvious puzzlement over French and Italian, she'd held little hope for the Greek or Latin.

Amazingly, he'd recognized the Latin. She was still astonished at that. True, her knowledge was from long-ago schoolroom lessons when she was a child, and Beren's grasp of the language seemed little better than hers, but at least they now had a way to communicate without the help of a five-year-old child who became bored after a few minutes. With stubborn determination and Beren's patience, Elizabeth had no trouble picking up his language after that.

And I can learn lots more when he comes back tomorrow. I won't be as nervous as today. After all, I now know what to expect.

But when Beren arrived the next day, her heart still thumped loud enough she was sure he'd hear. She didn't know how she got through the lesson without stuttering or blushing like a maid fresh from the schoolroom. It was embarrassing, even when their discussion revolved around such dry topics as parts of speech, pronouns, and verb tenses. Beren didn't call them that, of course, but Elizabeth remembered her own studies well enough to recognize what she was learning.

The following day, she learned the names of the animals and birds she saw from her window, and the day after it was the different types of trees in the forest behind the village. She expected—hoped—the visits would become part of a comfortable routine, but every time he arrived at her door, she found herself tongue-tied for a moment. They spoke in Latin at first, but after a while her grasp of Beren's language improved. She suspected it was some kind of Norse or Swedish dialect.

She could now chat with Runa, and one day learned Beren and Gudrin's mother wasn't from the village. At Beren's next visit, Elizabeth gathered the nerve to ask him about her.

"Runa said your mother comes from the South? Another country?"

He frowned. "Yes and no. Kiana is my heart-mother, but yes, we are from the South."

Elizabeth tilted her head. "What is heart-mother? How different from mother?"

He shrugged. "Kiana took care of me after my parents...died. When we traveled here, she met Tor and wed him and they took me as their son. They are parents of my heart, heart-mother and heart-father, as I am their heart-son."

"I see." She thought about relationships. "But Gudrin is their *daughter*, not...not heart-daughter? And your heart-sister?"

"Yes."

"Do you have other brothers and sisters."

He held up two fingers. "Olaf and Leif. They are traveling with Kiana and Tor. It is Leif's first voyage and Olaf's third." She opened her mouth to ask why he wasn't with them, but he hurried on. "Do you have brothers and sisters?"

Elizabeth smiled. "I have two brothers. Jason is three years older than me. He is married and will have a child by..." Was there a word for Christmas? "By midwinter. William is...smaller? No, younger by two years, and will soon join the navy."

She then had to explain what a navy was, and in turn learned about the trading voyages Beren's people made every year.

Over time, their conversations varied from village life to the food she ate and the weather. Her shoulder was healing, although she expected more pain and was surprised she was able to move her arm at all after such a crippling injury. However, she dared not attempt too much for fear of further damage and still fretted over how long it was taking to heal.

At last, ten days after Elizabeth woke from her fever, she sat in anticipation. Today the bandages came off, so Runa had promised, and Elizabeth wanted to be out, wanted to send word to the nearest English colony that she was alive and safe and ask them to come to get her.

She glanced at the empty cradle. The room was quiet without Ned—no happy giggles, no demanding cries. She missed him terribly but his presence exhausted her, so she hadn't complained when Runa offered to take him to the village nursery.

When Runa entered with the healer, Elizabeth stifled a sigh. Didn't these people believe in knocking first? At least Beren called out and waited for her reply before entering. She forced herself to smile at the women and slipped the robe off her injured shoulder.

"How Mikkel?" she asked Runa while the healer unwrapped the bandage.

Runa's face lit with happiness. She spoke too fast for Elizabeth to understand, but she got the impression the boy was mending well and was back out doing mischievous boy things. She smiled. A few more years and she expected Ned would also be a handful.

The last bandage fell away and the healer bent close to Elizabeth's shoulder, probed with gentle fingers, and sniffed the wound.

After that first sight before the fever took her, Elizabeth had refused to look at the wound. Either it mended or not, as God saw fit. No amount of worry on her part was going to change whether she lost her arm.

God, however, had decided to be merciful. She kept the arm, and each time the bandage was changed, the healer said "*Góðr.*"

Goather, good, one of the first words Elizabeth had learned.

Now the older woman straightened. After tossing the bandage into a bag she'd brought for that purpose, she nodded and stood back.

Unable to resist, Elizabeth tilted her head to view her shoulder. The cut was healed and a thin red line marked where the skin had been pierced. She touched the line in awe. No medicine in her experience left such a neat scar in such a short time. The fever must have lasted longer than she realized.

"Wonderful," she breathed. "*Góðr.*"

"Very good." Runa approached to stand beside the bed. "No bandage now."

"That *klengodd* is very strong," Elizabeth said in awe. "I have never heard of it before."

Runa smiled. "It is from a Shadow trade."

"Shadow?"

"Um…" Runa bit her lip. "A place we trade with."

A strange name for a country, but then so was *Turkey* or even *Wales*. "They are fortunate to have such a…a fine healing plant."

"Oh, it doesn't work from the ground." Runa chuckled. "The traders like to keep their secrets, but we understand they treat the root with something to make it heal better."

I wish Doctor McAndrew had something like this when Jason broke his leg. Jason hated staying in bed for weeks.

After the healer left, Runa helped Elizabeth put her robe back on. Elizabeth still wasn't used to people other than her physician or her maids seeing her unclothed. Even David had never seen her body. He preferred the privacy of darkness when he came to her in the night, and had done his duty without undressing her.

Struggling to control her embarrassment at the memory, Elizabeth wrestled with the drawstrings at the neck of her robe and decided now was as good a time as any to ask the favor she wanted. "Runa?"

"Yes?" The woman stopped straightening the blankets on the bed and gazed expectantly at Elizabeth. "You want baby?"

"No." Elizabeth shook her head. "I want…hot water?"

"To drink?" Runa raised her hand to her lips, fingers curled.

"No. I want clean…" She didn't know the word for bath. How to convey what she wanted? "Need water…to clean me." She rubbed her arms, her face.

Runa gave a delicate sniff, grinned, and giggled. "*Lauga.* Yes. Zabeth not clean." Elizabeth's face heated in dismay, but Runa laughed. "Wait."

Elizabeth had read that Vikings used communal bath houses. Was Runa going to take her there? The idea of leaving this room both frightened and excited her, but half an hour later Elizabeth gazed in delight at a huge wooden tub two strong women carried to her room, and the steaming water they'd hauled in buckets to fill it. Runa brought several large woolen towels and a fresh robe to change into, then gave Elizabeth her yearned-for privacy.

She stripped off her clothes and climbed into the tub.

The water was hot but not scalding. She lowered herself until she sat on the bottom. The tub was so big she didn't even have to bend her knees. Beside the tub Runa had set a small stool with a soft rag and a cream she'd indicated was a kind of soap. After soaking up the warmth for a few minutes, Elizabeth scooped cream from the jar and rubbed it on her skin. A rich lather formed, and a floral scent she couldn't identify lingered on her fingers.

She washed every inch of skin twice, then submerged until only her face was above water, allowing her hair to flow loose so she could unknot the tangles and wash it.

A voice sounded close to her ear. "Zabeth?"

Startled, she floundered upright and snatched one of the towels to hold in front of her. She hadn't heard Runa return.

The older woman clucked her tongue. "You have a good body, Zabeth. You don't need to hide it."

While Elizabeth sorted out the words, Runa studied the water in the tub. Elizabeth clutched the towel tighter, soaking it in the process. She'd never get used to the way these people regarded nudity as natural.

But Runa's next words alarmed her even more. "Not much hot water today. You'll have to share."

"Share?" Her voice came out as a squeak. Never mind the tub was cramped with just Elizabeth's own body. Under no circumstances was she going to share it with anyone.

"Yes, share." Runa winked and her grin turned saucy. "Share with a handsome young man."

A face popped unbidden into her mind, a dark face with gentle eyes and a braided beard, and a smile that lightened her heart. *Beren.*

The moment the irrational thought flashed into her head, Runa's mischievous grin hinted she guessed what Elizabeth was thinking. She didn't tease, however, but walked to the door and spoke in a low voice to someone outside. When she stood back, Gudrin toddled in carrying Ned.

Concern that such a small child was entrusted with her baby must have been evident on Elizabeth's face. "Gudrin is very strong for her age," Runa explained with a reassuring smile, "and she's fond of your son." She plucked the baby from her niece's hands, stripped away his gown and clout, and held him out to Elizabeth.

Her towel dropped into the water, forgotten.

"Now play," Runa commanded. She herded Gudrin out the door and shut it behind them.

Looking at Ned, Elizabeth couldn't help a rueful smile. "Well, little one, did you know Runa was such a tyrant? I suppose we'd better do as she says."

Ned entered the water with an enthusiasm that had her grinning. While his little hands splashed at the waves, an image of Beren sitting naked in the tub jumped into Elizabeth's mind. Shocked, she pushed the image away, but it kept coming back.

He'd have strong muscles and a broad chest covered in a mass of dark brown hair. There'd be muscles on his legs, too, strong thighs, and—

"Stop." Abruptly she sat up. The motion drew an indignant cry from Ned. "Sorry," she murmured. She leaned back again and forced herself to relax. After a while, only Ned filled her thoughts.

Half an hour later, clean and dry once more, she laid Ned in the cradle, then dressed in soft boots and a clean robe. The simple woolen garment clung to her legs and body when she moved, and revealed more of what lay beneath than she considered decent.

Her chemise and dress were too crusted with blood and torn from the battle to be worn again. Both had been cut up for bandages, but she didn't know what Runa had done with her corset.

This robe was modest enough but she wasn't happy with it. The simple shift covered her from neck to ankle, and this time there was an additional garment, a sort of overdress, like a large apron or the tunic Runa wore, dyed a pale blue. It fastened with a belt at the waist and converted the shapeless shift into something that more closely resembled a dress, but the lack of underthings to disguise what she considered a disappointing body increased her discomfort.

Her breasts were too large, her hips too wide for the current fashion, and when she walked, every inch of flesh jiggled and bounced in an unbecoming and embarrassing fashion.

She plucked a brush from the nearby table, stroked it through her tangled curls, and worked her fingers through the worst knots. Before, she didn't want to risk opening her wound by lifting her arm, but several times in the past few days she'd longed to ask one of the women to brush her hair for her. However, she didn't have the nerve to bother them with such a trivial request when they were all concerned about the injured boys.

Although surely they must be better by now.

Experimentally, she raised her injured arm above her head. Not even a twinge accompanied the action.

Amazing.

Ned cooed and gurgled. Elizabeth continued to brush her hair as she made her way to the cradle and gazed down at him. The little sleep robe tangled in his legs while he sucked on a toe through the fabric. When her shadow fell across his face, he let the toe pop from his mouth and lifted his arms to her.

A long-forgotten emotion swept through her then, and after a moment she had a name for it. *Contentment.*

No. She shouldn't be content. She was a widow, living on sufferance among a strange people, with a responsibility to her son to return him to safety and civilization. The blue robe she wore was a mockery. She should be wearing black, not this pale color.

A lump in her throat caused a strangled sob. She'd held it back, determined to be strong for Ned, but now an image of David as she'd last seen him flashed into her mind, his tall muscled body pinning the pirate to the deck, saving her life even as he lost his own.

He'd cared for her in his own way, as she'd cared for him—*still* cared for him. He was her husband, the father of her son. It wasn't fair he had to die and she still lived. How could she face his family? How could she tell them she'd run away, left him to die alone? How could she—?

A soul-searing cry escaped her lips. The brush dropped unheeded to the floor. She stuffed a fist into her mouth and stumbled away from the cradle, not wishing to upset Ned, but the sobs still came, faster, gasping on each breath.

Her knees gave way and she collapsed to the floor, hunched over, rocking back and forth. Tears streamed down her cheeks and great tearing sobs wracked her body. She couldn't stop bawling and gave up trying.

Grief washed over her, smothering her. Three words chanted in her head: *David is dead. David is dead. David is dead.*

Elizabeth wailed her loss, wailed the unfairness of it all. She didn't want to be a widow. She didn't want to have to raise Ned on her own. She wanted her life back. She wanted...she wanted...

I want to go home.

Chapter Eight

A long time later—hours, minutes, she wasn't sure—Elizabeth stirred and raised her head. She felt drained, so dry she didn't think she'd ever have tears again.

Weren't you supposed to feel better after a good cry? Weren't tears supposed to lessen the grief? The emptiness still haunted her, but...the pain didn't seem quite as sharp now.

Ned gurgled from his crib and she caught his gaze. He smiled at her.

"You're my sanity," she murmured.

She still had her son, and she'd do everything in her power to get him back home. His future was in England, with her family and David's. She'd get him the best tutors, send him to the best university, give him every opportunity for a successful life. She'd even try to find herself a wealthy husband to give Ned everything she couldn't. She'd do whatever she had to.

Ned was her future now. Not this village, not these people, and definitely not a barbarian named Beren.

Time to return to a normal life, or as normal as possible while she was here. She clutched the cross at her neck. "I don't think they have a church here," she told Ned. No one had mentioned a Christian worship place, and even though Beren spoke Latin, he'd explained they had no priest still living. "I don't even know what day it is," she continued, "but it doesn't matter. I can pray any day; it doesn't have to be Sunday."

Reassured by that resolve, she closed her eyes, knelt, and whispered a prayer for strength. Afterward, she rose to her feet, stiff from sitting in one position so long, and shuffled to the mirror, a burnished metal oval that may have been a shield in a previous life. She winced at the sight before her. Her eyes were red and puffy, her cheeks stained with tears.

"Zabeth?"

She jumped. Beren? What was he doing here? It was too early for their lesson. His voice was muffled by the door so at least he hadn't come into the room.

She swallowed. "A moment."

Using the remains of the bath water, she scrubbed her face until all trace of sorrow was wiped away. The brush lay where she'd dropped it. She scooped it up and dragged it once more through her hair. Finally feeling normal again, she raised her voice. "You may come in now."

The door swung open, and Beren peered in. His smile dimmed. "Are you well?"

All right, maybe some traces of her breakdown remained, but she gave a brisk nod. "Yes. Just a bit of…soap in my eyes."

"Ah." He gave the wooden tub a knowing look. "Soap is very dangerous. I think every warrior should carry a bar instead of a sword."

The unexpected joke drew a startled laugh from Elizabeth. *I didn't realize Beren had a sense of humor.* She felt better. "What do you want?"

He grinned. "Runa thought you might want to see the rest of the building, and join her in the kitchen."

The kitchen? What was an obviously high-born woman like Runa doing in the kitchen?

"I…" She paused.

The room felt stuffy, for all its chill, and she did want to see the rest of the building, but she couldn't go out with her hair loose. Gudrin's childish attempts at tying it back had kept it somewhat respectable in the privacy of her room. But in public… Even on the ship, when Maizy was busy elsewhere, Elizabeth had been able to tame her wayward curls into some semblance of control.

"One moment." She looked in the mirror, then pulled some strands of hair away from the side of her face—*not even a twinge from her shoulder*—and tied them at the back of her head with a blue ribbon.

She'd never learned to manage a bun on her own so let the rest fall free. It wasn't as formal a style as she'd wish, but it looked little different from the way Runa and the healer wore their hair on the days they didn't braid it.

Maybe I'll try a braid tomorrow.

With one final look in the mirror to assure herself she was presentable, she nodded to Beren. "I'm ready. Let me get Ned." She hurried to the cradle and picked up the baby. She smiled at him, then marched to the door, grateful for the warm kid-leather boots laced around her ankles.

Beren held the door open for her. Elizabeth nodded her thanks and swept through.

She stepped into a long hallway with wooden doors lining one side. Glowing torches provided a dim light that emphasized the shadows at either end. A blank wall faced her, broken a short distance to her right with a gap that stretched from floor to ceiling and as wide as two men.

"Which way?"

Beren pointed. She took a deep breath and turned left. When she reached the gap, she strode through the opening.

Another short hallway took her to a balcony that ringed a large open space higher than her father's manor hall. She stood at the narrow end of a rectangular-shaped room. It stretched twice the length of the ship she'd been on a few days earlier, and at least as wide.

Openings to other hallways led off each side, and stairs descended at regular intervals all the way around the balcony. A pair of enormous doors stood open half way down the right side of the space on the ground floor. Through it came the shouts of children at play.

Realizing her mouth hung open in awe, Elizabeth snapped it shut. "This is…big."

"This is the main Gather Hall." There was pride in Beren's voice and she glanced at him as he continued. "When it was first built many years ago there was just this one room. We've added to it since."

She raised an eyebrow. "You built all these other rooms? Yourself?" If he could make a joke, so could she.

He chuckled and swept a hand toward the nearest stairs. "This way."

She descended into the chamber, turning her head this way and that to take in her surroundings.

A wide bench hugged the perimeter of the room and stretched around all four sides two feet from the floor with a space beneath for storage. More hallways led off the main space. People bustled across the floor—women holding brooms, children of perhaps ten or eleven arranging narrow benches around several long tables near the end where she stood. It reminded her of her father's great dining hall.

One table was placed perpendicular to the others, perhaps meant to seat the leaders of these people. Instead of benches, wooden chairs flanked this table, with one huge chair at its center. She was too far to notice details, but it looked too big to hold one man. Carvings gave texture to the arms and back. She longed for a closer look, but not now. Later, she promised herself, once she was more at ease here.

Clean rushes covered the wood floor. A huge fireplace made of a circle of stones stood near the head table, with another of equal size halfway down the room. Wood crackled and popped in the hearth, supplementing the braziers, although the room held more light than could be accounted for by just the flames.

Curious, she searched for the source of the extra light and found it in the form of several globes hanging under the edge of the balconies. The globes flickered with an internal fire, but the fire was white, not the usual red or orange.

"How are lights made?" She hoped not by magic or witchcraft. Her hosts were heathens but she refused to believe they'd sold their souls. They were too kind to be worshipers of the Devil.

Beren shrugged. "I don't know. We traded for them several years ago. They stay alight for many days and when they dim, we show them the sun for half a day and they light up again."

"Show them sun?" Elizabeth had a vision of men lifting globes over their head so the objects had a good view of the sun.

Beren shrugged again. "That's what the keepers do." He glanced at the globes. "I never wondered how they worked before." He went silent, a thoughtful expression on his face.

Dismissing the mystery, Elizabeth switched her attention to the large doors that led outside. They looked tall enough to admit a man on horseback. Remembering her history lessons, she pictured a dark Viking warrior riding through those doors, challenging all who stood in his way. Somehow it didn't surprise her the Viking in her imagination had Beren's features.

She drank in the atmosphere, the sounds of everyday living. She'd missed those sounds in her quiet room.

Beren touched her arm and pointed to a hallway on her right. "That way. I have duties now but I'll join you later for our lesson." He gave her an encouraging smile, then strode through the outer doors.

"But—" Elizabeth raised a hand to stop him, to ask him the thousand questions spinning in her head, but he disappeared before she could say another word.

A burst of laughter echoed from the hallway, then a babble of women's voices. She recognized Runa's voice and followed the sound.

The hallway led to a large kitchen. Four women dressed in plain woolen tunics in various colors were gathered around a long table. Elizabeth spotted Runa at once, her red tunic covered with flour while she kneaded dough on a square wooden board. She didn't know the other women. All seemed about Runa's age. The two skinny ones showed traces of silver in their dark hair, but the plump woman's white-blonde tresses hid any gray. They all seemed in gay spirits, laughing and chattering.

Elizabeth had learned Runa's husband was one of their most

honored warriors. The equivalent of an English nobleman, he'd have servants and maids to cook and clean for Runa, yet here she was baking her own bread. Elizabeth had never set foot in the kitchens of her father's manor. She'd never thought about where her food came from.

Maybe it's time I learned.

Runa caught sight of her, smiled, and waved her into the room. "*Vel kommen*, Zabeth. It's good to see you strong now." She dusted her hands on a cloth draped over a nearby chair and pulled Elizabeth to stand in front of the plump woman. "Zabeth, this is Freya. She is wife to Garan, our chieftain."

Holding Ned with one arm, Elizabeth spread her skirt and dropped a graceful curtsey. "I am...happy...for your help," she enunciated each word, then cringed at the awkwardness of the phrase.

"Thank you." Freya smiled and motioned her to rise.

Bǫkk, Elizabeth repeated to herself. Next time she'd remember.

"You are welcome here, Zabeth. We're all glad you're healed." Freya ran a pudgy finger down Ned's cheek. The baby cooed. "This little one has made friends of us all. My own children are grown, but I hope for their children soon."

Elizabeth smiled, sharing a mother's pride. She imagined Ned with children of his own, and grinned at the absurdity of it. Her son was four months old and already she longed for grandchildren?

"Come and sit," Freya ordered, and shuffled her bulk along the bench to make room.

Thankful for the chance to sit, Elizabeth sank onto the bench. The walk from her room had tired her more than she expected.

Runa introduced the other two women as Ulla and Hulda. Their similar features proclaimed them sisters, and their familiar banter with Runa and Freya indicated they weren't servants. Where *were* all the servants? She refrained from asking. Curiosity was no excuse for plain nosiness.

"I help?" she asked after a moment.

Freya patted her hand. "No, child. You rest." She folded pastry around handfuls of berries and placed the little parcels on a flat wooden board.

Elizabeth sat Ned on her lap. He wasn't old enough to sit by himself, but with her supporting his back he rested his fingers on the table. He seemed eager to explore the texture of flour.

"*Keevah?*" Runa offered a mug. "It'll make you strong."

Elizabeth nodded. She had grown used to the warm milk over the last few days. It had a nutty taste, with a hint of cinnamon. At times she even found herself craving the restorative.

Runa concentrated on her dough for a while, kneading and patting it into a flattened ball. She placed it onto a wooden paddle and inserted the paddle into a small stone-lined opening beside the roaring fire.

"Gudrin," she called.

The little girl skipped into the room holding a wooden doll by one arm. She climbed onto the bench beside Elizabeth and stroked Ned's cheek. At a word from Runa, she sighed, stared at the ceiling, opened her mouth, and sang in a high clear voice. Elizabeth couldn't understand the words, but she guessed the song's purpose.

Before leaving for the Americas, she'd studied books and talked to sailors, soaking up knowledge about the land and the people who colonized it. Among the many interesting facts was that few pioneer women owned the luxury of a clock. Instead, they sang hymns.

At first Elizabeth believed the hymns were sung to give God's blessing to the food, but later she'd learned each hymn, sung at a specific pace, helped the women time their baking and cooking. Although the song Runa's niece sang sounded more a folk tune than a hymn, it probably served the same purpose.

Freya finished her pastries and leaned back against the wall with a sigh. Ulla and Hulda, cleaning rabbits and fish by the fire, grinned at her before returning to their tasks.

"These are so small, so difficult." Freya indicated the berry parcels, then tilted her head and regarded Elizabeth with open curiosity. "You must have many questions, yes?"

"Yes," Elizabeth answered, surprised at the woman's perception.

Freya smiled. "Ask."

Where to begin? How did Vikings end up on these shores? What had happened to the pirate ship? Why had she seen no sign of servants or slaves?

But first she needed to know where she was. She needed to send a message to her family and David's, reassure them she and Ned were still alive. Somewhere.

Before their fateful trip, David let her pour over maps of the east coast of America, and showed her the location of the colony they were headed for, a booming town called Hartford. There'd been rumors of rebellious talk, the colonists complaining about what they considered unfair taxes, but David assured her it was just talk and nothing else. As a member of the English nobility, she didn't need to worry what the colonists thought.

"But when we move to the Americas, won't we be colonists

ourselves?" she'd asked, but David never understood her reasoning.

Summoning her small store of words, Elizabeth asked, "Where are we?"

Runa sat down across from her. "Kitchen."

"No, where…?" She waved at the window, the village buildings visible through the opening. "Where village?"

Freya smiled. "We call it New Asgard."

Elizabeth shifted, annoyed she couldn't make herself better understood. "But where?"

Runa exchanged a look with Freya. The chieftain's wife regarded Elizabeth for a moment, then nodded. "It's time, I think. Take her. I'll watch your bread."

Runa stood and took Elizabeth's hand. "Come."

Chapter Nine

Beren strode across the courtyard so lost in thought he didn't see Eskil until his friend held out an arm to stop him.

"What has taken your interest this time," the younger man asked with a teasing grin. "Has the Shadow woman told you a tale of wonders?"

"Her name is Zabeth, and no." At least, not wonders of her world.

Why had he never given a thought to the light globes until she asked about them? They'd been in the Gather Hall for years, one of the first items gained once trade was established with one of the newer Shadow worlds. But it wasn't the globes that distracted him. It was the memory of Zabeth's face when she'd allowed him entry to her room.

She'd been crying, but there were signs she'd tried to hide the fact. His first instinct had been to take her in his arms and comfort her, but he'd remembered in time the words of his heart-mother.

If a woman doesn't want you to know she's upset, by the Lady, don't give her sympathy. Distract her, tease her, make her angry. She's embarrassed enough that you caught her crying so pretend you didn't.

So he'd come up with that pathetic jest about the soap. He cringed at the memory, but it seemed to have been the right thing to do. She was calmer when he left her in the Gather Hall.

Runa and her friends were the cure. He was glad his aunt had sent him on the mission to bring Zabeth to the kitchen, although how baking bread and chopping meat was supposed to cheer a woman up, he didn't know.

"Well, whatever you're thinking about," Eskil continued, "put it aside. We have archery practice."

Beren glanced at him. "We do? I thought it was our turn on patrol."

"Garan changed the schedule. We're due in the horse barn now."

"Who's training?"

"Lida's teaching the new women volunteers but she wants us to put the more experienced ones through a tougher session." Eskil scowled. "That includes Astri."

This should be interesting. Beren grinned and slapped his friend on the back. "Don't worry. I'll protect you."

Eskil aimed a return blow, which Beren easily avoided, and laughing, the two men hurried toward the barn.

~ * ~

Elizabeth lifted Ned away from the flour he found so interesting and ignored his annoyed cry. She brushed at his clothes while she followed Runa back to the large room.

At the doors to outside, they stopped. Runa grabbed a short woolen cloak from a peg beside the door and draped it around Elizabeth's shoulders, covering Ned in its folds. The air outside was crisp and cool. It smelled of autumn. She'd sailed in August, so it must be September by now. Did winter come early here? Or had she lost more time than she'd at first imagined?

She stood beside Runa at the bottom of a horseshoe-shaped courtyard. Skinny vines softened the austerity of the two solid side walls, while an empty street crossed the open end. Behind a waist-high hedge that divided a corner of the courtyard from the rest of the space, two women played with several toddlers. A nursery? This side of the building offered the same view as from her window, with scattered houses leading toward the sea.

Before turning onto the street, Elizabeth glanced back. The building she'd left was a larger version of those she'd seen from her window. Two stories high, its white plaster walls dazzling in the sunlight, it stretched as wide as a great manor house. Rows of windows stared from the upper story.

Elizabeth's contemporaries believed the Americas were populated by primitive savages. This building, this town, gave the lie to that belief.

But then, this particular part of the Americas is colonized by Vikings.

If you ignored their ferocious reputation and battle-scarred history, Vikings were known for great skills in shipbuilding and decorative jewelry. The remains of a Viking dwelling had been found buried in a field not far from her grandfather's manor, and its carvings and construction had impressed the scholars as much as the remains of the Roman villa standing near her own home.

Runa plucked at Elizabeth's sleeve, and she returned her attention to where they were going. At the end of the street, the view opened to forested hills and mountainous cliffs that surrounded the village on three sides. The green of trees blended into yellows and a touch of gold, beginning to turn to their autumn splendor.

They strolled at a leisurely pace, in deference to Elizabeth's still weak condition, down narrow but clean streets, winding a way through what seemed a maze. At last, they came to a square. A well stood to one side, and several women drew water from it to slosh into a wide trough that dominated the center of the space. Other women worked at the trough, washing clothes.

"In winter we use the wash shed," Runa informed her.

They crossed the square and turned down a long street. At the end, separated from the village by a large empty space, stood another imposing building, this one smaller than the hall they'd just left.

"Keeper Hall," Runa announced.

They mounted three steps to a covered porch and a young man limped forward from the shadows to meet them. Instead of the leather breeches and vest favored by the other men Elizabeth had seen so far, this one wore a coarse robe belted with a braided rope.

"This is Zabeth," Runa told the young man. "Is Keeper Magrim here?"

He nodded and led them along the porch and around the building. On the far side, he opened a door.

The room they entered was dim after the light of day, but Elizabeth's eyes soon adjusted. Tables and pedestals crowded into every corner, each holding a different item. Some Elizabeth recognized—a sextant such as the captain of her ship had once shown her, a telescope, a horse's bridle, even a pistol like David used to carry.

Strange machines lay in a row on one table—a blue rectangle with buttons on the top, a metal tube with a piece of glass in one end. Shelves lined the walls, stuffed full of books. Dozens of books. She recognized Shakespeare and Homer, a tattered copy of the Holy Bible, as well as other books in languages she didn't know.

To her mystification, some of the English texts had titles that made no sense. Who was Winnipeg, and why did he have yellow pages? Beneath the books, in smaller cubbies, were rolled scrolls, such as she'd seen in engravings of monastic libraries.

She spun in a slow circle, her gaze traveling from one exotic object to another until—

Oh my.

There, on a table in the far corner, displayed in all its embarrassing glory, sat her corset. She stifled a gasp. What on earth was her corset doing in a place like this? A museum exhibit? She wanted to run over and snatch it off the pedestal, hide it away where no one could see it, but a voice spoke from the shadows at the far end of the room.

"What brings you here, Runa Olafsdotter?" An old man strode forward.

He looked familiar, and when he stepped into the light from the doorway, Elizabeth recognized him as the gray-haired man she'd run into when she escaped the pirates.

Runa bent her head in a formal bow. "Keeper Magrim, I have brought Zabeth."

Keeper *must be a title.*

When the old man shifted his penetrating gaze to her, Elizabeth dropped a nervous curtsey.

He smiled at her. "Zabeth. Welcome."

Ned stirred against her shoulder and raised his head to gaze around with the curiosity of the young. She rubbed his back.

Magrim looked at Runa. "Is this wise?"

Runa spoke in a low voice. Magrim responded, but the only word Elizabeth understood was *forbid.* Did he mean she was forbidden to be here, or he was forbidden to tell her where she was?

After a brief exchange, Runa won her argument. With a doubtful look at Elizabeth, the keeper walked to the shelves against the side wall. He lifted a rolled scroll from one of the cubbies, spread the parchment on an empty table, and beckoned to Elizabeth.

The parchment, she discovered, was a map of the world. It must have been drawn hundreds of years ago. Some of the shapes were a little lopsided, and large areas of Eastern Europe and the Orient were blank space.

Magrim looked at her. "Where are you from?"

Excited, she pointed to England. "Here." She used one finger to trace the eastern edge of the island to a spot half way between the Thames estuary and the Scottish borders. "We...my father...has land."

She traced her finger around the south coast, down the west coast of Africa, and across the Atlantic to the Caribbean. "My family...travel here." She looked at the keeper and waved her hand over the east coast of the Americas. "Where now?"

Magrim frowned. With a wary glance at Runa, he moved Elizabeth's finger back to England and farther east, to the west coast of Denmark. "Here." He pointed at the rough coastline.

He doesn't understand. He's telling me where his people came from.

Elizabeth smiled and shook her head. "No, where now?" Again she waved her hand over the Americas, but again, more firmly this time,

Magrim dragged her hand back east.

"Here," he repeated. "Now. Today."

She stared at the map. No, that wasn't possible. He couldn't be saying she was in Denmark. For heaven's sake, they'd been in the Caribbean a few days ago. To return to England must take at least a month, and she hadn't been unconscious long enough to account for that length of time. Ned looked the same as when she'd fled the ship, and at the rate he was growing, she was sure she'd notice if he was older.

She shook her head. "No."

Magrim turned a helpless gaze to Runa, who shrugged her shoulders and took over. "Zabeth, look." She pointed to Denmark and said in a tone that allowed no argument, "This is New Asgard. We are here. Now." She shifted her finger to the Americas. "Not here."

Elizabeth's mind spun. How could she travel hundreds of miles in a few days?

As if he guessed her thoughts, Magrim muttered something to Runa, who smiled and turned to Elizabeth. "Fast ship. Very fast ship."

Elizabeth blinked. "Ship?"

"Yes." Runa nodded. "Our men, on the ship, found you and brought you here."

The explanation didn't sound quite right, but what other alternative was there? That she'd been transported by magic in an instant? Not possible. Not even the fabled magicians of the Orient were skilled enough to transport people over great distances. Coins, yes, and perhaps a fan or ribbon, but people? Never.

A fast ship. Hmmm. "I would like to see this ship," she murmured more to herself than the others in the room.

"Soon," Runa promised, but her eyes held a troubled look.

Elizabeth studied the map. Denmark wasn't far from England. Her heart beat faster at the implications. A fast ship could get her home in days. Days! With luck, she and Ned might be in time to celebrate Christmas with her parents.

"When you take me home?" She was unable to hide the eagerness in her voice.

Runa and Magrim exchanged a glance Elizabeth couldn't interpret. The keeper shook his head and shrugged. "Ask Garan."

"Garan? The chieftain?" Alarmed, Elizabeth glared at Runa. Despite the woman's earlier reassurance, Elizabeth still didn't trust these people. "Why? Am I...prisoner? Slave?"

"*No.*" Runa sounded shocked at such an idea. "I told you before, we have no slaves, no thralls. You're our guest, as Freya said. But we have only one ship, so we must wait until it returns."

"One ship? But there is ship on beach, small boats for fish."

The keeper chuckled. "The *Geri*—the ship on the beach—has a big hole. It won't sail far. Our carpenter cannot fix it himself. He has only one hand and many hands are needed. All are away on the *Freki* so it must wait for their return."

"And it's not a good time of year for small boats," Runa added. "Too many storms."

Elizabeth frowned, unconvinced. Why hadn't their carpenter fixed the one on the beach before the other ship left?

Magrim rolled up the parchment, then stared at her companion.

"I'm sorry, Keeper Magrim," Runa said. "We've taken up much of your time."

Elizabeth took the cue. "Yes, thank you."

She followed Runa from the room, thinking hard. Once outside, she stopped. "Why no ship now?"

Runa looked worried. "They should be here, but winter comes early. There are many bad storms. If they don't return soon, they'll have to wait until spring, when the seas are calmer."

We're stranded here for the winter? No, I won't accept that.

There had to be a way to at least get a message to her father. All she needed was to ask the right questions. "Runa, you…someone…tell my family where we are?"

Runa took Ned from her and resumed walking. "Perhaps you should talk to Garan. Would you like to see the beach?"

"Beach?" What was so unnerving that Runa was eager to change the subject?

"Sand. Water. Lots of fun for the baby." She grinned. "We'll be careful so you don't need to bathe again."

A day at the seaside. The idea appealed to Elizabeth after being stuck inside for so long. She also relished the thought of sitting again.

But not yet. "First Garan. Then beach."

Runa regarded her with an expression close to pity, as if she expected the chieftain to deny her request, but Elizabeth didn't care. She'd not give up until she'd at least asked.

At last, Runa nodded. "Yes, first Garan. Then you can enjoy the beach."

~ * ~

The arrow landed a hand's breadth from the outside edge of the target. Not bad for a beginner like most of the women Beren was helping Lida teach. *This* arrow, however, had been shot by Eskil.

"You call that a shot? My grandmother could do better blindfolded." Eskil flushed at Astri's taunt, but in fairness her

75

grandmother had been one of the best archers in her village—or so Tor and Runa often boasted about their mother.

While true Eskil wasn't the most accomplished archer, for the past hour it seemed he'd forgotten everything he learned. It didn't help that Astri goaded him at every turn, *accidentally* laughing just as he was about to shoot, or blowing in his ear. Eskil should be used to her tricks by now, but every time, he jerked the bow.

Beren, watching from the sidelines, sighed. "That's enough for today. Lida's class already left and it's almost time for the midday meal."

Eskil lowered his bow with a scowl but Astri shook her head. "He needs more practice."

"I do not!" The protest was accompanied by a glare Beren was sure had power to roast Astri in her boots if such a thing were possible. Eskil thumped the end of his bow on the ground. "If *someone* would stop interfering—"

"You won't always be shooting in a barn," Astri interrupted in a sweet voice. "There'll be all sorts of *interference* in a battle."

"And how many battles have you fought?" Eskil's face turned a strange purplish shade.

Beren thrust himself between them. "Enough." He glared at Astri. "When battle comes, Eskil is more than capable of focusing on what needs to be done. He doesn't need you to distract him in training." He spun on Eskil and caught the beginning of a smug grin. "And she's right. You do need more practice." The grin disappeared and the scowl returned. Beren continued before Eskil could protest. "Stay for another quarter hour." He glanced over his shoulder at Astri and narrowed his eyes. "Alone."

Astri pouted but was quick to recover. She winked at Eskil, slipped her arm through Beren's, and led him from the barn. That wasn't quite what Beren had in mind, but at least it gave Eskil some time to cool down and regain his mysteriously lost skills. Beren liked Astri but sometimes her antics annoyed him.

When they reached the square, instead of separating to their individual barracks to wash up, Astri walked him to the well before dropping her hand from his arm. "Has Eskil said anything to you about how he feels about me?" She dipped a ladle into the water bucket beside the well and stared at it as if it was the most fascinating object in the world.

Prepared to reject Astri's usual flirtatious advances, for a moment Beren found himself without words. Astri and Eskil? Was she the one his friend pined over? The humor of the situation struck him and he struggled to keep a grin from his face. Perhaps it was time to give

Astri a taste of her own back.

"So you think Eskil is more handsome than me?" He slapped his hand over his heart and continued in a dramatic tone. "I'm crushed, Astri. I thought you liked me."

She blinked in surprise. "I do, but—"

He held up a hand to cut off her protest. "I see I'll have to challenge Eskil for your favors."

"Challenge? Don't be ridiculous," Astri snapped. "It's just..." She sighed, rolled her eyes in defeat. "All right, I'd just like to know."

At her dejected look, he gave up all teasing. "I don't know, not for certain, either way."

She sulked for a moment, then she narrowed her eyes and curved her mouth in a grin that made Beren nervous. "I know how we can find out."

"Astri." He recognized that tone. It never boded well.

"No, it's not much. Pretend you're courting me."

He gaped at her. "You want me to...*what*?"

"It'll be easy, really." Her tone turned pleading. "And it's just play-acting."

Still. "Why?"

"Because..." She gave him a patient smile. "If Eskil does have feelings for me, he'll get jealous."

"And challenge me?" He shook his head. "I'm not going to fight my best friend."

"It won't come to that." She tilted her head and gazed at him from beneath her lashes. "Please, Beren?"

That look. That tone. He'd seen her use both on her father until Vider did anything she asked. What chance did Beren have? But by playing along, was he betraying his friendship? Not if Eskil did want Astri, as Beren suspected.

And perhaps this is the push he needs.

Beren pretended to consider the request. "I still don't think it's a good idea. What's in it for me?"

She pouted. "My undying gratitude?"

"I can't eat gratitude." He knew better than to give in without a protest. Astri was leading Eskil a merry dance. Let her worry for a while.

Only after she promised him a cask of her father's best wine did Beren agree to help her. No matter how this ended, he intended to share it with Eskil.

"Thank you, Beren!" She flung her arms around his neck and kissed him, and by accident dumped the ladle of water over his head. Without waiting to apologize, she skipped away.

Beren shook the water from his hair and sighed. *What have I done?* A familiar voice made him raise his head in time to see Runa turn into the road to the Gather Hall. Zabeth followed, her back stiff as if she smelled something rotten.

Had she seen Astri kiss him? He swore under his breath. He didn't want Zabeth to think someone else had a claim on him. Not that he wanted to court Zabeth, but… Curse it, he didn't know what he wanted.

As he left the well, a strange thought intruded. Why would Zabeth care about Astri unless…?

He stared after the departing figures, a flicker of something…hope?…teased a smile from his lips.

~ * ~

Elizabeth followed Runa back into the village. When they passed through the square, Beren was talking to a blonde woman dressed like a man in trousers and shirt. The woman suddenly threw herself at him and kissed him. Elizabeth stopped, her mouth hanging open.

Runa made a tut-tutting sound with her lips. "What is that girl up to now?"

"You know her?" Elizabeth stared after the woman—no, girl. She looked much younger than Elizabeth. Of course, any man would prefer someone younger than a matron with a child. Not that she cared. Of course not.

"My eldest, Astri." Runa sighed and resumed walking around the square. Elizabeth had to hurry to catch up. "She's always up to mischief, that one."

Runa's daughter? "So she's Beren's…cousin?" Elizabeth hoped she'd said the correct word.

"No." Runa frowned. "In a way. It's complicated. Beren's parents died many years ago and Kiana brought him with her when she came north. She and Tor adopted him formally when they wed."

"Oh. Heart-cousins." At Runa's surprised look, Elizabeth shrugged her shoulders. "Beren said how not…how different from true family." She smiled and offered a commiserating tone, mother to mother. "Children are always getting up to mischief, so my grandmother always said."

"She's sixteen. She should know better." The older woman shook her head. "Most girls her age are married with children of their own by now."

"At sixteen?" A different culture, Elizabeth reminded herself. And hadn't she been a mere two years older when she married?

"They don't *have* to settle down," Runa conceded. "The gods know *I* didn't until I was almost Beren's age but…Astri's my daughter." She sighed again. "Sometimes we indulge her too much."

Elizabeth glanced at Ned. "I think we all indulge our first child."

Runa gazed after the departing girl and shook her head. "Whatever it is, I don't want to know. Come, let's get you to Garan." She turned down a side street.

Elizabeth didn't know why the sight of Astri kissing Beren annoyed her so, but she had more important things to think of right now. Pushing her odd emotions aside, she hurried in Runa's wake.

In the Gather Hall, Runa led her to the chieftain's quarters accessed by a wooden door at one end of the hall. Before entering, Elizabeth took Ned from Runa. She needed her son's touch. Even that little support gave her courage.

Garan's main living space was a dark room, hot and stifling. Shelves lined the walls. One side displayed weapons—knives, shields, crossbows—the other, without doubt Freya's touch, held pots of various shapes stuffed with dried flowers or rushes.

The chieftain listened to Elizabeth's request to send a message to England.

"Keeper Magrim showed her maps," Runa explained. "He told her the storms are too strong for our boats this time of year."

"That is so," Garan agreed.

"But it is not far," Elizabeth protested. "A few days at sea. A short trip."

"No," Garan shook his head, but his tone was full of regret.

Elizabeth fought back tears of frustration. She wanted to plead, but didn't know enough words. Even Ned reacted to her distress. He fretted and whimpered, struggled to get down. Any minute now he'd start howling.

Elizabeth wanted to howl too. "Why? You can send…send man to my people. To tell them we are safe. *Please.*"

Garan rose from his chair and limped to the fireplace. Again he shook his head. "The sea is too rough and we have few warriors here. I can't spare anyone right now."

Elizabeth closed her eyes and pressed her lips together. She wouldn't cry. She was the daughter of a viscount, the wife…widow…of a duke's son. She was a lady. Ladies never showed emotion in public, not joy, not disappointment. She dug her fingernails into her palms and opened her eyes.

I. Will. Not. Cry. Not again. Not anymore.

After several moments, she composed herself enough to face Garan again. Summoning all her dignity, she dropped him a small curtsey. "I will wait. When you have a ship, more men, then I will go, yes?"

Garan gave a solemn nod. "Yes. In spring we'll send a message."

"In spring, I will go." She made it a statement. With or without his permission, she didn't intend to stay here any longer than she had to. *Half a year. A lifetime to wait.*

He inclined his head. "If you wish."

"I wish." Ned had had enough. He lifted his head and cried into her ear. Elizabeth flinched and rubbed his back. She looked at Runa. "We go to beach now?"

Runa nodded, relief evident in her expression. Before the door closed behind them, Elizabeth glanced back. Garan still stood at the fireplace, staring into the flames. He looked as unhappy as she felt and the flickering firelight suggested a hint of guilt in his expression.

Chapter Ten

The next morning the rising sun blazed through the barracks window straight into Beren's eyes. He winced and rolled off the cot to his feet. "Wonderful," he grumbled to himself. "At least something doesn't mind getting up today."

He'd slept little. Winter was closing in earlier than expected. The *Freki's* delay could no longer be ignored. It wouldn't be home before spring, and so the responsibility of protecting the village over the long winter fell to a handful of warriors, both men and women, and the few farmers who wintered in the village, bringing their livestock and families from the outlying areas. The only other men in the village were the elderly and those with injured or missing limbs. A village of cripples, as the chieftain had observed a few days ago.

After washing in the communal wash bowl in one corner of the barracks, Beren combed and braided his beard and shrugged into his clothes.

He snatched his bearskin cloak from a hook beside the bed, draped it about his shoulders and dashed down the street to the Gather Hall. Runa should be in the kitchens by now. With luck, she'd have spiced porridge simmering over the fire.

He pushed open the great doors and the scent of nutmeg teased his nostrils. He grinned and strode into the kitchen.

"Don't stick your dirty fingers in there." Runa slapped his hand away from the cauldron of porridge. "Use the ladle."

Impatient to fill his stomach, he grabbed the ladle from its hook and spooned some of the oatmeal into a wooden bowl Runa held. She slammed the bowl onto the table and tossed him a spoon.

Beren raised an eyebrow. "Did I forget a name day for one of your children?"

She wagged a finger at him. "You forgot to mention you were chasing Astri."

Beren choked on the spoonful of oatmeal he'd just put in his mouth. The scene in the square. Damn the instincts of a protective mother.

He coughed and swallowed. "We're friends, Runa."

"That's not what it looked like yesterday. Half the village is talking about it." Runa shook her finger at him. "Ulna said you offered for Astri and she was too polite to turn you down cold. Frankly, I didn't know she could be polite. She's certainly never shown me any respect."

Beren grinned. "You're her mother. You two are so close in temperament it's a wonder you haven't strangled each other by now."

Runa snatched his spoon away and slopped porridge over the table. "Mind your tongue with your elders." She waved the spoon. "Really, Beren, that girl's not right for you. Anyone can see she's too...too..."

"Impetuous?" Beren made a grab for the spoon but Runa held it out of his reach. "Runa, it's not what you think."

"What *I* think has nothing to do with this. It's what the village thinks." She glared at him. "Besides, if you wanted to offer for her you could at least have the sense to talk to Vider first. He is her father, after all."

"Heart-father," Beren corrected, then held up his hands in a placating gesture at Runa's scowl. "Runa—"

"Don't you *Runa* me in that tone, young man." She whirled away and stalked to the window, then spun around to face him again. "By the gods, Beren, Have you no sense?"

He tried again. "Runa."

"No. I don't want to hear any more." She turned her back on him.

Beren jumped from the bench and grabbed her arms. "Runa, Astri wants Eskil, not me."

Runa opened her mouth, then snapped it shut. Her brow furrowed in a puzzled frown. "Then why is she chasing you?"

"She isn't. She just wants Eskil to think she is." He ran his hands up and down her arms, soothing her. Runa was more a mother to him than Kiana had ever been, even after his warrior-guard had children of her own. Runa was family.

The corners of her lips twitched. "She truly wants Eskil? And he doesn't know?"

"Not yet," Beren muttered.

She laughed, slapped the spoon into his hand, and pushed him back to the table. "That's a relief. Astri's a nice girl, but not for you."

Beren shook his head at Runa's abrupt change of heart. A

moment ago Astri had been an impetuous troublemaker. What was it with mothers and daughters?

Runa narrowed her eyes with a speculative gleam. "I suppose we'd better plan a wedding for the midwinter feast."

The porridge stuck in Beren's throat and he coughed. "At least wait until Eskil is caught in her snare." He held up his bowl. "Could I have some more?"

While he was devouring the second helping, Eskil appeared in the doorway. "Thought I'd find you here."

Beren pointed to his bowl. "Want some?"

Eskil shook his head. "I ate earlier. I've been to the cove."

Beren paused with the spoon half-way to his mouth. These days, the one cove of any importance was where they'd found traces of the raider ship. He glanced at Runa. He didn't want to worry her. "Anything new?"

Eskil shook his head. "The waves are pretty high. No one in their right mind would brave the seas now. A Shadow engine might work, but no one has those but us."

"Hmmm." After finishing the porridge, Beren rinsed the bowl in a barrel of hot water, then motioned Eskil to follow him from the kitchen. They paused in the opening to the Gather Hall and observed the usual morning bustle. "We've got some time, then." He drew Eskil toward the doors. "We'll keep up the training, but I doubt the raiders will show their faces until spring."

A flash of blue caught his eye. Zabeth sat herself on one of the benches. Her blue robe rippled around her body when she smoothed the folds. She'd braided her hair this morning, and wound the braids into a knot at the base of her neck.From the tightness of the braids, it looked as if she'd been in an angry mood when she'd pulled her hair back. Her skin was pale, and there was a grim set to her mouth.

Was she still angry at him? She'd sent word yesterday asking him not to come for their regular language lesson. She hadn't said why but he could guess. Astri.

Beren paused. "Go on ahead. I'll be there in a moment."

Eskil grinned and sauntered on, but instead of leaving, he leaned against the doorframe and waited.

As Beren made his way to Zabeth, she clutched a drop-spindle he hadn't noticed before, and now twisted the raw flax onto the wooden shaft in clumsy threads that wavered from thick to thin.

He also spotted several knots in the skein, but decided it would be prudent not to mention that. "Good morning, Zabeth."

She looked up. "Good morning, Beren."

Not the warm greeting she'd used other mornings. He searched for something to say. "Another lesson this afternoon?"

She lowered her head and fumbled with the spindle and yarn. "If you want."

Yes, she was still angry. "What's wrong?"

Her knuckles whitened under her tight grip. She shook her head, then changed her denial to a quick nod. She stared at the tangle of threads in her hand. "I speak to Chieftain Garan yesterday."

Garan? So her anger wasn't directed at him? The rush of relief surprised him. He bent closer to hear her words, but before he had time to ask what they'd talked about, Astri called his name.

He straightened and forced a welcoming smile.

"There you are, Beren," Astri gushed.

Since yesterday, she'd been playing her part to make Eskil jealous with too much eagerness for Beren's comfort. He stole a sideways glance at his friend in time to see him storm out the doors. Astri smoothed her tunic, a smug grin on her face, and turned to Zabeth.

"You must be Zabeth." Astri grinned as if nothing had happened. Ignoring Beren, she dropped onto the bench beside the Shadow woman. "I'm Astri. My mother is Runa."

Zabeth nodded and returned her attention to the spinning.

Astri, irrepressible as ever, slid closer and took the spindle from her fingers. "I heard you spoke to Chieftain Garan." Astri positioned Zabeth's hands on the thread and guided her to the correct motion. "I'm sorry we can't help you get back to your family right away."

Zabeth's hands trembled, but the thread spun in smoother strands. "I want to go soon. Go home…"

Beren heard the yearning, the sadness, and a lump formed in his throat. She was so alone here and it was all his fault. He exchanged a look with Astri, who shook her head in warning.

So, they hadn't told Zabeth all of it yet.

Astri put an arm around Zabeth's shoulders. "We have lots of fun here in the winter. The time will go quickly, you'll see, and when spring comes—"

"When spring comes, we leave." It was not so much a statement as a vow. Zabeth raised her head, mouth set in a stubborn line, and the expression in her eyes defied anyone to contradict her.

The lump in Beren's throat eased. Here was no compliant maiden, content to let her elders decide her fate. There was steel in this woman, perhaps more of the Valkyrie than she realized.

Changing the subject, Astri positioned her arms in front of her as if cradling a baby. "Where's your son?"

Zabeth's expression softened. She pointed to a corner of the Gather Hall. "Runa take him there."

Despite Zabeth's inexperience with the language, she managed to spend several minutes conversing with Astri, exchanging women talk about children. Beren shifted from one foot to the other. He didn't need to stay but found himself reluctant to leave. At last, Astri rose from the bench. "We have work to do now."

Zabeth nodded. She looked from Astri to Beren and offered a polite smile. "I give you both good...good fortune."

"Thank you." Astri flashed a brilliant smile.

Gods. Zabeth must have heard the rumor of him courting Astri. Beren had an urge to explain, but Astri grabbed his arm and dragged him toward the door, calling over her shoulder, "We'll talk to you later."

In the courtyard, Beren pulled his arm from Astri's grasp. "What are you doing? It's bad enough everyone thinks I'm offering for you. Do you have to flaunt it everywhere you go?"

Astri stared at him. "That's the whole idea, isn't it? We have to make it look real."

He growled in frustration. "Why don't you tell Eskil the truth?"

Astri chuckled. "The truth? He'd run away faster than you could blink. No, we have to snare him, make him believe wanting me was all his idea. Until then, we'll show him he's not the only rabbit in the woods."

She strode away, leaving Beren to roll his eyes and follow with reluctant steps in her wake.

His friends spent the next hour sparring with each other, Astri teasing, Eskil reacting with his usual annoyance. Similar scenes over the past few days now made sense. Perhaps Astri's crazy plan was going to work after all.

When Beren at last emerged from the horse barn, Astri's coy voice made him jump. "Will you walk me back to the village?"

Eskil stood in the doorway of the barn, wiping his face and scowling at them. Beren forced his mouth into a smile. Strange, he'd never had trouble smiling at Astri before, but in truth he found this whole scheme uncomfortable.

Compared to Zabeth, Astri was still a child, spinning childish plots, while Zabeth had the confidence of a grown woman. Still, he had promised to help. "I'd be honored."

Astri slipped her hand into his and led the way. They stopped by the meadow to admire the sturdy plough horses galloping around the paddock, enjoying the last few days of warm weather before they were closed in the stable for the next few months.

"Will you be meeting Zabeth this afternoon?" Astri asked.

Beren looked at her, startled at the question. "For her language lesson, yes. Now she's stronger we'll probably use the Hall instead of her room. Why?"

"She seems nice. I'd like to get to know her better." She sighed. "It's so sad what we're doing to her."

"We saved her life."

Astri grimaced. "But we're lying to her. She went to Garan yesterday to ask someone to send word to her family she's safe, but Garan told her she'd have to wait until spring. She's worried they think she and her child are dead."

"Couldn't he have said we'd send a message?" That seemed the easiest solution.

"If it's safe enough to send a message it's safe enough for her to leave, and he doesn't want to lie to her."

"Why not tell her the truth now?" He wasn't surprised Astri was aware of the details of Zabeth's visit—the girl had an uncanny ability to learn every secret in the village—but he agreed it wasn't fair to keep lying to Zabeth.

Astri headed toward the village. "I overheard Keeper Magrim talking to Garan. No one knows how she'll react. She could be hysterical, or despair so much she might wish to take her own life. They want to observe her over the winter. Besides, by spring she will have enough of our language to understand when we tell her about the Shadow worlds." She glanced at Beren. "Imagine if we didn't know about 'Links or the God-Hold, and suddenly found ourselves in a strange land with people who didn't understand us."

Beren wanted to remind her that had happened to Tor and Runa, but she hurried on before he had a chance to even open his mouth.

"It must be frightening for her, yet she seems to be handling it well. Garan wants to make sure she is truly as strong as she seems before we tell her she has no choice but to stay here."

Choice. The word sent an unexpected jolt through Beren. Such a small word to hold so heavy a burden. He understood how Zabeth must feel, but he also understood the necessity of keeping silent. Zabeth was not only far from her home, but far from her time. How could she even understand what had happened to her? Still...

"Beren?" Astri tugged his arm. "Did you hear me?"

He nodded. "I heard you. I just hate the thought of lying to her."

"It's not lying if we don't say anything." Astri gazed ahead. "Besides, as long as Zabeth accepts Garan's ruling, she won't question anyone else, and there'll be no need for lies."

~ * ~

From the bench beside the Gather Hall door, Elizabeth watched a recovered Mikkel wrestle with his friends, and pondered the mystery of Runa's nephew.

Beren got on well with his cousin, and even with children as young as Gudrin. It seemed babies made him nervous. Or was it Ned who upset him? Perhaps when Ned was older—

No. Come spring, she and Ned would return to England. They'd never see Beren again, and she'd never again have to wonder why she had to fight so hard to ignore the way he affected her.

And he did affect her. Whenever he was near, she had to struggle to hold an intelligent conversation. Her heart sped up, her cheeks burned, and she had to wipe her hands on her dress several times. He even invaded her dreams, with his smiling mouth and admiring eyes.

She'd never experienced these sensations before and had to keep reminding herself she *shouldn't* feel this way. David had been dead less than a month. What kind of wife—widow—lusted after another man so soon after losing her husband?

She paused. Maybe not *lusted*. She'd never lusted after anyone before, so wasn't sure how it felt, but it couldn't be like this. No, it had to be nerves. After all, she wasn't used to being alone in a room with a man who wasn't a relative. She needed to accept these new customs, at least for a while, until she went home.

Besides, Beren was interested in Astri, not her.

She ignored the quick pang that reminder caused.

After the midday meal, Elizabeth played with her son, but as soon as Beren arrived for their lesson, Gudrin appeared to take Ned to the nursery. Elizabeth handed him to the young girl and sighed.

"He'll be safe with the other children," Beren said.

Elizabeth watched Gudrin until she vanished into the crowd at the far end of the Hall. "Yes, but he is all I have here. I do not like to be away from him long."

Beren didn't comment. Instead he began the lesson.

An hour later, her head stuffed full of new words and concepts, Elizabeth leaned back. The bench that edged the Gather Hall wasn't as wide at this point as elsewhere in the room. It was possible to sit with her back to the wall and her legs dangling over the edge, like a child sitting in a chair too big for her small body.

She gestured to the rest of the expanse of bench. "What is this? It is too wide for a chair and too low for a table."

"It is for sleeping."

"Sleeping?" She frowned. "But there are many rooms in here.

Why sleep on this?"

"In winter, it's more than the village. Most of the people gather here for the cold months." He seemed frustrated at his inability to explain.

She didn't know what gave her that impression, but ever since she'd first awakened to his presence in her chamber, she'd felt as though she understood him, that they were somehow tied together with an invisible bond.

Abruptly, Beren rose. He walked away a few paces, then turned back to her. "Runa said you enjoyed your time on the beach, yesterday."

She nodded, surprised at the change in subject "Yes. I grow...grew up by the sea and love the smell of...of..." What was the word for *salt*.

"Fish?" Beren suggested with a grin.

She managed to stifle an undignified snort but had to smile.

He laughed and offered his hand. "Come. I want to show you a special place."

The excitement in his eyes was irresistible. Despite her good intentions, Elizabeth found herself clasping his hand.

A sharp tingle shot up her arm and she jerked but didn't let go. She glanced up at him. His eyes had darkened. A sensuous fire burned in their depths and found an answering quiver low in her belly.

He tightened his grip and drew her to her feet until they stood toe-to-toe. She had to tip her head back to look up at him. Beren bent his head until their lips were inches apart. Caught in the snare of his gaze, Elizabeth couldn't look away. She parted her lips, waiting for...what?

No. This wasn't happening. This *couldn't* happen.

She took a shuddering breath and forced herself to draw away. Every nerve in her body screamed in protest, but she managed to ignore the traitorous clamor.

"What...what do you want to show me?" She cursed the hitch in her breath, the husky note that crept into her voice.

Beren stepped back, a wry expression on his face. He cleared his throat. His eyes lightened back to their chocolate brown shade, but the smile he gave her was pure heat. A good thing she still leaned against the bench, for her knees felt like melted butter and just as capable of supporting her.

"The beach." His voice was rough, although Elizabeth suspected those weren't the words he wanted to say.

He headed toward the outer door and tugged her after him. She'd forgotten he still held her hand. He released her long enough to throw a cloak around her shoulders and grab his own.

While they walked, Elizabeth glanced sideways at Beren until the question in her head burst from her before she had sense to pull it back. "What is it made of, that…cape?"

He fingered the fur at his neck. "My cloak? Bear fur."

"Bear?" Alarm shot through her. "Like the ones that attacked Mikkel?"

He grinned. "Bigger." He pulled her to a stop, released the clasp at his throat, and shrugged off the cloak. He held it up, his arms spread wide over his head. The cloak dangled an inch from the ground.

Elizabeth touched the fur. "Soft," she murmured in surprise. She'd expected it to be coarse, with sharp bristles, but it felt silkier than any lamb's wool she'd touched in the past.

"They are prized for their fur," Beren agreed, and after a few deft folds, swung the cloak back over his shoulders so it no longer touched the ground. "When a boy reaches a certain age, he hunts for his own cloak. It is a trial of manhood."

She shook her head and eyed the cloak. "But they are so big."

"If they were small, it wouldn't be much of a trial." Beren fastened the clasp. "Often it takes a few hunts before a boy is successful. It took three years before Kiana earned her cloak."

Elizabeth's mouth dropped open. "Your mother? But you said it was a trial for boys."

"Kiana is…" He paused, narrowed his eyes as if searching for the right words. "Different. She was raised a warrior."

"Do any of the other women have cloaks like this?" She hadn't seen any in the village.

He shook his head. "None they have earned themselves. Their men might give their own cloak as a courting gift. Any who go on the hunt go to support the more experienced and skilled hunters."

"Are you saying your mother fought a bear herself?" Elizabeth couldn't imagine a woman facing such a large beast.

Beren gazed at the forest that loomed at the edge of the village and grinned again. When he spoke, there was pride in his voice. "Oh yes. I'm told it was a magnificent battle. I was too young to see it myself, but the hunters who were with her were so impressed they created a festival song in her honor. You'll hear it one day."

Elizabeth didn't know what to say to that, so she remained silent.

"Come," Beren said. "Not much farther."

By the time they reached the beach, Elizabeth was breathing hard. She hated not having the energy for even such a short walk.

Beren stopped and let her sink onto a rock that edged the sand. "Rest. We'll go on in a moment."

Grateful for the respite, Elizabeth leaned back on her hands and stared around her.

A week ago, the sea had been crowded with small fishing vessels. Today all those boats were drawn up on the sand, upside down with canvas lashed over the tops to protect them from the weather. Several men sat on the pebbles farther up the beach and mended nets or chatted together in small groups. All had gray hair and skin turned to leather by sea and wind.

"Where are all the young men?" she asked Beren.

He gazed past the cliffs that protected the bay from the choppy waves farther out. "Some are farmers, still at their holdings, but the rest are on the *Freki*. The runes said this was a good year to trade, so they all went."

She tilted her head. "What does that name mean? *Freki*?"

Beren smiled. "It's named after one of Odin's wolves. The other ship, the *Geri*, was holed in a storm last month. It's named after the other wolf. Both lie beneath Odin's throne."

Hadn't she read somewhere that Odin had pet ravens? "I think...thought Odin had birds."

"True." Beren nodded. "The ravens are Odin's messengers. The wolves are his companions."

"Ah." She glanced at the *Geri*, then back at Beren. "Why you not go?"

He glanced away, as if uncomfortable. "Someone had to stay to protect the village. In summer, most of our enemies are busy planting or trading or harvesting. Only in early spring or late autumn do they come raiding."

Alarmed, Elizabeth jumped to her feet. "Raiding? Autumn? You mean, *now*?" She shot a glance at the sea, the cliffs, the hills behind the village. She half expected raiders to pour from the trees.

As if sensing her fear, Beren placed a hand on her arm. This time his touch didn't tingle. This time it burned.

She gasped, snatched her arm away.

Beren cleared his throat and tucked his thumbs under the edge of his belt, anchoring his hands in place. "Not now," he said, as if nothing had happened. "Sit. You are safe."

Reluctantly, she sank back onto the rock.

Beren continued, "There are few paths through the mountains and we watch them all. Raiders cannot come by sea at this time of year because the water is too rough." He gestured to the fishermen and the flotilla of beached boats. "If *they* cannot sail the sea, then no one can."

Reassured by his confident tone, Elizabeth stood again. "I am rested now. We go?"

Once again Beren took the lead, although this time he didn't hold her hand. She couldn't decide if she was relieved or disappointed.

Wet sand clung to her skirt, sucked at her boots. She took a deep breath of the salt air, savoring its taste on her tongue. The outbound tide had left several pools in the hollows of the beach. Some of the younger boys were gathered around the pools, dipping in cautious fingers and pulling up various treasures. Several cupped shells in their hands. One held up a starfish.

With a shout, all the boys ran toward the waves, splashing in up to their ankles. The boy with the starfish bent over and tossed the creature into the deeper waves.

"Watch your step here," Beren said.

Elizabeth pulled her attention back from the boys. The knife edge wall of a cliff blocked her path. Jumbled heaps of boulders softened the base, where cliff met beach. Water glistened off the rock, leaving a wet sheen where the tide had retreated.

Beren had already scrambled up one boulder. He offered his hand. "Let me help you."

Elizabeth shook her head. She didn't want a repeat of the last time she'd touched him. The effect was…disconcerting. Instead, she gathered her skirt in one hand and used the other to pull herself over the rocks.

Beren poised as if ready to grab her if she slipped. Elizabeth concentrated on her footing, testing each step before putting her weight on each potentially slippery spot. The last thing she wanted was to break a leg, or her neck. After a moment, Beren continued around the base of the cliff.

After negotiating one tricky stretch, she found herself standing once more on wet sand. She raised her head. "Oh my."

The cliff continued around the bay, but here a great gash tore through the rock. Two hundred feet above her head, a waterfall gushed from a vertical slash below the top of the cliff. Water cascaded down several levels, falling the last twenty feet into a deep pool bordered by rocks that sparkled in the daylight. A dark shadow on the cliff face cut off a few feet above the pool and showed where high tide buried the fresh water.

"I thought you'd like it." Beren stood a few feet away from her, grinning.

She breathed a sigh. "It is beautiful."

The sun peeked from behind a cloud at that moment and sent a shaft of light onto the water. Dozens of rainbows danced into view on every surface.

"Oh!" Elizabeth gasped and sat on a rock, heedless of the water that dampened her skirt.

For a while, neither of them moved. The play of water and color continued until another cloud covered the sun.

Beren sighed and sat at Elizabeth's feet. "In winter, you can see Bifrost, the rainbow bridge to Asgard."

"Asgard?"

He nodded. "Where our gods live."

Elizabeth stiffened and touched her cross. "There is only one God, not many."

Beren gave her a curious look and shrugged. "We know of your one god. You're from a different…land, and your gods are not our gods." He grinned, "But you'll still be able to see Bifrost. I'll show you when it comes."

Without waiting for her to respond, he jumped to his feet and scrambled back the way they'd come. Elizabeth rose more sedately. She was relieved he hadn't taken offense at her denial of his gods. He was more tolerant than she, and that shamed her. He'd shown her a wonder that left her breathless, and her response had been to reject his beliefs.

Glancing once more at the waterfall, she sighed, then turned away and followed Beren back to the village.

~ * ~

That evening, Beren sat in the Gather Hall with Eskil, listening to one-legged Audun regaling the group with tales of his youth. Zabeth had been tired after the afternoon's walk and stayed in her room for the evening meal, but now she sat with Runa and her children.

A twinge of guilt speared through Beren. He'd always found the waterfall gave him a sense of peace, but perhaps clambering over slippery boulders wasn't the best way to help an invalid recover strength.

"I don't know why you're so gloomy," Eskil interrupted his friend's thoughts. "Astri hasn't taken her eyes off you all evening."

Although the observation was delivered in a mild tone, there was an underlying note of irritation in Eskil's voice.

Beren stifled an urge to groan and peered across the room at Astri, who sat in regal splendor beside Runa. He'd forgotten the role he was supposed to play.

She'd shed her trews for a robe this evening. The rich green with gold thread edging the neckline and sleeves suited her. She'd even taken the time to braid gold threads into her hair and pile the whole mass on top of her head.

He had to admit Runa's daughter looked lovelier than he'd ever seen her, and sure enough, she was smiling at him.

Beren nodded his head in brief acknowledgement and turned his attention back to Eskil. "She has been very…attentive…these last few days."

Eskil scowled and his jaw tightened, as if he was grinding his teeth. "She makes herself look foolish."

Beren raised an eyebrow. "Oh? Have you told her?"

"No," Eskil snapped. "It's not my place to tell her." He narrowed his eyes at Beren. "You're the one she's being a fool over. Why don't you tell her?"

"I like my head just where it is, thank you." Beren took a swig of wine to hide his grin, then lowered the cup and shook his head. "I fear that one is not easily persuaded."

Eskil scowled. "That's nonsense. With a woman like that, you have to teach her a lesson."

"How?" Beren asked in amusement. "You think Vider would allow you to lay a hand on his daughter?"

"He'd thank me for it, but she needs more than a spanking." Eskil shot to his feet, grabbed his bowl, and disappeared into the kitchen.

Beren risked a glance at Astri. She hadn't missed Eskil's reaction. She even had the nerve to wink at Beren.

He had to agree with his friend. The little minx was asking for trouble.

At that moment, the door to the Hall burst open and a man staggered in, supported by a stout woman and a young girl of about fourteen. Beren recognized the family.

He jumped to his feet and rushed to offer his support. "What's happened, Dev? Raiders?"

"Worse," gasped the man, clutching his side. Blood poured from a gash over his hip.

Garan appeared beside them. He took the place of Dev's daughter and helped the older man to a bench at the table nearest the fire. Pillows were brought for him to sit on. Freya and Astri led mother and daughter to the table.

When Eskil returned from the kitchen he carried a large bowl of stew and three spoons, which he placed in front of the family. While they ate, Zabeth edged closer. Judging by the expressions darting over her face, curiosity warred with concern.

"Rest easy, Dev," Garan said. "Tell us what happened."

While the healer tended Dev's wound, Beren handed the injured man a cup of *keevah*.

"Bears," Dev said after he'd finished the cup. "A pack of five.

Giants."

Beren glanced at Mikkel, who had joined the crowd surrounding the farmer. The boy listened with rapt attention.

"They attacked the farm," Dev continued. He took another drink. "Broke through the walls like they were made of cloth instead of turf. We didn't stand a chance." He looked at Garan. "They must have been starved. They went for the food. Skara tried to fight them off, but he's an old man. They swatted him aside like a gnat. We couldn't do anything for him, but he gave us time to get away."

He shifted, winced from pain. His eyes held a bleak stare when he spoke of his old uncle.

"Did you fight them too?" Garan indicated the gash in Dev's side.

The farmer nodded. "I tried. The women stood between them and the food pots. I got them out of the way, but not without hurt." He shook his head. "In a way, it's a good thing they were so hungry. If they hadn't been intent on getting the stew, they'd have gone after us."

Garan patted his shoulder, then stood. He studied the people in the room, as if assessing what strength he had to face this newest threat.

At last, his gaze came to rest on Beren. "Set up a hunting party. Take Dug, Eskil, and Olav. I won't have my people threatened by rogue bears. It's about time we drove them back into the hills."

Beren nodded. "We'll leave at first light."

Dev raised a hand. "My helper, Bryn, disappeared a few days ago. Maybe the bears got him. Would you look out for him?"

"We will." Beren exchanged a look with Garan. If the bears had developed a taste for human flesh, more than the outlying farms were in danger. He pondered the threat as he strode back to his seat and picked up his cloak. He'd need his rest if they were leaving in a few hours.

"Beren? Remember your promise?" Mikkel stood beside him, an eager expression on his face.

Beren caught his breath. He'd promised to take Mikkel on his next hunt if the boy followed the healer's instructions. He hadn't envisioned chasing a pack of five rogues. Still, he'd given his word. Despite his misgivings, he ruffled Mikkel's hair. "Better get to bed. I'll call you before sun-up."

"Thank you, Beren." Grinning as if he'd won the treasures of the gods, Mikkel dashed from the Hall.

Eskil grabbed his own cloak from the bench. "You're taking Mikkel?" he asked in disbelief.

Beren nodded. "I promised."

Eskil stared after the departing boy and grinned. "Runa's going to kill you."

"I know." And with a mock shudder, Beren headed to his sleeping quarters.

Chapter Eleven

Yesterday's exertions on the beach, followed by the evening's excitement had tired Elizabeth more than she cared to admit, and she slept later than usual. For once, so had Ned. After the midday meal, Elizabeth sat in the Gather Hall and practiced her spinning. Back home it had never occurred to her the threads she used in her delicate embroidery came from the backs of sheep. Learning how to turn the coarse wool into fine twisted fibers was challenging but also…satisfying. The baby lay in her lap and waved pudgy hands at the dangling wool.

A childish voice interrupted her contemplation. "Mistress Zabeth, my brother Beren is not here."

Elizabeth looked up. Gudrin stood before her. "Yes. I know."

Elizabeth's mastery of the language was progressing, but although she was able to converse in simple terms with some of the other women, the children were her favorite teachers. They were more patient. Where the adults smirked at a mispronounced word, the children repeated the word with her until she got it right. Determined to master the language, Elizabeth had asked Gudrin not to use English unless Elizabeth was especially puzzled.

Gudrin had attached herself to the older woman, but Elizabeth suspected she was more attached to Ned, since the girl never tired of playing with him. Now she'd delivered her message, Gudrin reached for the baby.

"He went to hunt the bears, yes?" Elizabeth placed Ned in the child's arms.

Gudrin lowered him to a fleece rug on the floor. "Yes. Auntie says he'll bring home a big bear, then Mikkel can have the skin and make a big cloak."

"Did your brother go alone?" She struggled to keep the anxiety from her voice. There was no need for her concern. Beren was a full grown man, not a boy. *He probably hunts giant bears before breakfast every morning, but please, Lord, keep him safe.*

"No. With Eskil and Dug and Olav and Mikkel. Auntie wasn't happy Mikkel went, but he's a man now and men go hunting." Gudrin stated the last as an irrefutable fact and seemed puzzled her aunt objected. "I'll go hunting when I'm old enough."

Go hunting? Girls don't go hunting.

Before Elizabeth could voice the thought, the door opened and Astri walked in carrying a brace of hares. Dressed in tunic and breeches similar to the men, she seemed unaware of the scandalous sight she made showing off her legs. Elizabeth had been appalled the first time she'd seen one of the women dressed thus, and the shock had not lessened with constant exposure.

Gudrin watched Astri stride toward the kitchen. "I think she wanted to go too, but Eskil told Beren not to ask her."

Elizabeth shuddered. *Quite right too.* What man allowed a woman to accompany him on such a dangerous trip? Why would any woman want to go?

For a moment, her father's voice echoed in her mind. *I must be mad to allow you to read your brothers' books. What kind of wife will you make with your head stuffed full of things too difficult for you to understand.*

But she *had* understood them, more than her brothers. At the time she'd resented that word *allow*. Even David had sometimes mocked her love of reading. *You are a lady of privilege, not a scholar.*

Different cultures. Perhaps here a woman didn't need a man's permission to do what she wanted. If Astri wanted to go on the hunt, why shouldn't she? After all, Beren's mother had.

Elizabeth shook her head at the strange thought and pulled herself back to the present.

Gudrin dropped to her knees on the blanket and shook a chain of smooth wooden disks strung on a strip of leather. Ned squealed with laughter and grabbed for the rattling sound. When he succeeded in seizing the disks from Gudrin, he stuffed them into his mouth.

Runa bustled into the Hall carrying two brooms. She laid one on the bench and turned to her daughter. "Gudrin, find Liv and ask her to give me a hand with the sweeping."

"I can help." Elizabeth set her spinning aside and jumped to her feet. So far Runa had refused to let her help with anything, saying her shoulder needed strengthening, but Elizabeth wanted to do more.

"Do you feel strong enough?" Runa's tone was doubtful.

For answer, Elizabeth picked up the extra broom and applied it with great energy to the rush-covered floor. Clouds of dust billowed up, sending everyone in the vicinity into a coughing fit. Gudrin snatched Ned from his blanket and ran away with him toward the safety of the kitchen.

Runa took the broom from Elizabeth's hands. "It's good of you to offer, Zabeth, but this type of sweeping takes great skill and many years of practice."

The words were kind, but Elizabeth hung her head and made her way to the other side of the room with her spinning and Ned's rattle in her hands. She'd never felt so useless in her life.

A plump woman in her late thirties hurried from the kitchen and took the spare broom from Runa. The two of them swept, not the floor, but the bench, guiding the dirt and dust to the edge and onto the floor without stirring up a single choking cloud.

When they worked their way around the room to where Elizabeth sat, she put aside resentment for curiosity. "Why do you do this?"

Runa stopped, wiped the sweat from her forehead, and propped her broom against the bench. "Soon it'll get very cold. The water in the bay will freeze over, the storms will begin, and everyone will spend the night here."

Elizabeth studied the bench that circled the entire Hall, wide enough for a man of even Beren's height to lay on. He'd mentioned yesterday about the benches being used for sleeping. "What do you mean?"

"When it's cold, when the winter storms come, the outlying farms are cut off. Even the houses in the village can't be heated well. We keep all our animals in the horse barn, but for the people, it's more difficult. So everyone comes here and brings their bedding and sleeps in the Gather Hall. On very cold nights, even the people who live in this building sleep here."

"Everyone?"

Runa chuckled. "Well, not everyone. The Hall is big but even with small children we can't all fit. Those who come late put their pallets in the horse barn or the barracks. We also have other rooms behind the Hall, where the old stables used to be, but..." She paused and worry creased her forehead. "...some of our people are still away on a trading voyage. If they don't make it back before the snows, we may not need to use the extra space." She gazed into the distance for a moment, then smiled at Elizabeth. "It's common for us all to share the benches, so they need to be deep enough for sleeping."

Men and women sleeping together in a communal bed? Elizabeth had never heard of such a thing. "Why?"

"Because it's the only room that can be heated in such cold. As winter grows, many families stake out a space of their own and live here. We all sleep together, all along the bench." She patted Elizabeth's arm. "If you wish, you may share space with my family."

Elizabeth's mouth dropped open. "I will light a fire in my room. I will be warm."

"You won't. The fire will go out, and you'll freeze. And you can't let the baby stay up in a cold room. He should be here, with the other children."

Elizabeth shook her head. Sleep with a roomful of strangers? Good Lord, what if her mother learned of the situation? She'd have a fit. But... Runa seemed certain it was necessary, and someone who'd spent all her life here had to understand the vagaries of the weather just as well as Elizabeth knew what to expect at home.

"Zabeth?" Runa prompted. "You will sleep here when it is needed, yes? And Ned?"

Elizabeth managed a polite smile and inclined her head. "I do not want Ned to be cold."

"Good." Runa nodded in satisfaction, then retrieved her broom from beside the bench and went back to sweeping the rest of the platform.

Elizabeth's smile vanished when Runa turned her back. What kind of land was so cold people had to sleep together? If the maps were correct, the top of Denmark was not much farther north than southern Scotland. Was the weather so much different here?

At that moment, a loud pounding noise came from outside and the doors of the Hall burst open. A pack of fierce men surged through, shouting and waving swords.

Runa dropped her broom. "Raiders."

Raiders? Beren had told her it was too late in the year for raiders, but the fear in her friend's eyes told Elizabeth he'd been wrong. Runa closed strong fingers over her arm. "Run!"

Elizabeth hung back. Her gaze darted over the panicked villagers. "*Ned.*"

"With Gudrin. Safe. Hurry." Runa dragged her toward the hallway that led to the kitchens.

Men continued to pour in. They spread out around the walls, blocking the doors and the stairs to the upper floors. Runa's dash to freedom was stopped by two sturdy warriors. With relentless ease, the raiders pushed the villagers back to the center of the Hall.

In the confusion, the two women became separated. Elizabeth found herself jostled by old men and women she didn't know, while everyone was herded into a tight group in the center of the Hall. She counted twenty men surrounding them, all with bared swords and pitiless expressions. She pushed at the crowd, struggling to get to where she'd last seen Gudrin, but the people were packed too close together. She found herself wedged beside the farmer who'd arrived last night and his wife. Their daughter huddled in her mother's embrace.

"Silence!" The commanding tone of a muscular man wearing a wolf pelt over his tunic and breeches brought instant obedience. The man stood at least six feet tall. A large ring covered each forefinger and a medallion hung around his neck.

There was not a sound in the Hall, not even the whimper of a child or the sob of a woman. The group gathered in the Hall held fewer villagers than she expected. None of the remaining warriors were present, nor most of the young women. Had they escaped to the hills? Elizabeth had been shocked to learn six healthy fighting men were all who protected the village. She didn't count the women. After all, they wouldn't be able to do anything against armed warriors. It seemed her misgivings were justified.

Her thoughts fled to Beren and the warriors who'd gone hunting, but no. Despair filled her. They'd never find out in time to be of any help, and there were too few of them anyway.

A movement near the great outer door made everyone crane their necks. Chieftain Garan was thrust through the wall of armed men and forced to his knees before their leader. Two men held his arms, but Garan managed to maintain an air of defiance and authority that calmed his people.

He glared up at the triumphant man before him, then spat at his feet. "Creltak. So now the rats attack women and children?"

The man smiled, but the smile didn't reach his eyes. He struck Garan across the face. Blood spurted from a gash opened on the chieftain's cheek by one of Creltak's rings.

No one moved. No one cried. Elizabeth wanted to scream but stuffed a fist in her mouth instead. After a moment, she regained enough control to lower her hand.

Creltak wiped his bloodied knuckles on Garan's shirt. "Brave words from a fool. Where are your warriors? Chasing bears, perhaps?"

The chieftain stiffened. "You. You drove the beasts to Dev's farm."

Creltak shrugged. "Where are the Shadow-Links, old man?"

Shock filled Garan's face but he said nothing.

Shadow-Links? Elizabeth understood each word, but her meager vocabulary wouldn't translate the joined words. Something from that country called Shadow?

At that moment, several older men in brown robes stumbled

through the doorway, herded by three warriors. Elizabeth recognized Keeper Magrim and the robes from her visit to him. Assistants? Fellow keepers? Magrim looked more angry than frightened when the men joined the villagers.

Two other warriors entered, each carrying a large sack that bulged at strange angles. They set the sacks beside Creltak. The warrior leader transferred his attention from Garan to peer into the sacks. His grin widened.

"A good start," he crowed, "But I'm sure these aren't all of them." He turned back to Garan. "Where are the rest?"

Garan spat. "I don't know what you're talking about."

Creltak raised his hand, but dropped it again. "Don't try that with me. You've got all these wonders, ships that sail faster than the wind, medicines that can heal a killing sickness or injury." He glanced at the strange white globes Elizabeth had noticed before. "Lights that shine without flame. We've all seen them or heard of them and wondered. Now we know." Garan said nothing, so Creltak continued, "Your people are weak, old man. That farmer didn't last an hour before he was telling us about your Shadow-Links."

Garan paled. Elizabeth remembered Dev had asked the hunters to look for his helper who disappeared a few days ago. Was that who this raider spoke of?

"You've had these things long enough. Now it's our turn." Creltak lifted the sack and removed a small box the size of Elizabeth's jewelry case. He turned it over, poked at the buttons and little levers on one edge. "You're going to tell us where the rest of these are and your priests here are going to show us how they work."

Garan curled his lip. "You think you can just sweep in here and take over once we've done the hard work? You're more fool than I thought."

"Silence." One of the warriors slashed his sword across Garan's arm and drew a thin line of blood.

The chieftain hissed in pain but said nothing. Creltak returned the box to the sack and strolled around his kneeling enemy. He stopped in front of Garan and pulled a leather bag from his belt. After tugging open the top, he tipped the bag and let a dozen small pebbles cascade into his hand.

"See these? These will decide the fate of your people. Every time you refuse me an answer, I'll draw a stone from this bag. If the stone is black, I'll burn one of your elders alive." A murmur of dismay swept the captives. "If the stone is red, I'll cut one of your children to pieces."

Elizabeth's heart plummeted to her toes and for a moment she couldn't breathe. *Ned.*

"For white…" He paused and let his gaze rove over the assembled prisoners. "For white, I'll take one of your maidens and give her to my men for sport."

Elizabeth dug her fingernails into the palms of her hands. The woman beside her clutched her daughter tighter.

"The Shadow-Links," Creltak repeated.

Garan set his jaw and remained silent.

Creltak nodded, as if he'd expected no other response. He tipped the pebbles back into the bag and shook it, then reached in and withdrew his closed fist.

Elizabeth held her breath.

Chapter Twelve

Beren studied the steaming pile of bear droppings beside the trail. "Fresh. They can't be far."

"How many?" Mikkel asked.

"Two. A male and a female. See? One set of prints is smaller than the other." Beren straightened and studied the forest around them. The men backed up, but Mikkel crowded closer.

"What about the other three?" the boy asked. "Dev said there were five."

"It's rare they keep together. The fact they attacked in a pack is unusual." He frowned and murmured under his breath, "I don't like it."

Something wasn't right, but he couldn't pin down what was bothering him. Instead, he returned his attention to the tracks and raised his voice to continue Mikkel's lesson.

While Dug led the small party, he let Beren handle the boy's training. "These two are heading south. If we hurry, we should be able to catch them before sunset."

Beren began to follow the spoor, but a sound on the trail behind him made him stop. Someone ran up the trail, crashing through brush with no heed to stealth.

"Hide," he murmured.

They melted into the surrounding bushes. Dug and Olav cocked their bows, while Beren and Eskil drew swords. Mikkel clutched his knife.

They waited. A few moments later, a ten-year-old boy burst into the clearing.

Beren recognized him and sprang into his path. Unable to stop his headlong flight, the boy crashed into him.

Beren, braced for the impact, didn't even sway under the boy's weight. "Easy, Kai. You look as if Odin's hell-hounds are after you."

The boy gasped and bent over, hands on knees while he gathered his breath. "Village," he managed at last. "Raiders."

He didn't need to say more. Beren cursed. "Raiders. I should have known. They must have seen us leave."

The men took off at a run, Mikkel and Kai struggling to keep up behind them.

~ * ~

Creltak uncurled his fingers. In the middle of his palm rested a white pebble. *For white, I'll take one of your maidens and give her to my men for sport.*

Oh dear God.

He strode before his prisoners, studying each one. "Where are the rest of your women, Garan?" he asked. His gaze traveled to the balcony and the other hallways. "Hiding? We'll have some fun hunting them later."

He stopped before Elizabeth. His cruel smile twisted into a leer. A chill of dread skittered down her spine, but she lifted her chin and forced herself to meet his gaze without flinching. She'd met his type before. A show of fear goaded bullies into more cruel actions.

"Ah," he murmured, satisfaction lacing his voice. "This one's better. But a bit old for my purposes at the moment. Later perhaps." He swept his gaze over her body, back to her face. "Yes. Definitely later."

He spun away and grabbed the young girl who stood beside her. The girl's mother lurched forward, but two men stepped in front of her with swords raised. With a sob, the woman fell back into her husband's arms. Creltak dragged the girl to the center of the room.

He held her back pressed against his chest. With one arm around her shoulders and another around her waist, he forced her to face her chieftain.

"Look at her, Garan," he ordered. "So young. So innocent. Behold what your stubbornness forces me to do."

Garan's face twisted in hatred. If he were free, Elizabeth was sure he'd tear his captor to pieces.

Creltak shifted his hands to the girl's arms and thrust her toward a giant of a man with filthy black hair and a wild beard. The man caught her hair, forced her head back, and bent his own toward her.

Without warning, he jerked. His expression puzzled, he fingered the dark shaft that had appeared in his neck. Blood poured from the wound.

Taking advantage of the distraction, the girl jabbed her hand forward, then wrenched free and pulled a small knife from his stomach. He opened his mouth, but no sound came out. He slid to the floor and the girl scrambled back to her mother.

More dark shafts appeared in the chests and necks of other men. Garan shook off the raiders who held him and surged to his feet.

At first, Elizabeth couldn't understand what was happening. Shouts of "Asgard!" echoed around the room. The missing young women and the two remaining warriors ranged around the balcony.

They held archaic crossbows of a kind Elizabeth had seen in museums, and were led by a woman in her late thirties who directed fire and shouted orders. Several of the defenders continued to fire at the invaders, while others leaped down the steps to the Hall, swords drawn.

Women challenging trained warriors? Elizabeth cringed from the slaughter she expected to follow, but when the women fought their way across the floor, it became evident they knew what they were doing. They drove the invaders back, slashing against shields raised at the last moment.

Magrim and two of his keepers darted forward, snagged the forgotten sacks, and dragged them back to a safe corner. Above the noise and confusion, from the far side of the Hall, a baby cried.

Ned.

Frantic, Elizabeth dashed around the edge of the battlefield toward the sound. *If they've hurt Ned—*

A strong hand grabbed her arm and swung her around. She found herself facing Creltak.

"Oh, no," he snarled, and bared his teeth. She flinched from his foul breath. "I'll not leave here without at least one prize."

The next instant she hung upside down over the man's shoulder. She screamed and pounded her fists against his back while he carried her toward the door.

A body collided with them and they fell to the floor. Free of his grasp, Elizabeth scuttled away on hands and knees. She didn't stop until she was on the far side of the room. Gudrin huddled in an alcove with Ned in her arms. Elizabeth seized her son and hugged him close, then checked him for any harm. Satisfied, she switched her attention to the battle, ready to flee if danger threatened again.

Creltak was on his feet. Facing him, sword swinging in a blur, was Astri.

Across the room, Garan roared encouragement to his people. Someone handed him a sword and he hacked a way toward Creltak, his lame leg not seeming to slow him down at all. Two raiders leaped from the pack to confront him and he turned aside.

Elizabeth swung her gaze back to Astri. The young woman held her own until a man appeared behind her. He raised his sword hilt first and struck her on the side of the head.

Astri crumpled to the floor. Creltak bent and tossed her over his shoulder, then his gaze caught Elizabeth's.

"Another time," he mouthed. He flashed her a smile full of lethal promise, then disappeared out the door with his captive.

~ * ~

To Beren it seemed an eternity before the village came into view. Yesterday, he'd promised Zabeth there wouldn't be any raids until spring. Now she was in the middle of the very thing she dreaded and it was his fault. He should have known something was wrong with Dev's story about the bears. He should have suspected something.

Dug held up his hand and the others skidded to a halt behind him. They crouched behind some rocks to study the scene before proceeding. Not for the first time, Beren wished Tor hadn't taken most of the able-bodied men to the Southlands this summer. But he had, and now it was up to Beren and his few companions to try and save the villagers from the raider attack.

The village looked deserted. Where were the women he and Eskil helped Lida train? Prisoners? There was no movement, no sound…at least at first. Then Beren heard it, a rumble as of distant thunder, coming from the Gather Hall.

At a signal from Dug, he skidded down the hill and dashed across the bare patch of ground that surrounded the village to protect it from fires in the forest, his friends close behind. Along the streets he ran. The pounding of his footsteps and those who followed echoed against the close-spaced walls. The sounds from the Gather Hall were clearer now, shouts, curses, the clash of sword against shield. Beren clutched his sword and ran faster. *Zabeth.*

The sounds increased, as if the battle had spilled into the street. A little farther. He rounded the corner into the courtyard and caught a glimpse of men fleeing out the far side. Young Sven, one of the two warriors who hadn't gone on the hunt with Beren, fought alongside the blacksmith. Lida shouted orders inside the building.

Women with swords and bows, elderly men with cudgels and, in one case, a shepherd's staff, fought with raiders near the doors of the Hall, pushing the enemy out. Beren recognized the raider symbols on the shields. He'd been right. *Sjørotte.* He shouted a war cry and launched himself at the nearest foe.

With the addition of the hunters, it wasn't long before the rest of the invaders were driven off. When the last man took to his heels, a ragged cheer went up from the defenders.

Beren burst into the Gather Hall. His gaze swept the room, noting the bodies of several raiders scattered over the floor. When he saw

Zabeth, the tension inside him eased.

Beside her, Runa helped Freya with the wounded and ignored Zabeth, who kept trying to tell her something. Garan sat on the nearest bench, an expression of annoyed impatience on his face while the healer bound a slash on his arm.

Beren resisted an urge to go to Zabeth and instead sheathed his sword and followed Dug to his chieftain.

"What happened?" Dug asked.

"Raider tricks," Garan snapped and spat on the floor. "They drove the bears to Dev's farm, then waited for us to send our warriors hunting." He gave the men a sad frown. "They took Bryn, probably tortured him. He told them about the Shadow-Links so they came here looking for them. Good thing the God-Hold is hidden, but they would have taken the keepers with them. As it was, they wanted the rest of the 'Links, but we surprised them. They'll not be back soon, I'm thinking." He clapped a hand on Beren's shoulder. "The women did well. You and Lida did a good job. You should have seen them, charging the berserkers like avenging Valkyrie."

Beren shrugged. "Lida did the training. I just helped with this new batch." He lowered his eyes in guilt. "We shouldn't have gone after the bears. I felt something was wrong."

"Four more men wouldn't have made a difference." Garan gave him a long stare. "Beren, there is no blame here. You gave us fair warning when you found the traces. I should have anticipated they might attack in daytime." He shook his head. "I fear Bryn is lost to us. We'll look for him but I don't hold any hope we'll find him, at least not alive." He shook himself and glanced around the room, an impatient frown banishing his smile. "Is everyone here? Was anyone injured? I haven't had a chance to check."

At that moment, Zabeth pushed her way through the crowd. She clutched Beren's arm and pulled him around to face her.

"Beren—" she began, but he cut her off.

"You are safe?" He ran his hands up both her arms.

"Yes." She shook him off. "It's Astri."

"Astri?" He looked at Garan, who stiffened.

"Yes," Zabeth replied. "They take...took Astri."

Garan cursed and thrust the healer away. "We must find them. Call the men, Beren."

~ * ~

For the next hour, Elizabeth helped Runa and the healer look after the injured. Others tidied the hall, cooked a restoring meal, or dragged the dead raiders outside for burial—skills Elizabeth lacked.

Tearing strips of cloth for bandages and holding the hands of those who needed comfort, yes, that she could do, and the distraction kept her from wondering how Beren fared, whether he and his friends had managed to rescue Astri, and if he'd been injured during that rescue.

Runa and the healer bustled between patients, each murmuring soothing words, then barking orders at their helpers, Elizabeth among them.

Perhaps a lady of noble birth shouldn't be expected to act like a common servant, but in this place, at this time, Elizabeth ignored what her society expected and instead found satisfaction in being useful.

Still, even the work and the worry couldn't assuage her guilt. Astri's capture was a direct result of Elizabeth's recklessness. She'd run across the Hall with no thought of the danger, and because of that, the young woman was now a prisoner.

It should have been me.

"Zabeth, the bandages." Runa's snapped order penetrated Elizabeth's self-reproach, and she hurried to deliver a handful of cloth strips.

She was holding her finger on a twist of linen while Runa tied a knot to secure a sling, when a commotion at the door drew her attention. Astri marched in, her expression triumphant as she led her band of rescuers.

"Thank the gods." The whispered prayer came from Runa, but when Elizabeth looked at her, the older woman schooled her features into calm.

Earlier, she'd seemed so composed, as if there were no doubts of her daughter's safety once the rescue party left. The pretense had fooled Elizabeth, but she now realized it had been Runa's way of suppressing a panic that wouldn't have helped anything.

While the rescue party split off to other parts of the Gather Hall, Astri and the older woman who had been leading the archers headed for the chieftain. Beren followed, but Runa raised a hand and he nodded, murmured something to the older woman, then crossed to his aunt.

"Was she harmed?" Runa asked when he was within hearing distance.

He grinned. "You know Astri. Better ask how many of the raiders were harmed."

Runa huffed out a breath, but Elizabeth heard an echo of a relieved sob in the sound. Beren must have heard it too, because he pulled Runa into a hug. She clung to him for a moment, then pushed him away with a brisk shove.

"I suppose there'll be a ballad about it," she muttered.

"Of course. Lida will make sure of that. Her archers were a great help." He turned to Elizabeth. "And you are truly unhurt?"

She'd told him so earlier, but the question, the implied worry behind it, sent a thrill of pleasure down her spine.

"I am." She looked over at Astri, chatting with the chieftain. "And your…" The word *betrothed* stuck in her throat, dampening the earlier pleasure.

Runa glanced at her and then at Beren, and a chuckle escaped her. "I think you'd better tell Zabeth your secret, Beren. You'll never get anywhere if you don't."

To Elizabeth's surprise, a flush of red crept up Beren's cheeks He rubbed a hand over the back of his neck, then offered a rueful grin. "There's more to tell now."

He took a quick look around, as if making sure no one overheard. The one other person close enough was Runa's current patient, the only sound his soft snores.

When Beren said nothing more, Runa turned to Elizabeth. "Beren is part of a conspiracy. Astri has set her sights on Eskil but he's oblivious, so she's trying to make him jealous."

The pleasure Elizabeth had felt earlier returned. "So, Beren and Astri is like a…a play?"

Runa nodded.

"But Eskil's not oblivious anymore," Beren said in a low voice. "I don't know what he plans, but I think Astri is not going to like it."

"Oh." Runa studied him for a moment. "So Eskil likes her too?" At Beren's nod, she pursed her lips. "And you're in the middle." She shook her head and explained to Elizabeth. "My husband and I fostered Eskil for many years while he was training to be a warrior. The lad is quiet and a bit shy, but he has a devious mind. If he knows what Astri's about, and he wants the same result, he'll not make it easy for her."

"And in the meantime, I still have to pretend to pay court to her." Beren grimaced. "I promised to help them both, but now I'm not so sure that was wise."

"Wise or not, you have to continue." Runa patted him on the arm. "If we can help in any way, you let us know, right Zabeth?"

Elizabeth nodded. It was hard to say no to this woman. She didn't know Astri or Eskil, but being torn between two friends was a difficult position for anyone to be in and she didn't envy Beren.

A shout from the chieftain had Beren turning away. The man gestured him over and he sighed. "I have to report what I saw. The raider ship had these wooden wing things on either side to keep it from wallowing in the sea. Olav cut them off, so they won't be back soon, but

I expect Garan will want the keepers to study them."

Runa nodded and pushed at him with a shooing motion. "Go. We'll talk later."

He offered a short bow to her and a grin to Elizabeth, then hurried over to the chieftain.

The patient sleeping on the floor beside them gave a snort, opened his eyes, and grimaced. Runa made a soothing sound and the two women returned to their task.

Chapter Thirteen

That evening, Runa persuaded Elizabeth to join the celebration in the Gather Hall. Because the chieftain didn't want anyone to miss the festivities, he'd decreed the children attend also. A play area was set up near the kitchens for the younger children, while the older ones were allowed to sit at the trestle tables with their elders.

A quiet corner was set aside as a nursery. The wet-nurse, whose name Elizabeth learned was Kaya, and a plump young woman named Maili, took charge of the infants. Runa had carried Ned's cradle down from their room, and it joined the dozen other cradles already gathered in the area.

Elizabeth fed Ned in their room before leaving, and he'd fallen asleep soon after. Now she laid him in his familiar bed and covered him with a soft wool blanket.

"What will we do if they wake?" Elizabeth asked when she and Runa strolled arm-in-arm back to the main part of the room.

Runa laughed. "Then they can join the fun. But most of them will sleep through it all."

Elizabeth was doubtful, but she reserved judgement. An excited murmur of female voices drew her attention to the next bench, where Astri, surrounded by her friends, regaled them with the tale of her capture and rescue. All the women wore robes this evening instead of their usual breeches and tunic.

Elizabeth shuddered. Astri was lucky to be alive. She couldn't understand why the girl was so…excited about what had happened, as if it were an adventure instead of a cold-blooded abduction.

"Be happy, Zabeth." Runa handed her a bowl of stewed rabbit.

"This is a great day."

A long day, not a great day. She ate automatically, without tasting anything. When she finished, Runa took the bowls into the kitchen.

Elizabeth sat back. *What happens next?* Beren sat on the other side of the Hall, eating with the other men. He was deep in conversation with his friend. With Beren's attention elsewhere, Elizabeth allowed herself time to study him and search for any sign of injury he hadn't bothered to mention.

A shadow fell across the table and interrupted her thoughts. Astri sat beside Elizabeth on the bench. "I have not yet thanked you, Zabeth," she said, her expression solemn.

Elizabeth placed her cup on the table. "Thanked me? Why?"

"No one else saw the raiders take me. If not for you…" She gave an exaggerated shudder. She bent her head and lifted Elizabeth's hand to her forehead. "I am in your debt, Zabeth. For my life I owe you your greatest wish, if it is in my power to grant."

She waited, head still bowed. Elizabeth didn't know what was expected of her. "I didn't do anything," she protested. "It was chance I saw. And…and *my* debt. They took you, not me."

Astri lowered Elizabeth's hand and raised her head. "Perhaps, but that doesn't deny my debt." She smiled. "What do you wish, Zabeth? Furs? Wine? Shall I be your slave for a year? Do you need someone to scrub your back while you bathe?"

As the suggestions became more outlandish, Elizabeth found herself smiling back. "What I wish you cannot give me," she said.

Astri eyed her for a moment. "You wish for winter to be over so you can go home." It was a statement, not a question. The compassion in her eyes was undeniable.

Elizabeth sighed, then smiled. "You said I can have anything you can give. I wish you my friend."

Astri grinned. "Done." She rose from her seat. "Would you like to join the rest of us over there?" She pointed to the other young women she'd been sitting with.

"Oh, I don't think…" She didn't want to force her company upon anyone who'd only tolerate her for Astri's sake.

As if sensing her reluctance, Astri caught her hand and tugged her to her feet. "They're all anxious to meet you."

"Me?" Why? She was at least four years older than any of them. A mother. A *matron*. She winced at the image.

"You come from a land none of us have seen. Your people do things differently from us. And," Astri dropped her voice to a conspiratorial whisper, "they all want to know what the men are like in your land. Come, before the skalds make talking impossible."

"Skalds?" Another new word to learn.

"They sing the stories of our people."

Unable to think of an excuse, Elizabeth followed Astri to the next bench. The women made a space for her.

"This is Ghili." Astri indicated the slim woman on Elizabeth's right. "Her husband is on the *Freki*. You might have seen her daughter in the nursery area."

Ghili smiled. "Helga is four months old, near the same age as your son. We can compare how well they're growing."

The information shocked Elizabeth. Ghili couldn't have been more than seventeen, almost a child herself, yet she was a mother already? Astri introduced the other women. Anya was the blonde in the pale yellow robe. Catryn wore bright green and giggled a lot. The young woman with the amber necklace was Betina.

Elizabeth was surprised to learn most of them had husbands who were away on the trading ship, yet they'd been among the first to attack the raiders. She couldn't tell married from unmarried women, for all had a similar air of confidence and independence Elizabeth found intriguing, in particular as most were her own age or younger.

"And over there in the nursery is my friend Maili," Astri finished, pointing at the chubby young woman who hovered over the cradles. "She's much better with the younglings than I am, although I'm sure I'll get lots of practice when I have some of my own."

Elizabeth sipped her wine and let the conversation flow around her. Once in a while she was asked a question, but, perhaps sensing her shyness, the women left her in peace while ensuring she understood she was welcome to contribute whenever she wished.

They reminded her of the ladies of her own social circle at home, gossiping about their husbands, their children, the eligible men. However, the resemblance dissolved when the conversation switched to a discussion over the best way to keep a bow from warping or a sword from rusting.

Catryn poured herself another mug of *keevah*.

"No wine tonight?" Betina asked with eyebrows raised.

She giggled. "I'm seeing Sven after the feast."

"Ah." Betina grinned. "Try the horse barn. It's warm there."

Catryn laughed with the others. Elizabeth leaned toward Astri. "Why drinking *keevah* to meet Sven?" she whispered.

"None of us want children until after we're wed," Astri whispered back, as if that explained everything.

Elizabeth's face heated at the implication, but persisted. "I thought *keevah* was to make you strong when sick."

"Yes, but it has other uses," Astri explained. "It keeps us free of babes until we're ready for them."

"Oh." Elizabeth turned away, absorbing this new information.

She knew such things existed. Her mother had once told her there were ways for a woman to ensure she didn't have too many children, but Elizabeth hadn't had a chance to learn them. Her first duty had been to give her husband an heir. There'd be time enough in later years to discover such remedies.

At least, that had been her plan before all this. Now it was doubtful she'd ever have more children. Few respectable men wanted to marry a widow with a child already, and those who did, for the most part, were widowers with families of their own and no desire for more.

To her surprise, Elizabeth found she enjoyed listening to the women's chatter, even though she couldn't understand half of what they said. Perhaps it was the wine, but after a while she asked aloud the question that had spun through her mind for the last half hour. "Do your husbands know you can fight?"

"Who do you think taught us?" Ghili returned with a grin, then she raised her brows in surprise. "Do the women of your people not fight with their men?"

Elizabeth shook her head. "It is not thought..." What was the word for *decent*? "Our men fight to protect us. We do not need to fight."

Astri leaned forward, her face an expression of disbelief. "You mean they don't let you fight? What do you do, then?"

"We—" Elizabeth broke off.

What did the women of her social circle do? They gossiped, visited, drank tea together, embroidered pretty cushions, shopped for the latest gowns. For the first time in her sheltered life, she was exposed to women who did more than decorate a room, women who were as independent as their men folk. Shame filled her at the realization of how useless her life was.

She was saved from replying by a loud boom of drums.

"Oh, good." Astri shifted on the bench to face the open center of the Hall. "Time for the skalds."

Two men strode into the open space. Both were older than the chieftain, but were dressed in tunics and breeches dyed a bright orange. They looked a little ridiculous to Elizabeth. One sat on a short stool, a large narrow drum held between his knees.

Using his knuckles and the heel of his hand, he beat an intricate pattern of rumbles, booms, and taps. After a short introductory solo, the drummer tempered his beat to a low, persistent growl of distant thunder, while his companion stood and spoke.

Despite his age, the man's voice had a melodic quality, a power that carried his words to the farthest corner of the Hall, with actions so expressive as to make the words unnecessary. Elizabeth sat as mesmerized as her companions while he wove a poetic tale of the vicious invaders and the bravery of the men and women who drove them off.

Through the movements of his body, Elizabeth understood, if not every word, at least the general story, and she found herself reliving again the terror of Creltak's threats, the exciting attack of the archers on the balcony, the despair when it was discovered Astri had been taken.

The skald mentioned the name Zabeth and she blinked, startled. *They think I'm one of the heroes of the tale.* She wasn't sure if she was flattered or embarrassed.

Next came the description of Astri's rescue, how Beren had suggested splitting their forces and approaching by sea as well as land. Elizabeth glanced at the far table. As if sensing her gaze, Beren turned and caught her eye. He winked. Heat flooded her cheeks and she looked away.

The tale continued. Determined to avoid thinking of Beren, Elizabeth concentrated on the skald—a bard or minstrel in her own world. While she listened, it struck her how close they'd come to disaster this afternoon. The bard's voice receded into the background while her thoughts took her in a new direction.

No matter how much this evening's festivities might remind her of her home, no matter how similar the people seemed, this was not England. These people were not Christians. Their life was primitive compared to her own.

And dangerous.

She dug her fingernails into her palms. What if something had gone wrong this afternoon? In England, wild bands of outlaws didn't attack villages. No one threatened to burn old people or ravage maidens.

No one threatened to kill children.

A wave of horror swept over her so strong she felt ill. She closed her eyes. They might have killed her baby. Instead of celebrating a victory, she might now be grieving for her son.

Elizabeth turned away from the entertainment. Her eyes still closed, she forced herself to take deep breaths. According to the chieftain, she couldn't go home yet, couldn't even send a message, but there had to be something she could do, anything to keep her son safe.

She opened her eyes and glanced at Astri…and an outrageous thought tickled the back of her brain.

Could I...? No, it's too scandalous...isn't it? But it's for Ned, a chance to protect him...even if I have to abandon everything I've been taught growing up.

~ * ~

Later, when the villagers drifted back to their homes and rooms, Beren watched Zabeth carry her baby back to their quarters. He had seen Astri draw her into her circle of friends earlier, and Zabeth had relaxed for a while among the young women. He'd also seen her distress when the skald related the battle.

For the first time, he understood how terrible it must be for her, trapped in a land she didn't understand, facing dangers she couldn't comprehend.

"What troubles you, youngling?"

Garan's hand on his shoulder drew Beren back from his dark thoughts. Beren shook his head. "She saved Astri's life, and all she wants is to go home."

Garan sighed. "You know she can't. The 'Link is destroyed."

"But what if she could?" Garan narrowed his eyes, and Beren hurried on, "No, there was no trickery. I really did destroy the 'Link. But if what the keepers say is true, the 'Links open to different times. What if there is another one that opens close to the time when Zabeth came through the portal? Perhaps a few days or weeks later?" *Somewhere on land.*

Garan shook his head. "And how would we know? We don't even know where or when Zabeth came from, so how could we identify another place in her time?"

Beren opened his mouth to argue, then closed it. Garan was right. Even if they opened a thousand 'Links, they'd not recognize when they found the right one.

Garan squeezed his shoulder and released his hold. "Your heart is in the right place, warrior, but you'd best spend your efforts getting her to accept her place here instead of giving her false hope."

Dejected, Beren left the chieftain in the Hall. He wanted to give Zabeth hope, see the rare smile she sometimes showed that made his heart leap and his tongue refuse to form words. Something twisted in his chest. He wanted to give her hope but he didn't want her to leave. What *did* he want?

Chapter Fourteen

The next morning, Elizabeth searched the Gather Hall for Astri. If she must stay here for the next few months, she'd make sure no one suffered on her account if another attack came. Her parents might have been shocked at her decision; her husband would have disapproved, but she'd made up her mind.

She found Astri in the kitchen. Elizabeth took her aside and posed her request.

"Of course," Astri agreed at once. "But are you strong enough? You've only been out of your room a few days."

"Yes," Elizabeth said with a firmness she didn't feel. She was quick to tire, but they could take it slow, couldn't they? "When can we begin?"

Astri puckered her brows in concentration. "Lida has a class of students tomorrow morning."

"Lida?"

"She trains our women, both for fighting and defense," Astri explained.

Ah, the older woman she'd noticed leading the archers yesterday. Elizabeth frowned. "Is there a difference?"

"Oh yes." Astri gripped her sword. "Some of us want to fight with our men, to defend the village. We are strong and we can learn the skills for sword and for bow and arrow."

"But I not strong enough." Her brothers had taken up archery for hunting, but they'd been doing it for years and she remembered how hard they found it at the beginning.

Astri shook her head. "No, not all of our women want to learn that. The rest learn defense, what to do if someone attacks them or they want to protect their children. Mainly knife work and some unarmed moves to slip from an enemy's grasp."

"Yes, that is what I want," Elizabeth agreed with relief. "So I do not feel so…helpless."

Astri nodded. "We all started with those lessons. Every girl in the village learns as soon as they are strong enough to hold a knife."

Understanding dawned. "That's how that girl got away yesterday." Lida must be like a fencing master. It made sense for a woman to teach other women.

"So," Astri continued. "Tomorrow, after morning meal, you come to the horse barn." She pointed to the long building visible through the window. "But do not eat too much, just enough to not be weak, yes?"

"Yes. But do I need to wear…?" Elizabeth indicated Astri's trousers.

The girl laughed. "No, of course not. If someone attacks, you won't have time to go back to your room to change, so you must learn what to do in your normal clothes. But you might want to wear something older. It will get dirty quickly."

Relieved, Elizabeth nodded her thanks and left. She'd taken the first step in gaining control over her new life, no matter how temporary her stay here.

~ * ~

On his way to the barracks after the midday meal, Beren was waylaid by a whirlwind.

"Beren! Beren!" The shout was accompanied by a small body hurling itself against his leg. "Can we see the gray man today? Please?"

Relieved the emergency was nothing more serious than a child's wishes, Beren knelt before his sister and caught her arms to calm her. "You saw the gray man last week, Gudrin."

"But I want to see him *again*." Gudrin thrust out her lip in a stubborn pout, then immediately turned the pout into the brilliant smile that never failed to soften his heart. "You can play your flute. You haven't played it in *ages*."

Devious child. She knew he hadn't had a chance to play since Tor and Kiana left. "You just want to dance with the gray man." He brushed a finger down her nose and smiled. He didn't have any duties this afternoon. Perhaps an hour or so to indulge his sister…and himself, he admitted…wouldn't hurt.

Sensing victory, Gudrin flung her arms around his neck and kissed his cheek, then grabbed his hand and pulled him toward the barracks. "Come on. Let's get your flute."

Laughing, he let her lead him away.

~ * ~

As usual, Elizabeth ate the midday meal in her room and played with Ned. He didn't seem concerned with their primitive surroundings.

Perhaps she should learn from him, be satisfied with the simple things, like having enough food, a place to sleep, people who cared for him. Except...no one cared for *her*. She still felt a stranger here. Even the interest shown by Astri and her friends was in all likelihood nothing more than fascination with someone new in their lives.

She refused to think of Beren's seeming interest, or the unexpected sparks she felt in his presence.

I will not wallow in despair. Elizabeth took a deep breath and straightened her spine. Yes, she was a stranger, but she was taking steps to change that. She was learning their language, was going to learn how to defend herself if danger threatened again. There must be more ways to give back, to repay the hospitality these people offered.

She fed Ned and waited for him to fall asleep tucked against her shoulder. Careful not to wake him, she rose and made her way to the Gather Hall. Beren wasn't due for their lessons for at least another hour. She needed some air, some time to think, and if she stayed in her room she'd nap and get nothing done.

She found Maili in the nursery area, watching over two other sleeping babies. Several children ranging in age from newborn to two years spent the day there while their parents completed their chores. It seemed the whole village took responsibility for the children.

The young woman smiled at Elizabeth. "Do you wish to leave him here with the others? He'll have friends to play with when he wakes."

"Yes please." Elizabeth laid Ned on the fur rug with the other children. "I would like to walk...to take walk. Is there somewhere quiet I can go?"

Maili nodded and waved a hand. "There's a path at the south end of the village. It splits after a way. Take the left path, up the hill. The view is lovely from up there."

Elizabeth smiled her thanks. "Yes, perfect. I won't be long."

"Don't worry about this little one." Maili patted Ned's back. "I'll keep him safe."

Runa had explained the cloaks by the main door were for anyone to use, so Elizabeth grabbed one and flung it around her shoulders to ward off the chill.

The path was easy to find. It arrowed deep into the woods before splitting. As directed, Elizabeth took the left path and soon found herself climbing a gentle slope toward the mountain that loomed over the village. The closer she came to the mountain itself, the steeper ran the slope, twisting along the edge as it rose higher. Soon the path led her to a meadow with a stream trickling near the border of trees. The grass was sparse but from some of the withered stalks she suspected flowers grew here in the spring. The walk had tired her, so she rested on a nearby boulder. She leaned back, raised her face to the weak sun, and closed her eyes.

The peace of the forest was what she needed.

For a while she sat and soaked up the sunlight. She must have fallen asleep, because she dreamed she heard music, faint and enchanting. After a moment, she realized she wasn't asleep and the music was real. She opened her eyes, tilted her head to listen. Yes, music. Some sort of reed instrument? Too high to be an oboe. Maybe a flute of some sort?

Curious now, Elizabeth rose and turned in a circle. *There. That way.*

Lifting her skirt to avoid getting it snagged on the brambles that lined the path, she headed in the direction of the sound.

A short while later, she emerged from the trees at the edge of a plateau. A cliff loomed high above and the rocky ground in front of it was flat and disappeared into space.

Beren sat on a rock at the edge of that space. He held a thin tube to his lips and, eyes closed, fingers dancing over the tube, blew the notes that had drawn Elizabeth here. He seemed lost in the music. She'd never seen his expression so…peaceful, as if nothing in the world could break his concentration. With his face at rest like this, she was close enough to notice for the first time how long his lashes were, dark brown and looking like velvet against his cheeks.

She had always considered his features hawk-like, sharp and angular. Now they seemed softer, rounder, reminding her not so much of a hawk as a falcon. His skin gleamed golden in the pale sun. For an instant, when she first saw him, her heart had leapt to her throat. Now it settled but beat just as fast.

This wasn't the fierce warrior who had fought off the raiders, the patient teacher who helped her with her words, the generous friend who had shown her the rainbow waterfall. He was all those things and more.

So wrapped up was she in the wonder of this discovery, it took her a moment to notice the other occupants of the plateau. A flicker of movement in the corner of her eye drew her attention to the child dancing merrily around in circles. But it was who…or what…Gudrin danced with that made Elizabeth gasp aloud.

The man was as tall as Beren, but gray from his hair to his skin to his clothes. He flickered in and out of view while the child danced around him, always appearing in front of her. Gudrin reached for his hands, held palm out in a warding gesture, and pretended to hold them.

Bits of words formed in Elizabeth's head, too short to distinguish a language and cut off mid-syllable each time the man appeared and disappeared, "Warn—Warn—Warn."

At Elizabeth's gasp, Beren stopped playing. Gudrin continued dancing for a few more steps, then glanced at Beren with an annoyed frown before she noticed Elizabeth. She grinned and waved, but instead of stopping, she danced backward until the other man disappeared. Both she and Beren turned to Elizabeth.

Elizabeth stared at where the stranger had been standing. "What...who was that?"

"The gray man," Gudrin said, as if the words explained everything. She skipped over to Beren and picked up a small cloak.

Elizabeth approached where the man had last appeared but stopped a few steps away. Gudrin's footprints scuffed the dirt around the area, but there were no other prints.

"It's all right, Zabeth." Beren rose and came to stand beside Elizabeth.

She shook her head. "Who is he? How did he disappear like that? Like a...a ghost." She didn't realize she'd spoken in English until Gudrin responded in the same language.

"He's not a ghost." She repeated the word in her language, then turned to Beren with a questioning look.

He patted her on the head. "Go home, Gudrin. I will bring Zabeth."

She nodded and ran down the path Elizabeth had used.

Beren took Elizabeth's hand and led her to the rock. She sat, folded her hands in her lap, and waited. There was a secret here.

Beren speared his fingers through his hair, paced to the middle of the clearing short of where the strange man had appeared, then paced back again. His determined expression indicated he'd come to a decision. He stood with his thumbs tucked behind his belt.

"The gray man is a...a guard." Still she waited. He sighed. "I'll show you. Stay here."

He returned to the middle of the clearing, stopped, and looked over his shoulder at Elizabeth. "Watch." Then he took a few steps forward.

Suddenly, the strange man appeared before Beren, his hands still held in that warding gesture. The words she'd heard cut off earlier now came clear. "Warning. Keep back. This ship is guarded. Keep away."

Elizabeth gasped. "He spoke *English*."

Beren stepped back and the man disappeared. "He speaks all our languages, in our head."

"But who is he? Where did he come from?"

Beren said nothing until he stood before her again. "It is a tale of long ago, when Tor first came to this land. Perhaps we should wait until we get back to the village before—"

"Now," she interrupted. "I want to hear it now."

He shifted from one foot to the other. "Long ago, when I was a child, a ball of fire shot through the heavens and buried itself in the mountain. It brought Tor and his family through a hole in the sky."

A ball of fire? A hole in the sky? "I don't understand."

He shrugged. "It is a saga sung by the bards every autumn. You will probably hear it in a few days."

"I want to hear it from you." The bards were skilled storytellers, but she couldn't ask them questions.

"I am not skilled enough. It is best if you hear it from them." Beren gazed at the spot where the gray man had appeared. "But I can tell you about him, a little. The fire ship is there, in the mountain, behind those rocks." He gestured to the cliff wall. "The gray man guards it and warns people away. We don't know who he is or where he comes from, or how he appears and disappears."

Elizabeth leaned forward. "What is he warning about? Is the fire still burning?"

"No." The denial came on a short laugh. "This…*ship*…it is made of metal, and if you touch it, lightning burns you."

"*Lightning?*" None of this made sense.

Instead of answering, Beren stooped, picked up a small stone, and tossed it at the cliff wall. An instant before it hit, the gray man flickered into view, then disappeared when the stone passed him. Sparks flew when it touched the cliff and the rock shattered into sizzling pieces. Elizabeth jumped to her feet, but when nothing else happened, she lowered herself back to the rock.

"It is safe if you don't touch it." Beren offered a reassuring smile, quickly replaced by chagrin. "We should have told you sooner. It is a danger we all know but we didn't believe you strong enough to come this far yet." He faced her, his voice earnest. "If you see the gray man, do not go near any cliff behind him. Do you understand?"

She nodded, too shocked at what she'd seen to find words.

"Good." Beren held out his hand. "Come, we should get back home. It's almost time for your lesson."

Home? No, the village wasn't home, but she didn't bother to contradict him. She took his hand and let him help her to her feet. Awareness shivered through her body.

Beren frowned. "Are you well, Zabeth?"

She didn't answer. She was beginning to see Beren as more than just a handsome warrior. He had layers she'd never imagined: a tender heart as evidenced by his love for his sister, an artistic side with the music he played. Elizabeth's earlier feelings swept to the fore. This was a man she could fall in love with and—

No. It's too soon. It's too...easy.

"Zabeth?"

Annoyed with herself, she couldn't help but snap back. "My name is Elizabeth. Not Zabeth. *Elizabeth.*"

Beren stepped back at the ferocity in her reply, then shrugged. "As you wish."

Without another word, he led her back to the village.

She glanced once more at the empty space in the middle of the plateau before following.

Chapter Fifteen

While Elizabeth brushed her hair before bed that evening, she reflected on what she'd seen on the plateau. Perhaps it was no surprise that it wasn't the gray man who occupied her thoughts, but Beren.

Today she'd seen a side of him she'd never seen before, not just the older brother indulging a young sister, but a musician, one who played with his whole soul. With a jolt, she recognized the kind of man she'd hoped for when romance filled her dreams as a young girl, a man who was strong and brave, but also gentle and thoughtful. *Chivalrous*, that was the word to describe her dream lover.

That was the word to describe Beren.

She paused, the brush tangled unnoticed in her hair, and stared out the window. What was happening to her? She'd told herself before she shouldn't have these feelings. It had been not quite half a month since she woke from her fever, a little longer since her husband's death. This wasn't right. It wasn't proper.

If she was smart, she'd avoid him, ask Runa for someone else to teach her the language. After all, she'd progressed faster than she'd expected. She didn't need someone *patient* to help her anymore, and they'd long ago abandoned the need for Latin.

Besides, she had a new goal now: learning how to fight, or at least how to defend herself. That had to be more important than sitting in a corner of the Gather Hall memorizing words she could pick up through daily activities.

Yes, that's what she'd do. Concentrate on her new skills, and avoid Beren as much as possible.

~ * ~

The next morning, Beren strolled along the edge of the woods and searched for any signs of invaders. Now that the raiders knew about the Shadow-Links, they might not accept their defeat, and the guard around the village had been increased. He doubted anyone would attack with winter snows so close, but it didn't hurt to keep a wary eye out.

Unfortunately, even as he scanned the ground for tracks, his mind replayed his encounter with Astri before he'd left on patrol. It seemed Eskil wasn't following the rules. Instead of falling at her feet and proclaiming his undying love for her, he'd decided to do the *noble* thing—Astri's words—and not come between Astri and Beren.

So now, she'd said, they had to convince him Beren was really interested in someone else. That someone, Astri declared, would be Zabeth—Ee-lee-zabeth.

He savored the word, then shook his head. No, he'd try to use that outlandish name when he was with her, but he'd always think of her as Zabeth.

He'd greed to Astri's plan only on the condition that Zabeth be made aware it. She deserved to know the truth of his increased attention, but how to explain what was going on?

He was so focused on the question he didn't hear Mikkel until the boy called his name. He waited until Mikkel ran up to him, then continued walking. The boy had to trot to keep up.

"When will you be hunting again?" Since the raider attack, Mikkel had decided he was now old enough to contribute to the protection of the village. Even his mother had praised him, and that, it seemed, was enough to convince him she approved of his joining the hunters.

"Not for a few days yet," Beren replied. "Once we're sure the raiders won't attack again."

"They wouldn't dare," Mikkel pronounced with certainty. "We'll beat them off again."

Beren smiled. He remembered when he'd been Mikkel's age. There had been little doubt in his own mind he was invincible.

"How's your mother?" Best to divert the boy's attention from hunting.

"Bossy as usual." He grinned. "She's starting to teach Gudrin how to catch a husband."

Beren's steps faltered, but he recovered quickly and continued on. "Gudrin's only five." He cast Mikkel a sideways glance.

The boy shrugged. "She told Mother she's decided who she wants to marry, so Mother said she'd teach her what's needed in a wife."

"And what's that?" Beren asked, curious.

"How to cook and spin," Mikkel replied without interest. "You know. Women stuff."

"Oh." A wave of amused relief swept through Beren. "So, who's the lucky man Gudrin's set her heart on?" Knowing his sister, he'd always suspected it was the gray man, impossible as that was.

Mikkel kicked a stone out of the way. "The Shadow babe."

At that Beren did stop. He turned an astonished gaze on his cousin. "Zabeth's child?"

Mikkel nodded. "Gudrin says he's going to be good-looking when he grows up."

Beren blinked a couple of times. "But he's a baby."

"Gudrin says that's the best time to start training them." Again, Mikkel didn't show much interest in the news, as if he wasn't aware the same fate might await him. "She says she wants a husband who'll help her with the household chores, and if you start teaching them before they know it's not man's work, they won't object."

"I see." Beren resumed walking. His sister was in for a shock when she got older. He looked forward to this afternoon's lesson. He'd have to ask Zabeth what she thought about Gudrin as a future daughter-in-law. "Was there anything else you wanted to talk to me about?"

Mikkel scrunched up his forehead in an effort to remember. "Oh, yes. Zabeth asked me to tell you she won't have time for her lesson today."

Once more Beren's step faltered. "Is she not well?"

"She's fine. I think she's meeting someone in the horse barn." Mikkel kicked another stone. "I heard her telling Mother."

Beren's eyes narrowed. Next to the God-Hold, the horse barn was a favorite trysting place for the young couples of the village, more popular now the weather was too cold for outdoor sport. But... No. He couldn't see Zabeth having a tryst. That wasn't like her. There were other activities in the barn these days, but that wasn't like Zabeth either.

There was only one way to find out. He'd let Dug and Gunnar handle the patrol. As for himself, he experienced a strong need to visit the horse barn.

~ * ~

Elizabeth stood in the middle of the horse barn and took shallow breaths. The stench was overpowering. Her father had valued horses above everything but his family, so she'd learned early in life how to care for her own horse. However, the clean straw smell of her father's stables was perfume compared to the rich earthy scent of sweat and dung that clung to everything in this barn. Even the horses were different, squat, sturdy work beasts instead of the sleek thoroughbreds of home.

She'd left Ned with Maili and Kaya in the nursery. During the past two weeks, her son had blossomed. He'd be crawling soon. She wouldn't be surprised if he was walking before his first birthday. He took after David's side of the family, and promised to be as big and strapping as any of the youths in the village.

Not that he'd be growing up here, of course. As soon as the *Freki* returned in the spring, Elizabeth had every intention of returning to England. In the meantime, she'd contribute as much as possible to the safety of her temporary home.

A soft cough reminded her she wasn't alone. Earlier she had tussled with several young girls while Lida taught them how to slip out of various grasps. After they finished, Lida sent the girls away and instructed Elizabeth to remain for further lessons to catch up.

"Are you ready, Zabeth?" the trainer asked.

The stench in the barn discouraged taking a deep breath, so she nodded instead of answering aloud. A tall figure in shirt and breeches strode from the shadows. "Astri?"

The young woman came to a halt and stood, hands on hips, surveying her up and down. "Good. You have a strong body."

Elizabeth peered down at the brown belted robe she wore and felt her face heat.

If she'd known such skills before she came here, would David still be alive? At least she could have fought at his side, as she'd heard Astri had fought beside Eskil at the cove.

"Very well." Astri drew two wooden knives from her belt. She handed one to Elizabeth, who fumbled, dropped it, then picked it up and held it awkwardly. Astri sighed, grabbed Elizabeth's wrist and repositioned her grip on the handle. "No, hold it like this."

Astri demonstrated a slashing movement. Elizabeth copied her. Astri smiled. "Good. Now come at me."

"Come at you?" Elizabeth glanced at Lida, who waved her forward.

Astri dropped into a crouch. "Attack me."

Feeling foolish, Elizabeth waved the knife in Astri's direction.

Astri rolled her eyes. "Not like that, Zabeth. Like this."

She lunged forward. Elizabeth jumped back with a squeak of alarm. Her feet tangled in her skirt, and she sat down hard.

A sound almost like a laugh came from the shadows. She turned her head, but then Astri stepped in front of her and held out a hand to help her up.

"You must be quicker than that, Zabeth," Lida said from the side.

Astri nodded. "If I were a man I'd be on top of you already, taking my pleasure."

Elizabeth choked. "Pleasure?"

"Pleasure for the man."

Elizabeth shuddered, took Astri's hand and, once on her feet, brushed off her skirt. One of the horses shuffled in its stall. Another gave a soft nicker. Was that what she'd heard earlier?

Astri handed her back her knife. "Here, Zabeth. We'll try again."

Elizabeth took the weapon. An hour later, Lida called a halt. Elizabeth rose once more from the floor, where she was sure she'd spent most of the session, and brushed at the dirt on her skirt.

"I am not tired," she protested.

Astri grinned. "Perhaps, but I am."

Lida came over and patted Elizabeth on the shoulder. "You did well for your first try. Rest tomorrow. We will continue the day after."

"Why not tomorrow?" A thought struck her. "Or are you busy?" She hated to think she had forced Astri and Lida to neglect their duties.

"No." Lida grinned and touched a red patch on Elizabeth's arm. Elizabeth winced. "Tomorrow you won't want to leave your bed." She nodded to Astri and strode from the barn.

Elizabeth rubbed her buttocks and silently agreed with Lida's assessment. "I do not think I will be able to sit tonight."

Astri chuckled. She picked up Elizabeth's dropped knife and handed it over. "Practice holding that and throwing it against the floor. You're a quick learner, Zabeth. You'll soon understand what to do."

Elizabeth nodded, but she was reluctant to leave. She didn't think she'd learned enough for one lesson. She glanced around the stable, and for the first time noticed the target set up against a bale of hay in a dark corner.

Several arrow-shafts stuck out of the target. "Oh! You trained in here, you and the other women, before…before the attack."

"That's right. Garan didn't want the raiders to know we were preparing, and this building is large enough to provide the space we needed." She glanced at Elizabeth. "What did you think we were doing?"

Elizabeth ducked her head. The last thing she wanted to do was admit what she'd thought was going on—illicit couplings, brazen trysts.

Instead she changed the subject. "Was it hard to learn how to fight?"

Astri laughed. "No. We train with the boys from the age of eight until about thirteen. When the boys go through their manhood trials, the girls go through something similar. We learn how to please a husband—cooking, sewing, loving. We can all choose, boys and girls, what we want to do. Some continue in the traditional path, boys fighting and girls in the home. But some boys prefer the gentler arts and become skalds or healers, while some girls, like me, prefer to keep up our fighting skills. And some become keepers."

"Even the girls?"

"Of course. Why not? We're as smart as the men." Astri winked. "Sometimes smarter." One of the horses snorted. Astri slid her knife into its loop on her belt. "Now, let's see what Mother is planning for the midday meal."

~ * ~

Beren limped from the stall where he'd been crouched for the past two hours. His leg muscles screamed a protest, so he stopped for a moment to stretch out the cramp.

He hadn't known what to expect when he'd decided to find out what Zabeth was doing in the barn. It came as a great relief to discover the real reason for her meeting, and a surprise. She didn't seem the kind of woman who'd want to do something so…so physical.

What had given him that impression? In all the time she'd been here she'd offered to help in the kitchens and with the sweeping and spinning. She was bad at all those tasks, true, but she'd at least tried. He was proud of her for that.

As if it matters what I think. As far as Zabeth was concerned, all Beren was useful for was to teach his language. Why should his opinions matter to her?

But he enjoyed teaching Zabeth, enjoyed being in her company. Every time he saw her in that blue robe she favored, his heart felt a little bit lighter. Every time his hand brushed hers, so soft and delicate, the touch sent tingles up his arm. That was the one good thing about Astri's latest plan, that he and Zabeth be forced to spend more time together.

He checked the women were out of sight, then slipped from the horse barn and headed toward the barracks. A breeze nipped at his bare arms.

Shivering, he glanced at the sky. Clear. Not a cloud in sight. A cold night, the beginning of many, and snow soon to follow. That meant more time confined to the village, more time to muck out stables, to clear paths in the snow between buildings, chop firewood—all tasks he hated.

Yet when he walked away from the horse barn, Beren hummed a merry tune. Winter could come with all the vengeance of the gods, but he didn't care.

All that mattered was he had an excuse to spend more time with Zabeth.

Chapter Sixteen

Elizabeth stood at the side of the Gather Hall after the midday meal, trying to work up the courage to ask Runa to assign someone other than Beren to help teach her the language. Before she could make a move, however, Beren joined her. He looked...guilty?

Beren inclined his head. "I must ask something of you, Za— Eeleezabeth."

"What?" The sound of her name in his deep, exotic voice, made Elizabeth's skin tingle.

He sat on the bench, invited her to sit beside him. She winced when she lowered herself to the hard wood. *Must remember to bring a pillow.*

For a long time, he stared at the floor. She was surprised when a dull red flush crept up his cheeks. At last, he raised his head and gave her a sheepish grin.

"It concerns Astri." He paused, and Elizabeth nodded encouragement. "Astri and my friend Eskil."

Ah. The jealousy ploy. "Runa said we would help. Do you need me to do something?"

He nodded and again lapsed into silence. Elizabeth waited. When he continued, he spoke slowly, as if he had trouble putting into words what he wanted to say. "Astri likes Eskil, but she thinks Eskil won't let himself like her because he thinks she likes me. But he knows she doesn't like me. I mean, she does, but not in that way."

Elizabeth nodded. She knew all this from his confession yesterday. "She wants to make him...angry? Upset?" What *was* the word for *jealous*?

A look of relief came over his face. "Yes. But Eskil knows this and doesn't want her to...to win so easily. So he's told her, as my best friend, he doesn't want to hurt me."

Comprehension dawned. "Is that his plan to...punish her? To

make her think he…wants your friendship more than her…more than hers?" She hated the hesitations in her speech. It was so frustrating not knowing what words to use.

Elizabeth hadn't thought it possible, but when she looked at Beren again, the red on his cheeks darkened even more. He squirmed. She had a dozen questions, but let him continue uninterrupted.

"Astri has a new plan." He wouldn't meet her gaze. "She thinks if I pay attention to someone else, Eskil will see I don't care as much for her as he believes."

Elizabeth absorbed that for a moment. "So Astri likes Eskil but does not think he likes her. Eskil likes Astri but does not want her to know he likes her, not yet. So… Astri wants to…to make Eskil think you like someone else, so he will feel free to…to chase her?"

"Yes."

"Who?"

He shrugged, glanced away, then back at her. Elizabeth's heartbeat thundered in her ears. He couldn't mean…

"Me?" she squeaked.

He nodded. "Astri thinks it's logical. We spend a lot of time together already with your lessons."

Spend more time with Beren? No, not a good idea. Hadn't she decided to avoid him? Weren't things complicated enough without a pretend…whatever this was supposed to be?

But he looked so miserable, Elizabeth couldn't help it. She giggled, and slapped a hand over her mouth. She *never* giggled.

Beren stared at her. His mouth twitched. A moment later, he threw back his head and laughed. Elizabeth struggled to control her mirth, but the situation *was* funny, like a story from a bad opera.

Finally, Beren quieted. Under control now, Elizabeth asked, "What are you going to do now?" Her voice wavered as the giggles threatened to resurface.

He scowled, but there was a twinkle in his eyes. "Will you help me with this foolish plan of Astri's? She will expect to see us together."

She remembered her resolve, but the chance to spend more time with this man was compelling. And what was the harm? She didn't intend to get involved with anyone here. She was leaving in a few months, after all, so why not pretend for a few days?

She rediscovered her sense of humor and her smile at the same time. "Yes, I will help."

"Good. Thank you." He stood. "Now, I'd better get back to my patrol."

He lifted her hand and, like an ancient knight of chivalry, kissed the back of it. Sudden desire shot from where his lips touched to the center of her core. He raised his head and gazed at her while his eyes darkened. She held her breath, parted her lips. Would he kiss her?

He bent closer, closer. A burst of laughter somewhere in the Hall halted his approach. He stopped, blinked as if awakening from a dream, then a slow smile spread over his face. He released her hand. "How far do you think we should take this play?" His voice, low, seductive, sent shivers up her spine.

How far...? Her own voice seemed to have vanished, leaving her with her mouth open. The heat in his eyes dried her throat. She couldn't think of a thing to say.

As if confirming something he had guessed, Beren nodded. "I will see you soon, Eeleezabeth."

After he vanished out the door, she remained seated for a long time.

~ * ~

In the following weeks, the days grew colder. Cattle and sheep were brought in from the hillside pastures. Furs and warm blankets were taken from storage and aired. Children and babies were fitted for warm leggings and shirts.

Elizabeth found little time to puzzle about her new life. She was too busy living it. Ned's demands eased with the passing days while he alternated between breast milk and a warm milky gruel used to wean the children of the village. This gave Elizabeth more time for her own pursuits.

Mornings she spent half her time in the kitchen with Runa and Freya, learning how to turn flour and water into bread. Her first attempts looked more like bricks than loaves, but she was determined to master this one small task, and soon even Runa was forced to admit Elizabeth's bread was as good as her own.

The later part of the mornings she spent in the horse barn. Her lessons with Astri grew more enjoyable as her skills increased. She discovered strength and endurance she never realized she possessed. It gave her a heady feeling to know she was no longer as helpless as she'd been when she'd first arrived here.

Neither she nor Astri mentioned Beren and the little game they all played. Whenever Elizabeth saw Eskil, he was watching Astri but only when the girl wouldn't notice. Astri, on the other hand, took to snubbing Beren when he crossed her path, and ignored Eskil. It was a strange courtship, Elizabeth mused, with neither party willing to acknowledge the other.

Perhaps as strange was Elizabeth and Beren's growing

relationship. No matter how much she enjoyed her baking and fighting sessions, she looked forward to the afternoons with growing impatience, and her first sight of the dark-haired warrior sent her heart to beating as fast as a hummingbird.

The midday meal was always…interesting. Beren turned up as soon as Elizabeth sat down at a table. He'd lean toward her in a flirtatious manner and tell her of his day so far. She couldn't bring herself to respond in kind, but her blushes and lowered gaze seemed to satisfy Astri's requirements.

In the afternoons, Beren sat with her and taught her words. She was becoming more proficient every day. One day, she had an idea for how to give back to this community that was giving her so much. She'd seen many scrolls and books in the Keeper Hall and some of them were in languages she already knew. Perhaps she could translate them for the keepers.

"Can you teach me how to read?" she asked before she lost her nerve.

Beren had brought a collection of seashells to give her words to, but now he peered at her in surprise. "Reading is not easy. Some of our people never learned how."

"Oh, I can read," she assured him. "in my own language. I want to know how to read yours."

"I'll see what I can do."

From then on, the lessons included guidance through the arcane symbols that passed for writing among these people. Sometimes Beren brought her one of the parchment scrolls the keepers kept in their Hall. These held the sagas, songs Elizabeth recognized from the evening feasts, as well as more practical instructions for creating dyes, shaping metal, and observing the various rituals required by their gods.

One day Beren asked her about her home life. "It will give you more words if you tell me about your wo…land."

They sat in a quiet corner of the Gather Hall. Even after all these weeks, Elizabeth couldn't put aside her reluctance to be alone in her room with a man who was not her husband or family, even Beren.

Especially Beren.

Although few people stayed in the Gather Hall during the day, there was always someone bustling about, either cleaning the benches, tending the fire pits, or going to or from some business.

Elizabeth smiled. "What would you like to know?"

Beren gazed into the distance for a moment. "I have heard there are horses in your land that are not used for farm or pack work, that men ride for pleasure. Did you ride?"

"I had a pony." She grinned at the memory. "His name was Pashta, for a…a visitor my father brought home one year." She stopped and gazed in wonder at Beren. "You look like him."

"I look like a horse?"

"No." She laughed. "No, the visitor. He was a prince from Egypt."

"Ah. Why did you not marry him?" The question was asked in an innocent tone, but there was a mischievous twinkle in Beren's eye.

"Because I was eight years old." *And the man already had several wives.* She took a sip of water.

"And he was only a prince." Beren slapped a hand to his chest. "While I am a king."

Elizabeth choked. She stared at Beren, then chuckled. "You make joke." She pointed a finger. "Not funny."

He shrugged. "Is true. I will tell you some time."

"Tell me now." The idea intrigued her. How was this Viking a king?

He regarded her for a moment, then nodded. "My father was king of Zamad, a land far to the south." He gazed into the distance, as if remembering. "Many years ago the Usali attacked. I was just a child and Kiana rescued me from the palace. My parents were killed, and I was their only son."

"Oh." Sympathy filled her for the orphan forced to flee his home. "Will you go back one day, to regain your throne?"

To her surprise, he laughed. "Why would I do that? This is my home. Kiana went back a few years ago to see what had happened there. The Usali are actually very good rulers. The people are happy." He shrugged. "Besides, I'd rather study in the Keeper Hall."

"So you're really a scholar?" The image of Beren huddled over scrolls seemed unreal.

"No, I just like to know things." He paused, then continued. "What else did you do besides ride your pony?"

Willing to accept the change of subject, Elizabeth considered. "I read. I played piano. I painted. I sewed…" What was the word for *embroidery*?

"Climbed trees?"

She glanced at him, but he seemed serious. "No, of course not. That was not…" She couldn't think of the word, so finished in English, "…proper."

He tilted his head. "What is *proper*?"

How to explain? "Ladies do not do the same things boys do."

"Why not?"

She huffed out a breath. "We do not show our legs. It is not judged…right. The rules of my culture. We cannot climb trees in skirts. And we do not disrobe in front of anyone except our…our maid-servant."

He shook his head. "That seems…" He glanced at her, "…inconvenient."

She grinned. Inconvenient indeed. How often had she thought the same? But that was how she'd been brought up, and the lessons were ingrained enough to make her uncomfortable even now. She'd never get used to seeing young women like Astri wear trousers, but constant exposure ensured she no longer cringed at the sight.

"And yet you are learning how to fight. Is that *proper*?" He grinned when he spoke.

She shot him a startled glance. "How did you—? Never mind. It's not a secret." She took a breath. "At home, where I come from, the men learn to fight and the women stay home. But here it is different. I am staying for a while, and I was taught to respect the customs of the country I am visiting. Fighting is…normal here."

"And a good thing to know," he acknowledged with a nod. "All our women know the basics. It's good you will know also."

And so the days passed. They didn't neglect their play-acting for Astri and Eskil. Beren always sat a little too close, Elizabeth made sure to smile at him more than anyone else.

Not that Elizabeth minded the ruse. She enjoyed talking with Beren, learning there was more to him than skilled warrior, secret scholar, co-conspirator, loyal friend…

Yes, there was more to him. Perhaps she smiled a little more often than she needed to, and perhaps she looked forward to their afternoons together, but she needed to learn the language anyway, didn't she? What did it matter if her heart beat faster when Beren was near? What did it matter if she found herself dreaming of him some—all right, *most* nights? Dreams of her hands caressing his broad shoulders, of *his* hands stroking her hair. Dreams where he strode into the middle of the Gather Hall, swept her off her feet, and carried her out the door to the horse barn, where he made passionate love to her.

Stop. It doesn't mean anything. She couldn't allow it to mean anything.

In the evenings, Elizabeth honed her embroidery skills on Gudrin's dresses. The little girl had developed a passion for bright red roses after seeing one of Elizabeth's creations, and from then on every one of her tunics and robes had to have a row of roses around the hem. Elizabeth attempted to teach her the skill, but the child had no patience for her own ragged stitches, and after a while Elizabeth gave up. She didn't mind. Embroidery was one of the *useless* skills Elizabeth enjoyed. Her handiwork was even admired by the other women, as she learned one morning when she took Ned to the nursery area.

When Elizabeth turned to leave, Maili cleared her throat. "Zabeth, may I ask a boon?"

Elizabeth smiled. "Of course. What do you need?"

Astri's friend ducked her head. "I wondered if you would…if it is no trouble…perhaps decorate my dress for me? I think…" She blushed and her pretty face glowed with happiness. "I think there is someone who likes me."

"Really?" Elizabeth was delighted.

It had often bothered her men rarely looked beneath physical beauty. The young woman was plump but had a good heart and a sunny disposition.

It was about time someone other than her friends noticed that. "Who?"

"I don't know." Maili removed a small wooden carving of a daisy she'd tucked inside her tunic. "I found this outside my door this morning. There have been others, every day this week."

Elizabeth ran a finger over smooth wood. "That's wonderful."

Maili sighed. "I wish he wasn't so shy. I think I know who it is but I'd like to be certain."

Elizabeth patted her arm. "Don't worry. I'm sure he'll reveal himself soon. Be patient. Leave your dress in my room and I'll start on it tonight. What kind of decoration do you want?"

Maili didn't hesitate. "Daisies." She blushed again, tucked the carving back into its hiding place, and returned her attention to her charges.

After that, several women asked Elizabeth to decorate their feast day dresses.

Once Beren's duties finished for the day, he spent most of his time either in Elizabeth's company or nearby. He even suggested making his attentions more obvious, perhaps kiss her a few times. She'd rejected that proposal of course, not so much because she found the idea improper—which it was—but because she was afraid she might enjoy his kisses too much.

She was confused by her feelings for Beren. Whenever he was nearby, she became inexplicably clumsy. Bowls leaped from her fingers onto the floor, needles jabbed into unwary palms. She couldn't explain it, any more than her restlessness when he wasn't about, but as anything else one experiences all the time, soon her reactions became part of the daily pattern, one more thing to adjust to. The emotions had become comfortable, like a familiar, well-loved blanket to wrap herself in whenever she felt lonely or sad. Beren was the tonic that cheered her up.

And if, on occasion, she imagined acting on her feelings…well, no one could hear her thoughts, even though she often thought they could when her face heated for no obvious reason.

The situation between Eskil and Astri hadn't changed. Eskil still ignored Astri, and although Elizabeth sympathized with the frustration her new friend experienced, she wasn't disappointed. The pretend courtship let her enjoy Beren's company without guilt.

One day, a few weeks after beginning her reading lessons, Beren took Elizabeth to the Keeper Hall, where Magrim waited with a book in his hand.

As soon as Elizabeth entered the display room, he handed her the book. "Can you read this, Zabeth?"

She glanced at the title, *Commedia*, and flipped through the first few pages. Her excitement grew. "Yes. It is a poem by a man named Dante, very like your sagas." She smiled, proud she'd learned enough of Magrim's language now to be able to express most of what she wanted. "He wrote it four hundred years ago, in the fourteenth century, but this looks as if it was printed later. The Italian is more…new…than when Dante wrote."

"See?" Beren crowed to the keeper, as if her ability to read the foreign book was a direct result of his lessons.

Magrim's eyes glittered with excitement. "Can you translate it into our language?"

Elizabeth hesitated. "I cannot write your language well yet."

Magrim waved away the objection. "I have assistants who can write it down, if you can read the words."

Relief made her smile. "Yes. I can do that."

And so afternoon lessons with Beren were shortened and followed by hours in the Keeper Hall. Elizabeth told herself it was for the best. He was too…tempting. Their play-acting was now restricted to the evenings, but as each day grew colder, her feelings grew stronger until she itched with a need she refused to acknowledge.

Chapter Seventeen

One night, Beren stood at the window in the barracks and held back the shutter. He ignored the sharp bite of cold, stared at the cloudless sky above the hills visible beyond the roof of the Gather Hall, and sniffed. There was a promise of snow. The stars glittered like jewels in the heavens, undimmed by a dark moon. Odin's chariot raced across the milky path while the great hunter aimed his bow at a dim star.

The sky reminded him of Zabeth, bright and distant. Their *charade*, a term he'd learned from a Shadow world, was becoming more real to him every day, even though she held back. Time he showed her there was more here for her than just a new home.

Conditions were perfect.

He waited, watched. When the first wispy streaks of color danced across the sky, he dropped the shutter and dashed across to the Gather Hall. When he burst through the door, the few stragglers still awake stared in his direction.

"Bifrost," he shouted.

Without waiting for a reaction, he sped through the Hall and up the stairs that led to Zabeth's room. He pounded on her door. "Zabeth. Awake! Come see Bifrost."

He flinched at a wail from within the room. A moment later angry words sounded through the door, words he didn't understand but guessed at the meaning. Zabeth was not happy.

The door was flung open and Zabeth stood in the opening, her child held in one arm, a blanket wrapped around them both. "It is the middle of the night. Why are you shouting?"

No, she was not happy, but it didn't matter. "The surprise I promised you. Bifrost. I promised I would show you when it appeared."

She glared at him in disbelief. "In the middle of the night?"

"You can only see Bifrost at night." He grabbed her free arm and pulled her forward. "Hurry. You'll miss it."

She snatched her arm from his grip, but her impatience disappeared under the force of his enthusiasm. "Oh, for… Wait until I get a robe and shoes."

She slipped back inside the room, but returned before he'd paced the hallway twice. She wore a thick fleece robe over her thin gown, and the child was wrapped in a kind of sling she'd hung around her shoulder.

On her feet were warm rabbit-pelt boots. She gave him a challenging look. "Show me this Bifrost."

He grinned and led the way. The Hall was empty when they passed through. Everyone was already outside. The first appearance of Bifrost each winter was always honored.

He led Zabeth away from the Hall to the open area by the horse pasture. More than a dozen people had already gathered there, staring up toward the hills. Their breath made little frost clouds in the chill air. Beren stopped by the corral, turned Zabeth, and pointed. "Look."

The night sky above the hills was alive with color. Streams of red and blue and green rippled in the north. One long strand of blue escaped from the band to sway and fly free. One end remained tethered, giving the impression of a blue banner waving in the wind.

Beside him, Zabeth gasped. "Beautiful."

He repressed a smug smile. "Bifrost is the most beautiful thing in the heavens."

For a while, they stood without speaking while the fantastical display rippled across the sky. Around them, everyone was silent.

"Tell me more about Bifrost." Zabeth gazed at the sky.

"When the gods built Asgard, their home, they put it on a peak surrounded by deep chasms. They built a bridge across the chasm, a bridge made of rainbows, and called it Bifrost." He watched her upturned face, fascinated by the awe in her gaze. "In the winter, when the sky is clear and the air is cold, the gods let mortal men see the bridge so they know the gods exist. It'll appear many times over the next few months."

She sighed. "I have never seen anything like it."

In a bold move, he took her free hand. She didn't notice, or perhaps she didn't mind, for she didn't pull away.

"Do you like what you see?" he murmured.

She tilted her head to look at him. He stared down at her, her face so close to his. So close…

Without conscious thought, he closed the distance. His mouth covered hers, gentle, soft. Need shot through him but he forced himself not to react. He tilted his head, ran his tongue over her lips until they parted. She didn't move. Her eyes stayed open, gazing into his. She didn't return the kiss, but she didn't draw away either. He wanted to plunge inside, taste her, but knew it wasn't the right time. Soon though...

The baby whimpered, shifted against her shoulder, and she took a step back. Beren's gaze was drawn to the child. Ned opened his eyes, looked at Beren, and smiled. Beren smiled back.

Zabeth refocused her attention on the colorful display above them and didn't look at him again, but Beren didn't mind. He'd kissed her and she hadn't objected.

~ * ~

Beren kissed me.

The words circled through Elizabeth's head while she continued to watch the amazing colored strips in the sky. It hadn't been a world-shattering kiss. In truth, it had just been a touch of lips to hers, and yet it had felt so natural, so...*inevitable.*

She shouldn't have let him kiss her. Perhaps she'd been too surprised to object. Yes, that was it. Surprise. She wouldn't let it happen again.

But when she fell asleep later, the feel of Beren's lips on hers followed her into her dreams.

~ * ~

The snow arrived a few days later. It fell for hours, hours that stretched into days, until mysterious lumps of white were visible where once had stood sheds and boats and corrals. When the snow stopped, the cold descended on the back of a howling wind.

People arrived from the outlying farms and crowded into the Gather Hall. Ropes were strung from beams, blankets folded over the lines to separate each family's temporary home from its neighbors. All the little areas remained open to the front so heat from the central braziers and the great fireplaces could move through the Hall without interruption.

Each day, when Elizabeth scurried from her cool room to the warmth of the kitchen, more bodies occupied the benches, more piles of belongings shoved beneath.

One morning a corner of the Gather Hall was cleared of excess baggage and keepers filled the benches. The bundles beneath their sleeping platform bulged with the sharp angles of Shadow-Links. According to Runa, the precious tools fared ill in the cold, but from now until spring there'd be no more trade. Even Elizabeth's book translations were curtailed. She'd have to find other ways to fill her afternoons.

A few nights later, with frost crusting the furs on the walls, everyone in the bedchambers relocated to the Gather Hall. Elizabeth had long ago accepted the folly of staying in her room, and the practicality of sharing a sort-of bed with strangers. Now she stood at the foot of the stairs, uncertainty making her nervous. Ned's cradle, stuffed with clothing, was under one arm, her squirming son in the other.

Runa hurried past with an armful of bedding. "Put that in the nursery." She indicated a corner with her chin.

Kaya and Maili had set up a cozy area by one of the great fireplaces. Already a dozen cradles stood in a semi-circle facing the cheery blaze, while two pallets were spread in the open space. Elizabeth placed Ned's cradle at the end of the group. Several infants played on a fur rug between the pallets.

"Bring him here." Kaya patted a spot on the rug in front of her. She sat cross-legged on one of the pallets, while Maili tumbled around with the older toddlers.

Elizabeth looked back at the huge Hall and located Runa and her family on a platform by the kitchen. "Would it not be better for me to keep Ned with me? You have so many to look after here."

Kaya smiled and reached for the baby. "Nonsense. This is the warmest spot in the Hall. Would you deny your son the best?"

Elizabeth hesitated for a moment, then placed Ned in her waiting arms. "I suppose not."

She watched for a few minutes while Ned explored the fur. His attempts to crawl were unsuccessful. He had, however, discovered he could get where he wanted to go by rolling, so now he rolled away from Kaya toward a friend he'd spotted on the other side of the rug.

"Do you have somewhere to sleep?" Kaya asked.

Elizabeth nodded. "Runa said I could sleep with them." She retrieved her bundle of spare clothes and bedding from the cradle and threaded her way through the bustle in the Hall to Runa's group.

Elizabeth had come to accept the necessity of sleeping with the family, but she wasn't comfortable with the idea. For one thing, she hated being separated from Ned. For another, she couldn't help but wonder how many of Runa's family also shared the bench space. On the heels of that thought came another.

Where did Runa's nephew sleep?

~ * ~

The sun had set before Beren returned from the barn. Cows, goats, and sheep now shared space with the horses, so whoever was on stable duty had more to clean than usual. He was bone tired, and the short walk from the barn didn't do anything to refresh him.

Wind whistled through the streets, tore shutters from windows, thatch from roofs. Numb from the freezing cold, he stumbled through the small side door into the empty kitchen.

He shook the snow from his fur cloak while he tramped through the cold room and down the short hallway to the Gather Hall. Inside the entrance, a small cauldron bubbled. Hulda handed him a mug of hot *keevah*. Beren leaned against the wall while he sipped the restoring brew. Where was Zabeth?

Several women clustered around the group of cradles in the nursery area. Even though he couldn't see her, Beren knew Zabeth was among them.

Something was growing between himself and Zabeth. After that first kiss, they'd both drawn back, neither saying a word. Their afternoon language sessions continued, but there was a strain, an unspoken agreement not to mention what had happened, as if keeping silent eased the tension. Instead it did the opposite.

He wanted to pursue this odd feeling. Kissing Zabeth had been torture. He lay awake at nights remembering the press of his mouth to hers, wishing he'd stroked her hair, her cheek. He promised himself he wouldn't rush her, but holding back was driving him mad.

He pushed aside a vision of green eyes shining with wonder at her first sight of Bifrost and joined the other men around one of the large cauldrons in the middle of the Hall. After spooning up a bowl of stew, he hunkered close to the fire to thaw the ice from his bones.

While he ate, a hush settled over the Hall, and by the time he finished, most of the Hall's occupants had fallen asleep. Besides himself, the few still awake were those who'd drawn the losing lots to tend the fires and braziers.

Beren wandered toward the outer doors, checked to make sure they were secured against the storm, then studied the room. All the benches were full.

Near the middle of the bundled group of people was Runa. Mikkel had tucked in with the other boys instead of his mother. Kaya and Maili curled on the floor by the cradles.

He frowned. Where was Zabeth?

Beren wanted nothing more than to crawl under the nearest fur, no matter who it belonged to, and sleep for days. But first he had to know where Zabeth slept. He'd ceased questioning his need to be aware of where she was at all times. He just did, and wondering why wasn't going to change the way he felt.

He wandered around the room, and at last found her snuggled in between Runa and Gudrin. Zabeth had curled around the little girl, hugging her close against the cold.

Beren grinned. Even in sleep his Shadow woman protected the children.

His.

When had he started thinking of her as his? She was as much a part of him as Runa and Gudrin.

He gazed at the three of them, so similar yet so different. His aunt, who had raised him as much as Kiana. Fiery-haired Zabeth, with a streak of stubbornness rivaled only by the brown-haired Valkyrie in her arms. Little Gudrin, with the heart of a warrior. He loved them all in one way or another.

Loved? Beren stiffened, backed up a step. Wrong word. For Runa and Gudrin, yes, he loved them. But Zabeth? He tried the word on his tongue, whispered it to himself. *Do I love Zabeth? More important, does she love me?*

He pondered the questions while his heart fluttered in his chest. The answer to the first was…just out of reach. As to the second, he feared the answer was no, and until she did, he couldn't do anything about the first.

He turned his back on the family group and forced himself to walk to the bench shared by the single men, knowing he faced a sleepless night.

Chapter Eighteen

When midwinter's day dawned, Elizabeth found herself caught up in the excitement of preparing for the evening's festivities. This was the shortest day of the year, the longest night, when everyone celebrated the return of the sun.

The twenty-first of December, in her calendar, and Christmas a few days away. The twenty-fifth was just another day to her hosts, but that didn't mean she couldn't celebrate it on her own, with quiet prayer. She'd already braided a rag doll for Ned, which she'd give him tonight as was the custom here. The celebration was as much about the children as the adults.

She spent the day helping Runa and Freya in the kitchen. While the other women baked bread, stewed vegetables, and roasted meat, Elizabeth peeled and chopped, washed dishes, fetched wood from the pile already stacked in the storage room, and generally helped wherever she could. A year ago she'd never set foot in a kitchen. Now she spent as much time here as in the central hall.

Conversation revolved around the evening's activities. Three of the women planned to perform an ancient folk dance and swayed while they stirred cauldrons of soup, their feet shuffling miniature versions of the steps. Freya muttered to herself while she rehearsed the tale of Idunn and the golden apples that kept the gods young.

"Gudrin's harping is still rough, so I've agreed to accompany her on the drums." Runa pounded a lump of dough with a complicated flourish and kneaded it into a perfect ball. "What about you, Zabeth? What did you decide to do?"

"Didn't I say?" Elizabeth paused in her latest task, peeling root vegetables for the stew.

The lessons over the last few months had increased her comfort with the language. When told she'd be expected to participate, she'd at first been nervous until she told herself it was no different from the social evenings she grew up with, where everyone performed. Elizabeth played the pianoforte at those parties, but that was out of the question here. "I'm going to sing."

Freya looked up. "One of your people's songs?"

"Yes." She'd spent hours translating the words so they'd be understood, but now she paused, uncertain. "Should I learn one of your songs instead?"

"No," Freya assured her. "We'd love to hear what your people sing."

The reassurance kept Elizabeth buoyed until the moment, several hours later, when she stood alone in the center of the Hall and faced a circle of eager, interested faces.

Sudden panic held her motionless. She'd intended to sing a hymn to the Christ's birth, to celebrate this time of year, but how would pagans react to such music in their halls?

The answer came to her on a rush of understanding. They'd react as they always did, with enjoyment and appreciation.

Confidence straightened her spine. She faced the head table and dropped a curtsey to Garan and Freya. A movement on her right drew her attention to the table where Beren sat with his friends. He raised a mug at her, and smiled encouragement as if he sensed her uncertainty.

At once her nervousness vanished. In its place was a giddy warmth that left her grinning back. She didn't question the attraction anymore. She liked him, a lot, and only the reminder she'd be gone in the spring prevented the guilt. She could wait a few months. Nothing would happen in that short time, so there was nothing to worry about.

She turned the other way and smiled at Ned, who sat on Runa's lap, then took a deep breath and clasped her hands at her waist in the formal stance she'd been taught to assume when singing. A hush fell over the Hall.

Elizabeth licked her lips, took another breath, and began. "Whilst shepherds watched their flocks by night, all seated on the ground."

No one seemed bothered the words were about a different god than their own. Instead they appeared enthralled by the simple tune. Elizabeth's voice soared through the crowded Hall. She closed her eyes. The familiar carol transported her back to Christmas celebrations of her youth, and as the words flowed from her, she knew with certainty God had not deserted her. Even in this far away land, she felt Him all around.

"All glory be to God on high, and to the earth be peace. Good will henceforth from heaven to earth, begin and never cease." A tear slid down her cheek when the last note echoed into the silence.

The Hall erupted in roars of appreciation.

Elizabeth opened her eyes, blinked rapidly, and gazed around the room. Runa grinned. Garan pounded his mug on the table while Freya clapped her hands together with great enthusiasm. The men at Beren's table also banged mugs on the wood, but Beren sat motionless.

What had she expected? Approval? Delight? Neither came close to the expression of awe on his face. As if in slow motion, he rose from the bench, rounded the table, and stalked toward her.

She couldn't move. The shouts and applause receded into the background, the eager faces blurred. Beren filled her vision.

He stopped so close in front of her she felt his breath on her cheek.

His mouth opened and closed, but she heard nothing until he touched her arm and sound returned. "You sing well, Eeleezabeth."

She swallowed, took a shaky breath, struggled for something to say. It occurred to her she'd been waiting for Beren's praise, that all the applause and appreciation from the rest of the villagers meant little compared to those few words, *You sing well*.

"Come," Beren murmured. "You can sit now."

She nodded. *Sit. Yes.* She allowed him to escort her back to the bench beside Runa.

"That was lovely," said Runa.

Ned gurgled, as if in agreement. His babbling broke the spell. Elizabeth smiled and lifted him onto her lap. "Thank you. And thank you, Beren." She turned, but Beren wasn't behind her. He had seated himself in the small space beside her.

He didn't grin, but there was a twinkle in his eyes. "May I share your table, Eeleezabeth?"

She nodded, all at once lost for words. This man was getting under her skin, and…she didn't mind one bit.

A drum beat announced Freya's recitation. Silence again descended over the Hall. When Freya began, Elizabeth forgot her preoccupation with Beren, enthralled with the saga of how the trickster god Loki had lured the goddess Idunn into abandoning the safety of Asgard with her golden apples, which left her vulnerable to capture by the giant Thiazzi. The tale had all the elements of a great adventure, including magical transformations, betrayal, and a daring rescue.

While Freya spoke, Gudrin slipped from her seat beside Runa and marched to her brother. She tugged at Beren's arm, whispered something in his ear. He smiled, swung around to straddle the bench, and lifted the little girl to sit in front of him with her back to him. She placed a brush on the table beside them. Beren untied the ribbon that held one of Gudrin's braids together and unwove the strands while Gudrin worked on the other braid. He then took up the brush and stroked it through her now-loosened hair.

Freya's tale drew to a close, but Elizabeth missed the last part. Her gaze was fixed on Beren's large, strong hands brushing the tangles from his sister's hair. Elizabeth tried to imagine how she'd feel to have him brush her own hair.

Stop. You don't need such...improper thoughts. Elizabeth dragged her gaze away from the domestic scene and forced herself to concentrate on the entertainment. The tumblers took over next, and after them came the skalds. She'd already heard the tale of how Tor came to this land. *A ball of fire. A hole in the world.*

Of course it was all allegory, with as much truth as Freya's saga. Still, it had been entertaining and explained the gray man and his ship in the mountain, even if in their imagination. This time the skalds told a more traditional tale, and she settled down to enjoy it.

A few hours later, the presentations were over and all the musicians had gathered at one end of the Hall to play energetic tunes while the villagers danced, alone, in couples, or in groups. Ned's head rested on Elizabeth's shoulder, one fist stuffed into his mouth as usual.

"I must put him to bed," she whispered to Runa.

The older woman nodded absently, absorbed in watching the dancers. Gudrin had long since succumbed to the excitement of the evening and now lay half on Beren's lap with her head on her brother's chest. He gave Elizabeth a rueful shake of his head.

"I can't leave yet," he whispered.

She reached down and stroked Gudrin's hair. "I know. I'll be right back."

Elizabeth slipped off the bench and made her way to the nursery behind her. The sleeping benches huddled, almost deserted, against the wall, while the occasional lump under a pile of blankets announced the presence of a child or adult exhausted by the celebration.

Once she had Ned settled, she stood for a moment in the shadows, her gaze drawn to Beren still seated sideways on the bench. With one arm supporting Gudrin in a protective hug, he rested the other arm on the table while he watched Elizabeth.

She smiled at him and hurried back. When she slipped onto the bench beside Beren, he grinned at her, but her attention was caught by Eskil, seated on the other side of the room.

He glowered at the dancers and Elizabeth followed his gaze. Astri, laughing, pranced and skipped among the groups with Sven and Olav, two of the unmarried warriors.

Elizabeth glanced again at Eskil. She'd forgotten her play-acting with Beren was supposed to drive the young warrior into Astri's arms. Eskil knew of the plan, so Beren had said, but now he leaned forward, his scowl deepening, as if he'd forgotten the role he was supposed to play. He narrowed his eyes in speculation. It looked as though his patience was about to snap.

A faint premonition held Elizabeth motionless. Beside her, Beren laid a hand on her arm. When she looked at him, he winked and nodded in Eskil's direction. She returned her attention to the young man.

Eskil surged to his feet. His face tight with anger, he strode across the room, stopped before Runa, and bowed his head.

"I speak to you, Runa, in the absence of your husband." His tone was formal, every word clear. "I ask your permission to punish your daughter."

Runa widened her eyes and rose to her feet. Eskil held his ground. Outraged mother and angry warrior glared at each other for several seconds before Runa's face took on a thoughtful expression. "Explain."

Eskil pointed at Astri as she danced with wild abandon. "She shames your house. She shames herself. You have to admit she deserves to have her backside tanned."

Runa's lips twitched, as if fighting back a grin, "Only two men have that right, guardsman, her father and her husband."

Eskil raised his chin. "Vider is not here."

A snort of laughter was his answer. "No, nor is he that brave."

"Then permit me." Eskil swallowed once, crossed his arms.

Runa stared at him for a long moment. At last, she gave a short nod. "If you can, son, then you have my permission."

"My thanks." He bowed, turned around, and plunged into the crowd while Runa sank back into her chair.

Astri whirled and danced as if she didn't have a care in the world, but an over-bright glitter in her eyes indicated she wasn't as carefree as she seemed. No one else noticed the tension there—or perhaps Runa did. Her reaction to Eskil's outrageous request left Elizabeth with the impression the woman knew more about her daughter's feelings than she let on.

Curious to know what Eskil intended, Elizabeth waited for the drama to unfold.

Astri spun in a circle, laughing up at Sven. Eskil reached her a moment later. Without a word, he grabbed her around the waist and kissed her. She froze, her eyes wide, then her lashes drooped and she began to raise her arms to his shoulders. Eskil pulled back, regarded her smug expression, then slung her over his shoulder.

Astri gave a loud screech. The Hall fell silent. Eskil slapped Astri's bottom and she reared up, cursed. "Put me down."

"We have things to discuss," he said in a matter-of-fact voice. "Eskil!"

Instead of answering, he headed toward the outside door. The crowd parted to let him through. Astri bounced on his shoulder and Elizabeth winced.

"Eskil, put me down, right now." Astri's voice held a trace of surprise more than hysteria. She looked toward the table where Elizabeth sat beside Runa. "Mother!" Runa shook her head and remained in her chair. "Mother?" Demand had turned to confused plea. Elizabeth's heart went out to her.

Astri, however, wasn't going to allow Eskil to carry her away without a fight. She pushed herself up and twisted until she was bent around his shoulder. Teeth bared in rage, she bit his ear.

Eskil yelled. He slapped her bottom again and bounced her until she hung down his back once more. His free hand snaked around, grabbed her braids, and held her in place upside down.

Her screech was even louder. "Stop. How dare you, Eskil! I'll scratch your eyes out if you don't put me down. *Eskil.*"

Someone held open the Hall door. Someone else threw a heavy fur cloak over Eskil's shoulders. It covered Astri and smothered her protests. Eskil strode into the night, and the helpful villager shut the door behind him. The silence in the Hall stretched uncomfortably for several moments.

Then Garan rose, a broad smile on his face. "Continue the celebration. We'll be having a wedding soon."

Relieved laughter greeted this announcement. Conversation and music resumed.

"About time," Beren muttered loud enough for Elizabeth to hear.

She stared at the closed door. For a brief instant, she imagined Beren carrying her off like that. The thought left her breathless.

Was she falling in love with him?

No. It couldn't be. She couldn't allow it. She had to think of Ned, of England.

Didn't she?

She shifted her gaze from Beren to her son. At home he'd have all the advantages of his station, a good education, the comforts and privileges of nobility, more so if she made a sensible marriage. As a widow she'd have more freedom in her choice of a husband.

David had been dead for over four months, yet in that time she hadn't thought of him as much as a loyal wife was expected to. Yes, she mourned him, but no more than was expected in her social circle. Theirs wasn't a love match, nor was it a horrid marriage.

A laugh drew her gaze back to Beren, who listened to something his neighbor had just told him. *About time*, he'd said. Did that mean he was glad the play between himself and Elizabeth was at an end, that he could go back to his normal life? Without her?

The thought left her cold. No, she didn't believe that. His attentions were too...genuine, and, God forgive her, she feared her feelings were just as entangled.

Feared? No, more...hoped? But what to do about it? An unexpected idea entered her mind. She'd had scandalous ideas before, even acted on them, but this...

She'd be going home in the spring, and once there she'd never see these people again. She'd return to a life caged in manners and propriety, in expectations and obligations. But spring was months away, and who in England was to know what happened here in those months? Why shouldn't she, this once, enjoy a little freedom, a little...affair?

Oh Lord, what am I thinking?

It wouldn't mean anything, of course. Nothing...serious.

But to take that step, to give her fondness for Beren free rein...

She shook her head. *No, I'm mad to even consider such a thing.*

Beren laughed again and her heart gave a thump.

Then again...why not?

For the next few days she argued with herself, watched Beren, thought about Beren, and at last worked up the nerve to go forward with her plan, only to back away at the scandal—*that no one back home will know about*—and the impropriety of an affair—*that no one back home will even care about.*

Ten days after the midwinter celebration, Elizabeth woke to the realization it was the end of December. If the pirate attack had not happened, she and David would be in the governor's mansion in Connecticut preparing to host a New Year's Eve ball for their rich neighbors. Instead, she was one of several women helping Astri get ready to wed Eskil this afternoon.

And tomorrow begins a new year.

The revelation echoed through her mind. A new year, new beginnings.

Time to follow my heart.

Chapter Nineteen

During the feast after Astri and Eskil's hand-fasting, most everyone shared the task of turning the spit of roasting boar. It was when Beren took his turn that Zabeth approached.

"It was a good wedding," he ventured.

She stopped. Several expressions crossed her face in quick succession—indecision, nervousness, excitement. She nodded, once, and spoke as if it was the most important statement she had to make. "Yes. It was." She watched the couple who whirled around the central fire, trailed by a line of laughing villagers. "They look so happy."

There was a wistful note in her voice that made Beren stare at her. *Are you not happy?*

Maili separated herself from the revelers and approached. "My turn on the spit, Beren." Her gaze took in Zabeth, who shifted from one foot to the other, as if poised to flee. "Why don't you dance with Zabeth?"

Beren glowed with warmth. He stood, held his hand out to Zabeth. She stared at it as if it were a strange beast, then she took a deep breath and placed her small hand in his.

As usual, her touch sent a pleasant shock through his body, but he tried not to show it when he led her to the line of dancers and joined the end. Zabeth followed awkwardly at first, but soon picked up the rhythm of the music and the simple steps of the dance. After a while, she relaxed.

Beren moved without conscious thought—he'd been dancing these steps since he was six—and allowed his mind to wander.

Zabeth seemed uncomfortable in his presence. He couldn't understand why. They'd been companions for months now. Perhaps what she needed was a distraction. Winter was a time to look to the future, but he didn't want her to think of spring. He'd keep her so busy she wouldn't have time to remember her plan to leave.

Ideas flowed into his head. He'd teach Zabeth the board game he enjoyed playing in the evenings. When the first few nights of the deep cold passed, he'd take her skating on the river that was now frozen solid. There were lots of activities to distract her.

He glanced down at her and caught her looking at him. The expression in her eyes had him stumbling to a halt in the middle of the floor.

~ * ~

Now the time had come, Elizabeth wasn't sure how to proceed.

One step at a time, her mother always said.

So, step one…but not here in the middle of the dance floor.

She offered a tentative smile, caught Beren's hand, and led him to a quiet corner at the side. She indicated the bench and they both sat, he with a wary gaze, she with nerves threatening to still her voice.

She swallowed several times. "I wanted to ask…" No, not like that. "With Astri married, she will no longer have time or…or interest in continuing my training, at least for a while." There, a simple fact, leading to a logical conclusion. "I wondered if you…if you…"

She paused, her throat dry again.

"If I would take over your training?" His voice didn't tremble as hers had, but it came out so soft she had to strain to hear.

She nodded, still unable to speak. Her mother had provided all sorts of information on how to be a good wife. Elizabeth wished she'd also included how to start an illicit affair.

Beren nodded. "Yes, that would be a good idea. It will give Lida a chance to work with her more advanced students."

"Yes." Relief gave her voice. "Lida. Of course."

He smiled. "So…I will see you in the horse barn in the morning?"

"In the horse barn," she agreed. "In the morning."

He regarded her for a moment, then, with a short bow, he rose and rejoined the dancers.

Elizabeth let out a breath. Tomorrow. Lord help her, she was going to do it.

~ * ~

The next morning, Zabeth arrived looking as nervous as a newborn colt. She clutched her cloak about her, slipped through the half-open door of the barn, and pulled the wooden frame closed behind her to shut out the cold wind. She stayed by the door, still clutching the cloak as if it were a shield.

She looked around. "Beren?"

"Here." Beren stepped from the shadows of one of the stalls.

She licked her lips, a sight that sent his blood racing. "Um, I thought you might have changed your mind."

And miss the chance of wrestling with her? "Let me see what you've learned."

It took another few moments before she seemed able to convince her fingers to release their grip on the cloak. She slid the furs off her shoulders and hung the garment from one of the hooks beside the door. When she turned back to him, her face was flushed, her breathing fast and shallow.

Of course, the strong odor in the barn, a consequence of all the livestock that now shared the stalls, might be to blame. The area in front of the doors remained free of animals. Beren grinned. At least Zabeth hadn't been here earlier. He'd been on cleanup duty and had to endure worse.

Today Zabeth wore an ankle-length brown robe under a stained yellow tunic loosely laced at the sides. She slid her hand beneath the tunic and pulled a wooden training knife from a sheath strapped at the small of her back. Beren nodded approval. The knife was hidden, but easy to reach.

Zabeth held the knife in her right hand, knees bent, feet flat on the floor. Again he nodded. The stance was right, balanced so she was able to shift in any direction. The action calmed her, for her movements were more sure, more confident than before. It was obvious she'd learned how to maneuver in the long robes without tripping over the hem. Astri had taught her well. All she had to remember was to try to anticipate her opponent's moves and react accordingly.

She caught Beren's gaze and held it. All rational thought disappeared.

She'll never be able to anticipate my moves. I can't think of any to make.

Zabeth lunged forward, slapped the flat of the wooden blade across his stomach, and skipped back. The shock of contact wrenched him from his trance.

"Is that good enough for you?" She grinned and her eyes twinkled with amusement. The small victory appeared to have banished her nervousness.

Beren rubbed his abdomen and paced in a sharp circle until the sting subsided. He drew his own training knife from its sheath, stopped, and faced Zabeth. Wariness replaced amusement in her eyes.

"Not bad." Beren tapped his blade against the palm of his left hand. "But you won't kill anyone with love taps." He bent his knees, bounced on the balls of his feet.

She narrowed her eyes and raised her chin. "I do not want to kill anyone, just defend myself and my family. If this was for real I would have aimed lower and used the point."

Beren froze again at the image her words conveyed, but he was quick to recover. A grin spread across his face. Astri had indeed taught her well.

He sidled left, circling. She circled with him, keeping him in front of her. "Warriors usually wear protective armor there."

"Then I would aim at your eyes," she replied.

She again thrust forward, but he was ready for her this time. He sidestepped and grabbed her arm when she brushed past him. He turned, swung her with him, and swept her feet from beneath her. She fell, but when he released her she grabbed his shirt and pulled him down with her.

She rolled when her back hit the floor, so instead of falling on top of her, Beren found himself face down on the straw-covered dirt. A moment later, Zabeth was on his back with her knife to his throat.

"Is that better?" There was a hint of mischief in her voice.

He grabbed her wrist, jerked the knife away from his neck, and rolled over in the same movement. This time Zabeth was on the floor and Beren on top. He pinned her hands beside her head. She brought a knee up but he shifted to pin her legs.

The position reminded him of Astri's attack on Eskil last fall. He remembered how she'd distracted her future husband long enough to escape his grasp.

Beren stared at Zabeth's lips. Would she try the same trick?

Breathing hard, she glared up at him. No, he decided. Zabeth wouldn't try such tricks, and if he knew what was good for him he wouldn't let himself be distracted by the image.

"You still have much to learn." He hoped she wouldn't notice the husky note in his voice, or the hardness pressing against her lower body. He released her, rose to his feet, and offered a hand to help her up. She ignored him and scrambled up by herself.

She brushed the straw from her robe and retrieved her knife. "Very well. You have proved your point. Show me what I need to know."

Later, when the bell rang for the midday meal, both were covered in sweat and straw and breathing hard.

"We need the bath house," Beren said on a laugh.

Zabeth glanced at him but continued brushing off her skirt. "*You* need the bath house. It's men this afternoon."

Curious, he leaned against a stall. "What will you do?"

She straightened. The corners of her mouth twitched and spread into a slow smile. She glanced at him. "I've heard the old stables at the back of the Gather Hall are fairly warm."

The stables? They hadn't been used for animals in years and now served as storage for items that couldn't be left in cold rooms, like the Shadow-Links the keepers had brought from their hall, or items needed only a few times over the winter, like extra bedding for the deep ice nights.

And some wooden troughs used to wash clothes or children too small to risk in the bath house tubs.

His mouth went dry. *Zabeth lazing naked in one of the troughs.* He gulped. "The water will be cold."

"I'm told there is a tube from the forge to heat it." Zabeth picked up her cloak and walked to the door. "That's what Maili said anyway. And I can hang a blanket for privacy. But after…" She stopped, glanced at him over her shoulder, and lowered her voice. "After, I wouldn't mind if you brushed my hair."

When she slipped outside, Beren's mind went completely blank.

~ * ~

Oh Lord, what am I doing?

Elizabeth sat on a bale of straw beside the trough, twining and untwining her fingers. The former stable-turned-storage room was indeed warm. Bundles of all shapes and sizes lined the walls and filled the abandoned stalls.

One nearby stall held extra bedding, which she'd arranged in a pallet on the floor before she took her bath, and she couldn't keep her gaze from straying to the pile, visible in the light of three lanterns suspended from the roof.

As she'd told Beren, she'd hung a blanket over the front of one of the stalls with a trough. She knew some of the older women preferred to bathe here instead of making the cold trek to the bath house through piles of snow, but she was told it wasn't something the men indulged in.

Still, she hadn't lingered in the water, and was quick to scrub off the sweat and dirt accumulated during her session in the barn. Now, dressed in a clean tunic and skirt, she waited for Beren.

Ever since her decision last night, she'd been assessing the best place to put her plan into motion. At first she thought to invite Beren back to her room, but with ice on the walls and the coldest days still to come, that wasn't practical. By accident she'd stumbled across the secret of the storage room a few weeks ago when she'd followed Maili to give her the embroidered tunic she'd finished.

Although it wasn't such a secret—everyone knew about it, and everyone respected the privacy offered when a red cloth hung on a hook outside the entrance, a signal that the room was occupied. Elizabeth had done just that. She hoped Beren understood the warning didn't apply to him.

Now, though, she was having second thoughts. Did she want to go through with this? Taking a lover was a big step, at least for her. Other women in her social class might think nothing of it, but Beren was Elizabeth's first outside of marriage. Was she ready to take that step?

A low cough drew her attention to the entrance. Beren stood there, an uncertain smile on his face. *Funny, he seems as nervous as me.* That calmed her.

She rose, strolled to the stall with the bedding, sat on the pallet, and pulled her braid over her shoulder. She took her time, as much to calm her own nerves as his, and unwove the long strands. Beren watched her fingers as if mesmerized. When her hair hung loose, she ran her fingers through the crinkled waves and lifted the brush she'd placed beside the pallet.

"Would you?" She slipped off the pallet to the floor and knelt with her back to Beren. After an eternity, he sat behind her and gathered her hair in his hand. When the brush touched her scalp, she braced herself.

David had brushed her hair sometimes, but only after she'd begged him with a promise to have Cook make his favorite pudding. She recognized now he'd never done anything for her without promise of reward. It had never bothered her before, perhaps because she was used to coddling her brothers, but David was her husband.

He was supposed to be the strong one, yet more and more she found herself mothering him. The few times he'd brushed her hair, he'd tugged impatiently at the knots until either she'd stopped him or he'd grown bored with the activity and wandered away.

But Beren didn't tug or pull. The hypnotic strokes of the brush should have relaxed her. Instead, every sense tingled with awareness, and the awareness centered around one word, one name. *Beren.* She sat between his legs. Even as his name echoed in her mind, he grew harder behind her back.

"I thought I'd misunderstood," he murmured.

A rush of joy swept over her, followed by a heady sensation of power. She eased the brush from his fingers, then shifted around until she faced him.

"Make love to me, Beren," she whispered.

Chapter Twenty

The raw desire on Beren's face was enough to tell Elizabeth she hadn't misjudged. At the same time, she was shocked at her own words, even though it had been her plan all along.

"All right." Not, *are you sure.*

He said the words in the same tone he'd used when he'd agreed to teach her how to read his language. But the fire in his eyes, the tremble in his hands when he drew her to her feet, told her he wanted her as much as she wanted him.

Before she could lose her nerve, she reached for the first lamp.

"Leave the lights," he ordered.

She paused and looked over her shoulder at him. "Leave them? But…we can't do this in the light."

"Why not?" He grinned. "I want to see you."

Her mouth went dry. Beren watching her while he—

The image that rose in her head brought heat to her cheeks.

Beren stood and grinned a silly, lopsided grin that turned her stomach to mush. "I love it when you blush. It makes your hair flame brighter."

Her knees shook and it was all she could do to keep from falling over. *Who was seducing whom?* As if sensing her weakness, he took both her hands in his and tugged her toward the pallet. They stood together and gazed into each other's eyes. She wanted nothing more than to dive into the chocolate-brown depths of them, drown there. They grew bigger until they filled her line of vision when he bent his head toward her.

She opened her mouth on a gasp and his mouth closed over hers. The breath caught in her throat. Fire sped from their joined lips through the rest of her body. His beard rasped against her chin, soft and intensely arousing.

She sighed, sank closer to the heat, and opened her mouth wider to draw in more. When his tongue accepted the invitation, she was sure she'd go up in flames and collapse in a pile of ashes at his feet.

How romantic is that? She giggled, the sound muffled by his mouth, but he heard and pulled his head back to study her with curiosity.

"I didn't realize my kisses tickled," he said in a solemn tone.

Instantly contrite, she pressed a finger to his lips. "I'm sorry. I'll try to do better."

He raised an eyebrow. "Zabeth, if you do any better you'll have to scrape the ashes from the floor."

"You too?" The words came out in a surprised squeak, and she squirmed at her boldness.

He laughed and pulled back. Taking that as a signal, she turned her back and began to untie the lacings down the front of her tunic.

"No," he murmured. He circled her with his arms; covered her hands with his, and pulled her around to face him. She waited, and she felt the beat of her pulse speed up in anticipation. "Undress me first."

Her heart slammed into her ribs. *Oh my.*

She lifted trembling fingers to his tunic and fumbled with the knots that held it together. *I can do this. I want to do this.* Oh, Lord, would her fingers ever work properly again?

At last, she released the final knot. Beren raised his arms above his head. She tugged the hem of the tunic above his waist, up past the crisp expanse of dark hair covering his chest. He leaned toward her and she pulled the garment over his head. When he straightened, she stared at his bare chest.

He is magnificent. She trailed her fingers from his shoulders to his belly, ran her hand over the muscles of his stomach. He sucked in a sharp breath and caught her wrist.

"Now the trews," he croaked.

Amazed at her own daring, Elizabeth slipped her fingers under his waistband and slid them around before settling on the ties at the front. Once again, to her dismay, her fingers refused to work, but at long last the waistband loosened. With a single tug, she pulled the soft leather over his hips and thighs, and let it drop to his ankles.

She stepped back and looked down, amazed at the sight of him. *So this is what a man looks like.*

Beren's amused voice rolled over her head. "You look as if you've never seen a man naked before."

"I haven't." She couldn't look away.

He stiffened. "But your husband…"

"In the dark," she murmured. "Always in the dark, and always clothed."

He glided toward her. His legs tangled in the breeches still trapped around his ankles. With a grunt, he toppled onto the pallet, pulling her down with him. He cursed, struggled to pull off his boots while she lay beside him and tried to stifle her giggles.

Free of his clothes, he glared at her, then sat on the edge of the pallet and pulled her up to stand between his legs. Because of his height, she only had to look down a little into his eyes.

He gave her a wolfish grin that sent her heart racing. "My turn."

He looked as if he'd eat her in one gulp. She swallowed hard, forced herself to stand still while he stroked his hands over her, and untangled knots and laces with perverse ease. He grasped the edge of the dress at her ankles and lifted the hem until she had to raise her arms for him to pull robe and tunic over her shoulders.

Hands trapped above her head, still blind and shrouded in the soft linen, she felt him shift the cloth to one hand while the other echoed her earlier actions and trailed over her stomach, her breasts. She gasped, pushed at the cloth that imprisoned her.

He licked a nipple, the tip of his beard tickling her belly, and blew cool air over the moistness until the nipple puckered. She moaned and arched to get closer to him. His mouth closed over her breast and he suckled until she writhed with want. A sharp ache grew between her legs. She wanted to pull him closer, wrap herself around him, beg him not to stop, but with her arms still imprisoned above her head, her mouth muffled by the enfolding cloth, all she could do was arch closer, moan louder.

At last, with a low groan, he drew away. She wanted to cry at the sudden abandonment, but he finished lifting off the dress and released her. She wrapped her arms around his neck and latched onto his mouth with hers. She was a fast learner. Remembering his trick with the tongue, she thrust hers into his mouth, determined to torment him as he had her.

He gripped her buttocks, pulled her against him until his hardness pressed against her stomach, then he rose to his feet, lifted her, and deposited her on her back in the middle of the pallet.

She was dazed by the sight of him. Magnificent, she'd thought before. She was wrong. He was more than magnificent. He was...he was...

In one fluid motion, he climbed onto the pallet and over her, caging her between strong arms and muscled thighs. He lowered himself until he nudged the fire between her legs. She'd never felt this desire, this need. She'd never felt this wanted.

She spread her legs wider and invited him in. *Make love to me*, she'd said. And he did. Thoroughly.

~ * ~

Beren didn't know how long he'd slept, but from the smells wafting from the Gather Hall on the other side of the wall, the evening meal had begun. They'd missed the midday meal and slept most of the afternoon away.

Perhaps *slept* wasn't accurate. He'd made love to Zabeth, not once, but several times. She'd responded with all the passion she possessed, giving herself with a generosity he cherished. Everything he did to her, she returned with enthusiasm until they were both too exhausted to move. He remembered one moment, when she'd discovered how ticklish he was and they ended up on the floor, giggling like children.

She stirred and opened her eyes. Green as the sea, he'd thought when he first saw her those many months ago, but today they'd darkened to the mysterious depths of the deep ocean.

As they were doing now.

"What time is it?" she murmured in the same sultry voice she'd used earlier.

"Almost evening. Did you sleep well?" Trite expressions, but when she looked at him in that way, all intelligent conversation fled from his mind.

"Evening?" Sudden panic filled her eyes. "Oh Lord, they'll see us come out."

"What? Who?" It seemed more than conversation had fled his mind.

"*Everyone.*" She pushed away, scrambled after her clothes, and tossed each piece on when she found it.

Beren leaned back and studied her with amusement. "Zabeth, no one will notice. No one will care."

"Elizabeth," she corrected, then stopped, held the remainder of her clothes to her chest, and closed her eyes. "I forgot about this bit."

"What bit?"

She waved a hand. "The after-it's-all-over bit."

He wrapped a strand of her hair around his hand. "But it's not over. It's just beginning."

She jerked, then sighed. With a reluctant smile, she gathered her hair and started to braid it. "You're right. Beginning. I'm just not used to…to being so…public."

He chuckled. "We're hardly doing this in the middle of the Gather Hall."

She paused in her braiding long enough to flash him a nervous grin. "No, I suppose not."

A thought had him sitting straight up. "Are you sorry we did this? Do you regret—?"

"I regret nothing." She pressed her fingers over his mouth. A genuine smile replaced the grin.

Relieved, he kissed her fingers, then pulled on his trews. "Then there's nothing to be nervous about."

When they were both dressed, Beren straightened the pallet, then put an arm around Zabeth's waist. "Perhaps we could meet here again, when others aren't using the space?"

He held his breath while she thought about it. After what seemed an age, she gave him an unexpected saucy smile. "I don't see why not."

She pulled from his embrace, caught his hand, and led him back into the Gather Hall.

~ * ~

Returning to the Gather Hall took all the courage Elizabeth possessed. She imagined everyone knew what had happened, but no one looked up when they appeared. No one whispered behind her back after she passed by. A few of her friends called a greeting as if nothing had changed—as if her whole world hadn't altered irrevocably.

"Beren, Zabeth, come join us," Runa called from a nearby table. She patted the seat beside her. "Have you eaten?"

Beren squeezed her hand. "I'll get the food. You sit."

"Thank you." Elizabeth sat on the bench. Heat suffused her skin and she hoped the light was too dim for Runa to notice her blush.

She couldn't find anything to say, so sat in awkward silence while Runa finished her meal. Over in the nursery Ned cooed at something. The sound made her smile, and when Beren returned with a bowl of stew, she turned the smile on him.

He grinned. "If you're this happy with stew, I can't wait until the next feast."

Elizabeth ignored the blush that didn't want to go away, picked up the wooden spoon, and took a tentative sip. The stew wasn't too hot, thank goodness. After a few bites, she noticed Runa's amused expression.

"Fresh air does wonders for the appetite, doesn't it?" the older woman remarked.

Elizabeth wanted to slide under the table. From the twinkle in Runa's eyes, food wasn't the appetite she had in mind.

Chapter Twenty-One

Years later, whenever Beren remembered that winter, it was as fragments of happy moments. He and Eskil and Astri taught Zabeth how to slide down the snow-covered hills on a piece of tree bark. Often Runa and Zabeth pulled Gudrin and Ned in sleds on the ice-covered river.

One day, the four of them helped Mikkel, Gudrin, and the other children build a snow fort, then took sides, boys against girls, in the subsequent snow battle—that memory always brought a grin to his face, for Zabeth and Astri had led their army to victory and tumbled the losers in the snow until they looked like ice devils.

But the memories he cherished most were the quiet times. Many an evening, Zabeth sat by the fire in the Gather Hall sewing tiny flowers on Gudrin's dresses while the wind howled outside and he sat at her feet carving figures for his board game. Sometimes he spun tales of great Odin and his consort Frigga, trickster Loki, and the thunderous Thor, while Zabeth and her baby listened with rapt attention. Once, Zabeth fell asleep during one of the long feasts and her head dropped to rest on his shoulder.

Best of all, of course, were the hours in the storage area.

Days grew into weeks, weeks to months. Beren was never far from Zabeth's side, but as their time together grew more comfortable, the unspoken tension between them increased.

Beren's plan to distract Zabeth worked so well the appearance of spring took him by surprise. Ice cracked on the stream and slivered over the cliff in cascading daggers. Trees dripped onto frozen ground and drilled tiny hollows that grew into muddy marsh. Sunlight grew stronger, shutters were thrown open, blankets and garments appeared on rope lines behind the Gather Hall. The farmers returned to their farmsteads and the Gather Hall seemed empty without them.

It came as a shock to realize Zabeth spent more and more time looking out to sea, waiting for the *Freki* to return.

"Hasn't she been happy these last few months?" he wondered aloud from his position at the door of the barracks. He stared across the roofs to the upper level of the Gather Hall where Zabeth had returned to her room this morning.

Eskil looked up from the sword he was polishing. Even as a married man he was still expected to take his turn on duty, and the barracks were more convenient for caring for weapons. "Stop fretting. Enjoy the day."

Beren slammed his fist on the door frame. "Enjoy? How can I enjoy when Zabeth is thinking of leaving?"

Eskil placed the sword on his bed. "She can't leave."

"Of course she can," he snapped. "When the *Freki* returns—"

"Beren." Eskil stood and placed his hands on his friend's shoulders. He spoke in a patient tone, as if to a simpleton. "She cannot leave. Your own sword destroyed the 'Link to her home world."

Beren stared at him for a moment, then let his breath out in a long whoosh. His whole body, strung tight as a bow, released the tension. Limp, he sagged against the door frame and gave his friend a weak smile. "I'd forgotten."

Eskil chuckled. "And you thought I was obsessed with Astri. That's nothing to your obsession with Zabeth."

"I am not obsessed with Zabeth." *Am I?*

Eskil dropped his hands. With a shrug, he returned to the bed, picked up his sword, and slid it into the sheath on his belt. "Fine. You're not obsessed. Coming to breakfast?"

"No. I'll join you later." Beren flopped onto his bed and laced his fingers behind his head. Was he obsessed with Zabeth? Or was what he felt for her something more?

"Eeleezabeth," he murmured. The name came easier to his tongue now, although in his thoughts she'd always be Zabeth. The other name, her true name, had a musical quality to it, and whenever he said it to her, she gave him such a smile it made his heart leap with joy.

Obsessed? No. He was beginning to fear it was more than that. More, even, than simple lust. Was it so terrible, this…obsession? Once Zabeth accepted the truth, she might be more open to accepting a future with him.

He sat up, swung his feet off the bed. He imagined them together, in a house he'd build for her. They'd wake in the morning, tangled together. He'd reach for her, stroke her hair, her cheek. She'd snuggle into his embrace, fit herself to him as if they were made for each other. Later they'd curl up in front of a roaring fire, him and Zabeth and little Ned. It no longer surprised him the child had become a natural part of the dream.

He sighed, blinked away the image. Impossible. Zabeth would never be completely his. No matter how much he wished it, she'd never forget her husband, never allow herself to find pleasure in the arms of another man, at least for more than a short time. In a way he reminded her of Kiana, who always put duty before personal happiness.

But Kiana found a way to join both. The memory made him pause, but he shook his head. *That was different. I wasn't her own child, just someone she'd sworn to protect.*

No, Zabeth would have a hard enough time coming to terms with her exile here. Did he want to burden her with his growing affection for her? She needed time, so he'd give her time. Once she was settled, once she accepted her life here, then he'd reveal his feelings.

~ * ~

Now she was able to use her own room again, Elizabeth looked forward to the evening. After the meal, she'd take Ned upstairs, tell him a bedtime story, sit with him until he fell asleep, then shift a wooden screen in front of his cradle to shield him from what went on in the big bed if he woke in the night.

No more struggling to keep quiet in the storage area. At last, there was true privacy here.

At first she felt shy inviting Beren back to her room with Ned asleep a few feet away, but the thought of not being with Beren was even harder to bear. In anticipation of this moment, a few weeks ago she'd asked Per One-Hand to build the screen. When he'd delivered the panels, she was impressed by the beautiful, delicate flowers carved alone and in bunches over its surface.

In her opinion, no artist of her own world could have made better, and she told him so. Payment was settled with a promise to embroider Maili's betrothal gown. The romance between Astri's plump friend and the burly carpenter had taken everyone by surprise, including Maili herself, as she'd confided when Elizabeth delivered the betrothal dress.

"I never even knew he was interested." She sighed. "I hoped, but was afraid I was wrong. He was the one who kept leaving me the daisies."

"Are you interested in him?" Elizabeth asked.

Maili stuttered and blushed. "Yes, but everyone said he'd never take a wife because of his missing hand, that he didn't want to burden a woman with half a man."

"But you don't see it that way?"

Maili's blush deepened. "You don't need two hands to please a woman as long as you're skillful with the one you have."

Elizabeth joined Maili's giggles. "He's certainly skillful with his carpentry tools," she said after they'd both calmed down. "This screen is beautiful. He's very talented."

"That he is," Maili agreed, and dissolved into more giggles.

Now Elizabeth picked up the betrothal dress and studied the hem. Two more daisies left to finish it. Because of Maili's size, there was more material to embroider than usual, but Elizabeth didn't mind. She liked the cheerful tanner's daughter and wished her well.

For a moment an image swam into her mind, a baby with green eyes and golden sun-kissed skin. With a wistful sigh, she banished the image. She wanted children, lots of them, but not here, not now. She made sure she drank *keevah* with her evening meal to prevent any *accidents*, as the other women called them.

But is that what I want for the rest of my life? Sooner or later, she had to make a choice—return home to a second marriage sure to be more loveless than her first, or stay here with Beren and an uncertain future.

She closed her eyes. *Is the price of loving Beren too high? Can I give up a future for Ned?*

It meant living in sin without any promise of a Christian marriage, against all she'd been brought up to believe. She shook her head. *This is nonsense. There's no choice to be made. As soon as the ship comes back, I'm taking Ned to England. If losing Beren is the price, then so be it.*

A knock at the door announced Beren's arrival. Her heartbeat accelerated. She banished her doubts and called for him to enter.

He slipped inside, then closed and bolted the door while she gathered up the embroidery and put it away for the night. When he turned around, she was ready for him. She threw herself into his arms and kissed him. Tonight she'd have no doubts. Tonight she'd enjoy the moment.

"I missed you," she murmured when he let her go.

He grinned. "I was only in the upper meadow. Eskil wanted to practice his archery." He looked around the room. "Your son?"

"There." She indicated the screen, then pulled him toward the bed. "Are you tired?"

"What do you think?" He lifted her by the waist, tossed her onto the mattress, and followed her down.

A short time later, Beren shouted his release, but a fitful cry from behind the screen dampened Elizabeth's own climax. Instantly she squirmed from beneath Beren and padded naked to the crib.

Ned's eyes were closed. If it was Beren's shout that woke him, he'd returned to sleep at once. Elizabeth tucked the blanket under his chin. After one final look at her sleeping son, she emerged from behind the screen.

Beren lay on his side, his head propped on one hand as he watched her. The woolen blanket covered his lower half and left his chest exposed. "Aren't you cold?" The words were delivered in a tone reminiscent of a purr.

For a moment, Elizabeth's mind went blank. Why would she be cold?

Oh. Oh!

Her face hot with embarrassment, she scurried to the bed and slid under the covers. Beren chuckled and ran a finger down her bare arm.

"You know," he murmured, "if you have to have Ned sleeping here, we'll need to make other arrangements."

Outraged, Elizabeth sat straight up in bed. "Other arrangements? You want me to send my son away?"

A puzzled expression crossed his face. Then he smiled and shook his head. "You misunderstand." He tugged her arm and after a moment she let him pull her back down. "I know you want him with you. I'd never ask you to send him away, but we shouldn't always be afraid of waking him up."

"Oh." She had to admit the thought of Ned a few feet away tended to dampen her enthusiasm, maybe a little bit. Mollified, she caressed his cheek, rubbed her palm against his beard. "You're important to me, too, but I don't like leaving him in the nursery all the time."

"Not all the time, no, but perhaps occasionally?" He grinned. "As for the rest of the time, I have an idea."

Wary, she narrowed her eyes. "What idea?"

He gathered her hair in one hand and pulled her down to him. "Later."

Then he rolled on top of her and kissed her. When she was breathless, he used his hands and mouth and body to make her forget what she'd been about to say. They managed to stay somewhat silent this time, with soft moans and cries muffled by lips. This time Ned stayed asleep.

Later, she sighed, pushed against his shoulders, and sat up. "We should get some sleep. You need to leave."

He caught her hand. "One more time?"

She glanced along his length, then sighed. "It will be dawn soon. You have duties, and I have chores."

He echoed her sigh but rose, pulled on his breeches, and walked to the door. "Will you have Ned with you tomorrow night?"

The question made her wary again. "Yes."

He nodded. "Then I'll bring something to use as gags." She opened her eyes wide in shock. He walked back, kissed her on the nose. "That way, little minx, I can do all sorts of interesting things to you, and no one will hear you."

After he closed the door, she muttered, "Why couldn't you have thought of that in the storage area?"

Chapter Twenty-Two

Spring in Denmark, Elizabeth mused one morning, was almost as beautiful as spring in England. Brown grass turned green, flowers dotted the edges of the forest, leaves sprang out to cover bare branches. Even the sun had more strength these days, warming land and skin.

Astri had suggested a picnic. Beren was cloistered in the Keeper Hall but that didn't stop Eskil from bounding inside and dragging him out. He looked…annoyed, but the frown vanished when he caught sight of Elizabeth.

She stood at the top of the steps and held tight to a squirming Ned. She gave Beren a tentative smile. "Astri invited us to a picnic. Will you come?"

Astri didn't give him a chance to answer. "Of course he will. We need someone to help you with your packages."

Two bundles rested at Elizabeth's feet. The smaller one held things for Ned.

Beren returned her smile, then picked up the two bundles and shoved the smaller one at Eskil. "Lead the way."

Eskil smirked and took Astri's arm.

While they walked, Elizabeth stole sideways glances at Beren. Every time she saw him, he seemed more handsome than the time before.

They left the village by way of the southern trail, Eskil and Astri in the lead, holding hands, followed by Elizabeth and Beren. The trail twisted through the surrounding forest and eventually arced back toward the sea and the higher cliffs.

She heard the waterfall before she saw it. The trail gave a sharp turn to the left, and there it was.

A lake lay before them, round, as if a giant ball had scooped out the earth and filled it with water. From the cliff above, a waterfall dropped from an unknown source deep within the ground, emerged through a narrow chasm, and fell into the lake. At the opposite end, closest to the sea, a stream disappeared into the trees. Was it the one that fed the series of waterfalls Beren had shown her last fall?

"It's beautiful," she murmured. "A perfect place for a picnic."

Ned struggled and stretched his arms toward the ground. His intent was obvious. He wanted down.

Astri pointed to a wide stretch of mossy grass a few yards away. On one side a gentle slope led toward the lake. "How about over there?"

It didn't take long to get settled. Astri opened her bundle and unfolded the ends to unroll a large blanket. She laid it on the ground and spread out the food—a loaf of bread, a hunk of cheese, berries and dried fruit from the last of the autumn harvest, and some hand pies. Elizabeth's larger bundle contained strips of dried fish and venison, jugs of mead, and mugs from which to drink it.

Elizabeth held Ned by his waist and lowered him. His arms and legs were moving before he even touched the ground. The moment she let go, he crawled off, his goal the lapping waters of the lake. Laughing, she chased him and herded him away from the danger. Ned squealed, clearly enjoying the game. He crawled through Astri's legs and sat behind her, chattering in his secret baby language.

Beren chuckled. "He's fast."

Elizabeth circled behind Astri, but the child rolled onto all fours and sped toward Beren.

Beren swooped on the child, scooped him up, and tossed him into the air. Ned squealed with laughter. Beren caught him and set him back on the ground. Elizabeth's mouth dropped open in surprise. She'd never seen him act so…so carefree around her son.

"He used to do that to Gudrin, but not when she was so young," Astri observed.

Ned looked up at Beren, rocked onto his knees, grabbed Beren's trews, and hauled himself to his feet.

"Oh," Elizabeth gasped. Everyone stopped to watch.

Perhaps startled at finding himself standing, Ned looked at his mother, then took an uncertain step toward her. She held out her arms to him, but after one more step, he dropped back onto his bottom. He looked around, spied Beren again, and gurgled something in a demanding tone.

"You've started a habit," Elizabeth accused with a laugh in her voice.

Beren gazed at the child and Elizabeth swore a mischievous twinkle appeared in his eyes. He retreated. Ned crawled after him, stopped when Beren stopped, and held up his arms. Beren took another step back. Before long, he was skipping backward around the blankets while Ned chased him.

Astri burst into laughter.

Beren caught his foot in a root and sprawled on his back. Sensing victory, Ned crawled over his legs and up his body. He ended up on Beren's chest. The baby leaned forward and grabbed Beren's beard.

"Zabeth," Beren gasped, and she realized he was laughing so hard he couldn't speak more than that single word.

She hurried forward and lifted Ned. "Are you all right?" She wasn't sure whether she spoke to Beren or her son.

Beren grinned and gave a quick nod.

"Let's eat," Astri called. "I'm starved."

Elizabeth glanced at Beren once more. Until now, he hadn't had much to do with her son. His enjoyment with Ned had surprised her and her heart gave a leap. Had she found a man who would accept them both? Had she found a man who could love them both? Perhaps time would tell.

~ * ~

Beren sat up, chose a pie, and bit into it. He'd enjoyed playing with the child, more than he'd expected. When Ned gazed into his eyes, his heart had fluttered as hard as it did when he looked at Zabeth. Was his affection for the son as strong as for the mother?

Eskil plopped down beside Astri and took a bite of the fruit she held in her hand. He glanced over at Beren. "We can make him a pen under those trees after we finish eating. That should keep him away from the water."

Beren nodded. Ned crawled into Zabeth's lap and made sucking noises. She opened the smaller bundle and removed a water skin. Runa must have given it to her, since she was the only one in the village who had such things. The other women were suspicious of any Shadow trade that concerned their children, although they'd embraced the things called *diapers* one of the female keepers had traded for three summers ago.

Zabeth attempted to feed her son and herself at the same time. The baby kept grabbing at the pie she held, and once she almost dropped it, but instead of being angry, she laughed and shifted the pie out of reach.

Eskil stood. "Come on," he said to Beren. "Let's build that pen."

While he and Eskil wove green saplings into an airy fenced area, Astri played with the baby, which allowed Zabeth to finish her lunch in peace.

Once the pen was finished, Zabeth transferred the food to one blanket, carried the other to the pen, and spread it on the ground inside. Astri placed the child on the blanket. He crawled around for a few moments, exploring this new space, then, as if exhausted by the day's activities, he curled up with his thumb in his mouth and closed his eyes.

Astri and Eskil returned to the picnic area and began to disrobe. Zabeth looked the other way. When they were down to their undergarments, they linked hands, ran toward the lake, and plunged into the water.

"Cold." Eskil gasped. Astri laughed and flung herself at him so they both toppled into the deeper part of the lake.

While his friends played, Beren leaned back on his hands.

Zabeth watched the two frolic in the water. "They seem so happy together."

Beren nodded. "Astri was right. This was meant to be." On impulse, he turned to Zabeth. "Is that what it was like between you and your husband?" He hadn't meant to ask, but he didn't regret the question. He wanted to know.

He held his breath.

~ * ~

The query took Elizabeth by surprise. She glanced at Beren, but by his expression and tone it was genuine interest, not idle curiosity, which had prompted the question.

All winter she'd managed to keep her relationship with Beren lighthearted. She'd convinced herself this affair was a surface thing, short term, without commitments, but Beren wasn't a casual acquaintance.

She craved him like a miser craved gold, and it was madness, for soon she'd have to leave him. She couldn't allow anything serious to grow between her and this Viking warrior. By the end of winter she'd almost managed to convince herself she felt nothing for him, but each time she saw him or heard his voice or, God help her, made love to him, her heart fluttered with joy, as if she were still a maid fresh from the schoolroom.

At those times she forced herself to remember her son, her obligations. It hadn't worked then. It didn't work now.

She'd never seen Beren so handsome, with his warm eyes gazing at her with interest, but what intrigued her at that moment was a hint of anxiety in those brown depths. Was the man jealous?

A sense of power slid through her, but she repressed the urge to smile. After all, there was no future for her with Beren, so why encourage the man?

Instead she thought back over her two years with David. Two years. Was that all it had been? It seemed like a lifetime.

"I thought so, at first," she said at last. "David was always attentive, always so…kind."

Beren shifted closer, as if offering silent support.

"We met at our wedding," she continued. "I'd seen him before, at local balls, but we traveled in different social circles. He was the son of a duke. My father was only a viscount. I was never so surprised than when my parents told me they'd contracted a marriage with him."

"You didn't meet your husband until the day you wed? How could you marry someone you didn't know?" Beren sounded confused.

"That's how it always works in the aristocracy." *I shouldn't be surprised at Beren's reaction. Different cultures, remember?* "At least David was close to my age. Some of my friends were married to men decades older than them. Unlike most couples, we liked each other, and the more I got to know him the more I grew to respect and admire him. He took care of me. He was gentle. We laughed together often." She paused and glanced at the pen where Ned's reddish curls were visible through the lacy fence.

"What changed?"

She sighed. "I gave him an heir. All David's attention switched from me to Ned. Oh, I didn't mind," she hastened to add. "But...I suppose I'd grown used to being the center of David's world. When Ned was born, David became...I don't know...aware of something outside his immediate world. He'd always been a dreamer. He was the youngest of three boys, you see, and had no obligations to make him serious. Even when we married, he just exchanged a mother to look after him for a wife to do the same. I made sure his home was ordered, his needs were met. But when Ned was born, I think David realized he had a responsibility to someone other than himself. He was still kind to me, but his focus was all on Ned."

"And that made you sad." It was more statement than question.

She shook her head. "No, not sad, not exactly. Perhaps a little jealous, and also a little hopeful."

"Hopeful?"

She gave a small smile. "As I said, David was a dreamer. He had this dream to move to the Americas, build a rich empire for himself there. When Ned was born and David began to change, I thought he'd given up that crazy idea."

"He hadn't," Beren guessed.

"No. A month after Ned was born, David told me to prepare for the move. Ned's birth reinforced his dream. I was still very fond of him, but...not as much. When he died—" She broke off, took a few deep breaths.

Beren leaned forward and rested a comforting hand on her arm. Desire zinged through her.

So much for not letting him affect me.

Beren's voice was full of concern. "Don't go on. If it hurts you…"

"No." She straightened her back, swallowed. "No, I have to say this. It's been eating at me for months." She shook off his hand and raised her chin. "When David died, I grieved, I really did. But deep down, I felt…relieved. And that made me feel disloyal, to my husband, my marriage vows…"

"You felt guilty."

She nodded. "I didn't realize, not at first. And when I did, I tried to deny it." She looked at Beren and her lips curved in a puzzled smile. "I don't know why I'm telling you this."

He smiled, a gentle smile full of understanding. "Do you feel better?"

She was silent for a long moment. Did she feel better? "Yes," she said. "Yes, I do, a little. I was dreading telling his family when we got home, but now, I think I can face them."

He was silent for a few moments, then he asked, his voice soft and hesitant. "Would you like me to visit you after…after you go home?"

"Yes." She didn't have to think about it. The idea of never seeing Beren again disturbed her more than she imagined. If he'd still visit…it wouldn't be so bad.

Going home wouldn't be bad? What had put that into her head? Going home was good. Going home was what she wanted. Her life was there, as was Ned's. She was doing this for Ned, for his future. Whatever she wanted was nothing compared to his needs.

What my son needs and what I want for myself are two different things. If she was honest with herself, she wanted to stay here, and if not for Ned, she would. She might even let her friendship for Beren grow into something more.

It already has.

Abruptly she pulled back from that dangerous precipice. She didn't need to choose between Beren and Ned. Her son was her first priority. He needed to grow up in a civilized land, a Christian land, and he needed his mother there to look after him. After all they'd been through, she couldn't bear to surrender him to a governess or nanny. He was her son, her flesh and blood, while Beren was just…

The meal she'd eaten formed an aching lump in her stomach.

Beren was just the man she loved.

She stared at him now while he watched her, his eyes full of concern. Why did she suspect once she got home she'd never see Beren again? He wouldn't visit her—he had more important things to do with his life—and she wouldn't be allowed to visit him. It would be over. All of it.

Soon she'd be home, and the one man she'd ever love gone from her life forever.

Beren raised his hand and ran a finger down her cheek to wipe away a tear she hadn't felt until now. "Eeleezabeth?"

He traced her jaw line, slid his finger under her chin, and tilted her head up. She stared into his eyes. She'd never before noticed the tiny flecks of gold swimming in the brown, flecks that swirled and danced and drew her into their depths. His cedar scent enveloped her when he leaned closer.

Pulse pounding, she parted her lips to gasp a breath. His beard tickled her chin and she swayed toward him. *Kiss me.*

Lips touched, feather light, burned. Heat flared deep within her. There was a roaring in her ears, a deep drone as of a thousand trumpets in a fine orchestra. Beren stiffened and raised his head.

Not a thousand trumpets. One trumpet, a horn that echoed against the hills around them.

"Odin's eye," Beren muttered. He rolled off her and rose to his feet.

Still drugged from the overwhelming emotions, she couldn't understand what was happening. Why had he stopped? Why—?

"The *Freki*," Beren said. The harshness in his voice made her look at him and she thought she saw a flash of disappointment in his eyes.

Elizabeth sat up. Euphoria receded. Confusion reigned for a moment, then it, too, disappeared. "The *Freki*? The trading ship?" Her way back to civilization. Ned's way home. She'd waited months for the chance to go home. That chance had arrived.

Shouldn't she feel excited?

Astri and Eskil dashed up to them, dripping water.

"Did you hear?" Astri pulled her tunic over her wet underthings. "The ship's back."

Eskil grabbed his trews. "It's about time."

It's too soon.

But Elizabeth rose and gathered up Ned's things. Beren dumped what was left of the picnic foods into a blanket and bundled it up. When Elizabeth lifted Ned, still sleeping, from his pen, she was surprised to find her hands shook.

Beren stepped beside her and held out his arms. "I'll take Ned."

She stared at him. It was the last thing she'd expected him to say, but she studied his face. There was calm reassurance in his eyes. He understood this was important to her. With a grateful sigh, she transferred Ned to Beren. Ned woke, then snuggled against Beren's chest and fell back to sleep.

Astri and Eskil finished pulling on stockings and boots and picked up the bundles. Beren turned toward the trees. Strangely empty, Elizabeth trailed behind him.

She was going home. Why did the thought make her sad?

Chapter Twenty-Three

Beren arrived at the beach in time to see the prow of the *Freki* appear from behind the headland. Zabeth had decided not to come to the beach. He suspected she was nervous about meeting the crew of the ship she expected to take her home, so had taken Ned back to their quarters.

If only the *Freki* hadn't returned so soon, but Tor always did have an uncanny sense of timing.

"Did you lose Zabeth?" Eskil pushed through the crowd.

"She said she'd meet everyone at the welcome feast tonight." Beren glanced around. "Where's Astri?"

Eskil jerked his chin toward the far end of the beach. "She wanted to talk to Runa."

"There it is!" Gudrin jumped up and down beside Beren. He hadn't noticed her dash up. "Can you see them? Can you see?"

Beren grinned at his sister's enthusiasm. "I can see. There, at the bow."

Gudrin strained her neck to look where he pointed. The *Freki* had cleared the headland now. Over two hundred feet in length, it had been constructed from pieces of *The Hammer*, the ship Tor had brought to this new world, and wood cleared from the forest when the village had expanded.

Sleek and fast, the vessel combined the swiftness of a warship with the deep hull and large storage of a trading knorr. Its length required two square sails, each reinforced by horizontal strips of red, and the power of a Shadow engine installed in its stern. When the ship angled into the shelter of the bay, both sails swung on their masts until they were parallel with the long edge of the ship. The crew worked in unison to lower the sails and lash the canvas to the cross-beams.

Men lined up on the deck. The ship was still too far to recognize faces, but Beren didn't need to see his heart-father's face to recognize Tor.

A giant of a man stood at the prow of the ship. One hand rested on the neck of the dragon-carved bow. His blond hair hung in several braids across his shoulders, and his beard came to three braided points on his broad chest.

Tor Olafsson, captain of the *Freki*.

Beside him stood a slim woman in black leather. Her long black hair hung, as usual, in a tail down her back, and left her golden-hued features bare to wind and spray. Beren smiled. Kiana was more than Tor's wife. She was his equal in fighting, intelligence, and curiosity, and the closest thing Beren had to a mother since he was five.

Already greetings were shouted. Closer came the ship, skimming over the shallow water despite the deep hull.

The ship scraped bottom, and half the crew jumped over the side and surged toward shore dragging ropes which they flung on the sand. Several women in the crowd dashed into the water, Runa among them. They flung themselves upon the men, kissing and hugging, laughing and crying. The crew who remained on the ship hurried to secure it to the anchor poles before they, too, abandoned the deck.

Olaf and Leif scrambled over the side and loped up the beach. Before Beren realized what his brothers intended, they surrounded him with a combined hug and squeezed until he gasped for breath. He laughed, pushed them away at arm's length. To his surprise, he had to tilt his head to look up at Olaf. Leif hadn't gained inches but he'd filled out. No longer the lanky fourteen year old, his body had caught up with his long legs and arms.

"You've both grown." Beren clasped arms with each brother, approving the strength in their grip, the new muscles rippling under skin.

Both babbled at once, trying to out-do each other in the telling of their adventures.

"Enough." The single word, spoken in a calm voice, silenced the two. They glanced at their father, who had followed them off the ship. Tor smiled to take the sting from his reprimand. "There'll be time enough for tales later." He glanced at Gudrin, who had gone quiet. "No greeting for your father, little imp?"

She stared up at him, eyes wide. "I forgot you were so big." At the men's laughter, she turned to Kiana. There was no hesitation here. She flung herself at the woman. "*Mama*."

Kiana knelt on the sand and enveloped her daughter in a hug. She buried her nose in Gudrin's hair and sniffed. "Oh, you smell so good, little one." She threw Tor a smile full of laughter, "I've yearned for the smell of something other than sweaty men." Gudrin giggled, although Beren was sure she didn't understand the jest.

"Did you see my dress?" Gudrin pulled back and spread the ends of her dress wide.

Kiana and Tor dutifully admired the dress. Kiana traced the embroidered edge. "Are those roses?" she asked.

"Zabeth made them." Gudrin hurried on, oblivious of the puzzled looks from her parents. "She does *em...embroidery*." She spoke the last strange word in Zabeth's language, and Kiana raised her gaze to Beren. "And she lets me look after Ned. He's growing too and almost walking."

Tor kissed his daughter's cheek. "It seems you've had as many adventures as we have. You can tell us all about it later." He glanced at Beren, the unspoken command clear to read. *You can tell us about it now.*

"Why don't you show Olaf and Leif where the bath house is," Kiana suggested to her daughter. "I'm sure they've forgotten where to find it." She smiled at the boys, who grinned and followed Gudrin to the village.

Already most of the crowd had dispersed, families taking their husbands and wives, sons and daughters, home for a private reunion after so long apart. There'd be a huge celebration tonight, but for now it was enough just to be home. Runa passed close to Tor but didn't seem to notice her brother. She had her arm around the waist of her husband, Vider, and the two disappeared up the beach in the wake of the rest of the village. The small family was left alone on the beach. For a few moments no one spoke.

Beren braced himself and straightened his shoulders. "Welcome home."

"It's good to be home." Tor studied his adopted son. "So, who are Zabeth and Ned?"

Guests from a Shadow world. Beren opened his mouth to say as much, but the words that came out were, "Zabeth is the woman I'm going to wed, and Ned is her son."

~ * ~

Elizabeth stayed in her room until it was time to descend to the Hall. She changed twice, discarded a plain brown robe for the more formal blue robe Astri had given her for the banquet nights. Tonight she'd meet the captain of the ship that came in today. She'd have to persuade him to take her home as soon as possible.

Oh, it wouldn't be right away. They'd been gone a long time. The crew would want to spend time with their families before they set sail again, but *she* wanted to get a promise from the captain tonight. Everything depended on her persuasive powers. Garan didn't believe it safe to sail so soon after the end of winter, but she was determined. So much depended on tonight. No wonder she was nervous.

It had nothing to do with Beren, or the fact the captain was Beren's father. No one knew what was between them. *Nothing* was between them, she corrected, just…just physical attraction.

She glanced at where Ned crawled on the furred carpet. The sight of his small, lovable face strengthened Elizabeth's resolve. She was going to take him home, to his family, no matter what it took. Not even her …fondness…for Beren was enough to stop her.

She finished braiding her hair and ran shaky fingers down her robe to smooth away the wrinkles. She stared at herself in the mirror. She couldn't do any more. If she wasn't ready now, she'd never be.

"Mama, Mama," Ned chanted. A tug on her skirt made her look down in time to see him use her skirt to clamber to his feet and lean unsteadily against her legs. "Mama, Mama, Mama."

"Oh, Ned." Laughing, she scooped him into her arms and settled him onto her hip. He grabbed one of her braids and used it and the back of her arm to steady himself. "Are we ready?"

Her voice shook, but she quelled the emotions. She'd waited for this day for months. She trembled because she was excited. There was no other reason for her to have to fight back tears.

Ned shoved a fist into his mouth and drooled around a happy smile.

"You've got another tooth?" She removed his fist and ran her finger inside his mouth along the gum line.

Sure enough another sharp point announced a new tooth ready to break through. She picked up the wooden rattle he loved and let him chew on that.

"You'll be ready to eat bear steak soon." She took a deep breath to fortify herself, then strode to the door. "Right. Let's get this over with." She settled Ned more firmly on her hip, opened the door, and headed toward the stairs.

The Hall had never seemed so full. Even at midwinter, when all the village slept together, the Hall had looked half empty. Not so now. With the return of the warriors, the village had almost doubled in size.

Elizabeth descended at a slow pace, searching the crowd for familiar faces. Runa sat with a blond-haired man near the middle of the first table, with Mikkel, Astri, and Eskil beside them. That must be Runa's husband. What was his name again? Oh yes, Vider.

Garan and Freya sat at the head table, with another man and woman beside them. Gudrin sat on the man's knee and cuddled into his arms. These had to be Beren's parents. The man looked like a typical Viking, with blond hair and beard, but the woman's dark hair and skin showed an unmistakable resemblance to Beren.

All of a sudden, Elizabeth was overcome by shyness. She hesitated on the bottom step until Beren approached. "Would you sit with me, Eeleezabeth?"

Relief mingled with excitement when he held out his hand.

"Be-be-be," Ned gurgled, and stretched out his arms.

Beren glanced at him, smiled, and plucked the child from her. To her surprise, he lifted Ned onto his shoulders and held him there with one hand. Ned giggled. Elizabeth's nerves settled.

She placed her hand in Beren's and allowed him to lead her through the crowded benches. Many of the faces were familiar, but many were not. The crew of the *Freki* watched her with open curiosity.

Strange. Weren't they the ones who'd rescued her and brought her here in the first place? Their expression suggested they'd never seen her before.

Conversation died away when she moved farther in. Beren led her toward the head table. When nerves overtook her and she pulled back, he squeezed her hand.

"It's all right. They don't bite." He leaned closer and whispered. "Unlike me."

She choked back a laugh and tightened her grip on his fingers. She must be hurting him but he didn't say a word. She raised her chin and marched forward. At the empty space before the table, Beren stopped.

"Thank you, Beren," said Garan.

Beren nodded and squeezed Elizabeth's hand again, silent reassurance he wouldn't abandon her.

The man who sat beside Garan rose and came around the table to stand before her. Taller than Beren, he had a square chin, deep blue eyes, and a scar on one cheek. His resemblance to Runa was striking, though unlike his sister, a few gray strands streaked his blond hair and beard.

"So you are Zabeth." He had a soft, gruff voice.

"Yes. You must be Tor, father to Beren and brother to Runa. I've heard many things about you." She didn't know where she got the courage to speak in such a bold manner, but she wanted to show she knew how to be as courteous as he.

He grinned. "You cannot believe half of what is said, and even less from my family. They see all my flaws."

She smiled in return. "I've heard nothing but good about you, sir."

He raised an eyebrow in disbelief. "That I find hard to believe. I am a hard task master, a tyrant of a ship's captain, and a bully of a father. Not to mention a stubborn and impossible brother and husband." He grinned, tossed a wink over his shoulder at his wife. "But I welcome your astute judgement and hope you will teach my critics how to look beyond the surface." He turned to Ned. "A handsome child. May I?"

Without waiting for permission, he held out his hands. Ned hesitated, clung for a moment to Beren's hair, then peeked up at Tor.

"Well, little one?" Tor asked in a soothing tone. "Do you want to come to this old man?"

Ned squirmed, leaned forward over Beren's head, and launched himself into Tor's arms. The older man swung the child in a circle over his head. Ned squealed in delight.

"Come Beren, Zabeth. Join us." Tor strode back to the table, sat, and perched Ned on his knee.

Elizabeth glanced at Beren, who gave her a smile of encouragement. She followed Tor.

The woman rose and hugged her. "I am Kiana. I'm pleased to meet you. Has my son been treating you well?"

"Um, yes." Memory of their nights together flashed into Elizabeth's mind. Her face heated and she prayed the dimness of the hall hid the telltale blush. "Yes, very well, thank you."

When she was seated, she turned to Tor. "I want to thank you for rescuing us and delaying your voyage to bring us here."

Tor looked puzzled for a moment, then smiled, as if he'd forgotten. "It delayed us little. I'm glad you've recovered." He shifted to allow Ned to bang his fists on the table. "Eat now, before the food gets cold."

The celebration that followed was even bigger than the midwinter feast. Rabbit, fish, quail, and venison all made their appearance at the table, along with platters piled high with vegetables—carrots, corn, peas, and cabbage. Bread and jars of honey battled for space with bowls of nuts and berries.

While she ate, Elizabeth looked over the company. Many of the single men and women were paired off now with others from the ship—husbands, wives, lovers. Children gathered around long-absent parents. Mothers fussed over sons and daughters who'd experienced their first voyage.

The sight reminded her Gudrin had learned English from her mother, and her mother, Kiana, sat right next to Elizabeth. She leaned toward the woman and, for the first time in months, spoke English. "I want to thank you for teaching Gudrin English. It was very helpful when I first arrived."

Kiana smiled. "Ah, my little surprise," she replied in the same language. "Gudrin is a quick study."

"She speaks it well. Have you been to England?"

"No, but I travel a lot and meet many people who speak many languages."

"Ah." *Wouldn't it be amazing if Kiana had met Jason on his Grand Tour?*

But Kiana denied meeting Elizabeth's brother.

Curiosity prompted Elizabeth's next question. "Why is Gudrin a surprise?" The comment had puzzled her.

Kiana laughed. "My boys came quickly and I expected no more children, but then nine years later Gudrin decided to join us so...a surprise."

They both laughed, and then Kiana asked about Ned.

The two women spent the next few hours trading baby stories. Kiana told Elizabeth about Olaf's first word, *no,* and shared the tale of sleepless nights when his first tooth came in. Soon Elizabeth knew she'd found another friend.

As the evening progressed, couples drifted away. Even the newly-returned skalds begged release from duty to recount the adventures of the trip until the next night. They too had spouses to go home to.

Every time Elizabeth thought about asking Tor when he'd take her home, either her nerve failed her or someone distracted her. When she noticed her son had fallen asleep in Tor's arms, curled against his lamb's-wool vest, she realized she'd run out of time. She'd have to wait until tomorrow.

"I'd best put him to bed." She lifted Ned from Tor's arms. He fussed a bit, but soon settled back to sleep on her shoulder.

Kiana rose. "I'll walk you back to your rooms."

There was no reason to refuse, so, with an apologetic smile at Beren, Elizabeth nodded and led the way.

They chatted as they climbed the stairs. Kiana opened Elizabeth's door for her and followed her inside. After laying Ned in his cradle, Elizabeth covered him with a blanket. Kiana stroked a finger over his reddish-blond hair.

"So soft, and such a lovely color." She gave a wistful smile. "I'll have to wait for grandchildren before I can feel this again."

Back in the main part of the room, Elizabeth walked Kiana to the door. "Thank you for...for everything. If your ship hadn't come along when it did, Ned and I wouldn't be alive."

"I'm glad you're safe." Kiana looked around the tidy room.

"You seem to have settled in nicely. Do you like it here?"

Elizabeth smiled. "I do. But I'll be glad to get home." She hesitated, then plunged ahead. "Do you know how long before someone can take me?"

Kiana shrugged. "Let's talk about it tomorrow."

"Of course." This was Kiana's first night on dry land. It was natural she'd want to spend time with her family. "I'm sorry to take up your time." Elizabeth offered her hand. "I hope we can be friends, for the short time I'm here."

Kiana looked at Elizabeth's hand, then clasped her wrist in the Viking manner. "I hope so too."

Chapter Twenty-Four

The next morning, Beren sat with his parents, Chieftain Garan, and Keeper Magrim in Magrim's quarters in the Keeper Hall. A fire burned in the small grate and a tube of glowing purple lit the room. Despite the warmth, Garan was wrapped in a heavy shawl. From the way the chieftain rubbed his leg, Beren suspected it pained him more than usual.

"So." Tor glared at the chieftain. "You've had all winter to tell her. Why haven't you?"

Kiana laid a hand on his. "Don't shout, love. We don't want the whole village to hear."

He grumbled something under his breath.

"I've been hoping she'd settle here before we had to tell her the truth," Magrim said from his seat beside the fire. He exchanged a look with Garan. "She didn't know enough of our language at first, and then winter came and it never came up."

"Beren said she saw the gray man," Garan offered.

They all turned to Beren and he explained how Zabeth had seen Gudrin dancing.

"That child." Kiana chuckled. "She's infatuated with the creature."

"And she didn't think it strange?" Tor asked.

Beren shook his head.

"She has a strong mind," Kiana noted. She lowered her voice, her next words for Beren alone. "I like her."

Flustered, Beren forced himself to continue as if he hadn't heard. "I also told her about the sky ship, so she didn't stumble into it unawares."

"What did she say to that?" Tor asked.

Beren shrugged. "I don't think she understood."

"She's stubborn," Magrim said. "I've talked to her a few times when she was translating some of our scrolls and books. She…how can I put it? She doesn't allow herself to believe everything she hears. She needs proof."

Tor thumped a fist on his knee. "Then that's the solution. We show her an actual trade, through a Shadow-Link."

"Even that may not work." Kiana held up a hand. "I've seen it before, even among my own people. Those who won't believe or don't want to believe don't see the magic. They come up with all sorts of silly explanations."

"Still," Garan said. "It can't hurt to try."

Tor nodded. "She has to accept it sooner or later." He shot a look at Beren. "Nothing can go forward until she does."

He means she won't accept me as her husband. Beren clenched his hands into fists. *This has to work.*

~ * ~

Later that morning, after leaving Ned in the nursery, Elizabeth met Runa in the kitchen. The older woman looked tired but happy. Her whole body radiated an indefinable contentment Elizabeth realized had been missing the last few months.

"Good morning, Runa." Elizabeth sat in her usual place on the bench by the wall and took out her embroidery. She'd promised Gudrin she'd stitch roses on the dress the child's father had brought back from the trip.

Runa raised her attention from the dough she worked. "Is that Gudrin's dress? You shouldn't indulge her so, Zabeth. You'll spoil her."

Elizabeth smiled. "Blame your brother. He's the one who brought her the dress. I'm just adding a few stitches."

Runa sighed. "Yes. Tor spoils all his children."

"Even Beren?"

"Of course." Runa's expression was puzzled. "He treats all his children equally."

"Then why—?" Elizabeth broke off. "Sorry, it's none of my business."

Runa paused in her kneading. "You do not need to be afraid to ask questions. How else will you learn?"

Encouraged, Elizabeth continued. "I wondered why he—Beren—didn't go on the trading voyage. I would have thought as the eldest it was his right."

Runa frowned and concentrated on her dough. "That is a question you must ask Beren."

"Oh." Was it that sensitive? Elizabeth returned to her embroidery. She threaded a thin steel needle Runa had told her came from a land far to the east. There were several seamstresses in London who'd give a fortune for such a fine needle. She'd have to ask if they traded such things in England.

For a few minutes, the two women worked in silence while Elizabeth made the delicate stitches of the tiny red flower and Runa flexed her muscles while she prepared the dough for tonight's meal.

There weren't as many people eating in the Hall today. Families who'd stayed there while their warriors were at sea had now gone back to their own homes, so the dough was half that needed all winter. Enough people remained, however, to require the usual kitchen duties.

At last, Elizabeth took the last stitch and bit off the end of the thread. "Do you think I could talk to your brother today?" She shifted the hem of the dress and began another flower.

Runa looked uncomfortable. "Do you wish to leave us so soon? The seas will still be rough. It might be dangerous to take Ned on such a dangerous voyage."

Surprised, Elizabeth looked up. "The ship looks stable enough. It got home safely."

Runa wiped her flour-covered hands on her apron. Her expression was troubled. "The seas are still rough. Vider said they should have waited another month for them to calm before attempting the return, but everyone was anxious to get home. Still, I suppose you could talk to Tor today. He might not want to sail again so soon."

"Oh, I don't expect him to leave right away." Although she wished otherwise, it was unreasonable to expect everyone to bow to her wishes so soon after coming home. "I want to ask, to know when…" *When I can leave this paradise and go home to a stable, respectable, dull life.*

Runa lifted the shaped loaves onto the paddle and slipped them into the oven. "I suppose it can't hurt to ask. He'll be busy with the ship for the next few days, though. I understand the keepers are going to attach the wooden wings they retrieved from the raider ship."

As if she sensed when she was expected, Gudrin appeared in the doorway. At a nod from Runa, she climbed onto the bench to sing. She'd grown over the winter.

The first time Elizabeth had seen Gudrin on this bench, her short legs had dangled halfway to the floor. Now her toes grazed the stone flags.

Elizabeth finished the second rose, but before she could leave to search for Tor, Astri burst into the kitchen. She flung herself at her mother, hugged the woman, and swung her around in a circle.

"I saw Sonja, as you suggested, and she said yes!" Astri almost sang the words.

Runa gave a happy cry and kissed her daughter on the cheek. "I'm so happy. Have you told Eskil?"

"Right now." Astri hugged her mother again and danced from the room.

Runa sank onto the bench beside Elizabeth, still smiling.

"Good news?" Elizabeth asked. From the glow on Astri's cheeks and the brief conversation, she already guessed the answer.

"Astri is with child." Runa laughed, jumped to her feet, and spun in a circle. "I'm going to be a grandmother."

Elizabeth rose and hugged her friend. "Congratulations. You'll make a wonderful grandmother."

Runa fanned her face with both hands. "Look at me. I'm as giddy as a spring maid." Her eyes widened. "Oh! Wait until I tell Vider." She tugged off her apron, turned to the door, then spun back. "The bread."

"I'll take it out when Gudrin finishes. I've been doing it all winter." Elizabeth shooed her friend toward the door. "Go."

With a laugh, Runa dashed out.

Elizabeth glanced at Gudrin, who had watched the interchange with interest. She didn't stop singing but rolled her eyes as if the antics of adults made no sense.

Later, just after Elizabeth placed the baked loaves on the trestle table to cool, Gunnar approached and asked her to attend Garan in his chamber in an hour.

Finally.

Hope made her hurry to her room. She stood in front of the wooden chest Runa had given her for her clothes. What to wear? She'd worn the blue last night. The brown was serviceable, but this might be the most important interview of her life.

She settled on the white robe and the white overtunic with blue edging. She'd embroidered the tiny bluebells on the tunic herself.

Elizabeth brushed her hair until it shone, then braided it into one long plait and wove blue ribbons into the strands. Swinging the braid back over her shoulder, she tucked in a few stray strands of hair and headed to the nursery.

She wouldn't take Ned with her. She'd need all her persuasive talents today and, while she loved her son more than anything, she didn't need the distraction. However, she wanted to see him before she left, to remind herself of the stakes.

When Elizabeth reached the nursery, Maili waved and pointed to Ned, who babbled away at two other infants.

"He and his friends are exchanging the latest news," Maili

explained.

Elizabeth raised an eyebrow. "What news?"

Maili laughed. "Only the gods know. Men may deny it all they want, but they're bigger gossips than us women."

Elizabeth smiled. Careful not to step on any of the children, she made her way to Ned, picked him up, and rested him on her hip. When had he grown so heavy? She could have sworn that yesterday he weighed less than a feather.

But then he's almost a year old. His cradle had been replaced by a sturdy crib, small to fit his size but with high sides so he couldn't fall out in his sleep. It had taken him but a few moments to discover how to crawl out on his own.

However, Runa had anticipated the need and had the village carpenter build a pen similar to those used in the nursery to restrain curious toddlers from exploring beyond the safety of their minders' watch.

Since those two tentative steps he'd taken by the lake, he'd no longer been satisfied with crawling. Now every time Elizabeth saw him he was standing up against something, or staggering a few drunken steps before he lost his balance and dropped onto his padded behind. Ned, it seemed, had inherited his mother's stubbornness and determination.

"We're going home, love," Elizabeth murmured. "Soon you'll see your uncles again, and your grandparents."

An image of Beren slipped into her mind, accompanied by a twinge of regret, but, with a determined effort, she banished it. Beren was the past. Ned was her future.

He looked at her with wide eyes. The green hue had deepened as he grew older, the emerald color brighter, more pronounced, not as muddy as in his early months. He regarded her for a moment with an expression that looked almost solemn, then stuck his thumb in his mouth.

Elizabeth shook her head. So much for a serious conversation. She lowered him to the floor and he scuttled back to his friends. With a smile, she headed to Garan's quarters.

The smile faded when she stood outside his door. What if he refused to let her go home, just as he'd refused to send a message last autumn? No, that was ridiculous. Everyone assured her she wasn't a prisoner, and this time the ship was here. She smoothed the wrinkles from the front of her dress, raised her hand, and knocked on the door.

"Come." That deep voice sounded like Tor, not Garan.

She lifted her chin, opened the door, and stepped inside.

Tor stood by the fireplace, Magrim and Kiana beside him. Runa and Freya sat on the long bench opposite Garan.

"Come sit with us, Zabeth." Runa patted the seat beside her.

Elizabeth glanced about the room. So many people, so many solemn expressions. A movement by the window drew her attention away from the tableau in the center of the room. Beren.

Alarm flared through Elizabeth. All her earlier fears rushed back. She couldn't imagine why the chieftain had asked all these people to attend. Tor, yes. He commanded the ship that would take her home. But the rest?

"Zabeth," Runa repeated, her tone gentle, patient. "Come sit with us."

This isn't good. Something's wrong.

With a sinking heart, Elizabeth crossed the room and sat on the bench between Runa and Freya. Both women shifted a little closer until their shoulders brushed hers, offering comfort.

Something was definitely wrong.

Garan cleared his throat and drew her attention. His expression was…sympathetic. If she hadn't known Ned was in the nursery, she might have worried something had happened to him.

"Zabeth, we asked you here to discuss your future." The chieftain's voice shook, as if what he was about to say pained him.

Elizabeth narrowed her eyes. "You're not going to let me go home, are you?" She could think of no other reason for such an odd delegation. It surprised her how calm her voice remained. Inside she screamed with fear and outrage.

Garan exchanged a look with Tor and Magrim before answering her question. His expression, if anything, became more apologetic. "Not for the reasons you might think. We can't."

For all her bravado, she hadn't expected that answer. Stunned, she stared at him. Freya and Runa shifted closer, but Elizabeth leaned forward, away from them. Anger replaced fear.

"Why?" she demanded.

Again Garan exchanged looks with his friends, then he took a deep breath, as if girding himself for a battle.

Battle? He didn't know the meaning of the word battle. *If this is to be a war, I'll be damned if I'm the only one to come out of it bloodied. Nothing will keep me from returning home. Nothing.*

"It is difficult to explain," Garan began, but again broke off.

"Tell her about the trade," Magrim prompted.

Garan swung him an annoyed look. "I will. Don't rush me." He turned back to Elizabeth. "Do you remember the skald's tale of the sky ship?"

She gave a cautious nod. "The hole in the world." She tried to smile at the absurdity of that notion, but the smile wouldn't come. "It was a fine tale."

"It isn't a tale," Magrim declared. "It really happened. I, myself, sailed with Tor. Beren says you've seen the sky ship."

She glanced at Beren, puzzled for a moment until she remembered. "The metal wall that shoots lightning."

"Yes." Magrim pursed his lips. "There was…cargo on that ship. Shadow-Links."

"What the raiders were looking for?"

He nodded. "The 'Links open holes to other…places, other times. You came to us through such a hole, Zabeth. This world you see may look like your own, but it is not. From what you have told us of your land, you have come from far in the future."

Elizabeth snorted. "That's nonsense." Her voice trembled but she took a breath. She was fine. She was not hysterical. *She was not.* She rose to her feet and fixed Garan with an aristocratic glare that would have made her mother proud. "I don't know why you're telling me these wild stories, but it's not going to work. I want you to take me home. Now."

Beren stepped forward. She switched her glare to him. He flinched, but continued closer.

The expression in his eyes frightened her—not amusement, not contempt, but pity, as if he believed Garan's crazy ramblings.

"We cannot take you home," Garan said in a gentle voice. "Your home is not there."

"I don't believe you." Tears pricked her eyes, but she fought them back. "You're lying to me. Why are you lying to me?"

Freya stood and wrapped her arms around Elizabeth's stiff shoulders. "We have no reason to lie to you. Sit. Listen. Let us explain."

She urged Elizabeth back to the bench but Elizabeth resisted.

Beren took another step closer. "Eeleezabeth, please listen to Garan. We have tried to help you in all things. At least listen to what we have to say."

She shook off Freya's arm, straightened her spine, and returned to the bench. She'd humor them, for now, until she figured out why they played this cruel game. She glared at Garan in defiance. "All right. I will listen. But don't expect me to believe."

The tension in the room eased. Garan leaned back in his chair. He looked at Magrim. "Did you bring the 'Link?"

From a sack at his feet Magrim removed one of the strange Shadow-Links the raiders had displayed. He rose and placed it on a nearby table, with the cone-shaped front aimed at the far wall. He touched the top of the box. Across the room, a circle appeared, about twelve inches in diameter, and within it the image of a room. Strange banners decorated white walls. Other than a metal table with clear sides and a birdcage containing a bright yellow canary, the room was empty.

Magrim nodded to Tor, who stood and drew his sword. He strode across the room and stopped in front of the hole.

Tor raised his sword, thrust it into the hole, and tapped it on the metal table.

Elizabeth gasped and shot to her feet. *Impossible.*

"I told you," Magrim said. "A hole. We trade through the 'Links."

Through the 'Links. She approached the hole, walked around it. On the back side of the hole was nothing but a blank circle. Tor's sword had disappeared. She circled to the front and stared inside. The sword did, in fact, rest on a table. "There's another room in there."

Tor nodded. "As real as here, but..." He glanced at Magrim. "But not just a different *here*. Also a different *when*."

She had a swift memory of the smoke on her ship, the light, and the sudden appearance of the room with stone walls. Her breath caught in her throat. One minute on her ship, the next here. A different world. "I came through one of these, to here?"

"Yes." Garan gave a sigh of relief.

"But it's so small."

"Well." Garan shrugged and looked at Magrim.

"We did an...experiment, to make it bigger." Magrim smiled in satisfaction. "It worked."

Elizabeth shook her head, then concentrated on the other fantastic words. "Different here and when. What time? When?" This had to be a dream.

"When we left our home, when the sky ship brought us here..." Tor paused, frowned. "Our seer said it was...it was the year *anno Domini* nine hundred and seventy-two." He stumbled over the Latin, then continued. "We've been here sixteen winters, so it is now..." He paused again.

"988," Kiana said when he began counting on his fingers.

He sent her a grateful smile. "Yes, *anno Domini* nine hundred and eighty-eight." He looked at Elizabeth. "What is the year you came here?"

988? 988 A.D.? Shock had the words circling in Elizabeth's head. *It can't be.* "No," she said aloud.

"What year?" Tor repeated, his tone gentle.

Stunned, she stared at him, then the number tumbled out. "The year of our Lord 1764." She shook her head. "But that can't be right.

That's over seven hundred years. I can't be seven hundred years in the past."

"More than that." Kiana spoke this time, drawing Elizabeth's attention to her. "Zabeth, my people ruled a land long before your time, long before Tor's time. We are not in nine hundred and eighty-eight. We are much earlier."

For some reason, Elizabeth felt like a bird mesmerized by a snake. She couldn't look away from Kiana but dreaded asking the next question. "How much earlier?"

"No one is certain, but the seer thought about three thousand years before Tor's time." Kiana looked at Magrim for confirmation, who nodded.

Three thousand years. The words, the number, seemed meaningless. Except… No, it didn't matter. If this was true, there was an easy fix. "You say I came here through a Shadow-Link," she said to the chieftain. "Then you can send me home through it as well."

He dropped his gaze. "We cannot."

"But it's right there." She waved her hand through the hole and felt nothing, not even a tingle in her fingers. "All you have to do is open the one I came through."

"We destroyed it." Beren's tone was bleak. "*I* destroyed it."

"You?" Elizabeth swayed. When Beren started to approach, she shook her head, locked her knees. *I will not faint.* "Why would you destroy the only way I have to get home?"

Garan cleared his throat. "I ordered him to. My decision. You were followed by…bad men. Violent men. I would not risk them attacking my village."

The pirate. "But…"

"Never before have we opened a 'Link that big." He shook his head. "Never again will we do so." The words were a vow. Implacable.

Beren laid a hand on her arm. "It wouldn't do any good even if it was fixed. It opened onto empty ocean. Your ship being there was pure chance."

She stared at him. "That…doesn't even make sense. If you use these things for trade, why would they open in the middle of nowhere?"

Beren blinked. Elizabeth stared at the faces around her. Most held pity, but also sadness, regret. It was a good act. She still couldn't understand why they spun this fantastic tale. And it *was* a tale. None of it was true.

She shook her head. "It doesn't matter. All right, say I believe you, that I came here through one of your…your holes. Say I believe Tor came here in his ships. Those are large holes, and if you did it once you can do it again. Even if you can't, I can crawl through something that size. But," she hurried on before anyone could say a word, "three thousand years? No, that I won't accept."

Magrim shook his head. "We cannot change where the 'Links open up. There are hundreds of them and we have no way of knowing if any others open to your time."

How convenient. Coming to a decision, she stood and faced Tor. "I want you to take me to England, to my home. By ship."

He frowned. "But we've told you, we can't take you to your home. It's not there."

She lifted her chin. "It will be there, and when it is, my father will reward you for taking care of me, for...for saving my life."

"And if it's not?" Kiana asked.

Elizabeth glared at the woman. "It will be."

Kiana exchanged a look with Tor, who nodded. To Garan he said, "I'll take her in the *Freki*."

Relief made Elizabeth's knees weak, but she refused to sit. "How long will it take?" If the ship was as fast as it looked, she'd be home in a week.

Tor walked over to Magrim. "Did you bring the map?"

The keeper nodded and withdrew a parchment from the same bag the 'Link had come from. He spread it on the table in the middle of the room, the same map he'd shown her the first day she'd visited the Keeper Hall, and beckoned her over. "Where is your home?"

She studied the map, then pointed to a spot half way up the east coast of England. "My father has a holding south of here. A river runs from the coast inland past the manor."

Tor placed a finger on the map, ran it back to the west coast of Denmark. "Two days at most, less if conditions are favorable."

Elizabeth gasped. "Two days? But..."

"The *Freki* is a fast ship," Kiana explained with a smile. "And it uses a Shadow engine."

"Shadow engine?"

Kiana indicated the room still visible through the nearby hole. "We call those places Shadow worlds, and the people we traded with called it an engine. It attaches to the rudder and makes the ship go very fast."

Shadow worlds. Not another country. Another world.

Garan cleared his throat. "How many men will you take?"

Tor tapped the map. "Twenty should be enough. We won't need the oars until we get to the river."

"I'm going with you." Beren stepped forward.

Tor and Kiana stared at him as if he'd said he was going to fly, but Elizabeth wasn't sure how she felt. One thing she did know. She couldn't stay here.

"All right." Tor exchanged a look with Kiana. "We'll provision the ship, give the men today and tomorrow while we fit the wings, leave the day after."

Satisfied, Elizabeth turned to the door. There was never a choice. Ned came first. Even if it meant leaving Beren forever.

Chapter Twenty-Five

The ship plunged into a deep trough. Beren staggered and clutched the rail to keep his balance. Salt water sloshed over the sides. He looked at the vista of endless waves and cloudy skies. The new wing structures attached to both sides of the ship were supposed to help it maintain a smooth balance on the rough seas, but when his stomach lurched, the reassurances fled his mind.

He spun and leaned over the rail. His body cramped and jerked while he spewed the remains of his breakfast. What madness made him volunteer to come on this hellish trip? He wiped the spittle from his mouth and the tears of shame from his cheeks, then straightened and turned around.

Zabeth stood behind him. She held a wet cloth. "Put this behind your neck. It helps."

Wonderful. The last thing he wanted was for her to see him like this. He scowled, snatched the cloth, and slammed it against the back of his neck. The ship pitched to the side and his stomach decided to leap into his throat. He spun back to the railing. This time Zabeth held his shoulders while he retched. *Dear gods, can it get any worse?*

"Why in Odin's name did you decide to come, boy? You know how the sea affects you." Tor's voice held sympathy, not scorn, which made it all the more difficult to hear.

Beren gritted his teeth. "Not helping."

From the moment he'd stepped aboard the *Freki*, his stomach had rebelled. The first few minutes were bad enough when they fought the surf, but once they cleared the headland and hit open water, it felt as if his whole body wanted to turn itself inside out.

A mug appeared in front of his nose. "*Keevah*," Kiana said. "It might help."

It never had, but he obeyed and took a sip…and at once threw it all up again on the deck.

"You'd better lie down," Zabeth said.

She took one arm, Kiana the other, and helped him stagger a few paces away from the side. Someone, Tor perhaps, had built a narrow pallet on the deck, and Beren collapsed onto it with a groan.

For the next few hours he suffered and wished for death. Zabeth and Kiana tended him like a sick child. If he hadn't been so miserable he'd have died from the humiliation alone.

They told him they'd put him in the exact center of the ship, half way from bow to stern and between the sides. This was supposed to be the most stable place, least affected by the pitch and roll of the ship.

It didn't work.

He wasn't unconscious, and listened to their conversations when they thought he slept. His embarrassment grew.

"I wondered why he didn't go on the trading trip with you." Zabeth tucked a blanket around his shivering form.

Kiana sighed. "It wasn't as bad when he was younger, for short trips. But the longer ones…"

Zabeth clucked her tongue. "Yes. I suppose Vikings aren't supposed to get seasick."

"No." Kiana was silent for a moment. "Why do you call him…us…Vikings?"

"Because that's what you…are?" Zabeth looked from Kiana to Tor while the question hung in the air. "It's what my people have always called the raiders from Norway, Sweden, Denmark. In our history books."

Tor chuckled. "I have heard of such books. But we do not call ourselves Viking. That is what we do, not what we are. There is a word, *víkingr*, which is someone who goes *a víking*. But we call ourselves Norse."

"Oh." Zabeth sounded dismayed. "I'm sorry if I insulted you."

"You didn't," Kiana replied. "But you're right. Beren's problem isn't so much he cannot sail, as that he thinks it shameful he cannot."

Well, it is shameful.

"But he can do so many other things." Zabeth sounded eager.

What other things? I'm a warrior who can't set foot on a ship and defend my people.

"He's a great warrior," Zabeth continued. "He defended the people in the Gather Hall when those raiders attacked. And he's hunted bears, the big ones you have here."

"True," Kiana said, pride in her voice.

"And Keeper Magrim tells me he has great skill with the Shadow-Links." Tor's voice. Was that pride? Did he truly not mind that

Beren couldn't sail with him? That he preferred the scholar's path?

"I got the impression you didn't approved." Zabeth again.

Tor chuckled. "Approve? That my son is a great thinker? That he can help us solve the mysteries of those boxes? Anyone can be a warrior, girl. Few can be keepers."

Few can be keepers. The unexpected words were the last Beren heard before sleep took him.

~ * ~

Elizabeth woke the next morning determined to hide any trace of uncertainty about what she was doing. She emerged from the small cabin in the hold of the ship in a clean dress, her hair brushed until it shone and braided into a neat knot at the base of her neck. She wanted to be presentable, the proper lady, when she greeted her parents.

She turned to mention that to Ned, then laughed at herself. Ned wasn't here. Runa had convinced her to leave him behind.

"The seas are still rough," she said, "and the *Freki* is not designed for small children. If you find your family, they can send one of their vessels for him. It will be safer."

Not if. When.

Remembering the harrowing trip through the surf to launch the ship, and the size of the waves when they reached open sea, Elizabeth was glad she'd listened. This vessel was no place for an adventurous child learning how to walk and eager to explore.

Beren stood at the bow. After a restless day and night, broken by occasional retching, he had at last fallen into a more restful sleep. Now, when he smiled at her, he was less pale than yesterday, although strain still showed in his eyes.

"How are you?" She walked up to stand beside him. "You look better."

"I feel better." He seemed surprised at the answer.

She nodded. "Maybe it took time for you to get your sea legs. My brother William had the same problem, but once he got used to the water, you couldn't keep him away from it."

A dull flush darkened Beren's cheeks. Elizabeth placed a hand on his arm. "Thank you for coming. I appreciate having a…a friend with me."

"A friend." He said the words as if they tasted strange.

"Yes." Unsure what else to say, Elizabeth stared at the empty sea. Beren was a friend, just a friend. Yes, there was an ache in her heart at the thought of parting from him, but she suppressed it. She couldn't afford to indulge her own wants. What she did today was for Ned, even if it tore her apart.

The cry of gulls drew her attention to the top of the mast, where several birds circled.

Beren followed her gaze. "We're close to land."

A moment later, the cry came from one of the men on lookout. Elizabeth gazed ahead at a line of dark that speared through the sea-mist.

She leaned forward. "How soon?"

"A few hours yet," Beren said. "We'll be striking land north of where you want to go, so we'll have to travel the coastline for a while."

Elizabeth remained at the prow and refused to leave even for the midday meal. She chewed her bread and cheese without tasting any of it, her gaze fixed on the growing shoreline.

When they were within half a mile of the coast, Tor steered the ship south. Elizabeth stared ahead while they sailed past a deserted shore. She expected to see fishermen already on the sea, smoke from the villages that lined the beaches for miles north of her father's manor. Instead there was nothing, but the absence didn't arouse her curiosity as much as it might. All her attention was on finding the entrance to the river that ran at the foot of her father's grounds.

Finally, "*There.* That's the headland up there." Elizabeth waved her hand at a point of rock that jutted into the sea a quarter mile ahead. "It's called Stag Tor, because it's shaped like the head of a stag with those two boulders on the edge like stunted antlers. Once we round that point, you'll see the river." She shaded her eyes. "We need to sail up it about two miles."

Behind her, Tor give the order to lower the sails. They'd use oars in the narrow passage up the river.

Elizabeth's position at the prow of the ship was deliberate. She was known, recognized by everyone in the area. If they saw her on the ship of her own free will, they'd know the Vikings came in peace and wouldn't attack.

At least, that was the reason she gave to Tor. To herself, she acknowledged that while she stood at the prow with her back to the crew it was less easy to be distracted by Beren. Not that the sight of him affected her resolve, but there was no point in making this harder on herself than she had to.

The ship rounded the headland and there was the river mouth. Tor angled the ship into the delta and gave the order to reduce to half speed.

Elizabeth leaned forward and studied the familiar landscape. Only…it wasn't familiar. At least, it was, but it was…different. Trees she knew as a child were nowhere in sight. Others, taller, thicker, older, stood in their place, unfamiliar yet looking as if they'd been there for centuries.

A cliff jutted into the river and forced the ship to make a wide sweep around it. Elizabeth remembered that cliff. It stood above the ruins of the Roman villa that should come into view any moment now. But the cliff she remembered was softer, more rounded. One side had sheared off centuries before and left tumbled boulders and pebbles where she and her brothers had played as children. The surface she looked at now was sharp and new, as it might have looked before the quake that shifted the rocks.

Puzzled, Elizabeth searched the bank for the ruins.

"Are you all right?" Beren stood beside her. She hadn't even heard him approach.

She nodded but the uncertainty persisted. "I guess I've been away longer than I thought. Things look…they don't look the way I expected." She pointed. "See that rock? Just past there, there should be some stone steps leading up from the river. The Romans built a villa there centuries ago. From the river you can see some of the columns. They're covered with ivy now, but…"

The ship slipped past the rock, but the bank remained unchanged. There was no sign of steps, stone or otherwise, carved into the sides.

"Maybe it's farther up," she muttered.

Beren curled his fingers around her hand. Without thinking, she returned his grip, steadied by the solid touch of him. Something wasn't right, but she refused to acknowledge the tale of her fall through time. She felt rather than heard Tor move up to her other side.

"Zabeth." His voice was gentle. "Remember what we told you. This land…this is not the land you know."

"Don't be ridiculous. I grew up here. I should know where I used to live." But a twinge of doubt fluttered her stomach.

Tor exchanged a look with Beren. "Where, yes. This is where, but it's not when."

"Not that again. Does this look like three thousand years in the past?" Even as she said the words, reality proved her wrong.

Beside them the bank flowed past in unbroken greenery. No Roman ruins. No broken steps. They'd arrived at the stretch of river where she'd grown up. She'd recognize the curve of that land anywhere. She used to sit for hours under that overhang studying her brothers' books while they splashed the afternoon away in the water.

Above the overhang was a patch of bare ground where one could glimpse the roof of her father's manor. She glared in fierce concentration at the land and willed it to show her what she wanted.

There was nothing there.

"But…it should be here," she whispered, bewildered.

Tor ordered the ship close to the bank. Beren jumped over the side into the shallow water and held up his hand.

Elizabeth didn't hesitate but followed him over the side. Not even the shock of the cold river water in her boots eased the numbing chant that circled through her head. *Home should be here. Home isn't here. Home* should *be here.*

When they climbed the bank and more of the landscape became visible, the numbness receded. Elizabeth ran, pulling Beren behind her, faster and faster, through a meadow full of bright daisies and sunny buttercups, past a group of saplings where a grove of ancient trees used to stand.

She tore free of Beren's grip and dashed past more trees before stopping in the middle of a bigger meadow. Refusing to believe her eyes, she spun around and around, seeking the familiar, finding nothing of what she knew.

Gone. Gone. Gone. The chant resumed in her head.

"No!" The cry escaped, torn from her very heart. She stopped spinning, sank to her knees. "It can't be gone. It can't be gone." Over and over she whispered the words, as if repeating them could change reality.

"Eeleezabeth." Beren's voice. An anchor.

She raised her head. He stood, an indistinct figure blurred through tears, an arm's length away, then he dropped to his knees in front of her, but didn't touch her. She stared at him.

"Where did it go? My father's home, my family? This…" She stared around her at the unbroken meadow. "This is where it should be." She gestured. "The stables are there, the chapel there, the kitchens—" Her voice broke and she couldn't go on.

Beren pulled her into his arms and held her while she struggled to regain control.

"Where is it?" she whispered. "Where is everyone?"

"Nowhere," he replied.

She pulled her head back to look at him. His expression was somber, his eyes filled with…pity?

She shoved him away. "It's not true. Tell me it's not true. Tell me!"

Unable to stop the impulse, she threw herself at him and pounded his chest with her fists. He didn't defend himself, but held her until finally, exhausted, she collapsed into tears. He gathered her close and rocked her gently.

"I didn't know what you would find," he murmured. "None of us did."

"My home. Where did it go?" She had to know what had happened.

"Nowhere. It didn't go anywhere." When she looked up, searched his face, he continued, his expression troubled. "It isn't here yet. A different time, remember?"

"Time—?"

"Can you walk?" He took her arm.

The question had no meaning for her. "Walk?"

He helped her to her feet and led her back to the river. "We'll talk on the ship."

Elizabeth was too stunned to resist.

Moments later they clambered over the side and onto the deck. Tor thrust a mug of *keevah* into Elizabeth's hands.

"Drink," he ordered.

She downed the liquid without protest, but unlike previous times it didn't ease the pain within her, the numbness. She let Beren lead her to her cabin, let him help her sit on the edge of the bed. Tor and Kiana followed close behind.

"I'm sorry, child." Kiana sat on the bed beside her. "We did tell you."

"It's all true, isn't it?" Elizabeth pressed the heels of her hands to her eyes.

"Yes." Beren squatted in front of her, pulled her hands away from her face and held them.

"I'm never going home, am I?" She forced herself to ask the question.

Beren ran his hands up and down her arm. "No. Is it so terrible, having to stay here? You told me once you were sailing to the sunset lands, what you call the New World. You wouldn't have been able to see your family then, either."

"At least I'd know they were still alive."

He leaned forward. "But they are. Don't you understand yet? They're in a different world, a different time. They haven't died. They haven't even been born yet."

He was in on this...whatever this was. This conspiracy. The sense of betrayal left her breathless until the numbness vanished on a wave of rage. "You knew." She jumped to her feet, pushed at Beren. "*You knew.* All this time and you didn't tell me."

He held up his hands, took a step back. "You didn't have the words."

"I had enough to understand *you're trapped here.*" She pushed him again. "Get out. I don't want to see you anymore."

Beren's widened his eyes. "But—"

"You lied to me." Beren opened his mouth but she pointed a finger at him. "Not telling me things—that's a lie of omission and it's still a lie." She glared at Tor and Kiana "Out. All of you. *Out.*"

Without a word, Tor opened the door of the cabin and slipped out, Kiana behind him.

Beren backed toward the door. "Zabeth—Eeleezabeth—you are not thinking clearly. I know this is a lot to understand. When we get back to New Asgard, things will look better."

On a wordless scream, she snatched her wooden training knife from her belt and hurled it at him. He slammed the door before it hit.

Chapter Twenty-Six

The return journey was faster than the outward. The wind was behind them now, and aided the Shadow engine with a steady push on the sails, as if it knew they needed to get home as fast as possible. To his surprise, Beren found himself enjoying the voyage.

Once in a while, they hit a deep trough and his stomach threatened rebellion, but the threat felt weak and he was able to ignore it. Perhaps all he needed was a long enough exposure to the sea to overcome that embarrassment.

Zabeth hadn't left her cabin since they'd departed her land. She'd refused to see anyone, refused to eat or drink.

Beren paced the deck and cast frequent glances at the hold and the silent cabin. Was she all right? Was she sad? Angry? He wouldn't blame her. She'd had no choice in what happened to her. His only consolation was that if he hadn't enlarged the hole, if the 'Link hadn't brought her here, she and her son would be dead. Now they were alive and if the gods were kind… But he had a bad feeling the gods would not be kind.

The next morning, the *Freki* arrived at New Asgard. To Beren, the village had never looked so good. Already people ran to the beach and shouted to their friends. He shaded his eyes while he looked for Runa.

Yes, there she was, with Vider beside her and Gudrin at her feet. Even young Ned stood on the ground instead of being held. He leaned against Runa's legs, his fists wrapped around her skirts for balance, much as he did with his mother.

A noise behind him made Beren turn his head. Zabeth stood on the deck. She'd re-braided her hair but now let it fall down her back. She held her head high, but there was an unnatural brightness in her eyes that tugged at his heart. He wanted nothing more at that moment than to stride over and take her into his arms, promise not to let anything bad happen to her, ever, if she'd smile at him.

As soon as the ship entered shallow water and the crew spilled over the side, Zabeth strode forward. She allowed Tor to lift her to the wooden dock, then stood there and stared around her.

"Mama, Mama." The high-pitched voice drew her attention, and with a cry, she ran to her son, lifted him, and hugged him tight. She buried her face in his hair, but not before Beren glimpsed a sheen of tears.

A moment later, she straightened. Runa said something to her, but she shook her head. Holding tight to Ned, she hurried toward the village.

Tor placed a hand on Beren's shoulder. "She's going to need you. Stay close."

"I will." He'd be there for her, whether she wanted him or not.

But she wasn't in the Gather Hall, or her room. In the end, one of the women by the well pointed him toward the forest.

Why did Zabeth go up there?

While he ran, memories invaded his thoughts—Zabeth bewitched by the rainbow falls, learning how to fight, and weeping at the loss of her home.

And then another memory slipped into his head—Ned clinging to his trews, taking his first tentative steps, and trying to say his name.

Beren stumbled, caught himself in time and continued on, but that last memory left him dizzy with discovery.

Was it possible he loved the boy too, not just tolerated him for his mother's sake?

The answer came like a burst of light. Yes. *Yes*!

He stumbled again, trembled. Gods, how could he have been so blind? Zabeth and Ned were one. He couldn't separate them, wouldn't want to separate them. Zabeth wouldn't be the person she was—stubborn, willful, protective—if not for Ned.

And Beren wanted them both. She was his lifemate, Ned the family he'd always yearned for. Joy filled him and threatened to make him stumble again. Impatient to see them, he forced himself to run faster. He had to catch Zabeth, had to tell her what he'd discovered.

But what if she still doesn't want me?

His steps slowed for a moment, then sped up again. It didn't matter. He'd still love her, love them. If she didn't want to have anything to do with him, he couldn't blame her after what she'd been through. After all, he was the reason she was here, the reason she was *trapped*—her word—here.

No matter what she decided, he still had to tell her how he felt. If she didn't want him after that…

It will tear me to pieces, but I'll let her go.

~ * ~

With Ned on her hip, Elizabeth picked her way over the protruding roots and fallen leaves that slicked the trail. Another woman might have run blindly into the forest, bent on finding a place to sort through her tangled thoughts. Another woman wouldn't have stopped to claim her son, instead preferring solitude.

But Elizabeth didn't consider herself to be like other women. She prided herself on her intelligence, her ability to think things through in a logical manner.

All right, perhaps she hadn't been very good at the logical part these last few months, but now she couldn't afford to make a hasty choice. Not that there was a *choice*. If she couldn't go home, what could she do? Ned was part of her life. She needed him with her now, to remind herself of the reasons on which she based her decisions.

The trees parted to reveal the sparkling reflection of the lake and the splashing waterfall. Was it only a few days ago she'd been here? The day the *Freki* returned to New Asgard, the day Ned took his first tentative steps…the day Beren kissed her and she'd come perilously close to abandoning her plan to go home.

As she stood by the water, she remembered the way Beren had pretended to run away from Ned. He'd been relaxed around her son, then. To her it meant there was hope.

Ned squealed, struggled to be let down.

"No, you can't go in the water." She carried him back up the bank to the edge of the trees.

The saplings Beren and Eskil had woven together still formed the crude playpen. Elizabeth lowered Ned onto the grass inside the pen. At once he crawled to the saplings, pulled himself up, and sidestepped around the pen using the fencing for balance. A caterpillar just out of reach caught his attention and he sat to watch the fuzzy creature.

Satisfied he couldn't do himself any harm, Elizabeth walked a few steps away and stared at the lake. She crossed her arms under her breasts and watched the wind-blown ripples while she tried to make sense of her situation.

She couldn't think on the ship. The shock had been too fresh, and she'd been unable to order her thoughts. Now, though, she felt calm enough to look at her situation. Her world had been flipped upside down. Fantastic as it seemed, she had to believe what she'd seen. She'd come here through a hole in space…*and time*. And there was no way back. She and Ned were on their own. No family. No home.

No obligations. No expectations.

No, not on their own. There were others here who were friends—Runa, Astri…Beren. Some, perhaps, more than friends.

We can leave, try to find another village where we'll be welcome, where they don't hide the truth.

But…*this* village felt like home now. She contributed already by working with the keepers. She translated their texts and if she stayed, once she'd mastered their script, she'd be able to write down the translations without someone else to help. Ned could grow up here and adopt their ways, become a Viking.

Just like Beren.

The thought made her pause. Beren wasn't born a Viking, yet he'd grown up with these people, adopted and accepted their ways, as they had adopted and accepted him. He was a good man. Strong, intelligent, thoughtful. Loyal to his friends. Yes, he'd hidden the truth from her, but who'd believe such a fantastic tale? When it came to it, he was the man she couldn't get out of her dreams.

And what about Ned? In all the time she'd known Beren, he'd shown remarkable patience with her son, and also with Elizabeth's protective instincts.

Her room in the Gather Hall was filled with the shells she'd collected from the beach, the dresses she decorated for her friends.

She remembered a phrase from her childhood lessons: …*where you live, I will live. Your people are my people, your God*— No. She clutched her cross. She'd not go so far as to follow their gods. That she *would not* change, but other things… Yes, she was willing to change other things. This was her home.

"*Zabeth.*" Beren stood at the edge of the forest. His face was flushed and he panted as if he'd run all the way from the village. *Which he probably had.* Dirty and sweaty and looking every inch the barbarian he was, nevertheless, the sight of him made her heart beat faster.

"Zabeth—Eeleezabeth—please listen to me." He strode into the clearing, then stopped, clearly unsure of his welcome.

Elizabeth took a step toward him but forced herself to stop. He was the one at fault here. Let him come to her.

He came forward at a slower pace this time. In his eyes she read desperation and…something else. Fear?

Elizabeth raised her chin, but it took all her control to suppress the hope. "That's close enough."

He stopped a few feet away. He looked miserable. "I'm sorry. You were right. We should have told you sooner."

"Yes, you should have." The way his voice trembled broke her resolve. "I understand why you did it, but…I should have insisted."

He licked his lips. "We were wrong. Can you forgive us, forgive me?"

A harsh voice answered from the trees behind them. "Too late for that. Right now he'd better want to keep you and your brat alive."

Beren stiffened at the same time as Elizabeth whirled toward the sound. At first all she saw were three dark shapes in the shadows of the trees. Then one of them moved and the sunlight glinted on metal. The man held a knife in one hand, and he clasped Ned to his chest with his other arm.

"*Ned.*" Elizabeth lunged forward, but Beren caught her around the waist and held her back.

"Don't," he whispered in her ear. "Raiders. They'll kill him if you move."

Heart thudding in her chest, she had no choice but to watch when the three men emerged from the shadows. Two others appeared behind them. All but the one who held Ned drew their swords. Beren's arm twitched and she knew he longed to draw his own sword. Instead he pulled her closer to him until she felt the pounding of his own heart.

She wouldn't panic, wouldn't repeat the mistake she'd made the last time she'd seen these raiders. She forced herself to calm and assessed the situation. She and Beren were still far enough from the men that if Beren pushed her out of the way, she'd have time to run for safety while he engaged the raiders. He might be able to hold them off, perhaps even defeat them, but he wouldn't be able to stop them killing Ned first.

It occurred to her Beren's heart beat in fear for her son's life as well as her own. Ned stood between escape or capture. Beren had chosen capture.

In that instant, she loved Beren more than ever before.

"What a pretty couple you make," sneered the warrior who led the pack. He pressed the point of his sword under Elizabeth's chin and forced her head up. "I told you I'd be back for you."

Creltak. She hadn't recognized him under the layer of grime and filth he'd used to blend into the forest. The raider's gaze swept over her body, and Beren's arm tightened around her waist. Every muscle in his body tensed. His breath hissed against her ear.

Creltak chuckled and shifted his sword to Beren's throat. "Drop your sword, boy, or I'll have my men spit your brat in front of your eyes."

They think Ned is Beren's son. Is that good or bad? It doesn't matter. At the moment, everything is bad.

Ned squirmed against the man who held him. "Mama," he wailed, reaching for her.

Creltak spared Ned a brief glance, then turned back to Beren.

"Your sword, boy."

Beren released Elizabeth. With slow movements, as if reluctant to follow orders, he pulled his sword from its leather scabbard. He didn't drop it, but bent and placed it on the ground, never taking his gaze off Creltak. When he straightened, one of the raiders darted forward and snatched the sword.

Beren glanced at Elizabeth. "I'm sorry," he murmured.

She nodded, gave a half smile. This was no time to indulge in hysterics. She needed a cool head.

"You will take us to the Shadow-Links now," Creltak ordered. His gaze flicked to Elizabeth and her stomach churned in sick disgust. "If not, this woman of yours will die, very slowly, very painfully. After my men and I have taken our fill of her."

Two of the men strode forward, grabbed Beren's arms and forced them behind his back, then bound his wrists with leather cords. He didn't struggle, but he glared at Creltak with a hatred so intense Elizabeth was surprised the raider didn't burst into flames.

"Mama! Mama!" Ned's wails escalated to screams. The raider shook him, but Ned didn't stop.

"Shut him up before someone hears him," Creltak snapped.

"No!" Elizabeth leaped forward, but Creltak caught her and pulled her against him.

Beren struggled but was knocked to his knees. She stared up at Creltak in fear.

"Please," she begged. "Give him to me. He'll be quiet with me, I promise, only don't hurt him. I'll do anything you want if you spare him."

Creltak was a bully. If he believed he controlled her through Ned, just as he controlled Beren through her…

"Wait," Creltak ordered.

The man froze in the act of raising his knife. Creltak studied Elizabeth. "Please," she whispered. She didn't have to pretend her terror.

A calculating glint appeared in Creltak's eyes. "Anything?"

Don't panic. "Y-yes. Anything."

A wordless cry erupted from Beren. "Touch her and I'll never show you the way."

Creltak smiled. Without removing his attention from Elizabeth, he addressed the frantic Viking. "I'll do more than touch her if you don't cooperate, boy." He ran a finger down her cheek. She shuddered. He released her, stepped back, and jerked his head at the screaming child. "Go get your brat."

Elizabeth wanted to run to Ned, but she forced herself to walk toward the man who held him. "Come to Mama, love," she crooned, and lifted her arms.

The man released his grip and Ned flung himself at her, buried his face in her shoulder, and sobbed. She rubbed his back, murmured soothing words.

"Enough," Creltak ordered. "You, boy. Lead the way. Your woman will be right behind you. Lead me wrong, or try anything I don't like, and you know what I'll do to her."

Beren glared at him, then shuffled forward. When he passed Elizabeth, he gave her an encouraging smile. Her own smile was strained.

"Don't do anything foolish," she murmured.

He shook his head. "Nor you." Then he was past her and headed into the trees.

Elizabeth avoided Creltak and hurried after Beren. The five raiders followed her. Ned, safe once more in his mother's arms, soon settled down, but he kept looking at the strangers behind them. Did he wonder who they were and somehow knew they meant him harm?

Her heart still raced. They'd survived so far, but they weren't safe. There had to be a way to help Beren, but all she had was a useless wooden training knife, not even sharp enough to cut the bonds that tied his hands.

Without knowing where the Shadow-Links were stored, she couldn't tell if they headed in the right direction. Every once in a while Beren stumbled. With his hands bound behind his back, he seemed to have trouble keeping his balance. Did he have a plan? Were there hunters in the hills he led them toward?

They reached a short incline covered in mud. Beren took two steps up. His feet slipped from under him. He fell and slid back down. Elizabeth rushed forward to help him up.

"Be ready to run when I tell you," he whispered.

Leave him? "But you're tied up."

He stared deep into her eyes. "I can slow them down. Get back to the village. They'll protect you there."

Creltak grabbed Elizabeth's arm and pulled her away. "Stop your whispering," he snarled. "Or I'll forget how nice I'm being."

She shook free. "At least let me help him up."

He glanced at Beren, who struggled in vain to regain his feet. He chuckled. "Why not? You're not going anywhere."

He shoved her toward Beren. She only just managed to keep her balance, and Creltak chuckled again.

She placed Ned on the ground with a stern warning not to move, then stepped behind Beren and slid her hands under his arms and around his chest.

Heaving and slipping, she finally managed to get him back on his feet. She retrieved Ned, who for once had remained where she'd left him, and resumed her place behind Beren.

Two of Creltak's men pushed past her and pulled Beren up the short incline while the rest of them followed. They released him at the top and drifted back to their former positions. Beren stumbled forward again.

Creltak stalked up behind her and she braced herself. He touched her between her shoulder blades, ran his hand down her back and squeezed her buttocks. "I'm wondering, girl, just how much you care for that child of yours."

She shot him a glance filled with all the hatred in her heart. "Enough."

"Enough to…" He bent his head and whispered in her ear.

Bile rose in her throat. Lida's words from her first training session came back to her. *There are ways to disable a man when he's that close to you.* Several of those ways presented themselves to Elizabeth, but none of them took into account a child in her arms.

Creltak raised his head and laughed. "Get used to the idea, girl. We'll have a chance soon enough to test that so-called mother-love you claim."

He dropped back a few paces and left her to shudder and struggle to breathe.

A few minutes later they came to another slope, this one going down. At the bottom, a narrow log spanned a stream strong with the force of spring melt racing toward the distant ocean.

Beren threw Creltak a scathing look, sat on the slippery mud at the top of the incline, pushed off with his bound hands, and slid to the bottom.

It looked as if he'd tumble into the stream, but he slewed around at the last minute and skidded into the brush that lined the trail.

Creltak grasped Elizabeth's arm and pulled her to the side of the trail where it wasn't as muddy. There he released her to make her own slow way down the incline, while he and his men followed on both sides of the trail.

At the bottom, she once again helped Beren to his feet.

Creltak arrived beside her and pulled her away from Beren, then stared at the narrow log.

"That doesn't look strong enough to hold the brat, let alone a man." He spun on Beren. "What kind of trick is this?"

"No trick. This is the way. The log's stronger than it looks." Creltak's expression remained skeptical. Beren shrugged. "If you don't believe me, send one of your men over."

Creltak scowled. "What kind of fool do you think I am? That log gives way and I lose a warrior."

"And then there'd be only four of you to handle a bound man and a helpless woman," Beren jeered.

The raider's face flushed deep red. He hauled back his hand, turned, and struck Elizabeth. She staggered and fell, but twisted to keep from falling on top of Ned. Beren jerked forward but Creltak's sword was already at his throat.

He froze. Stunned, tasting blood on her lip, Elizabeth pulled herself to her feet. Ned whimpered, but she murmured a few words and he calmed.

Creltak stood back, sheathed his sword. "Your woman crosses first."

"Wait—" Beren began, but Creltak grabbed Elizabeth's arm and shoved her toward the log.

"Move," he snarled.

She stared at the log. From bank to bank it stretched perhaps ten feet, but it might as well have been a hundred. It was wide enough to place one foot in front of the other if a person was careful.

She took a step forward but Creltak snatched her arm. "Wait." Before she knew what he intended, he plucked Ned from her arms and thrust him at one of his men. "Try anything and I'll kill your brat. Understand?"

Mouth dry, she nodded.

"It'll be all right, Eeleezabeth," Beren murmured.

That was all the reassurance she needed. She placed one foot on the log. It didn't wobble, didn't roll. It seemed sturdy enough, despite its flimsy appearance.

Creltak took a pace forward. "Woman—"

"I'm going." She took a deep breath and lifted her other foot onto the log.

It held, but for how long? She inched her way farther. The frothing water that rushed beneath made her dizzy, so she forced herself to look at the far bank. She continued forward, sliding first one foot ahead of her, then bringing the other one behind. No sound came from the men behind her.

Step. Slide. Step. Slide. It became a chant in her head and drowned out the sound of the water, her own nervous breathing. At last, she reached the end of the log, and with a sigh of relief she stumbled off and turned to flash a grin of triumph at Beren.

Creltak grunted and pointed to the smallest of his men. "You next. Take the brat."

The man glanced at the log, then at Elizabeth. "If she can do it, so can I."

He sheathed his sword, slung Ned over his shoulder like a sack of grain, and ignored the child's indignant squawk. Then he stepped onto the log and strode across it with confidence to the other side. As soon as he reached the bank, she darted forward and took Ned from him.

"Now you, boy," Creltak ordered, and thrust Beren toward the log.

He hung back. "I can't cross it tied like this. I'll fall in and you'll lose your guide to the Shadow-Links."

Creltak snorted. "Nice try, but I'm not about to free you. Valtr, take him over."

A wiry man, not much bigger than the first man to cross, grabbed Beren by the collar of his tunic and shoved the Viking onto the log. They shuffled forward.

Beren swayed, as if he couldn't keep his balance. At the mid-point of the log, he staggered, then, with a yell, knocked into the other man and both fell sideways into the water.

Chapter Twenty-Seven

Elizabeth screamed.

Creltak cursed and sprang to the edge of the stream. She also dashed to the stream. The raider on her side of the river followed and stood beside her. His sword was still sheathed, but she took little notice. She scanned the churning water and searched for a dark head. The stream hadn't looked too deep. Why was it taking them so long to surface?

A man on the opposite bank shouted and pointed. She followed the direction of his finger. A body tumbled through the water farther downstream.

She clutched Ned with one hand and stuffed her other fist into her mouth. *Beren*. The body didn't move, didn't attempt to swim but…she stared. The body wasn't as big as her Viking, and the hair was a different color and unbraided. *Not Beren*. Where was he?

"Find him," Creltak roared from the other bank.

One of the remaining men edged onto the log. As he passed the middle, a hand appeared from the water, closed around his ankle, and jerked him backward. The man yelled and flailed his arms, then crashed into the stream.

A moment later, Beren surged from the water at her feet. The remains of the leather cords still dangled from his wrists. A knife, somehow obtained from the first guard, gleamed in one hand.

He threw the knife. The man beside her gurgled, clutched at his chest, and toppled forward. Beren pulled himself from the river. On the other bank, Creltak cursed and sprang onto the log.

Beren bent over the dead raider and drew his sword, then jerked the knife from his chest and shoved it into Elizabeth's hand. "Run."

She needed no further urging. She ran. The trail ahead opened into a cleared space where another trail crossed it. She glanced at the sun to get her bearings. The sea was somewhere to the west, so she turned left and plunged into the trees. The shouts faded behind her but the clang of swords echoed through the forest. She stumbled, lurched to a halt.

She remembered those sounds on the ship when David was killed. *Run*. David had wanted her to run, and he'd died.

Beren had told her to run, but by the time she returned from the village with help...

A sob escaped her. He couldn't die too!

Ned squirmed in her arms, whimpered. She had to get him to safety. If Beren failed, they'd be after her next and she wouldn't let Creltak get his hands on Ned again.

But she couldn't leave Beren. She rocked on her heels, stared ahead, then back. What to do? Which way?

She looked at Ned. Could she leave him? He might be safe here if he didn't move, didn't make a sound. If she went back to help Beren, the odds were good they'd both die. Ned would be left with no one, and what if he wasn't found? He'd die here in the forest from starvation or exposure?

But if anything happens to Beren, I don't know what I'll do. She couldn't live without him. It was the same choice all over again. Beren or Ned? The answer wasn't as clear as it had been a few days ago.

The sound of footfalls on the trail coming from the direction of the village pulled her from her trance. Had the raiders gone around her? She placed Ned on the ground, ordered him to stay still, and crouched in front of him, the bloody knife slick in her hands but held steady, the way Astri had taught her.

Two figures emerged from the trees. Relief flooded through Elizabeth. "Runa. Thank God."

The older woman rushed to Elizabeth. "What is it? What's wrong?"

"Raiders...Beren...fighting them." Elizabeth managed to get the words out between frantic sobs.

Runa turned to her companion. "Gudrin, run to the village. Tell them raiders are here."

Elizabeth picked Ned from the ground and straightened. "Wait. She can take Ned—" But the little girl was already sprinting back the way she'd come.

"He'd slow her down," Runa explained. "You go on." She pushed Elizabeth in the direction of the path.

Elizabeth expected Runa to follow her, but when she didn't hear the woman behind her she glanced over her shoulder. Runa stood on the path, her head raised to the heavens in prayer. In her hand she held a short sword.

"No." Elizabeth dashed back and grabbed Runa's arm. "What

are you doing?"

When Runa faced her, her fierce smile made Elizabeth drop her arm. "I'm going to help my nephew. It's been a while but I'm sure I remember my training. I still have my sword." She touched the point of the blade and added in a low voice. "I always have my sword."

Elizabeth was horrified. "You can't go there. You'll be killed!"

"He's my nephew. His mother saved me many years ago. Now I can repay the debt." Runa strode toward the trail.

For a moment, Elizabeth stared after her, her mouth open in shock. Ned whimpered in her arms and drew her attention. She glanced at him, than at Runa's retreating figure. "Runa." She didn't shout the words. Perhaps that was why Runa stopped and turned around. She raised an eyebrow.

Elizabeth drew a breath and calm descended like a blanket. "Six months ago I'd have let you risk your life on my behalf. Six months ago I didn't have a choice. I do now."

Runa's brows creased in puzzlement.

Elizabeth walked toward her. "I'm not the person I was six months ago. I'm not Elizabeth. Today I'm Zabeth."

"What do you mean?"

She reached Runa and thrust Ned at her. Instinctively the woman dropped her sword to clutch the child. "I'd give my life for Ned. I won't let anyone else give theirs. Take care of him for me." She kissed Ned's forehead. "I love you, my handsome little lord, but you don't need me as much as he does right now. Be a good boy."

Ned looked up at her, a solemn expression on his face that almost fooled her he understood. Tears blurred her eyes and she stood back.

Runa shifted him in her arms and touched Elizabeth's hand. "Would you leave him motherless?"

Elizabeth shook her head. "This village is his mother. *You* are his mother. I know you'll love him and raise him to be strong." She wiped away the tears with the back of her hand and offered a watery smile. "Besides, I don't intend to die. *My* training is still fresh."

"At least take the sword."

"I don't know how to use it." She headed back up the trail toward the distant clang of swords.

"Remember your targets," Runa called after her.

Elizabeth didn't answer. She was already running toward the sounds of battle.

~ * ~

Beren dodged another blow from Creltak and skipped sideways, keeping an eye on the fifth man who still edged his way over the slippery log. Soon he'd face two opponents instead of just the one.

Under normal circumstances that wouldn't be a problem, but Creltak was a big man, stronger than Beren, and faster than his size suggested. Beren had to dance aside to avoid being skewered on Creltak's sword.

At least Zabeth got away. She'd be safe in the village by now. Beren had made sure his route kept them all close to the bay.

Creltak slashed downward and forced Beren to dodge away. His heel skidded on a rotting leaf. Beren struggled to keep his sword up and managed to stay on his feet, but a sharp pain in his ankle told him the effort had wrenched it—not surprising, as that was the leg he'd broken when a child, and it had never been very strong.

He forced away the pain and lurched toward Creltak. All he had to do was survive the next few minutes, give Zabeth time to raise the alarm, and for the warriors to come.

The two men circled each other, paused, attacked in a flurry of slashes and parries, then fell back to circle again and assess the damage. The last series of strikes left Beren with a gash on his shield arm, while blood poured from a wound in Creltak's thigh.

Beren tensed for another attack, but he caught a movement from the corner of his eye. He changed direction, swayed aside when a heavy blade crashed toward his head.

Creltak's last man had reached the near bank.

Faced now with two foes, Beren let instinct take over. Muscles and habit moved faster than thought. He struck at openings his conscious mind was too slow to notice, deflected blows from two directions.

Holding his sword two-handed, Beren whirled, slashed, blocked. The clang of metal on metal warred with the roar of the flooded stream, the thunder of blood pounding in his head.

"You're dead, boy," Creltak snarled during a lull. "You can't fight off both of us indefinitely. You're bleeding, getting weaker. Soon that sword will feel ten times heavier than it should. You won't be able to lift it off the ground."

Beren let the words flow over him unheeded. While Creltak taunted him, the other raider glided to the left to outflank him. Beren faced Creltak and pretended not to notice the maneuver.

Without warning, Creltak surged forward, but instead of retreating, Beren dodged to the right. The second man's sword sliced through the air where Beren had been, and buried itself in the ground.

Creltak charged past. Beren swung at his back, but the second man managed to jerk his blade from the soil. It swung up and blocked Beren's blow but without any control behind it. Beren twisted, slid the blade of his sword under the other man's guard, and plunged the point into his chest.

Creltak roared in anger. Beren jerked the sword free and turned to face his final opponent.

"It's the two of us now," Beren taunted, and beckoned Creltak forward.

The big man sneered. "You think so?"

A movement by the river edge drew Beren's attention. The man he'd pulled off the bridge waded through the water, sword drawn, teeth bared in berserker madness. The distraction was all Creltak needed. The raider roared a battle cry and leaped toward Beren.

Beren was too exhausted to deal with them both. He dodged sideways and his heel caught a root buried under the fallen leaves. His ankle twisted again, something snapped, and he fell.

He landed on his back, all the air driven from his lungs at the impact. By instinct, he kept a grip on his sword and gasped for breath. The two raiders charged forward from opposite directions.

At that moment, a slim figure dashed from the trees and hurled itself at the raider near the river. Both went down, but the smaller figure rolled out of the way and was on her feet in an instant.

Zabeth! Like a flame-haired Valkyrie, she kicked the man's sword from his hand and jabbed at his eyes with her knife. The man screamed, clutched his face.

Creltak loomed above Beren. The raider's blade slashed downward. Beren rolled away.

Concentrate.

But the throbbing in his ankle—broken, he suspected—made it difficult. He'd never be able to get back on his feet to face Creltak. Instead, he scurried backward on all fours and drew Creltak away from Zabeth. The raider leader stalked after him.

Beren felt the bark of a large tree behind him. Nowhere else to go. He pressed his back against the trunk. To either side were more trees and brush so thick it was impossible to push through.

Beren used his good leg to help him stand, then leaned back against the trunk, and balanced on one foot. Creltak stopped a few paces away, the point of his sword aimed at Beren's throat. No longer snarling, he actually smiled at Beren.

"I see your woman came back, boy. That saves me the trouble of chasing after her." He lunged forward.

Zabeth screamed. At the same time, Beren hurled himself toward his enemy. Unable to stop his momentum, Creltak impaled himself on Beren's sword. His arm jerked, and Creltak's sword cut deep. A burning pain seared Beren's ribs. Then blood gurgled from Creltak's mouth and he collapsed.

Zabeth dashed forward and flung herself down beside Beren. "Oh God, you're hurt."

"Just a…scratch." He raised a hand to her cheek, used his thumb to wipe the tears from her eyes.

"Lie down." She placed a hand under his head and eased him sideways until he lay on the ground.

There was no pain now, nothing at all. A vague darkness crept at the edge of his vision. A sense of urgency took him. He clutched Zabeth's arm. "Listen…must tell you…"

"Shhh. Don't speak."

"Must." He gasped for breath. "Zabeth, I…love you. Love…Ned."

She sniffed back the tears. "I know."

"Want to be…father to him." She began to speak but he lifted his hand, pressed his fingers to her lips. "Want to marry you."

"Shhh. We'll talk about it later." She clutched his hand.

"May not…be…later."

"Don't say things like that." The command was uttered with such ferocity he had to smile.

"My stubborn…red-haired…Valkyrie." His eyes closed, her voice faded, and the darkness took him.

~ * ~

Shock raced through Elizabeth. "No! Don't you dare die on me, Beren Torsson. We're not finished here."

When Eskil and the other warriors roared into the clearing, Elizabeth didn't even look up. She knelt beside Beren, rocked him in her arms, and repeated over and over, "Don't die. Don't die."

He didn't move. His body was cold, so cold, and there was so much blood. Only his faint ragged breathing told her he still lived. Hands gripped her shoulders and Tor's voice murmured words she was too numb to understand. Eskil knelt on Beren's other side and probed the gash that tore Beren's side open from shoulder to belly.

Elizabeth flinched, flung out a hand. "Don't. You'll hurt him."

"He's beyond pain at the moment," Eskil soothed.

"Come Zabeth." Tor tugged her away. "Let the healer look at him."

She looked up. Two women accompanied the warriors. One was the healer, who nudged Eskil out of the way and opened a pouch of herbs. The other was Kiana.

Elizabeth didn't want to leave Beren's side, but Tor gave her no choice and pulled her away.

"He can't die." She looked up at him, silently pleading with him to agree.

"The healer will do what she can." Tor, his face pale, glanced at Beren. "Come, let's get back to the village."

When they left the clearing, Eskil ordered someone to bind the prisoner and someone else to bring the bodies. She stumbled. Was Beren now one of the bodies? Eskil's voice came again, this time directing someone to make a sling to carry Beren back.

Not a body. Not yet.

"He'll make it," Kiana said at her side, as if she'd read Elizabeth's thoughts. "Pray to your gods, Zabeth, and we'll pray to ours."

Elizabeth remembered little of the next hour. Kiana took her to the Gather Hall, where Runa made her drink a mug of *keevah*. When they carried Beren in a short time later, Elizabeth insisted on accompanying him. They put him in an empty chamber on the ground floor. The healer shooed everyone from the room, but Elizabeth, Kiana, and Tor refused to leave.

Runa bustled in with a bowl and cloths. She gave the visitors a stern look and pointed to a bench against the wall. Like meek children, they sat. The healer cut away Beren's shirt and Runa hurried forward with the bowl, cutting off Elizabeth's view.

Tor laced his fingers with hers, the gesture somewhat reassuring. Kiana, on his other side, leaned her head on his shoulder. Tor raised his free hand to clasp hers. "Reminds me of another time," he said in a soft voice.

"Hush," Kiana whispered. "No bad thoughts."

Elizabeth wanted to pace. It was maddening. She wanted to do something. *Anything.* At least Runa helped the healer, but for Elizabeth there was nothing to do but listen to the wet gurgle of blood that at first gushed, then thinned into a trickle, and the horrifying sound of flesh as it was sewn together.

Once the worst of the wounds was tended, the healer inspected the rest of Beren's body. Elizabeth had already noticed the swelling in his ankle.

"It's the same leg he broke before," Kiana said.

Tor squeezed her hand. "He'll be fine this time too."

The healer probed the flesh, then she gripped his foot on either side of the swelling and gave a sharp twist. A loud *pop* filled the room. With deft hands, she bound a straight stick to either side of the ankle.

"Not broken. Dislocated. That should set better." She wiped her hands and resumed her inspection.

Through it all Beren didn't move, didn't make a sound.

At last, the healer straightened and turned to Tor. "I've done all I can. It's in the hands of the gods now."

She left, and, after a swift glance at her brother, Runa followed. And so they sat, the three of them. Kiana leaned against her husband while Elizabeth stared at her lover and prayed.

After a while, Elizabeth stirred herself. "I…I think I'd better see what's happened to Ned."

Kiana placed a hand on her arm. "Gudrin has him, with Kaya. Don't worry. He's all right." She raised her head and looked at Elizabeth. "Has anyone asked if you're injured?"

Elizabeth shook her head. "I'm fine."

Tor shifted his shoulders. "You should sleep, Zabeth."

"No. I'll watch over Beren. I want to be here when he wakes up."

"It could be days," Kiana warned.

Elizabeth didn't reply. After a moment, Kiana and Tor rose. "I'll bring you an extra blanket," Kiana said, then followed Tor out the door.

Elizabeth stood and staggered to the bed. She looked down at Beren and studied his pale face, determined to memorize every feature, every line and blemish. What would he look like without his beard? It didn't matter. She didn't love him for the way he looked.

"I love you for being you," she whispered. She brushed a lock of hair from his face, bent, and placed a gentle kiss on his forehead. "I love you, Beren Torsson, so hurry and wake up so I can tell you."

Hours passed, then a day, another. Elizabeth sat in Beren's room and refused to leave. Runa brought her meals, ordered a cot brought in, although most of the time Elizabeth fell asleep sitting on the floor beside Beren, her head on the bed, resting on her crossed arms.

Twice a day the healer removed the bandages to check the stitches and the progress of the *klengodd* root poultice as it sealed and healed the cut. Runa visited at every meal, but her family kept her occupied and distracted from worrying about her nephew. Tor and Kiana came more often, stayed longer.

Once, Runa brought Ned into the room. He'd been fussing and even the sight of Elizabeth didn't calm him, but the moment he saw Beren, he waddled up to the bed and patted his face. "Be-be-be," he chanted.

"Well," said Runa, bemused. "And here I thought it was his mother he missed."

"He's grown attached to Beren." Elizabeth pulled an edge of the blanket up to Beren's chin. "It's taking too long. Why is it taking so long?

I thought this…this root was supposed to help any injury."

She didn't expect an answer and was surprised when Runa replied. "Some injuries are deeper than others."

"Deeper? I almost lost an arm and you said I wasn't unconscious this long. All he did was dislocate an ankle."

"And nearly get gutted." Runa sighed. "Losing an arm won't kill you. Losing half your side might. Give it time, Zabeth. All will be well."

When Runa took Ned away, he didn't fuss, and she told Elizabeth afterward he'd been no problem since.

On the third day, Beren opened his eyes.

Chapter Twenty-Eight

When Beren regained consciousness, his first sight was of Zabeth hovering beside him. Relief flooded through him. She was safe. She was here.

"Good morning...Eeleezabeth," he croaked. His throat was dry, and his voice all but non-existent.

"It is afternoon," she corrected, but her face was split by a wide grin and tears filled her eyes. "And you can call me Zabeth." He lifted his hand, but she clutched it, lowered it back to the bed, and swiped the tears from her face. "Don't move. The healer said you need a few more days yet."

"Days?" He looked around, confused. "Have I been ill?"

She sniffed, shook her head. "Not ill. Wounded. Don't you remember fighting the raiders?"

He frowned, and a memory tickled the back of his mind.

"You were very brave," she continued, her tone teasing. "You defeated five of them all by yourself."

The memory surfaced. "I think I had some help."

She smiled. "I did what Astri taught me—go for the vulnerable spots. I couldn't reach the one I was aiming for, so chose the second target."

"You did well." An urgency gripped him and he tried to sit up. "Ned?"

"He's fine." Zabeth pushed him back down. "Now, rest."

He caught her hand. "Don't go."

She smiled. "I won't."

He wanted to say more. He wanted to tell her he didn't mean *don't go from this room*, but *don't go from my life*. He wanted to say so much more, but he couldn't keep his eyes open. He fell asleep still clutching her hand.

When next he woke, a hushed babble of voices surrounded him

and he sensed others in the room. He clenched his hand, found he still held Zabeth's. She squeezed back before easing her fingers from his grip.

"He's awake again," she announced.

He opened his eyes and looked around. Tor stood beside the bed and beamed at Beren as if he'd healed his son himself. Kiana, Runa, and Vider stood by the window. Garan and Magrim were on the other side of the bed, while Freya, Eskil, and Astri sat on the bench by the wall and played with little Ned.

Tor leaned down. "How do you feel, son?"

Beren shrugged, winced when a dull pain throbbed in his side.

"Careful." Zabeth glared at Tor, who took a quick step back. Then she placed a hand on Beren's arm. "You might tear the stitches."

He looked down at his chest, swathed in bandages. "Will I have a scar?"

Tor chuckled. "Even *klengodd* root has its limits. Oh yes, you'll have a nice long scar to impress the girls."

Beren scowled. He didn't care about *the girls*. There was only one girl, one woman, who was important, and she wasn't impressed by scars.

He glanced at her. She looked so pale, so tired.

Garan stepped forward. "You're a lucky man. The healer said another few inches and you'd have lost your arm as well as your insides."

Beren swallowed, took a quick peek to the side to reassure himself the arm was still attached.

"Zabeth told us they were after the Shadow-Links," Garan continued. "You did well, drawing them away."

Beren frowned. "Why were there so few of them? I would have thought they'd come back in force."

Garan shook his head. "The prisoner told us Creltak believed a few might succeed in stealth where force had failed."

"Prisoner?"

"The man Zabeth wounded." There was pride in Garan's voice.

Beren's gaze swung to Zabeth. She gave a weak grin, but her face was pale. She might have the fury of a Valkyrie, but she'd no taste for blood.

"Be-re," piped a high voice.

All heads turned toward the bench. Ned strained away from Astri's hold, reached toward Beren. "Be-re," he repeated, the urgency clear in his voice.

Astri glanced at Beren, and at his nod she released Ned. The child staggered across the room. The top of his body leaned forward, seeming to move much faster than his tiny legs, until he fell against the bed. He looked up at Beren from eyes as green as his mother's, and stretched his arms to be picked up.

Beren stroked the boy's reddish curls. "I can't lift you, Ned."

Ned regarded him for a moment, dropped his arms, and leaned his head against Beren's arm. Zabeth stood behind him.

Beren looked up at her. His stomach clenched. After what happened, he'd no doubt she wouldn't want anything to do with him. Her son's life had been threatened, again, her own almost lost.

Yet she came back to help, a small voice reminded him. She'd risked her own life to save his. He smiled at her and mustered the courage to speak, but at that moment the healer bustled into the room.

She glared at the visitors. "I said no more than five minutes. There's too many of you in here. Out. All of you."

Amid half-hearted protests, Tor shepherded the younger people from the room, while Garan followed at a slower pace. Soon only Zabeth, Ned, and the healer were left. The healer stood back and tapped her foot.

Zabeth lifted Ned onto her hip. Beren's mouth went dry, but he had to speak, had to say…something. He caught her hand. "Zabeth, wait." She paused, her expression puzzled. "I…I wanted to tell you…to ask you—" He broke off, swallowed.

Her expression cleared. "Have you forgotten our bargain?"

Now it was his turn to be puzzled. "What?"

Ned tugged at Zabeth's arm, but she ignored him. "Back in that clearing you asked me to marry you. You fainted before I could give you my answer."

Beren's heart raced. Ned wriggled. Zabeth lifted him off her hip and sat him on the edge of the bed. He pulled his legs up under him and crawled up beside Beren to sit in the curve of his arm and pat his chest. "Be-re."

Beren unconsciously rubbed Ned's back, his attention on Zabeth. Her chin was up, her shoulders set, defiance in every line of her body. "We made a bargain, you and I."

"I don't remember."

She flashed a quick, nervous smile. "You were unconscious at the time. We didn't say anything aloud."

"Oh." He didn't understand, but it didn't matter. Only her answer mattered.

Again that determined glint appeared in her eyes. "You promised you wouldn't die, and I promised to marry you. You kept your promise. I have every intention of keeping mine, so don't think you can wriggle out of it now."

For a moment, Beren couldn't understand what she'd said, then his heart leaped and he gave a great shout of joy. He grabbed Zabeth's hand and dragged her down to him. She flung out her other hand and stopped herself before she fell on top of Ned. Laughing, crying, she regained her balance, and leaned over to kiss him.

The door burst open. They sprang apart when Tor and Kiana rushed in. Beren glared at them over Zabeth's shoulder. They halted.

The healer stepped from the other side of the bed and headed for the door. "I'll be back in a few minutes." She pushed the others out the door before her.

Zabeth sniffed back her tears and sat up. Beren held her hand in a tight grip, afraid to let her go. "I didn't think you would want to have anything to do with me."

She shrugged. "What gave you that idea? I love you, and I know you love me and Ned. With all that in our favor, how could I give it up?"

He tilted his head. "How do you know I love you both?"

She stroked Ned's arm. "You risked your life for Ned. You could have escaped with me, but you stayed to protect Ned. I knew then you had to love him. As for loving me..." She paused, gave him a teasing grin. "I knew *that* the moment you stepped on board the *Freki*. Why else would you suffer so much if not for me?" She bent her head and kissed him, a long, lingering kiss that made his head spin. When she drew back, her eyes were deep emeralds. "Do you deny it?"

He shook his head. "Never. I love you Zabeth. I never want to be parted from you."

"Then you won't." She slipped from his arms and stood beside the bed.

Ned patted Beren's chest again, looked at his mother. Zabeth smiled. "Time to go, little one. Beren needs his rest, and you need a bath."

Ned squealed and bounced on the bed. "Ba."

"Sounds as if he knows that word." Beren grinned at the child.

Zabeth plucked Ned from the bed and laughed. "He's discovered he can blow bubbles."

Beren caught her hand again and stopped her from turning away. "You'll be near?"

She nodded. "Outside the door. Now let the healer look at you. We can talk later."

"I love you." The words came easily now, and never more true.

Tears glistened in her eyes and she sniffed. "I'm turning into a watering pot." He frowned, puzzled by the strange term, and she smiled. "I'll explain later. I love you too."

She swept out the door as if on a whirlwind.

The healer stepped inside and gave him a scathing look. "If you're finished courting, Beren Torsson, I'll get on with my work." A twinkle in her eyes belied the scolding tone. Beren grinned and surrendered to the inevitable.

~ * ~

A week later, Elizabeth stood on the beach under a spring sun. Her hair hung loose, a circlet of flowers perched over her forehead like a crown. She wore an ankle-length gown of pale green silk which clung to her above the waist, but rippled and flowed in the gentle sea-breeze. Beside her, Beren leaned on a crutch Tor had cut for him. All their friends and family, everyone from the village, crowded the beach around them.

Today was her wedding day, and Elizabeth had never been so happy.

She and Beren faced the chieftain's wife. As priestess of Frigga, Odin's consort, Freya claimed the right to join them.

The words of the ceremony, although different from those Elizabeth was used to, still conveyed the same hope for a long and happy future. The one disconcerting note was when Freya pricked their wrists and held them together for their blood to mingle. Elizabeth didn't know if there was any truth in the belief of bonding their souls in this manner. She did, however, feel a faint tingle throughout her body, as if Beren were indeed becoming one with her.

Finally Freya signaled to Astri and Eskil. They stood behind Elizabeth and Beren, and each held one end of a woven garland of spring flowers. They walked forward now, draped the garland around Elizabeth's left shoulder and Beren's right, crossed it in front of them, and held the ends so the bridal pair were bound by the fragrant blossoms. Freya pronounced the final words of blessing. Beren raised his left hand, clasped in Elizabeth's right, and broke the garland rope as required.

"It is done," proclaimed Freya in a clear voice. A cheer erupted from the gathered crowd.

Beren pulled Elizabeth into his arms and kissed her. The world spun around her, as it always did when he kissed her, and Elizabeth melted into his embrace.

When they parted, breathless and grinning, Beren whispered, "We'll make a better job of it tonight."

Elizabeth shook her head in affection. *Damn the man.* Even now he still made her blush.

"Mama. Be-re." Ned's demanding voice interrupted her reverie.

Beren laughed and, balancing with the crutch, scooped Ned into his arms. "When I build our house, Ned will have the finest room of any child in the village."

"What? You don't want him sleeping in our room with us?" Elizabeth teased.

Beren scowled, but there was a twinkle in his eye when he lowered his voice. "So you liked using the gags?"

Her face heated with embarrassment and she punched him—lightly—on the arm.

Tor appeared beside Beren and clapped him on the shoulder. "Odin's blessing on you, Beren, and on you, Zabeth." He reached for Ned, who launched himself into Tor's arms. "And is my new grandson looking forward to spending a few days with his old grandfather?"

"And grandmother," Kiana added. She slipped her arm through Tor's and kissed Ned on the cheek.

Elizabeth brushed a lock of hair from Ned's forehead. "Are you sure he won't be too much trouble?"

"Nonsense. We'll be fine, won't we boy?" Tor nuzzled Ned's neck and drew a squeal of giggles from the child. Kiana shook her head.

Elizabeth laughed. Beren put his arm around Tor's shoulder and leaned close to Ned. "Behave yourself, little boy," he said in a stern voice.

Ned grabbed Beren's beard with one hand and Tor's with the other and tugged. Both men roared in mock pain and Ned giggled.

Elizabeth regarded the three of them with a fond smile. Three generations, all unrelated—father, son, and grandson—and she loved all three, each in his own way.

Someone beat a drum. A flute and harp joined in the merry rhythm, and in an instant the beach was filled with dancing couples who laughed and jigged on the sand around the central fire.

My people. Wonder filled Elizabeth. *My home.*

Beren freed his beard from Ned's fingers, stepped away from his father and son, and limped the short space separating him from his wife. Elizabeth's heart soared at the sight of him. "Greetings, husband." She dropped a small curtsey.

"Greetings, wife." He pulled her close and gave her a quick kiss, then stepped back. "Let's dance."

"Dance?" She looked at his crutch. "You can barely walk."

"We'll manage." He wrapped his arms around her and swayed to the beat of the drum. "Tonight," he whispered in her ear, "We'll dance a different tune."

She laughed, and her heart expanded in a glow so overwhelming tears sprang to her eyes. "I love you, Beren."

He squeezed her against him. "Keep telling me that, my love, and I'll keep telling you. I love you, Zabeth, and always will. Until my dying day, you are my love, my lifemate."

Elizabeth wrapped her arms around his waist, rested her head on his chest. "My love, my lifemate. Until my dying day, and beyond."

The music swelled. Dancers swirled around them, and Elizabeth and Beren were whirled into the rhythm of life and love in the village of New Asgard.

Epilogue

From the sidelines, Gudrin watched the dancers whirl on the sand.

One day that'll be me and Ned.

The flames of the central fire leaped with the dancers, but, eager to *See*, she concentrated on the smoke. She'd inherited more than a gift for languages from her mother. She'd also inherited her grandmother's Sight.

There. The two of them stood just like Zabeth and Beren before the priestess. As expected, his hair was reddish-gold, braided and flowing down his back. He turned his head and she caught her breath.

He didn't have a beard. *Everyone* had a beard. Why didn't Ned?

And then she looked more closely at the woman by his side. Her hair was long and brown, but not as dark brown as Gudrin's, more a golden brown, and her face...

Not my hair. Not my face. Not me!

Angry now, the child narrowed her eyes, pushed her will into the flames. Ned was supposed to marry *her*. The woman should be *her*.

Slowly the figures in the smoke changed. Satisfied, she watched the image of herself, grown to womanhood, stand before the priestess.

With a man who wasn't Ned.

Acknowledgments

As always, thanks go to all my friends and family who have listened to my crazy ideas, read snippets of scenes, and supplied invaluable suggestions. Your faith in me has been a constant encouragement.

Special thanks to my fantastic editor, Renee Wildes, whose guidance made me a better writer. Also for coming up with this great title.

To my publisher, Cassie Knight, and the team at Champagne Book Group, and to my cover artist, Sevannah Storm, thanks for turning these words into an amazing book.

To Keith Willis, who mentored me through the esoteric world of publishing, marketing, and costumes, I hope we meet at a Ren Faire one day. I really enjoyed reading your *Knights of Kilbourne* series (https://www.keithwillisauthor.com/).

To Ron Hore, for helping me navigate the intricacies of working with a publisher in a different country. Also, your *Housetrap Chronicles* satisfy my love of paranormal detective stories. I look forward to reading your other series (https://www.ronaldhore.com/).

Finally, to my wonderful husband, Alan, for your encouragement and support. And especially for your ability to find those pesky typos I missed after reading the same sentence fifty times.

About the Author

Maureen Castell has been writing most of her life and loves meeting the characters who pop into her head. A finalist in several writing contests, she specializes in fantasy and science fiction romance. Sharing left- and right-brain skills, Maureen studied mathematics, computer science, and Shakespeare at university, and spent her working life as a technical writer.

Her first book, *The Viking Who Fell Through Time*, was released in 2022 and this book, *The Viking's Shadow Lady*, is the second in the series. Both combine three of her favorite subjects: Vikings, time travel, and romance.

Maureen lives with her husband in Manitoba, Canada.

To learn more about Maureen's work, to sign up for notifications of upcoming events and releases, or to send her a message, visit any of her links below.

Website/Blog: https://maureencastell.com/
Facebook: https://www.facebook.com/Maureen-Castell-Author-102629802446032

~ * ~

Thank you for taking the time to read *The Viking's Shadow Lady*. We hope you enjoyed this as much as we did. If you did, please tell your friends, read another book by Maureen, and leave a review. Reviews support authors and ensure they continue to bring readers books to love.

Turn the page for a peek inside *The Viking Who Fell Through Time*, book 1 of Maureen's Vikings in the Bronze Age series.

They were born three thousand years apart, but fate brought them together.

Dragged into the ancient past by a crashing spaceship, Tor and his fellow Vikings face starvation in an autumn that is six months too early. When exploring their new home, they meet the mysterious Kiana and the villagers whose winter shelter has been destroyed by the spaceship.

Uneasy allies at first, these two leaders find unexpected love as they join forces to build a home together, until Kiana's enemies threaten her new life.

CHAPTER ONE

North Atlantic, 982 A.D.

Tor Olafsson wrapped both arms around the groaning mast and shouted into the howling wind. "Curse you, Odin, punish *me* if you will but leave my people alone."

A huge wave crashed over *The Hammer*'s side, cascaded along the sloping deck of the ship, and swept a bleating, flailing goat toward the far railing. The remains of its tether dragged behind it. Tor lunged for the frantic animal and managed to snag the rope around its neck. They'd already lost one goat to the sea. He'd not lose another. They needed every animal they brought with them if they survived to make landfall.

"Got you." He pulled the goat to him and clasped it under one arm. His own tether tightened around his waist, but when he jerked to a halt, it snapped. His heart plummeted into his stomach. "No!"

His shout swallowed by thunder, he skidded along the deck, clawing for a hold with frozen fingers. A precious water barrel tumbled past him and crashed through the railing. His legs slid through after it. Tor grabbed the rail with his free hand, instinctively tightened his grip on the goat, and stared, mesmerized, at his legs dangling over the angry ocean. Shoulders strained, fingers slipped—

Someone grasped his wrist. For a moment he hung, suspended over the watery abyss. Time stopped. His rescuer squeezed Tor's hand, dragged him onto the deck, and back to the mast. Tor swiped wet hair from his eyes and nodded thanks to his best friend and first mate.

Vider held out a length of rope. "Never curse the gods."

Tor passed the goat to a crewman to join the animals in the shallow oar pit. After he attached the new tether, he focused his attention back on Vider. "They've done nothing to help us."

His friend shrugged. "They've kept us alive so far."

"Alive?" Tor ground his teeth and glowered at the battered longship, at his exhausted crew rowing and bailing for their lives. *My fault. They trusted me.*

"Perhaps we should also petition Jorvik's Christian god." Vider grinned at Tor's immediate scowl.

"If our own gods won't help us, why would his?" Not for the first time, he wished he'd left the priest behind. No matter he worshipped the one god—many of Tor's men believed the more gods they prayed to the better—but he also claimed to be a seer and spouted dire predictions before they set out on this journey. Why bother to come with them if he thought their exile doomed before it even began?

Tor again shoved wet hair from his face. The storm had struck with such sudden ferocity there'd been no time to braid the whipping strands that stung his cheeks and blinded him.

The ship lurched sideways. A wall of water rose on the right.

"To starboard," he shouted.

The crew strained at the oars while two helmsmen struggled with the steering oar and aimed the ship into the towering swell. The bow lifted, but not enough. They plunged through the wave.

Tor held his breath. *We're going under.* He and Vider clung to the mast and each other.

The ship, built by men familiar with these waters, emerged battered but afloat. When they straightened again, Tor glanced at the tent still anchored against the stern. If they got out of this alive, he'd add a hold or a cabin or…something…*anything* sturdier than cloth. At least Emund's trading vessel boasted a hold, now crammed with most of the livestock and his own family.

Tor raised himself to examine the surrounding sea. *Where are the other ships?*

After what seemed an eternity Emund's *knorr* appeared on the crest of a wave, the clumsy vessel recognizable by its width. A moment later, Beade's longship came into view farther away. His brothers were experienced seamen, but as the eldest it was impossible for Tor not to feel responsible for their safety. That the three ships still traveled together was a miracle.

"We're together still." Vider echoed Tor's thought. "Spring storms are always the worst."

"As if winter wants one last chance to conquer us," Tor muttered.

"This storm will pass, as all storms do." Vider helped Tor to his feet. "We have weathered worse."

The screaming wind failed to muffle the fearful wails of the women and children. Tor grimaced. "Not with our families aboard."

"True." Vider glanced at the flimsy hide tent that had miraculously defied all attacks of the wild waves. "Look."

A tall blonde woman crawled from the tent. She remained on her hands and knees as she made her way toward him, her woolen dress plastered to her like a second skin. Tor clenched his jaw in an attempt to keep admiration from overwhelming his annoyance.

Even thus, crawling like a dog, her body heavy with child, his twin sister shamed the fiercest warrior with her courage. At least she had the sense to tie her tether to the lines strung from mast to stern.

When she reached the two men, Tor knelt beside her and wrapped one arm around the mast, the other above the bulge of her belly. Her skin was ice cold. She buried her face in his chest to avoid the stinging wind.

"I'll...go help the men bail," Vider muttered.

Tor didn't miss the longing glance Vidar threw over his shoulder before returning to the lower deck. If only he had been there to offer for her before she found herself carrying Ottar's spawn. If only Tor had been able to protect her from the bastard.

"Go back to the tent, Runa," he shouted into her ear. "It's not safe out here."

"It's no safer in that tent. The wailing is driving me mad." She flashed her annoying try-to-stop-me-brother grin. "If I'm going to die, it will be by your side. We took our first breath together, and we'll take our last the same way."

Pride warred with exasperation. His stubborn sister challenged even death itself to get her way. Tor hugged her. "We're not going to die."

Another wave, bigger and more powerful than the ones before, loomed over the ship. No time to aim into it. He tightened his grip on mast and woman. The wave fell. The world vanished in an endless flood of water. The ship tilted.

He lost his footing and dug his fingers into the wood. After what seemed an eternity, the wave passed, and he was able to breathe again, though he shook with cold.

"Go back." Fear for Runa's safety added a harshness to his voice.

She squeezed his waist. "My place is here, as always."

Gods, why did I go on that last trading voyage? It took him away from home for almost a year, and in that time… How could opening a new trade route compare with losing his father in a so-called *fair* fight with a man half his age, the same man who dishonored his sister and then cast her aside? Until she proved to be with child.

Tor wanted to keep Runa safe, but her will was as strong as his. Hard enough to get his siblings to obey his lead, but when the most troublesome of them all was only minutes younger than he, authority was just a word. At least he had no wife or children of his own to worry about.

The ship lurched beneath them. He shouted orders to his oarsmen, who were already compensating. The deck tilted, straightened, then tilted the other way. He wanted to be down there, rowing with them, but they knew their jobs better than he. As captain, he hadn't lifted an oar in years, nor pitted his strength against the sea, and in truth one more oar would be of little help. Just keeping the ship from capsizing was a heroic feat.

Despair filled his heart. He touched his forehead to Runa's and whispered, "Odin has abandoned us."

She cradled his face in her hands. "Then we will spit in his face."

A bark of laughter escaped his lips. The corners of his mouth lifted, tugging at the scar on his left cheek. *Ah, Runa, ever the defiant one.*

A loud clap of thunder made her jerk away. Her eyes widened at something behind him. He twisted his head.

Black clouds filled the horizon. Between the clouds and the ship, the air shimmered as if with heat. Something smooth, shiny, and *big* emerged from the shimmer, first a stubby point like the edge of a shield, then a curve of metal, more, until finally the entire object hung in the sky before the three ships.

The shimmer dissolved.

Longer than all three of Tor's ships lined end to end, the object resembled a child's ball after being battered by a giant hammer. Around its edge lightning spun, shining with a blinding radiance. Strange metal spears bristled around the sphere, making it appear more war mace than ball. Without warning, a dark square appeared in the front part of the object and within that square Tor glimpsed startled faces. *People?* A moment later the square vanished, leaving smooth metal in its place.

The crew's shouts broke Tor's trance. Some cursed, others prayed.

Runa trembled in his arm and again hid her face in his shirt. "Odin, forgive me. I didn't mean it."

Anger flooded him. He staggered to his feet, hauling his sister with him. "I will not lie down like a dog to die." Using his body to brace her behind him against the mast, he drew his long-sword and waved it in defiance at the giant ball. "Come, Odin, do your worst!"

As if it heard him, the object shot straight up into the black clouds. A moment later it reappeared and dove toward his ship.

Runa screamed. The men on the oar deck scrambled toward the stern. The object shot overhead and passed a hand's breadth above the mast.

The air shimmered again. A circle opened in front of *The Hammer*. Around the ship, waves crashed in fury, threatening to overturn the battered craft. Through the circle, far below—at least half the length of Tor's ship—the water lay calm, a bright sun shone among a few scattered white clouds, and a silver beach protected by high cliffs and a colorful tree-covered mountain beckoned.

"Asgard." The wind snatched his words.

The metal ball flew into the circle and dragged the churning water—and Tor's ship—behind it.

"Hang on!" He turned, gripped the mast with both hands, and pinned Runa against it with his body.

A moment later the ship tilted and rushed over the waterfall of storm water. A quick glance showed his brothers' ships pulled in his wake. At last, with a jolt that threw everyone to the deck, *The Hammer* landed on the calm water.

Everything stopped. The ship lay still. No roar of thunder or waves battered Tor's ears. *Have we all gone deaf?* Behind him, the circle vanished.

As if awakening from a dream, the men crept forward, staring at the heavens. Tor followed their gaze. The object had stopped its fall toward the beach. For an instant it hovered above the water before lurching inland. It shuddered once, then plunged into the mountainside, burying itself deep in the earth. The screech of twisting metal thundered through the air. A shock of sound rocked the ships, pressed against their eardrums as if to deafen them.

Then there was silence.

~ * ~

Farther along the shore

Kiana swung her sword at an invisible opponent, honing skills she had little opportunity to apply these days. Her prince's enemies were unlikely to find them this far north, but she was his sworn protector and thus responsible for remaining in top fighting condition. She gave a final stab at the imaginary foe and stepped back.

A sudden roar filled the air. Startled, she spun around, stared at the mountain looming over the village. Something too big to make out buried itself in the rock, spewing broken trees and dust into the air. The ground shook with the impact, but years of training helped her keep her feet and her weapon. With one final spurt of flame, the object disappeared under the collapsing peak.

Beren is up there.

She shoved the sword into her back scabbard and raced through the summer village. A mindless keening screamed through her head. *Not Beren.*

"Are we under attack?" Lida called from the training ground.

"Unknown," she shouted back, then slowed. *By the Lady, think. Don't dash like a raw recruit into danger. Always assume the worst.* "Set up guard around the village, just like we trained. Arm the nets."

Lida veered away to assemble her fighters. Most of the men were still at sea on a final fishing run, so only the few trained women defended the village. Fortunately the fishing nets proved strong enough to trap any enemy.

Miri ran from her hut, lacing her overtunic and struggling to keep her tangled skirts from tripping her. "I'm coming with you."

Kiana shook her head. "No. It's too danger—"

"Eskil's up there." Miri tightened her mouth in a stubborn line, a mother determined to rescue her son.

Beren and Eskil weren't the only children on the mountain. Young Eskil had gone with his friend and the older boy Arkin to clean the caves. "Try to keep up." Kiana signaled to two of her trainees. "Guard her."

Unencumbered by a skirt, Kiana soon outpaced the others. How bad was it?

Dear Lady, let it not be bad.

Arkin was a responsible lad for his twelve years—he'd look after the younger boys—and Beren was smart enough to seek shelter. If he had time.

She stumbled but bore down and kept going. *Hold on, Beren. I'll be there soon.*

~ * ~

Runa pushed against Tor's back and peered beneath his arm. "Where are we?"

"Dead." He stared at the perfect beach, the broken forest, the dented mountain. *Or mad.*

Why hadn't he been more diligent in the evening rites? The gods wouldn't welcome such as he to their paradise.

"We can't be dead." Runa shoved him again. "Look at the fish."

Puzzled, he turned his gaze to the breach in the rail and the water surrounding the ship. The salt tang of the ocean filled his nostrils, along with the stench of scorched metal, burning vegetation, and another smell, familiar but...

Fish?

He stumbled to the railing. Hundreds of fish floated belly-up on the waves, killed by the shock of the object's crash. *No. Wait.* As if waking from sleep, they stirred, flopped, and swam away. Soon the ocean was once again clear.

Not Asgard then. Even there, fish didn't die and come back to life.

Time to make some decisions. "We need to get to shore. We'll need food, water, shelter for the night, and we have no thralls to help us."

"But where are we?" Runa's question echoed the growing murmurs of the crew.

He had to stop the rising panic. Tor faced the crew and raised his voice. "Odin has heard our prayers and brought us to a land of peace."

"Aren't we dead?" one anonymous voice asked.

He'd thought the same moments earlier but the need to reassure his crew overrode his own fear. "Do you feel dead?" Tor straightened to his full height. "Do the dead feel pain? Are you not still wet and cold? Do your hands not bleed from the oars, your back ache from rowing? Wherever we are, we are destined to be here."

He studied the welcoming shore, the cliffs curving to either side of the cove—a natural harbor. To his right, the cliff jutted out a few feet from the beach, then dipped into shadow before it continued out to sea for perhaps a mile.

Tor infused his voice with all the confidence of a desperate man hoping to be right. "Ottar sent us into exile, to starve and die, but the gods brought us to a new home." He gestured to the beach. "We will survive. We will *thrive*."

The murmurs subsided. Someone gave a ragged cheer.

"Will we be safe here?" Runa rubbed her distended belly.

Tor smiled. "Safer than in that storm. Safer than under Ottar's rule."

He stared again at the land. A shiver of unease slid down his spine. There was something about the trees.

Colors. In spring, trees burst green with new growth, but these... A few spruce were scattered through the forest, but most of the trees were oaks, with some alder and maple mixed in. Orange, yellow, even red. The colors of autumn, of harvest.

How can that be? Three days ago it was spring. How can we lose a whole summer?

No, impossible. Think about it later. Right now they needed to make sure the land was safe for them. They couldn't stay at sea forever. "Let's get a scouting party ashore."

~ * ~

Even running, it took Kiana an endless fifteen minutes to reach the base of the mountain and begin the climb to the winter caves. Generations of villagers had smoothed the path, but to her the trail stretched forever. The acrid stench of burned leaves and pine needles stung her eyes and made her nose itch. Once she stopped to cough and catch her breath.

Thank the Lady this morning's rain quenched any fires.

When she finally rounded the familiar boulder, she skidded to a halt. A single entrance protected the series of caves the villagers used for winter quarters. That entrance—easy to defend and shore up against the blasts of ice night storms—no longer existed. Piles of shattered rocks filled the space, the fall so deep it covered half the plateau.

"Beren!" she shouted. She didn't expect an answer. How could anyone survive that avalanche?

"Here." A child's voice, weak and fearful.

Shocked, she spun in a circle. Not Beren. "Eskil?"

The thundering of her heart deafened her so she had to strain to hear the answering call. To her left. Oh, thank the Lady, to her *left*, not in front, not under that mass of earth and rock.

She squinted through clouds of lingering dust. There. A large rock marked the far edge of the plateau, and peeking from behind it, a pale shape. Relief and fear shot through her at sight of the child's ashen face.

"Here, Kiana." He waved to draw her closer. "We're here."

We. She swallowed the leap of hope and sprinted to the boy. When she rounded the rock, she understood why he hadn't run to meet her.

The rock leaned over his head to form a shallow cave between its bulk and the edge of the plateau. Somehow the boy had wedged himself into the cave. The angle of the balanced rock deflected most of the debris over his head and into the trees below, but some had fallen close enough to form a solid barrier that left an opening a hand's-breadth wide.

Eskil crouched close to the opening, the space behind him

hidden in the dark. With Beren's dusky skin he'd blend into the shadows, and where was Arkin? Eskil shifted and a ray of daylight allowed her to glimpse the other figures huddled behind him.

"Beren." She breathed the word, terrified all over again when the figure didn't move.

"We're stuck, Kiana." Eskil's voice shook. "There was a fire in the sky, and Arkin carried us here but now we can't get out."

She squinted at the dark shapes in the shadows behind him. "Are you hurt? Beren, are you hurt?"

"He hit his head when I pushed him in here." Arkin answered this time. "Some rocks came down on his leg, but he breathes. I just can't move him. And we can't get out." His words ended on a squeak, and Kiana recognized the imminent panic. Young as he was, the boy had protected the two children half his age.

"I'll get you out. Eskil, your mother's not far behind, and she has some of the warriors with her, so we'll all get you out." She touched his hand to calm the boy. After all, at five he was just a year younger than Beren.

Eskil clutched her hand, but his eyes weren't quite so wide and white now, and when he spoke, the tension in his voice was noticeably less. "I didn't know if anyone would come," he confessed. "Arkin said so, but I didn't believe."

"Of course we'd come." She forced a teasing smile. "We need strong warriors like you to keep the village safe."

The boy said nothing, but his grip on her hand eased.

How badly was Beren injured? To distract herself, she studied the barrier trapping the three boys. Several large rocks blocked them in, but dirt and many smaller rocks and stones made up the bulk of the pile. Thank the Lady, it wouldn't take long to clear away.

"Tell me about the fire in the sky," she ordered, more to keep herself sane than to distract the boys. "How did you see it before it hit the mountain?"

"We were leaving, but Beren forgot his flute." Arkin's voice no longer trembled. "We turned back, but the sky... It was such a strange color, just for a few moments, then this big ball of fire came straight toward us and we dove under the rock."

The other women arrived, panting. No time to worry about the mystery of the object.

Miri ran to Kiana. "My boy?"

"Mama." Eskil pressed his face close to the opening, and his mother reached for him.

"Miri, stop. He's stuck." Kiana drew her away. "We have to

loosen the rocks first or you'll hurt him."

Tears streamed down the woman's cheeks. "Thank the gods you're alive."

"Aw, Mama." Eskil sniffed and drew back.

"Eskil was very brave. He stayed with Beren and Arkin and looked out for them while they waited for rescue." It didn't matter Eskil had no choice about waiting, and the compliment soothed him some more. Kiana peered over his shoulder and winked at Arkin.

The older boy smiled.

Miri stared past Eskil into the shallow cave. "Arkin? Beren?"

Eskil answered first. "Arkin's all right. He saved us by pushing us in here. But Beren's hurt, Mama."

Kiana touched Miri's arm. "We need to lift these rocks. Can you help?"

Miri bared her teeth in a fierce grin. "Of course."

They set to work. It felt like eons before they'd cleared enough debris for Eskil and Arkin to crawl out. Kiana thrust her head and shoulders inside and let her vision adjust to the dimness. Beren lay on his side, his face toward the opening.

"Beren, I'm here." She didn't know if he heard her. His eyes were closed, but his chest rose and fell in a steady rhythm.

She skimmed her hand down his leg and discovered his ankle trapped under a large rock. Just one, thank the Lady, not a cluster. Let it not have crushed the foot as well.

She backed out of the space and turned to the other women. "All right, let's get the rest of this out of the way. Slowly."

When the opening was big enough, Kiana squeezed in and wrapped her arms around Beren's chest. "Now lift while I pull."

Ignoring his moans, she dragged the boy onto clear ground and bent to examine him. Blood on his forehead. A lump in his hair above his left eye. *He'll have a headache.* He wore the sleeveless tunic and short leggings of the locals. Scrapes and bruises on his arms and legs but nothing serious.

His ankle was another matter, swollen to twice its normal size. Kiana cut away the constricting hide boot and probed the flesh. She let out a breath when bone shifted beneath her touch.

"Broken, not crushed," she reported to the others. "We'll have to carry him back. I don't want that ankle to move more than it has to." *Can I carry him that far?*

"I'll do it." Kari, one of the trainees, fished with her father, heaving the loaded nets aboard his boat, and could easily manage Beren's slight weight.

"Good. Let me prepare the ankle first." Kiana needed to ensure it didn't move. Even dangling from gentle arms might cause a weakened bone to snap. "Get me some short branches, a dozen or so, about the length of my forearm."

The two trainees hurried into the forest. Miri, after settling Eskil and Arkin on a boulder at the edge of the plateau, approached. "Can I do something?"

Kiana studied her woven overtunic. The trainees, like Kiana, wore leather, too stiff for the purpose she needed. "Yes. Cut some long strips off your tunic to wrap around this leg."

Miri drew her bone knife from under her belt. When the other women returned with a handful of branches each, Kiana sorted through the offerings until she found the four straightest. Using those and the strips of cloth Miri handed her, she soon had Beren's lower leg strapped to the branches. Satisfied the ankle was safe from jolts and bumps, she backed away, nodded to Kari.

The woman lifted the boy in her arms, then headed down the trail with the other trainee. Kiana took a step to follow but a shout from Miri made her pause.

"Wait, Kiana. There's something you need to see."

Kiana wanted to brush her off, to rush after Beren, but the urgency in Miri's tone told her not to ignore the woman. "What is it?"

"In the cove."

From the edge of the plateau, the mountain curved toward the cove two miles north of the village. The air was still thick with settling dust, but clear enough to reveal three strange ships floating near the shore, easily visible from this height.

"Did they bring the fire ball?" Arkin asked.

If they did, the village was in more trouble than just the loss of their winter shelter.

Chapter Two

Tor stared at Emund's ship and cursed. With its deep hull, the *knorr* had run aground on a hidden sandbank, tearing a hole just above the waterline where the storm waves had weakened the wood. Tor hurried to the stern of his ship and cupped his hands around his mouth to shout toward his other brother's longship.

"Beade, drop anchor." The longships were shallow enough to clear the obstruction, but they'd be too far away to protect Emund if it came to a fight.

Beade nodded and turned to give orders. Tor's crew released their own anchor. Soon both ships bobbed close to shore in the protected cove.

"Right," he said. "Let's see what's ashore. Vider and…" He studied the crew huddled over the oars and pointed. "You three. Come with me."

Tor and the others jumped over *The Hammer's* side and landed waist-deep in water little warmer than what the storm had tossed at them. Five more men joined them from Beade's ship, although Beade himself remained aboard as war-leader in Tor's absence.

"What about Emund?" Vider stared at the beached *knorr* while they waded ashore.

"No." Tor didn't look at his brother's ship. "He'll need to inspect the damage. Besides, he's got all those animals, and they're bound to panic if water starts coming in."

Once ashore, Tor gauged the distance to the ships and studied the beach. Only a narrow rim of wet sand edged the water. High tide.

His spirits rose. "We can wait for the tide to withdraw, then unload the women and animals. Dry land will be closer to Emund then, and they shouldn't get too wet."

Recalling how they arrived there, Tor squinted at the mountain. No sign remained of the metal orb, now buried under rock and rubble.

Even the fires in the surrounding trees had burned themselves out.

What about the people in the orb. Did they survive?

He shrugged. They posed no threat at the moment. Once everyone was safe, he'd take time to check it out, but practicalities came first.

"Ivar, take two men and search inland." To two of Beade's men, "Follow the shoreline north. Vider and I will head south." He turned to the remaining three. "Stand watch here. This land looks empty, but let's make sure. Shout if you see anyone."

With a nod, they strode off.

While he walked, Tor's mind crowded with problems. Mentally he counted them.

First, daylight. The sun, overhead not long ago, now edged toward the western horizon far out at sea. With luck they'd have time to set up a camp before full night.

Second, trees. It shouldn't be autumn, but the color of the leaves... He had pregnant animals on his ships ready to birth so any milk needed to be shared with the newborns if the flock was to grow. Casks held grain and seeds ready to plant, but no time to grow anything before winter.

So, third, food and shelter. If there were settlements, trade was a possibility, or outright theft if the natives proved hostile. Only then might his people survive.

As to how they lost a summer in getting here... Never mind. Time enough later to worry about that.

"I doubt there's a threat," Vider murmured after a few minutes. "We saw no smoke from settlements, and it's cool enough to need a fire."

Thinking of his third problem, Tor hoped he was wrong. "You can never tell."

Vider's gaze strayed to the mountain again. "It flamed. Why didn't the trees burn longer?"

"Feel the air." Vider sniffed, and Tor continued, "It's damp. Maybe just rained."

"We might have problems getting the wood to burn, then. Campfires will be needed tonight."

"Perhaps you should be leader instead of me," Tor teased. "You've a more level head."

Vider shuddered. "And deal with all those people? No, friend, it's you they followed into exile. I'm just glad I had no family to bring. You have more than enough, with those brothers of yours and their wives."

"Not to mention Runa," Tor added with a sideways look at his friend.

Vider shrugged but ducked his head. Tor chuckled.

They climbed the tree-covered hill bounding the southern edge of the cove. Vider stopped every few paces to mark their back trail by bending branches or carving a slice of bark from a tree trunk. Leaves crunched underfoot. The crisp air caressed Tor's skin and reminded him of the first spring day that promised the end of winter.

Or the first day of fall.

He frowned.

"Do you see something?" Vider drew his sword.

"No." Tor was unwilling to pursue that other worry yet. "Best to be wary."

They proceeded with more caution, swords at the ready. The hill descended in a gentle slope into woodlands. Trees closed over their heads and the sun dimmed to occasional shafts of light spearing through breaks in the leaves. Tor, in the lead, estimated they'd walked for half an hour without seeing so much as a curious squirrel or hearing the chirp of birds. No surprise with the presence of humans.

"Do you smell something?" Vider murmured.

Tor sniffed. "Wood smoke?" People.

He raised his sword and took another step. Without warning, the ground erupted beneath him. He lost his grip on his weapon and it flew out of reach before woven ropes closed around him and dragged him into the air. His arms and legs fell through the gaps, leaving his body trapped inside a strong net. Vider shouted and leapt forward. Another net sprang up around the first mate, but he managed to keep a grip on his sword and was able to hack his way out. He headed toward Tor, but a spear landed quivering at his feet, forcing him back. A second dug into the ground beside it.

"Go," Tor shouted. "Warn the others."

Vider paused. An arrow skimmed his ear, drawing blood. With a helpless shake of his head, he turned and ran.

The rain of spears stopped. The forest stilled. All was silent save for the creak of the ropes around Tor. A moment later, five women emerged from behind the surrounding trees.

"Who are you?" He regretted the question immediately. He should have stayed silent. Curiosity showed weakness.

The women crept forward without speaking. They were all as fair-skinned and blonde as his own people. Three were dressed in serviceable skirts and carried barbed spears. The remaining two wore men's trews and had bows strung and ready, aimed at him. One drew a knife and sliced through a length of rope stretched beside a tree.

His prison fell to the ground. He gathered himself to attack, but someone hit him from behind, enough to daze him. The women pulled his hands behind his back and secured them with leather thongs.

I don't believe it. On shore less than an hour and captured by a handful of women.

He struggled and cursed, but the women stood back until he tired of the fruitless effort.

When they at last hauled him to his feet and pointed their spears at him, he had no choice but to stumble along before them. Not a word was said. Their intentions were clear.

He fumed. *Stupid.* Blundering around a strange land with a single companion—what had he been thinking? Whether he freed himself or Vider came, Tor's pride was already lost.

Five minutes later they entered the village. A scattering of huts draped in hides sprawled over a sandy area leading to a shallow beach where several fishing boats lay. Like the cove with his ships, cliffs jutted out to either side of a sheltered bay. Farther out to sea, a white line of wavelets marked a reef, protection from the rougher water beyond.

Women, some with babes in their arms, lounged against doorways and stared at him with suspicion. Two old men paused in mending their nets, while several children ran toward the newcomers, dancing and pointing.

Tor fought a sudden impulse to duck his head in embarrassment. *This must be how a slave feels when first displayed to its captors.*

Instead he raised his chin and stared forward. His guards marched him toward a larger hut near the center of the village. *Few men in view. Good. Easier for Vider and my crew to take over when they arrive.*

One woman led the way into the large hut while two others pushed Tor through the entrance. Inside was dark, but he blinked until the room came into focus. The women pushed him forward, and two men, both of middle years, took his arms.

Several old men stood around the edges of the hut. In the center sat a massive wooden chair, with legs and arms shaped like the feet of a great beast, and a tall back carved into intricate lines and curves. It probably was meant to convey importance, but dwarfed the man who sat in it. This, then, must be their chieftain.

He appeared of an age with Tor's father, his blond hair and beard sprinkled with gray. The man's muscles declared him no soft politician, but if he'd ever wielded a sword in battle, he'd escaped with no scars. This was a man used to hard work, a farmer or fisherman, not a warrior. He wore clothes similar to Tor's, but around his shoulders draped a huge cloak of dyed wool decorated with a collar of claws, each the length of a short dagger.

A chill swept down Tor's spine. *What kind of animal has claws that long?*

The two men forced Tor to kneel before the great chair. The woman who preceded him into the hut now bowed before the chieftain, then whispered in his ear. When she finished, both stared at Tor, who bared his teeth in a silent snarl. The chieftain said something to the woman and waved her from the hut. She left without a backward glance. The chieftain glared at Tor and spoke.

The words were strange, familiar but...*twisted*...somehow. Tor remained silent. He guessed he was being asked where he came from, but even had he understood the words, he'd not give the man the satisfaction of an answer.

Several times the chieftain spoke, his tone louder and angrier with each phrase. Still Tor refused to say anything. He was prepared to wait until his men arrived.

This chieftain wouldn't be so confident once seasoned warriors surrounded his village.

~ * ~

The village was in uproar when the rescue party returned. Miri took charge, herding the children and the trainee carrying Beren toward the healer's hut. Kiana paused, wondering at the cause of this latest crisis.

A woman dressed like Kiana in men's clothing ran from the chieftain's hut. "You must come at once. Uncle Soren requests your presence."

"Not now, Lida. Beren needs me." Kiana sidestepped past her friend.

Lida shifted to block her path. "It's because of the prisoner."

Prisoner? Kiana stopped, heart pounding. *Has Ajmal found us?* She clutched Lida's arm. "This prisoner. Is he dark-skinned, like me?"

"No, yellow hair, light skin."

Releasing her hold, Kiana suppressed a sigh. *Not Ajmal.* She frowned when a more probable answer sprang to mind. The strangers in the cove?

"Chieftain Soren requests you go straight to the council hut when you return," Lida continued.

Soren *requested*, not ordered—a small victory.

The expression on Lida's face drew Kiana's attention. "There's more?"

Her friend cleared her throat. "The man wasn't alone. The other escaped."

"Ah." Kiana cursed under her breath. "He'll be back. Best gather everyone together and arm anyone who can hold a spear or bow."

Unable to do anything for Beren, Kiana was grateful for a task she *could* help with.

Her first sight of the prisoner after entering Soren's hut gave her pause. Two guards, the last men left in the village who weren't children or ancients, flanked the kneeling man. Tangled blond hair hung down his back to below his shoulders. With his hands bound behind him, arm muscles strained. She imagined those hands crushing an enemy's throat.

Kiana grimaced. This man brought danger to her new home, to Beren. He caused what the boys called a fire ball to batter a mountain onto the heads of innocent children. This wasn't a man to admire.

He was, however, a warrior, proud and fierce, and in another life one she might have gladly fought beside. Tall, even on his knees, he braced, shoulders back, chin raised. No doubt he glared defiance into the chieftain's eyes.

Soren sat in the great chair he'd purchased from a travelling merchant last summer. There was nothing like it in the village, but from the scowl on Soren's face it failed to awe this stranger with the chieftain's importance and power.

Kiana strode forward and bowed. "How may I be of service?"

Soren gestured to the man. "He doesn't speak nor seem to understand me."

She turned. Avoiding his face for now, she studied the man's clothes.

These were familiar, similar to those the village fishers wore—leather leggings over hide boots, a sleeveless leather tunic laced together with leather ties over a long-sleeved cloth shirt in a faded red. Salt stained his clothes in patches. A woven belt, tied at his waist, held a horn at one side and a loop for a sword on the other.

Good. Lida remembered her training and had taken that from him first thing. A hardened warrior, then. Kiana wondered how her raw recruits had managed to capture him. *Ah, there.* A few strands of thin rope were caught in his sleeve. The sturdy nets were used to haul in the largest sea beasts in these waters, not just seals but whales and even giant squid, so were strong enough to hold a man. Satisfied, she resumed her study and at last raised her gaze to the man's face.

Shock had her clamping her lips together to smother a gasp. *It's him, the man in mother's augury.*

Her heart thumped in her chest. *Breathe.*

Two years ago her mother had shown Kiana this man's face in her temple fires, a light-skinned barbarian with hair the color of the desert sands and eyes a brilliant blue. He looked older than her then-eighteen years, perhaps in his early twenties? She judged his features pleasing, even with a scar on his left cheek and covered by a thick beard.

Her mother's next words left her breathless. *He is your destiny.*

The priestesses were gifted prophets, none more so than her mother, but this? This was impossible.

Kiana had scoffed at the time. *My destiny is with Ajmal.* Ajmal was her future, not some stranger from who knew where. Ajmal.

Until he betrayed everything she held dear.

Now there knelt this same man, yellow hair, yellow beard, scar. He appeared the same age he'd looked in the smoke, but she was now two years older, and he didn't seem so ancient. In build and features he resembled her hosts, his skin pale beneath a sea tan. His eyes were a deep blue, reminding her of the waters of the inland sea her people had sailed for generations. His expression, however, was different, not the languid, smoldering stare that still haunted her dreams. The bared teeth and set jaw showed hatred and determination.

She made herself stare into those eyes, daring the man to drop his gaze. He did, at last, but not before a flicker of uncertainty creased his brow.

"Who are you?" There was no answer, and no flash of recognition for the language of her adopted home, nor for her own language or any of the other languages she knew. Nothing. She wagered the man understood none of them.

So it was up to her to learn his.

As a daughter of the king's wizard and the high priestess, she possessed a special gift, the gift of tongues. If she heard just a few words, the language blossomed full-blown in her memory as if she was born to it. That talent, perhaps more than her warrior's skills, had placed her in the queen's personal guard.

But to learn the prisoner's language he had to speak, and he refused.

"Hold him," she ordered the guards.

Each seized an arm with one hand and placed the other on one of his shoulders.

He tensed and frowned, wondering, perhaps, what torture they planned for him.

Kiana stood in front of him. Even kneeling his head was on a level with her own. She cradled his face in her hands and curled her fingers into his beard to keep his head still. While it appeared coarse, the hair was softer to her touch than she expected, and she itched to stroke it.

No, not now. Not yet.

She bent forward and kissed him.

A shock like lightning coursed from her mouth to her core. The touch of his lips on hers tingled with short bursts of fire. Only firm will kept her from reacting, even though she wanted to moan in pleasure. The man flinched. Had he felt it too?

It doesn't matter. I can't let this distract me.

She opened her eyes, surprised she had closed them, and found herself staring into the man's half-closed eyes, his expression dazed.

Languid. Smoldering.

Forcing down her uncertainty, she concentrated on the success of the first part of her plan. She kept a half smile on her face when she stepped back. The man focused his gaze on her, and his own lips began a slow smug curve upward.

Kiana yanked on his beard.

Chapter Three

The man roared—there was no other word to describe the sound—and reared back, but the guards' grip on his arms and shoulders prevented him from surging to his feet. Kiana released her hold, and his roar changed to curses.

She needed two or three words for her gift to give her the knowledge, but the words coming from this man's mouth made no sense. Oh, she understood them, but their grouping...dragons spawned from she-devils? Pigs with horns? Or...by the Lady, *fangs*?

At last the words she sought slipped into her mind, and she interrupted the man's tirade with a snapped order. *"Á sér sitja."*

He stopped speaking, and his mouth hung open.

Satisfied she'd used the right words for him to be quiet, Kiana faced Soren. "What do you want to know?"

"How many men does he have, and how long before they attack?" Having seen Kiana's talent at work when she first arrived in the village, Soren showed little surprise or even approval at her success.

She doubted the man would answer the question, but she turned to him, refusing to flinch at the raw hatred in his stare. "We hold your life," she began. "Do you understand your danger here?"

His eyes widened, then narrowed. "How do you speak my tongue?"

"Do you understand your danger here?" she repeated in the same flat tone, ignoring his question.

He was silent for a moment, then dipped his head in a stiff nod.

"Good. Answer our questions, and you may live. Refuse and we can make you wish for death." Not even the toughest fisher in the village had the stomach for torture, nor did she, but the man didn't need to know that. "How many men do you have?"

His mouth thinned even more. He raised his chin and shifted his gaze to stare over her shoulder. She sighed. *Why are men so stubborn?*

She expected more silence, but after a moment he swung his gaze back to her and curled his lips in a fierce grin, white teeth flashing through his beard. "Thousands."

Her heartbeat thundered in her ears. She gasped. She didn't believe the number, but that grin... That grin shot heat to her core, sweat to her palms.

Enough. She narrowed her eyes. "Those ships are too small to hold thousands."

He blinked, then flashed his grin again. "My ships are bigger than they look."

A twinge of admiration for his bravado threatened to undermine Kiana's resolve. *Focus.* She curled her fingers against her legs. "How many men?" she repeated.

He continued to smirk.

What to do next? He'd shown them no threat so far, but there was a chance he'd come to raid the village. This place was hers, at least for now, and she'd not allow another invader to drive her from her home.

Not even one who invaded her dreams.

She turned to translate the man's words, but at that moment Lida rushed in.

"Men in the woods, around the village." Her hands shook on her bow, but her voice remained firm.

Soren rose and jerked his head at the prisoner. "Bring that one." He strode from the hut.

The guards wrenched the man to his feet and shoved him toward the door. He towered over them, and had to bend to exit through the doorway.

Holy Inanna, even her dreams hadn't shown the true size of the man.

Everyone in the village gathered around the central hut. The injured and ill from the healer's hut huddled near the wall. Dangerous, keeping them all together, but easier to defend.

Beren sat with Inga, unconscious still, a cloth around his head and his leg covered in thick wrappings. Anger filled Kiana. By the Lady, if these raiders planned to hurt her prince, her friends...

She drew her sword and strode to the front of the outer circle, between Soren and the prisoner, once again on his knees. She placed her sword at his throat. If his men attacked, he'd be the first to die.

Several strangers hovered at the edge of the forest, armed but their weapons sheathed. A movement in the woods drew her attention to the right. From the trees emerged three people. Two—no, *one* warrior. The other man, perhaps twenty years older, with eyes that squinted in the sun and a body better suited to lifting pebbles than swords, was dressed in a plain brown robe. Between them walked...a very pregnant woman.

Their prisoner surged forward and almost impaled himself in Kiana's sword before his guards pulled him back. "*Runa.*"

~ * ~

Tor struggled against the men who held him. The woman's sword nicked his throat, and he stilled. Something in her stance, in the way she looked at him, warned him not to underestimate her. A shield maid, for certain, although he'd never met one who stirred his blood as this one did.

Runa approached, reminding him of the danger. He had no choice but to watch his sister stride into the middle of the enemy camp.

What is she thinking? She was no fool, but this action made him wonder if madness ran in the family. First his own lapse of judgement that resulted in his capture, now this. If a bargain needed to be made, why, by Odin's beard, weren't Emund or Beade here? Why weren't his brothers leading this...this foolish meeting, not his irritating sister? She should be back in camp, safe.

"Get out of here," he shouted.

One of his guards dragged his head back by the hair and shoved a dirty rag into his mouth before releasing him. Tor's protests turned into muffled growls. Runa spared him a glance, her expression warning him not to interfere, before turning her attention to the leader of these people.

The man might not be a war leader like Tor but, despite the vanity shown by that ridiculous chair in his hut, he'd not be a man to cross.

Runa strode toward the chieftain, Vider on one side of her and Jorvik, thin and pale, on the other. Tor understood why Vider was there. His first mate was a warrior able to protect Runa to the death, but why Jorvik? Even as he asked himself the question, the answer came. The seer knew many languages, so perhaps not surprising Vider had brought him.

Runa paused before the chieftain. "We come in peace." She held out her empty hands. The woman beside Tor murmured to the chieftain, who stared first at Runa, then at the two men beside her, and last at Runa's belly. He said something in return, and Jorvik frowned in concentration.

"Well?" Runa asked.

"I'm not sure," he admitted with a frown. "The words are like ours or the Danes, but not quite. I think he asked about a child?"

"He said you must love your husband much to risk your child to his enemies," the shield maid corrected.

Tor glanced at her, at the tension in her shoulders, despite her seeming calm.

"You speak our language?" Runa asked in surprise.

The woman gave a brief nod but said no more.

Runa shrugged and bowed her head to the chieftain. "Please tell him we don't wish you harm. We are traders, not enemies. If my foolish brother has offended, we will make reparation."

Tor struggled, trying to shout a protest. Foolish? Reparation?

She shot him a quelling glance. "Let me handle this."

Anger and fear for Runa turned the world red. He sputtered, strained against his captors. Madness to risk her child.

The village woman spoke to the leader. Tor jerked his gaze to her. Strange. Was there less tension in her body now?

While the chieftain and Runa conversed through the woman's translation, Tor studied the surroundings. All the villagers clustered around this central area with few men in the group. Some women held bows or spears. He'd not underestimate women warriors, but these held their weapons loosely, as if unseasoned. The woman beside him, though, who now withdrew her sword from his throat…she'd not hesitate.

He returned his attention to Runa and the conversation. To his surprise, she was explaining how they arrived in this place. "We were in a great storm and a great metal ball of fire appeared in the lightning. It made a hole in the air and pulled us through to this land, or at least to the sea off this land."

Surprise, disbelief, filled the village chieftain's eyes. "This fire ball—you didn't bring it to attack us?"

"*No.* It captured *us* and brought us here." Runa waved her hand at the village huts. "I didn't see it attack here. It went straight to that mountain over there."

After the woman translated the words, she and the chieftain conversed together for a few minutes.

At last Tor managed to spit out the rag. "Runa. What are you doing?"

"We need allies, brother. The more we tell them about us, the less they might be inclined to kill you." Her voice was dry with sarcasm.

His guards tightened their grip but didn't bother replacing the gag.

The chieftain turned to Runa, stopping any further conversation. "We have no wish to be enemies," he said through the woman translator. "We will speak further." He glanced at Vider and Jorvik, and for the first time a smile twisted his lips. "You may keep your protectors, but perhaps you should also have brought a midwife."

Runa grinned, a true grin, not feigned. "I still have some time. This child isn't ready to come into the world yet." She turned to Vider. "Send the men back to the ships."

"No." Odin's beard, Tor didn't know whether he wanted to strangle his sister or his friend. At least they had the sense to bring more men with them, but to now send them away? "This could be a trick." He glared at Vider. "And since when did you take orders from my sister?"

Vider opened his mouth, but Runa interrupted. "Since Vider is a warrior, and we need a peacekeeper."

The woman with the sword slipped it into a sheath on her back and nodded to the men behind Tor, who released his arms. She drew a dagger and cut his bonds. When he surged to his feet she stepped back. He wanted to...he didn't know what he wanted to do, but he'd not give her the satisfaction of being the one to break this truce.

The woman waved to the central hut. "Come."

He didn't want to *come*. He wanted to rage at Runa, at Vider, at anyone but himself. The gods knew he wasn't a prideful man, but these last few hours proved he wasn't the level-headed trader he considered himself. Coming through that strange hole from the storm must have addled his wits. It made perfect sense to deal with these people. Hadn't he wished for just that when he and Vider set out from the cove? Of course these people defended themselves. Why, then, was he so bad-tempered?

Yet one look at *that woman* brought the memory of that amazing kiss surging back, and all his common sense vanished. He glared at her and planted his feet.

She glared right back, then shrugged. "Come with your sister, then."

Turning, she marched into the central hut, annoyance in every line of her body. Ah, what a body. Similar to the women who had captured him, she wore leather trews and a sleeveless vest, but her skin, unlike everyone else in this village, was dark, almost golden, her arms strong with muscle yet still feminine. Instead of blonde curly hair, hers was black as night and hung straight as water in a tail down her back. It reminded him of women he'd seen in the Southlands. Even her eyes fascinated him...dark, mysterious, and that gaze so easy to fall into and be lost. Unbidden, another memory of her kiss came to mind and his lower body hardened. He dug his fingernails into his palms, the pain a welcome distraction.

Tor took a deep breath. No matter how fascinating the woman, he'd rather forget that moment of weakness. He'd deal with her later. Right now he needed to find out what madness had taken his sensible first mate.

He strode to the trio still arguing in the clearing. Well, Runa and Vider argued, while Jorvik stood well back. Smart man.

"Go back to the ships, Runa," Tor ordered when he joined them. "We'll take care of these savages."

Runa glanced at him and placed her hands on her hips. "How? By attacking women and children? Don't be absurd, brother. We need them. We can't afford to make any enemies now."

"Of course I'm not going to attack them. What to you take me for?" He turned to Vider. "And why isn't Emund or Beade leading this…this…?"

"Rescue?" Runa finished. That wasn't the word he intended, but she carried on without giving him a chance to protest. "Because they can't." She hunched forward, her face flushed, gaze fierce. "Beade was injured in the storm, hit his head, and sees double. His wife is caring for him, and Emund stayed back to protect the families should I have misjudged."

"Misjudged?" Tor clenched his teeth. "Woman, we're standing in the middle of a village where I was held prisoner, still am if these people turn treacherous."

"They found two warriors wandering close to their wives, their children. What did you expect them to do? Welcome you with open arms?" He winced, and she held up a hand, closed her eyes for a moment. "I'm sorry, brother, but we *need* them. We have to try it this way first."

Tor turned to Vider, but his friend just sighed in resignation. "She has good reason, much as I hate to admit it, but I don't like sending everyone away. This could turn at an instant."

"Perhaps," Runa said, "but we have to risk it. We still need to make friends with them." She glanced at Tor, then returned her attention to Vider. "Have the men withdraw to that clearing we passed on the way here. They'll still be close enough to hear us if we need them."

Vider turned to Jorvik. "You tell them. I'm staying here."

Tor bristled. "I am still your leader."

"Then lead with your head, not your pride." Runa waved around them. "What do you see?"

He spared the surroundings a quick glance. "A village."

She sighed. "Around it."

Around it? "Trees." *Ah.* The reason he'd hoped to find a settlement in the first place. Autumn. Food.

He'd lived through one winter five years ago after a harsh summer where plants withered for lack of water, leaving a harvest too sparse to feed them through the cold months. Meat they had in plenty, and fish, but still, many of the elderly and children starved that year before an alliance with the Danes across the short ocean allowed them to trade for much needed fruit, vegetables, and bread.

They needed that from these people now.

Sanity returned, and Tor sighed. "Yes, we need them. Somehow we've lost a summer. Our stores won't last if winters here are as long as they are at home, and we'll need more than fish." He frowned. "All we have to do is think of something to trade with. We didn't leave home with much."

Runa stroked his arm, the familiar gesture soothing his worries. "We've been given a second chance at life here. We left Ottarshavn because of Ottar's bloodthirsty, treacherous ways."

"We left because he raped you and got you with child." Tor at once regretted the harsh words, and softened his tone. "And you'd not let me challenge him." That still hurt.

Runa paled, then firmed her lips. "I'd not have you die as our father did."

Tor closed his eyes. He didn't know how Ottar had defeated Olaf Strongarm, but not even the priest believed the fight had been fair. Why else did so many follow Tor into exile?

He opened his eyes and gathered his dignity. "Very well. I'll speak with them, and we'll find out if these people in fact do want peace."

"*I* will speak with them," she corrected. He stiffened but her expression softened, turned pleading. He wasn't fooled for a minute. "Tor, I know you. Your pride has been hurt and that may affect your skill with your tongue." She paused at Vider's snicker, rolled her eyes. "You know what I mean. You're not calm enough right now to negotiate."

Tor bristled. "I'm calm."

Runa just stared at him. Again he sighed. He hated it when she was right. This whole experience left him unsettled. Where had his trading skills disappeared to?

As if reading his mind, she stroked his arm again. "If you were silver-tongued like Jorvik we'd not be in exile."

"Then why isn't *he* doing the talking?" Tor shot Jorvik a glance, but that wise man had been backing away while they argued and now stood close to the trees. He cast Tor a sickly grin, then turned and fled into the forest.

Runa chuckled. "Because he has the courage of a field mouse."

Tor had to smile. She brushed past him to stride toward the central hut.

Out Now!

What's next on your reading list?

Champagne Book Group promises to bring to readers fiction at its finest.

Discover your next
fine read!
http://www.champagnebooks.com/

We are delighted to invite you to receive exclusive rewards. Join our Facebook group for VIP savings, bonus content, early access to new ideas we've cooked up, learn about special events for our readers, and sneak peeks at our fabulous titles.

Join now.
https://www.facebook.com/groups/ChampagneBookClub/

www.ingramcontent.com/pod-product-compliance
Lightning Source LLC
Chambersburg PA
CBHW060910250626
47159CB00008B/2941